SOUL THIEF

ALSO BY JANA OLIVER

The Demon Trapper's Daughter

SOUL THIEF

A Demon Trappers Novel

JANA OLIVER

St. Martin's Griffin
New York

SOUL THIEF. Copyright © 2011 by Jana Oliver. All rights reserved. Printed in the United States of America. For information, address St. Martin's Press, 175 Fifth Avenue, New York, N.Y. 10010.

www.stmartins.com

ISBN 978-0-312-61479-9

First Edition: September 2011

10 9 8 7 6 5 4 3 2 1

To

Michelle Roper

who taught me to find humor

in the small things

Acknowledgments

There are many wizards behind the curtain making the magic that becomes the book in your hand. Here are a few of those souls.

I owe a big shout-out to Jennifer Weis (my editor) and her assistant, Mollie Traver. They are there for me in all the ways that count. I am blessed to have the amazing Meredith Bernstein as my literary agent. She always has my back and will often call just to ask, "How's it going?"

My fellow authors and critiquers deserve praise as well: Nanette Littlestone, Dwain Herndon, Aarti Nayar, and Harold Ball. My beta readers (who slog through a really muddy version of the early manuscript, usually at breakneck speed) are totally fearless and so I send my thanks and hugs to Jean Marie Ward, Michelle Roper, Cate Rowan, and my dear spouse, Harold. William MacLeod kept Master Angus Stewart's lilting Scottish accent honest and, as usual, the great city of Atlanta and Oakland Cemetery provided excellent backdrops to Riley's adventures. Without all this support my life would be immensely crazy, and not in a good way.

For they both were solitary,
She on earth and he in heaven.
And he wooed her with caresses,
Wooed her with his smile of sunshine . . .

—SONG OF HIAWATHA,
Henry Wadsworth Longfellow

ONE

2018
Atlanta, Georgia

The Grounds Zero Coffee Shop made the most amazing hot chocolate in Atlanta, maybe even the whole world. It appeared Riley Blackthorne would have to wade through Armageddon to get it.

"The end is near!" a man called out to passersby. He stood at the shop's entrance holding a homemade cardboard sign that proclaimed the same thing. Instead of having a scraggly beard and wearing a black robe like some biblical prophet, he was wearing chinos and a red shirt.

"You've got to prepare, missy," he said and shoved a pamphlet toward Riley with considerable zeal. The tract looked remarkably like the one she had in her jacket pocket. Like the one the angel had given her right before she'd agreed to work for Heaven to save her boyfriend's life.

"The end is near!" the man shouted again.

"Is there still time for hot chocolate?" Riley asked.

The End Times guy blinked. "Ah, maybe; I don't know."

"Oh, good," she said. "I'd hate to take on Hell without fueling up."

That earned her a confused frown. Rather than explain she jammed the tract in her pocket and pushed open the door to the coffee shop as the man went back to exhorting his audience to prepare for the worst.

The Grounds Zero didn't look any different from how it did the last time she'd been here. The smell of roasted beans hung in the air like a heady perfume, and the espresso machine growled low and deep. Customers tapped on laptops as they enjoyed expensive coffee and talked about whatever was important in their lives. Just like every day. Except . . .

Everything is weird now.

Even buying hot chocolate. That used to be easy: Place order, pay for order, receive hot beverage. No hassles. That didn't appear to be the case today.

The barista kept staring at her even as he made the drink, which wasn't a good thing, because he nearly scalded himself. Maybe it was the multiple burn holes in her denim jacket, or the ragged slice down one sleeve that revealed the T-shirt underneath. Or the fact that her long brown hair had a frizzled, been-too-close-to-a-flame look, despite two shampoo sessions and a lot of conditioner. At least she'd changed her jeans, or the guy would be staring at all the dried blood. Blood that wasn't hers.

"I saw you on TV. You're one of them, aren't you?" he asked in a shaky voice, brown eyes so wide they seemed to cover most of his face.

On TV? Riley had no choice but to own up. "Yeah, I'm a demon trapper." *One of the few lucky enough to survive last night's slaughter.*

The guy dropped the ceramic cup on the counter, sloshing some of the brown goodness over the side and onto the saucer. He backed away like Riley had horns coming out of her skull.

"Whipped cream?" she asked, frowning now. Even if the world was ending, hot chocolate had to have that glorious white stuff on top or what was the point? He reluctantly added the topping, keeping his eyes on her rather than the cup. Some of it actually went inside. "Chocolate shavings?" she nudged.

"Ah . . . we're out," he said.

It's just one creepo guy. No big.

But it wasn't just him. Other customers stared as she made her way to an empty booth. One by one they looked up at the television screen high on the wall, then back to her, comparing images.

Ah, crap.

There, courtesy of CNN, was last night's disaster in glorious color: flames pouring out of the roof of the Tabernacle as demons ran everywhere. And there she was, illuminated by the raging fire, kneeling on the pavement near her injured boyfriend. She was crying, holding Simon in her arms. It was the moment she knew he was dying.

Oh, God. I can't handle this.

The saucer in Riley's hand began to quake, dislodging more of the hot chocolate. It'd been bad enough to live through that horror, but now it was all over the television in full and unflinching detail.

She paused near a booth as a picture of Simon appeared on the screen. It must have been his high school graduation photo, since his white-blond hair was shorter and his expression stone serious. He was usually that way except when they were hanging together; then he'd let his guard down, especially when they were kissing.

Riley closed her eyes recalling the time they'd spent together before the meeting. They'd kissed, and he'd admitted how much he cared for her. Then a demon had tried to kill him.

Riley sank into the booth and inhaled the rich scent of the hot chocolate, using it to push the bad memories away. The effort failed, though it never had in the past. Instead, her mind dutifully conjured up the image of her boyfriend in his hospital bed, tubes everywhere, his face as white as the sheets.

Simon meant so much to her. He'd been a quiet, comforting presence after her father's death. Losing him so soon after her dad was unthinkable and Heaven had known that. What else could she do but agree to their terms: Simon's life in trade for Riley owing Heaven a favor. A Really Big Favor. Like stopping Armageddon in its tracks.

"Why me?" Riley muttered. "Why not someone else? Why not Simon?"

He was religious, followed all the rules. He'd be the perfect guy to keep the world from ending. They could have made the deal with him when he was injured.

Instead they chose me.

To Riley's annoyance, the hot chocolate had cooled beyond what was acceptable drinking temperature, but she sipped it anyway. She kept her eyes riveted on the cup's contents, away from the television screen. Someone scraped a chair across the floor to sit at a table, and Riley jumped at the sound, half expecting a horde of demons to pour through the front door at any moment.

The cup trembled in her hands, reminding her how close she skated near the edge. Too much had hit her in a short period of time. Too much more and she wouldn't cope.

I have to find my dad. That she could do. Maybe. Still, it was something she could focus on. It was unlikely his body was buried under the rubble at the Tabernacle, not when a necromancer went to all the effort to summon him from his grave. That's what necros did: they reanimated corpses and sold them to rich people as unpaid servants. By now someone would be lining up to buy Master Trapper Paul Blackthorne, if he hadn't been sold already.

What is it like to be dead and walking around like you're still alive? Besides the creep factor, it had to be truly weird. Did her dad remember dying? Did he remember the funeral and being buried? Spiky cold zipped down Riley's spine. She had to get her head in the game.

I'll find him. I'll get him back in the ground, and that'll be the end of it.

Her eyes wandered back to the television. A different reporter was doing a play-by-play of last night's horror. He had it mostly right—the local Trappers Guild had held a meeting at the Tabernacle in downtown Atlanta, just like they always did. In the middle of the meeting the demons had arrived. Then it got bad.

"Eyewitnesses say that at least two different kinds of Hellspawn were involved in the attack and that the trappers were quickly overwhelmed," the reporter said.

Three different kinds, but who's counting?

Riley frowned. The trappers hadn't been overwhelmed. Well, not completely. They'd even managed to kill a few of the things.

When she went to pick up the cup of hot chocolate, her hands were still shaking. They'd been that way since last night and nothing she did made them stop. She downed the liquid in small sips, knowing people were watching her, talking among themselves. Someone took a picture of her with his cell phone.

Ah, jeez.

In the background, she could still hear the reporter on CNN. "A number of the trappers escaped the inferno and were immediately set upon by a higher-level fiend."

The higher-level fiend had been a Grade Five demon who'd opened up deep holes in the ground, spun off mini tornadoes, and caused the earth to shake. All in an effort to take out one trapper.

Me.

If it hadn't been for Ori, a freelance demon hunter, the Five would have killed her just like it had her dad.

"We have interviewed eyewitnesses who claim they saw angels last night," the reporter continued. "We've had Doctor Osbourne, a professor of religious studies at UC Santa Barbara, review the videos. He's with us here today, via satellite." A solemn gray-haired man appeared on the screen. "What's your take on this amazing event, Doctor?"

"I've watched the videos, and all that is visible is a circle of incredibly bright light that surrounds the demon trappers. I have colleagues in Atlanta who've claimed to see angels in your city. They appeared throughout the Bible to Abraham, to Jacob. Sodom and Gomorrah rated two of them. In this case, they were actively protecting the trappers from Hellspawn. I'd say that's biblically significant."

Tell me about it.

Riley dug in her messenger bag, retrieved a pen, and began a list on a crisp white napkin.

Find Dad
Bust Holy Water Scam
Save the World
Buy Groceries
Do Laundry

As she saw it, if number three on the list didn't work out, the last two weren't going to be an issue.

TWO

Feeling a tickle in his throat, Denver Beck coughed deeply in an attempt to purge the stale smoke from his lungs. It did little good. In the distance, firefighters moved across the Tabernacle's rubble, working on the hot spots and searching for charred bodies in the mounds of broken bricks and burnt wood.

I should have died last night. In the past it wouldn't have mattered. Now it did. It was his fear for Riley that had driven him out of the smoke and flames.

To his right, Master Trapper Angus Stewart leaned heavily on his cane in the late-afternoon sun. His usually ruddy face was nearly the color of his white hair, pale against the bloodstained bandage tucked into his hairline. They stood near one of the many holes in the Tabernacle's parking lot, the stench of burnt asphalt hanging heavy in the air. Beck bent over and stared into the crater's maw, which was laced with tangled wires and debris. It was a good ten feet wide and three times as deep. A thin column of steam rose from its center.

"How does a demon do this kind of damage?" he asked in a soft Southern drawl.

"The Geo-Fiend just waved its hands and this abyss appeared. They have some strange power over the earth and the weather," Stewart said in his rich Scottish accent. It was still noticeable, though blunted by a decade in Atlanta.

As Beck straightened up, the demon wound in his thigh cramped in protest. The dressing was leaking and the drainage had soaked into his blue jeans. He needed more aspirin—his temperature was up and every now and then his teeth would chatter. Like a mild case of the flu with claw marks as the bonus.

Everythin' has changed now. He knew angels were for real; he'd seen them around Atlanta. Most were the ministering kind, the most prolific of Heaven's folk, who came and went doing whatever God wanted them to do. He'd never seen any from the higher realm, the ones with the flaming swords. He had last night.

Beck shook his head again, unable to deal with how eerie the things had been. At least seven feet tall, clothed in eye-blinding white with shimmering alabaster wings edged in gray, their fiery swords had roared like summer thunder and filled the night air with the crisp tang of ozone.

"I've never heard tell of Heaven steppin' in to protect trappers," Beck said in a lowered voice, mindful of a television news crew on the other side of the parking lot. They were all over the city now, trying to get a handle on one of the biggest stories to hit Atlanta since the 1996 Olympics. "Why're the demons workin' together now? It feels like a war's brewin'."

"So it does." Stewart cleared his throat. "Seein' the angels make ya a believer?"

Beck blinked at the question. *Had it?* He'd never really thought much about God, and he figured the feeling was mutual. "Maybe," he admitted.

Stewart huffed in agreement. "The city will be wantin' action."

"Master Harper will take care of that, won't he?" Beck asked. Harper was the most senior trapper in Atlanta and Riley's master. From what Beck could tell, he was a serious piece of work but a good trapper when he wasn't drinking.

"Nay, not with his ribs bein' the way they are," Stewart said. "I'll have ta take the lead. With Ethan dead, I'll need yer help."

Ethan had been one of the master's apprentices, but he'd not made it out of the Tabernacle alive. "What about yer other apprentice? Rollins. Where's he?"

"He quit. Canna handle this sorta thing. I respect that." Stewart paused a moment, then added, "I'm pleased ta hear young Simon's gonna make it. That's good news for Riley."

"Yeah," Beck replied, unsure of where the old master was heading with that last comment.

"She and Simon have taken a fancy ta each other, did ya know? They were holdin' hands and kissin' before the meetin'. They didn't know I saw them."

"Kissin'?" Beck felt something heavy form in his chest, like a stone weighing on his heart. Had to be because of the demon wound; they always made you feel sick. It wouldn't do for him to think of Riley as more than just Paul's little girl.

"Ya didn't know?" the master asked, all innocence.

Beck shook his head. He'd known Riley and Simon were spending time together: They were both apprenticing with Harper and saw each other every day. But he hadn't realized their relationship had gone that far. She was only seventeen, and now that both of her parents were dead he felt responsible for her. Sort of like a big brother. Sort of something more.

"Yer frownin', lad," Stewart observed.

Beck tensed, uncomfortable under the old trapper's scrutiny. "Simon's better than some she could date," he acknowledged. "But he's not what she should be thinkin' about right now. I'll have a talk with him once he's better. Warn him off." *Let him know if he goes too far with her I'll rip his damned head off.*

The master gave him a fatherly smile. "Let *them* sort it out, lad. Ya canna keep her in a bubble the rest of her life."

Wanna bet? It's what Paul would have wanted and, if he was honest, the only way Beck could sleep at night. As he stared at the broken land-scape and the savaged building, his mind filled with images from the evening before. Of demons and the trappers battling for survival. Of Riley in the middle of the flames and how close he'd come to losing her. Beck shuddered, ice shearing through his veins.

Stewart laid a heavy hand on his shoulder, startling him. "I know ya stayed inside that furnace until the very last. That takes stones, and I'm damned proud of ya."

Beck couldn't meet the master's eyes, troubled by the praise.

The Scotsman's hand retreated. "Ya can't carry it all on yer shoul-ders, broad as they are."

He sounded just like Paul, but that made sense: Master Stewart had trained Riley's father, who in turn had apprenticed Beck. From what Paul had said, the Stewarts were some of the best demon trappers in the world.

This man thought he'd done all right last night. *He's just bein' nice.*

As if knowing a change of topic was needed, Stewart asked, "Any idea who pulled Paul from his grave?"

That was the other thing hanging over them. Though he'd been dead for two weeks, Riley's father had appeared at the trapper's meeting, summoned from his eternal rest by a necromancer. He was a reanimated corpse now, money on the hoof providing he'd made it out of the Taber-nacle in one piece.

"Riley did everythin' she could to keep him in the ground," Beck complained. "She sat vigil every damned night, made sure there was a consecrated circle around his grave. Then some bastard steals him the one time she isn't there. It just sucks."

"She have any notion who did it?" Stewart nudged.

"I didn't get a chance to ask her." Which wasn't quite the truth. Beck could have. They'd huddled together in her family's mausoleum in Oak-land Cemetery until dawn, on hallowed ground in case the demons came after them. She'd been so upset about Simon and the others, she'd cried herself to sleep. At the time it didn't seem important to know who'd resurrected Paul, so he'd just held her close, kept her safe, thanking God she'd survived. Trying to work through his feelings for the girl. When he'd left her this morning she'd still been asleep, dried tears on her cheeks. He hadn't had the heart to wake her.

Stewart shifted position again: He was hurting more than he let on. "I canna help but believe there's a connection between the demons' attack and Paul's reanimation," the old trapper mused.

"How could there be?"

"Think it through. Wouldn't he have gone off with the necro who summoned him rather than droppin' in for a wee visit with his old mates?"

"I don't know," Beck said, swiping a hand through his blond hair in agitation. "But I'll know soon enough. I'll find the summoner who did it and we'll come to an understandin': Paul goes in the ground or the necro does."

Stewart stiffened. "Be careful on that account. The summoners have wicked magic and they'll not appreciate ya gettin' in their business."

Beck didn't respond. It didn't matter what happened to him; Paul Blackthorne was going back in his grave, and that was that. He hadn't been able to keep him alive, but he could honor his friend's memory in other ways. He'd do it for Paul's daughter, if nothing more than to give her peace of mind.

"I hear that Five went after Riley in particular," the master stated. "I wonder why."

Beck had no answer to that. Grade Five Geo-Fiends were the big boys of Hell who generated earthquakes and spawned mini storms as easily as he took a breath. A Five had killed Paul, and he was willing to bet it was the same one who'd gone after his daughter during the battle.

Beck *was* sure of one thing: The demons were taking too much of an interest in Riley, calling her out by her name. Hellspawn didn't do that as a rule. *Maybe I should tell Stewart. Maybe he would know what's goin' on.*

But if he did, it'd only add to Riley's long list of troubles. Before Beck could make a decision, the master's phone began to buzz inside a coat pocket.

He pulled it out, frowned, and opened it up. "Stewart."

Beck turned his attention to the hole in front of him. One of the trappers told him that the Geo-Fiend had thrown Riley into this very pit. That same trapper hadn't known how she'd managed to escape, said there'd been too much smoke to see what had really happened.

Why didn't the Five kill ya, girl? There was one possibility, but he didn't want to think about that. No way Riley would have sold her soul to Hell to stay alive.

What if she'd fallen into that hole and never come out again?

Before Beck could admit to himself what that loss would mean to him, Stewart ended the call.

"That was Harper. The Guild's representatives are ta meet with the mayor in two hours. We need ta be there."

"We?" Beck said, caught off guard. "Me too?"

"Certainly. Ya gotta problem with that?"

Hearing the challenge, Beck shook his head. "Can't the city at least wait till we bury our dead?"

Stewart huffed. "Of course not. Politicians wait for no man when they can lay the blame on some other poor bastard."

THREE

Riley knew that finding a parking place near the Terminus Market was never easy, but today was worse since the market was so close to the site of last night's tragedy. After trolling up and down the street for what seemed an eternity, she finally caught sight of a scooter pulling out leaving a thick blue cloud of exhaust in its wake. She edged her car into the open space, nervous she might clip the stall ahead. It was full of knitted hats and scarves, most sporting Georgia Tech or Georgia State logos. The owner, an older black man, kept a wary eye on her progress. Once she turned off the engine, the knitted-hat guy relaxed and gave her an appreciative thumbs-up. She returned it.

When Atlanta joined the growing list of bankrupt cities across the country, the city planners mined every possible way to make money. They'd sold off the school buildings, put a tax on cigarettes, alcohol, day-care centers, Holy Water, homeschooling, almost everything. As the parking spaces went empty because of the excessive price of gas, the city turned them into "retail opportunities," which meant there were a cluster of mini shops where once there were cars. Each store lived within the white lines of a parking spot, like the guy with the knitted hats and scarves. Some vendors rented more than one, which was why there was a music shop on Peachtree Street called The Five Meters.

Riley crawled out of the car at half speed, her denim messenger bag

in hand. It felt like her body had been ambushed by a particularly sa-
distic army of karate experts. When she'd showered this morning she'd
been astounded at all the bruises. Holy Water was only good for demonic wounds, so she'd be a patchwork of yellow and brown spots in a
few days. Luckily most of them were hidden by her clothes. The one on
her left hip was particularly painful, courtesy of the malevolent Grade
Five demon and the door handle of a Volvo.

Riley trudged into Centennial Park on the wide brick path, favor-
ing her sore hip. When she was a kid this place was just a park, though
pretty cool as far as green open spaces went, especially one in the center
of a major city. It had the five Olympic Ring fountains to play in, and
vendors sold ice cream and other yummy goodies. It was still a cool
place, but there was a lot more to it nowadays. Over time, vendors moved
into the market with portable campers and a small city sprang up inside
the bigger one. Now the Terminus Market, as it was called, was a year-
round thing.

Right before she entered the market, Riley paused on the walkway,
allowing the past to catch up with her. Closing her eyes, she swore she
could hear her mom's voice, jesting with her father about his need to
buy *just one more book* on the Civil War.

"I miss you guys," she whispered. *Wish you were here.* Then she continued into the chaos of the marketplace.

Originally there had been a plan to all this—food vendors in one
section, crafts in another, and so on. That plan was ignored as the market sprawled in every direction. The tents came in all different colors,
ranging from deep black to brilliant red; some were plain, others were
adorned with flags and streamers. All had some form of lighting, since
the merchants were usually open until after midnight.

Riley paused in front of a tent where a dead animal hung from a
spit over a large wood fire. A boy was in charge of turning the spit, and
Riley could tell it took all his strength, his muscles straining with every
rotation. The sign on the tent said it was pork, but you never knew.
Sometimes they sold goat. It smelled good, whatever it was. Her stomach

complained, reminding her there hadn't been a lot of food it in all day, besides the hot chocolate.

Later.

A bit farther on was a guy selling used furniture—chairs, tables, dressers. Some of it was in worse shape than the thirdhand stuff in her cramped apartment.

"Riley?" a voice called out.

She turned, knowing that voice anywhere. The body, too. Clad in a black T-shirt, jeans, and a steel gray duster that swept the ground, the man striding toward her was over six feet with shiny ebony hair and bottomless dark eyes. Definitely yummy. What she liked best was his attitude: It told the world to take a number and wait its turn.

What am I doing? She really shouldn't be checking out other guys when she was dating Simon, especially when he was in the hospital. *Still, it can't hurt to look. . . .* That wasn't being unfaithful.

"Ori," she called out. "What are you doing here?"

"Still trying to find a proper sword," he said.

Riley smiled at that. The first time she'd seen him he was at the tent that sold all sorts of sharp pointy objects. He'd been holding a sword, looking like a hero out of a romance novel. *He still does.*

"How are you doing after last night?" he asked, his full attention on her now.

"I'm okay." It was her default answer.

Ori's jet-dark eyes searched her face. "Try again," he said softly.

She sagged. "The truth? Life sucks. There're lots of dead trappers, and, just to make things really special, my dad's been reanimated."

Her companion looked surprised. "By whom?"

"No clue," Riley said, holding up her hands in defeat.

"I'm truly sorry." Ori moved closer to her, sending little tingles through her skin. She never understood why that happened, but it felt good. He sounded genuine, which caused her conscience to nag at her. Many of her memories of the previous evening were hazy, however one in particular was crystal clear: Ori pulling her out of the crater as he threatened the Grade Five demon, making it back off. If he hadn't, she'd be lying next to her parents now. One of them at least.

Feeling awkward, she dug the toe of her tennis shoe into the dirt. "Did I . . . thank you for . . . well . . . saving my life?"

"No, but you just did," he replied, like it wasn't a big deal.

"Don't go all modest," she protested. "You saved me. I owe you."

A twinkle appeared in his eyes. "You do."

"I know it sounds weird, but I don't remember what happened after I reached the car. Next thing I knew I was at the cemetery."

"It happens. When the mind is confronted by something too big for it to deal with, it shuts down."

"Wish it worked that way with the nightmares."

His hand touched hers. It was warm, and she could feel the heat radiate through her skin. It wasn't a grabby sort of gesture, more a gentle one.

"Not many apprentice trappers would challenge a Geo-Fiend," he said.

"I just wanted it to stop killing the others."

"Which was really brave. Don't sell yourself short."

She felt a rush of warmth on her cheeks. *He thinks I'm brave. How cool is that?*

"Don't worry; the next time I will kill it," Ori said, his voice rougher now.

"Do you think it'll come after me again?"

A determined nod. "I'm counting on it. So don't be surprised if you see me hanging around a lot." He delivered a sexy grin. "The only thing I'm stalking is the Hellspawn."

She couldn't stop the smile. "Why didn't you just nail it last night?"

"I wanted you out of harm's way," he replied. "And I won't show off in front of the trappers. It'll be *my* kill, on *my* terms."

"I know you don't like them, but the Guild is shorthanded right now. I bet you could get a job really easy."

Her companion shook his head. "I work alone."

Which is what she expected he'd say since Ori was a freelance demon hunter, a Lancer. Trappers couldn't stand Lancers because they didn't play by the Guild's rules. Rome's Demon Hunters didn't like them, as they wouldn't pay homage to the Vatican. They were a force all their own, each Lancer his own master, and they dealt with demons as they saw fit.

In a few years maybe she would go out on her own. The trappers didn't like her anyway; she might as well work for herself.

"How is your boyfriend doing?" Ori asked.

Riley blinked. "How did you know Simon and I are dating?"

"I saw you with him right before you went after the Five. You weren't crying over any of the other trappers, so I assumed there was something between you."

She couldn't argue with his logic. "Simon's much better today. He's going to make it." *Because of me and the angel.* A warm glow fluttered through her chest at the thought.

Ori paused near a bookstall. After a moment's hesitation, he reached into a display and removed a paperback. It was Dante's *Inferno*. He glanced at a few of the pages and frowned.

"He got it wrong; the Ninth Circle of Hell is *not* a skating rink." He thumped the book closed in disgust and returned it to the rack.

"Have you ever seen angels before?" Riley asked.

"Lots of times."

"Oh." Maybe it was just her. She'd only seen one in her entire life.

"You're talking about the ones from last night, aren't you?" Ori asked, somber. When she nodded, he explained, "Those were the . . ." He paused and searched for a word. "Warrior angels. It's been a long time since they've been deployed."

Deployed? Military guys used terms like that. Had Ori been in the Army?

He glanced away at that very moment, frowning as if something had distracted him. "I'd best be going. It's good to see you again, Riley," he said.

It was like he was suddenly keen to be somewhere else. Had she said something stupid?

"Thanks . . . again. I won't forget what you've done for me."

"It was my pleasure."

Riley watched him head down the row of tents, his duster flapping behind him. Women turned and watched him pass; he had that kind of magnetic pull. She had a lot of questions about this guy, but there was no one she could ask. She'd promised Ori not to tell any of the trappers that he was in Atlanta, which seemed odd, since he'd definitely been right in the thick of the action last night.

"I'll think about that later." Her dad came first. Then she'd figure out Mr. Hunky Mysterious Dude.

Riley kept moving toward Bell, Book, and Broomstick, the witches' store. It was easy to find, the gold and silver stars on the midnight-blue canvas glittering in the late-afternoon sun. To her relief, Ayden was arranging bags of incense at the end of the counter. The witch wore her usual Renn Faire garb—peasant blouse with a laced bodice, a full skirt, and a heavy emerald-green cloak in acknowledgment of the chilly January weather. Most prominent was the large dragon tattoo that began at her neck beneath her russet brown hair and went all the way down into her ample cleavage. In the midst of the market, she seemed ageless, like a fairy queen.

"Ayden?" Riley called out, stopping a few feet away.

The witch looked up then raced out from behind the counter, springing at her like a mother does a missing child. The embrace wasn't a quick one, but the kind that tells you the embracer is thrilled to see you're alive. Riley returned it with just as much fervor.

"Goddess, you had me worried," the witch said, releasing her.

"Sorry. My cell phone got toasted so I didn't have your number. I'm using my dad's phone now."

"And you lost my business card, too?" Ayden chided.

"Ah . . . no." It was at the bottom of her messenger bag somewhere under all the other stuff. "I didn't think of that."

I'm sorry.

"It's okay," Ayden said. "You're alive. That's what counts."

"Dad's gone. Someone pulled him out of his grave last night. He was there, at the Tabernacle, and he . . ." Riley's shoulders began to heave.

There was another embrace, and this time her tears soaked her friend's shoulder. When they broke apart, Riley fumbled in her messenger bag for a tissue.

"Come on. There's a guy down the way who sells hot cider. I think we both need some."

Riley blew her nose while following her friend through the winding paths of the market. The cider merchant's tent reminded Riley of a Turkish bazaar. Red fabric, possibly silk, hung underneath the traditional canvas, and it was shot with gold threads. An incense burner sat in the corner wafting something aromatic into the air. The vendor was dark-skinned, Middle Eastern, maybe, and she could tell he had his eye on her friend by the way he smiled at her. Ayden returned the smile, but not quite as warmly, collected the drinks, and herded her toward the back of the tent away from the other patrons. They sat on large, plush pillows near an electric heater. The cider tasted wonderful and warmed Riley from the first sip. Not quite as luscious as hot chocolate, but still good.

"Tell me what happened with your dad," Ayden said.

Riley settled the thick mug on her lap. "I had to go to the meeting, so the cemetery had this new volunteer sit vigil. A necro sprang a huge magical dragon on the guy. He was dragon-phobic, so he freaked and broke the circle. The cemetery people don't have any idea who did it."

"It was probably Ozymandias, especially after you dissed him."

Riley groaned. A couple nights earlier Ayden had been sitting vigil with her at the graveyard, watching over her father's grave while they shared a bottle of the witch's potent homemade wine. Riley had gotten seriously ripped, and when Ozymandias, the creepy necromancer who resembled one of the evil dudes in *The Lord of the Rings*, showed up, she'd smarted off to him. She was inside a protective circle, so what could he do?

Steal my dad, that's what. "I was sooo stupid," Riley admitted.

"No argument."

"Hey, it's partly your fault. I blame your wine; it was wicked strong."

"I blame your mouth," Ayden retorted. "Either way, your dad's on the loose for the next year. There's not much you can do about that."

"I'm not letting him stay aboveground."

"Don't even think you can tangle with a necromancer and come out ahead," the witch scolded. "Especially if it's Ozymandias. I wasn't blowing smoke when I told you he's into the dark stuff. Just let it be, okay?"

Not okay.

Riley fell silent to avoid an argument. Ayden took that silence as acceptance and turned her attention to the remainder of the cider in her mug.

"Do you want to talk about what happened inside the Tabernacle?" she asked in a low voice.

Riley shook her head immediately. How do you explain what it was like to see people you know being ripped apart and eaten? What it felt like to think you were going to die the same way?

Ayden's comforting hand touched her arm. "When you're ready, I'll listen."

"I don't know if I'll ever be," Riley admitted. "It was too . . . horrible."

"Is Beck okay?" her friend asked.

"He got clawed up, but he's alive. Simon—" Riley jammed her lips together. Just thinking of him made her want to cry.

"Is he going to make it?" the witch asked. Her hand was still on Riley's arm, warm and reassuring.

"I . . . yeah. They didn't think he was, but now he is."

Ayden frowned, like she didn't understand Riley's verbal gymnastics. "Anything else you want to tell me?"

Riley couldn't hold it back. Someone had to know her secret. "Ah, well, you see, I made a deal with this angel, and . . ."

The witch's frown deepened. After a quick glance around to ensure they weren't being overheard, she leaned closer. "What do you mean by *deal?*"

Riley told her about the agreement with Heaven.

"My Goddess," Ayden murmured. "You sure it was an angel?"

Riley nodded. "And she came through. Simon's getting better."

"Once Hell finds out you're on Heaven's team, it could get complicated," her friend warned.

Riley snorted. "More complicated than last night? That Five was after me. It was the one who killed my dad and the same one who tried to flatten me at the law library."

"Which happened before your deal with Heaven," Ayden said. "Oh, Goddess, you are in trouble, aren't you? Have you told Beck any of this?"

"No, and I'm not going to. I'll work it out on my own."

"It's not showing weakness to ask for his help."

"No way, not from Beck," Riley retorted. "End of subject."

Ayden walked with her as far as the witches' store. "Try the Deader tent two aisles over," she suggested. "The man there might have heard about your dad."

"But you said I shouldn't go near the necros."

The witch raised an auburn eyebrow. "I know you're not listening to my sage advice, so I might as well steer you in the right direction."

"And if that guy doesn't know anything?"

"Then work through the summoners who were hounding you at the cemetery. Minus Ozymandias. Do not go near that man, do you understand?"

"Got it."

"Really got it or just saying that to make me happy?" the witch pressed.

"Don't know yet."

Ayden rolled her eyes, then reached for something on the counter. After giving Riley another hug, she handed her a small plastic bag full of herbs. "Brew yourself a cup of tea with this right before bed; one teaspoon should do it. It helps clear your head and might keep you from having nightmares. I'm thinking you need that right now."

Riley smiled. "Thanks, Ayden, for everything."

The witch traced something in the air between them. It looked like a complex symbol.

"What was that?"

"Just waving away a mosquito," Ayden replied.

In January? You are so lying.

FOUR

The Reanimate Palace, as it was called, wasn't doing much business. Four Deaders stood in a row, staring at nothing, a grayish tint to their wan faces. From what she'd heard, if their bodies were treated carefully they could remain outside the grave for almost a year.

If her dad's body had been in pieces after his battle with the Five, no necro would have wanted him. Instead he'd died from a single shard of glass driven into his heart by the demon's windstorm. A pristine Dad meant a potential reanimate. Her father was one of a kind: It was rare any trapper ever made it onto the reanimate market.

Riley cocked her head, studying the four forlorn figures—two males, two females. One of the guys was about her age. One minute he was dead, then he was standing inside a tent while people decided whether to buy him or not.

That so has to suck.

The government outlawed slavery in 1865; that date had been drummed into her head by her father, the history teacher, but the dead were another matter entirely. Recent court cases had ruled the deceased had no civil rights, so there was a bill in Congress to rectify that big hole in the law. It was stalled in committee, the victim of a well-financed lobbying campaign by the necromancers. Meanwhile people like her dad were stolen out of their graves and trafficked to those who could afford to buy them.

Riley took a deep breath to calm her nerves and walked into the tent. The salesman immediately moved forward with oily ease.

"Good afternoon. Can I help you?" he asked. It sounded like he sold bootleg designer purses. Anything but dead people.

"My dad was reanimated last night, and I need to know who did it."

"The summoner should have left a notice at the gravesite, if it was a legal reanimation."

"It wasn't," she said. "I didn't give anyone permission to do that."

"Ah . . ." the fellow said, moving back behind a folding table that served as a makeshift desk. He riffled through a stack of cards and then offered her one.

"Contact this guy. He's the summoner's ombudsman in Atlanta. He handles all complaints about ripped-off corpses."

The card was familiar. A number of them had been left just outside the circle that once protected her father's grave. Of the necromancers she'd encountered, Mortimer Alexander had been the nicest, always polite. He'd claimed he wouldn't reanimate a corpse without the family's permission. If that was true, then he'd be her best bet to find her dad.

Riley studied the address on the card. "Little Five Points?"

The sales dude grunted. "Necros like it there. They say it has a kind of magical vortex or something."

"Is there?"

The guy shrugged. "If Mort can't help you . . ." He handed over another card.

GONE MISSING DETECTIVE AGENCY. YOU LOST 'EM, WE FIND 'EM.

"They charge for this?" she asked dubiously.

"Sure. There's always money to be made in death," the guy remarked.

Riley hurried out of the tent before she hit him.

Ori followed the girl's movement through the market from his position near the five fountains. After they'd talked, Riley had gone to the witches' tent, where she met someone who apparently was a friend, given the intensity of their greeting. Then they'd moved to the tent that served drinks. Now she was speaking with someone at the tent where they sold corpses. Others might not see it, but he could tell she was hurting, both inside and out. That wasn't a surprise after the death of her father and last night's battle.

"Too close," he muttered. By the time he had realized what was happening at the Tabernacle, he'd almost lost her to the demon. "Won't happen again." He would be following her from this point on. It was only a matter of time before the Five came after her, and he'd be waiting. At least her boyfriend was out of the way for the moment.

One less complication.

Ori scratched his chin in confusion. Higher-level Hellspawn were always on the lookout for souls to harvest. Why hadn't the demon made her a deal—her life for her soul? Then the fiend could use that valuable bargaining chip to buy favor with others of its kind. That was how Hell operated—an endless line of favors owed all the way up to the Prince of Hell himself.

Riley was on the move again. Ori tracked her to her car and watched as she pulled away. No sign of the Geo-Fiend. Sometimes he couldn't get a break if he tried.

Riley's hope that she could zip into the hospital, spend some time with Simon, and then retreat without anyone else seeing her was just not in the cards. Her father had once remarked that after every disaster there is a time of reckoning. After the smoke clears and the bodies are toted off, the survivors and their families need time to come to terms with what has happened. Put things into perspective.

Since Riley was one of the survivors, her boyfriend's family wanted to hear her story. Before she realized what was happening, she was shepherded into a private waiting room set aside for the Adler family. There were ten of them, and they all looked like Simon—lanky and blond.

Someone whispered, "She's a demon trapper?"

Riley was getting used to that. It came with the territory.

Simon's parents didn't rise from their seats; their faces were pale and lined. They appeared more exhausted than when she'd met them this morning. The others settled in around the couple, talking quietly among themselves and shooting furtive glances at Riley. One of the women carried a sleeping infant. In the midst of the group was a toddler who wandered from person to person showing them his stuffed dog. It had big blue eyes, just like the little boy. As he made his rounds, he received lots of hugs and kisses.

I could so use a hug right now. Ayden's had worn off.

When the little one stopped in front of her, Riley smiled and touched his blond hair fondly. "He looks so much like Simon," she said.

"Just like him when he was little," a young woman replied. It was Amy, one of Simon's sisters. "He used to drive me crazy following me all over the house." She had her hand placed protectively over a noticeable baby bump that pushed against her blue knit top.

"Come here, son," the child's mother urged. The toddler wandered in her direction, babbling and waving his little toy.

Mrs. Adler stirred. She had a kind face. "When Simon first mentioned a trapper named Riley, I thought you were a boy. You look so young to be catching demons."

"Lots of people think that," Riley replied.

"I'm sorry about your father," the woman added. "You must miss him deeply."

Riley could only nod. She took a long sip of water from a plastic cup. She didn't remember where she'd gotten it, but there it was. The Adlers didn't press her for answers as she organized her thoughts.

How do I tell them that everything went wrong? That the demons weren't supposed to get across the line of Holy Water. That they had coordinated their attack like an army.

Just get it done.

"Ah . . . we didn't see it coming," she began.

Simon's father leaned forward in his chair, brows furrowed.

"Simon and I met before the meeting. He'd just put down the ward, you know, the Holy Water circle we do to protect ourselves from the demons. Then we went outside for a while." And that was about as much as she could say about that. It'd been his idea to go around the back of the building. His idea for them to kiss and hold each other close and talk about the future. She remembered how good that had felt, how she'd never wanted it to end.

"Riley?" Mr. Adler prodded.

"Sorry." She cleared her throat. "We went back inside for the Guild meeting." Riley hesitated. This was where she'd told the trappers about the Holy Water, how some of it was counterfeit. The Adlers didn't need to know that. "The demons just appeared out of nowhere."

"How did the fire start?" Simon's father asked.

"Pyro-Fiends. There were a lot of them. They just went crazy. It was the Threes that broke through the Holy Water ward."

"Threes?" Amy asked, perplexed.

"They're . . ." How could she explain these things? They were so much a part of her world now. "They're Grade Three demons. They're about four feet tall," she said, indicating their height, "and all teeth and claws. They eat . . . everything."

There were gasps around her.

"That's what hurt my son?" the man asked, his voice edged with a quaver.

She nodded. "They broke through the ward, and one of them got between us. Simon shouted for me to run, and it went for him. If he hadn't said anything . . ."

It would have come for me instead.

That would have been okay. Better than watching the thing tear into him like a big cat, shredding and clawing, Simon's blood spraying into the air in a fine red mist.

She shuddered at the memory, the cup shaking in her hand. "I hit it with a chair and then one of the trappers carried Simon outside."

Which wasn't all that had happened. She wasn't telling them about the others—the ones that were burned or torn to pieces. Ethan, Morton, Collins . . . so many.

Mr. Adler touched her hand gently, jarring her out of her dark thoughts. Riley looked into the eyes of her boyfriend's father. Simon would look like this in thirty years or so. He would age well, as long as he stayed alive long enough to do it.

"It is not your fault," he said softly.

Wish I could believe that.

"The Guild's doctor said someone treated my son's wounds with Holy Water and that's why they're not infected," his mother said. "The surgeons sewed up all the damage, and from what we've been told, he's healing really quickly."

"Holy Water does that." Providing the wound was caused by one of Hell's fiends.

"They don't know what to make of the fact that his brain is working again," his mother continued. "Father Harrison said it was a miracle."

That's the truth. Her boyfriend's family would be making funeral arrangements if Riley hadn't agreed to Heaven's terms.

"He was so brave last night." Riley's heart swelled at the memory. "He didn't back down at all."

"Sounds like our son," his dad said, smiling faintly at his wife, a glint of tears in his tired eyes.

"He's a really nice guy," Riley said, then felt foolish. They knew that.

"He likes you a lot," his dad replied. "He smiles whenever he says your name."

Riley didn't reply. If she said anything more, she'd start to cry, and she wasn't sure she'd ever stop. The energetic toddler wandered over again. He patted her knee with a chubby hand.

Riley bent and hugged him, feeling his warm breath on her shoulder. The tears came anyway. Then she got hugs from every member of Simon's family. All of them said they were praying for her.

Like I'm one of them.

Simon's hospital room was less crowded with equipment than it had been this morning. The machine that had helped him breathe was gone, and in its place was the soft hiss of oxygen.

Her boyfriend's wavy blond hair held flecks of dried blood. His gorgeous blue eyes were closed, and he was breathing deeply, just like the night he'd fallen asleep at the graveyard. The same night he'd held her as she wept for her dead father.

Would Heaven have let him die if I'd said no?

There was a slight moan from the bed. Both of Simon's hands and arms were bandaged, and the image of him trying to fend off the demon's slicing claws returned before she could block it.

Riley carefully took one of his hands in hers. Simon painstakingly pried his eyes open.

"Hey there," she said. His gaze finally settled on her face, and he gave her a bewildered look.

"Water?" he croaked.

Riley hunted around until she found a glass of ice on the bedside table. She remembered this from when her mom was sick, and after fumbling with the electronic controls to help him sit upright, she gingerly placed a piece into his mouth. He sucked on it, but his bloodshot eyes never left her. After three more pieces, he pushed the spoon away and she returned the cup to the table.

"Riley," he whispered.

"You scared me, guy. You can't do that again," she said, smoothing back a lock of hair. It refused to stay in place. Dried blood wasn't a great styling product.

"You're alive," he said. It sounded like he hadn't been entirely sure on that point.

"Because of you," she said.

"No." Then he grimaced, extracted his hand from hers, and slowly pulled down the blanket. It was hard going, what with the thick bandages. He wasn't wearing a gown, but a pair of drawstring pants. Riley barely suppressed the gasp—his chest and stomach were covered in a patchwork of bandages.

"Itches," he said, wincing, carefully scratching near the edge of a piece of adhesive tape.

"Tell me about it," she said, pasting a false grin on her face. Her demon-clawed thigh still demanded a lot of lotion to keep it from driving her nuts. "It means you're healing."

It hurt so much to see him like this. He'd be marked for life.

Like me.

"You killed that demon," he said simply, letting his arms fall on the bed as if the scratching had depleted his energy. "You saved my life."

"I didn't like seeing my guy getting chewed on."

Simon shivered in memory. "Its claws burned like fire," he said, not looking at her now. "I thought it was going to . . ." His voice trailed off.

You thought it would eat you alive. Like the Three that had attacked her a few weeks back. She still had nightmares about that, still felt its claws imbedded in her thigh and its rancid breath in her face.

Riley gently squeezed his hand again, waiting for the questions that were sure to come.

"How many . . . ?" he whispered.

He'll have to know eventually. "Thirteen that we know of. There're probably more in the rubble they haven't found yet. Another four are in bad shape."

"Who died?"

"Simon, I—"

"Who?" he demanded, his attention returning to her.

Riley gave him the names, and with each his face grew more solemn. He closed his eyes when she told him about Ethan, one of their fellow apprentices.

"He was so happy," Simon whispered.

Ethan had a reason to be happy. He and his fiancée were looking for an apartment and were planning a wedding sometime in the summer.

Now he was dead.

"Who else?" Simon asked, his voice so quiet she almost didn't hear it.

"That's it. Both of the masters are hurt: Stewart has a concussion, and Harper's got a couple of cracked ribs."

Silence. Not the good kind.

She offered him more ice and he took it. Once it was gone, he sucked in a thick breath. "I must have put down the Holy Water wrong."

"No way. You did it perfectly. The demons shouldn't have gotten through."

But they had. It was a good bet he would carry that horrendous guilt forever, no matter who said he wasn't to blame. Simon would always second-guess himself.

More silence. She held his hand, knowing he needed to think things through.

Eventually Simon closed his eyes, and she took that as a hint he wanted to be alone. After a kiss on his forehead, she whispered, "You get better. You hear?" No reply.

When she reached the door Riley paused and looked back at him. A single glistening tear rolled down his pale cheek.

It was a match to her own.

FIVE

When he was young, Beck had spent time in the high school principal's office, hauled in for swearing, roughing up bullies, threatening teachers, and vandalizing a skinhead's truck. Same drill in the Army, though most of the time that had been on account of his drinking. Even now, at twenty-two, he knew what it was like to be called to account for his sins. That's what this felt like.

As they waded through the throng of newshounds outside Atlanta City Hall, he shot a look at Stewart. From the expression on the master's face, he could see the man agreed. They were going to be held responsible for this disaster.

Reporters churned around them, shooting questions at them like bullets. As the pair made their way toward the massive building that housed Atlanta's civil administration, Beck did his best to clear the path in front of Stewart, knowing the master's leg was troubling him. Truth was, his was just as bad, but at least he had age on his side.

Once they reached the top of the stairs, they turned as one and were greeted with an amazing sight: Mitchell Street awash with satellite trucks, their masts high in the air like overzealous daisies. Across the street, in the park, the police had formed a viewing area for the curious citizens of Atlanta. Signs were everywhere. "Prepare to Meet Your Maker!" one said in bright red lettering. Others cited Bible verses. Then there was the Demons Have Rights group with fake horns on their heads. They even carried plastic pitchforks and wore pointed tails. That bunch was separated from the rest, probably to keep them from getting beaten up.

"So what ya seein' here?" Stewart asked.

"A whole lot of crazy people," Beck replied sourly.

"A few, maybe. Frightened people do stupid things, lad. Keep that in mind in the days ta come."

Beck didn't reply. He knew the old trapper was right. As long as the Guild stood between the dark scary things and the public, the good folks of Atlanta had been okay with that. Now it looked like the trappers were losing the battle, and that scared their fellow citizens out of their minds. *Hell, it even frightens me.*

Beck caught a glimpse of flaming red hair billowing around a woman's shoulders, stirred to life by a light breeze. She wore a chocolate-brown pantsuit and stood near a news van. From this distance it was hard to tell the color of her eyes, but he'd bet they were vivid green to match her blouse. She stood out like a fiery beacon in the midst of a monotone crowd.

There was a nervous cough from behind them. It came from an earnest young man in a suit. "Sirs?" he said. "If you would follow me. The council is ready."

Stewart waved their escort forward. " 'Lay on Macduff, and damn'd be him that first cries, "Hold, enough!" ' "

"What?" the young flunky asked, bewildered.

"Never mind, lad. Show us the way, will ya?"

"Yes, sir."

As they walked into the building Beck wondered aloud how the solid metal doors had remained in place. "These must be worth a fortune."

"The last three fellows who tried ta steal them were given a one-way trip ta Demon Central," Stewart explained. "Word gets 'round."

They kept walking, which only made Beck's leg throb.

They were shepherded into one of the smaller meeting rooms. It wasn't fancy, nothing more than a long table and a few padded armchairs for the council and folding chairs for the audience. The master trapper sank into a chair near the front, his forehead sweaty.

"Ya okay?" Beck asked, worried.

"Nothin' that a little whisky won't cure," the man replied gamely. Stewart's eyes met his. "Ya keep that temper on a leash, ya hear?"

That was going to be difficult. Beck was dog tired, he had a raging headache, and his body ached like he'd been in a mosh pit. With demons. *Keep it cool,* a voice said inside his head. It was Paul's voice, guiding him like he had since Beck was sixteen.

Ezekiel Montgomery, the mayor of Atlanta, entered from a side door. The politician sported a noticeable paunch and was accompanied by a few council members, a couple of assistants, and a pair of Atlanta cops. The officers positioned themselves on either side of the long table, facing toward the audience like they expected trouble.

"They brought backup," Beck murmured. He heard a snort from his companion.

"This isn't all of 'em," Stewart observed. "The council president is missin'. I wonder why the others aren't here."

As the council settled themselves, Beck took a seat next to the master and waited, drumming his fingers on his knee to work off some of his tension. When he brushed a hand over his forehead, it came away wet. He wanted to peel off his leather jacket, but then everyone would see the sweat rings and how his shirt clung to him because of the fever. He'd changed clothes before this meeting, taking care to tightly bandage his left thigh in an effort to keep the jeans clean. The way the leg throbbed, he suspected the bandage was a waste of time.

God, I feel like crap. At least in another twenty-four hours he'd be better. Until then, he just had to tough it out.

"Which one of you is Harper?" the mayor asked without looking up from the paperwork in front of him.

Stewart cleared his throat. "He's out with an injury. I'm Master Trapper Angus Stewart. I'm empowered ta speak for the Guild."

"Could you stand when you talk?" the mayor asked. "It makes it easier for us."

"But not for me," the Scotsman said, remaining in his chair. "Tell 'em why, lad."

Beck pulled himself to his feet. "Ah, what Master Stewart means is that he's injured. It's best he sit."

The mayor frowned, then gave a curt nod. Beck's attention moved to the young man right behind Montgomery. He looked like any other young political assistant, but something about him felt off. The guy wouldn't meet his eyes but kept his full attention on his boss.

"So who are you?" the mayor asked, scrutinizing Beck like he'd just discovered him breaking into his house.

"I'm Denver Beck. I'm a journeyman trapper."

"Mr. Buck," the mayor began, "we offer our condolences for the losses the Guild has incurred."

That's just fancy talk for "As long as it isn't my ass that's hurtin', I'm good with it."

"The name's *Beck*," he said. Grudgingly he added, "Thank you."

The councilwoman sitting three seats down from the mayor issued a faint smile. She was African American, with caramel skin and bright eyes. There was no nameplate in front of her, so Beck had no idea who she was.

"I want to know what you intend to do about these demons," Montgomery demanded.

Beck looked over Stewart, who waved him on. *Why am I doin' all the talkin'?*

"Master Harper called the National Guild, and they're sendin' us another master so we can train new apprentices."

"How does that solve the immediate problem?" the councilwoman asked.

"It doesn't," Beck admitted. "We've put out a call for other trappers to move to Atlanta for the time bein'."

"How many were in the Guild to start with?" the councilwoman asked.

Beck gave Stewart a quick look, and the master whispered the answer.

"Fifty-six," Beck said, feeling like a talking puppet. "Not all are active. Right now we have about twenty trappers who can work." He'd never felt so out of place in his life. What did he know about all this political stuff? He hadn't even voted in the last election.

"What about the demon hunters? Why can't we have them take care of this?" a balding councilman asked.

Stewart finally spoke up. "I talked with the Archbishop about that this mornin'. The Church's position is that we can handle it."

The mayor's assistant leaned forward and whispered in Montgomery's ear. The mayor shook his head, causing the man to repeat whatever he'd said. This time there was a nod.

"I must respectfully disagree with the Archbishop," Montgomery replied. "The governor has been in touch with the Vatican, and they've offered to send a team of demon hunters to Atlanta. I think we should move forward on that offer."

The muscles in Beck's jaw tensed, causing him to weigh his words carefully. "I'm sure the big boys are good at what they do, but they don't know Atlanta or her demons. Our fiends aren't the same as the ones in New York City or L.A. . . . or Rome for that matter."

"So you're saying that your knowledge of the city will be better for this situation than the Vatican's expertise?" the councilwoman asked.

The lady was feeding him the right questions, and Beck loved her for it. "Yes, ma'am. We got ambushed last night, and that won't happen again."

"If last night was an example of how the trappers work, we're in deep trouble," the mayor insisted.

One of the other council members nodded. "I agree. We should request the hunters come to Atlanta. They'll get the job done."

"The trappers have dealt with our demon issues for as long as the city has existed," the councilwoman protested. "Bringing in an outside force will only make things worse. The hunters aren't locals, and they don't have to answer to anyone but the Church."

"We need to get this behind us," Montgomery replied. "We've got major industries looking at moving to this city. Unless we get this settled as quickly as possible, those opportunities are going to dry up." The mayor began to shuffle papers in front of him, clearly agitated. "We're having this problem because of the Guild. The trappers had their chance and they blew it. We need professionals, not amateurs."

Stewart's face turned blood red at the grave insult. His mouth opened, but no words came out. Beck was sure the man was going to have a stroke.

After a quick motion, which was seconded, the vote went in favor of the demon hunters. Only one nay vote was cast: The councilwoman had held to her principles.

"Motion passed." The mayor gaveled the meeting to a close and then rose from his seat. "Go bury your dead and call it a day, gentlemen," he said. Behind him, his assistant wore a sly smile, like he'd just won a major victory.

Beck's temper burst out of its restraints. He took a step forward, his fists clenched, but he was immediately blocked by the cops, hands on their firearms.

"Don't, lad," Stewart said from behind him. "Give it up. They're not listenin'."

Once they'd waded through the crowds and were inside the truck, the master produced a silver flask from a pocket and took a long swig. He offered it to Beck, who did the same. The whisky burned his raw throat as it went down. "Thanks," Beck said, and handed the flask back. As he pulled away from the curb, he asked, "Why did ya let me do all the talkin'? I'm just a journeyman."

The old trapper took another swig of his flask, then smacked his lips. ". . . Who'll be a master someday. Ya might as well learn the ropes now. It's not gonna get any easier, that's for damned sure."

"But I'm not . . ." *what ya think I am.*

Stewart glared at him. "Paul Blackthorne only trained the best. Ya wouldn't want ta be insultin' his memory now, would ya?"

The master had him by the throat: No way Beck could diss his friend. "No, sir."

"Good. First thing, take me home. I need sleep. Pick me up about eight tonight, and we'll go ta Harper's. We need ta find a new meetin' place, start the insurance paperwork, all that."

"But if the hunters are comin' to Atlanta . . ."

"All the more reason ta get our own house in order."

SIX

Oakland Cemetery. It was the *last* place Riley wanted to be, but here she was, trudging along the asphalt road that led into the boneyard. The cemetery sat east of the city and had been there since the mid-1800s. Since the Victorians had a thing about graveyards and designed them like parks, Oakland was known for its massive magnolia trees and stately mausoleums.

Over the last couple of weeks Riley had spent almost every evening here, safely tucked inside a sanctified circle of Holy Water and candles, guarding her father's grave from the necromancers. As long as the circle had remained intact, no one could have touched him. Once the moon was full, he'd have been safe from any summoning spell.

But he never made it to the full moon.

"I should have been here," she grumbled, her breath puffing out in a thin white stream as she tromped deeper into the graveyard. Nothing would have scared her into breaking that circle.

She turned left onto the road toward her family's patch of ground. The air was still at the moment, the moonlight draped across the ancient gravestones like thin silver icing. Beneath each of those stones was someone who'd lived in this city, walked its streets. Now all they had was a bit of red clay to call their own.

Back when the Blackthornes had money—one of her relatives in the 1880s was a banker—they'd constructed the family mausoleum. It was one of the finest in the cemetery. Sitting on an island between two roads, it was built of red stone, so solid it had withstood a tornado. In true Victorian fashion the builders had really pimped out the place—heavy bronze doors, stained-glass windows, and lurking gargoyles on the roof.

Now Riley thought of the mausoleum in terms of hours and hours of sitting vigil for her father. Of last night with Beck after the trappers had been killed. She'd fallen asleep inside the building, nestled in his arms, safe on holy ground. She didn't think he'd ever closed his eyes. He'd smelled of smoke and blood and righteous anger. Denver Beck was a stick of dynamite waiting for a match, and she hoped she wasn't anywhere near when he exploded.

Riley halted in front of the mausoleum and peered up at the gargoyles. Their bizarre lion faces glowered down at her as if she were an intruder. They had always creeped her out.

Since the building was full of dead relatives, her parents' graves were on the west side looking toward the state capitol dome. Though it hurt too much to think about, Riley knelt in front of her father's grave. It was still a mess, like a giant mole had dug itself out, mounding dirt on either side in its frantic effort to escape. The damaged coffin was gone. Apparently the cemetery people had taken it away.

She took a deep breath, feeling the cold saturate her lungs, causing her to cough. Her mouth still tasted of soot. Blinking to clear the tears, she whispered, "Sorry, Dad. It wasn't supposed to be like this."

He was supposed to be alive, teaching her how to be a trapper, laughing at her jokes and taking her out for pizza. Calling her a sleepyhead when she woke up late. Being there for her. Now there was just an empty hole in the ground that matched the one in her heart.

Riley remained silent for a time, pulling memories from the corners of her mind like someone might detangle yarn. She never wanted to forget her father's gentle voice, his face, how his hair refused to behave. As long as she held those memories close, he wasn't really gone.

Then she began to talk to him. Though his body was missing, maybe somewhere his spirit would hear her. It wasn't like she hadn't been close to her mom, but her father had been a trapper, so she told him what had happened over the last twenty-four hours. She knew he couldn't answer, but somehow the talking seemed to help.

"I saw some of them die," she said, shuddering. "Beck's okay but pretty beaten up. Simon's—" Her voice caught. "He's going to make it, but only because, well . . . just because."

There was a sigh of wind in the trees around her, like her father had heard her and was offering his sympathy. His calm voice floated through her mind. *It'll be okay.*

When she was a child she'd believed him. Not anymore.

Once she'd talked herself out, Riley rose, dusted off her knees, and headed back down the road to the Bell Tower, where the cemetery had its office and gift shop. She would wait there for the volunteer who'd failed her and her father so spectacularly.

Boredom quickly took hold, and she dialed her best friend. She didn't have many friends, at least none like Peter. He was more like a big brother than a buddy. Unfortunately, the last time they'd talked they hadn't parted on good terms.

"Hello?" her friend asked, his voice hesitant.

She'd forgotten she was using her dad's phone and he wouldn't know the number.

"Hi Peter. It's me."

"Hey. Where are you?"

"The cemetery."

"Still grave-sitting?"

Peter didn't know. They'd last spoken when she was at Beck's place the morning after the Tabernacle fire. Upset that she'd nearly gotten herself killed, Peter had hung up on her and she'd never had a chance to tell him about her dad.

"No, I'm done with that." Then she told him why.

"That bites. You go to all that work and . . ." He swore into the phone. "I'm so sorry, Riley."

"Yeah, it sucks. I'm trying to find him but none of the necros are talking."

More silence on the other end of the phone.

"So what's up with you?" she said, hoping to spark more of a conversation.

"Not much. It's tense here right now. I really should go."

"Ah, okay. Maybe we can talk tomorrow."

"Sure. That'll work." He hung up.

Was he upset because of her nearly dying at the Tabernacle or was it something else? No way she would know unless he was willing to talk, which didn't seem to be the case. She shelved that away as another potential problem.

A quarter of an hour later—Riley kept checking her watch every few minutes—the cemetery dude arrived. He was younger than she'd expected, about twenty-five, and wore glasses. His heavy coat hung off a thin frame. He moved up the road like someone who'd been viciously mugged and expected to be a victim again.

This was the volunteer who'd failed to keep her father safe. Last night she could have happily thrown him to a demon, and tonight wasn't much better. Still, she'd almost broken the circle twice herself, only catching Ozymandias's clever ruses at the last moment.

The guy stopped a good ten feet from where she was sitting on the steps that led to the cemetery office. It was easy to see the look of devastation on his ruddy face. He was a walking apology. They stared at each other for a time, neither willing to speak first. At any little noise, he jumped, casting a worried glance in the direction of the sound. What had it taken for him to come here tonight?

This was too painful. "Tell me what happened," she said.

He winced. "I . . . did everything like I was supposed to."

Oh, God. He sounded just like her after the disaster at the law library. She'd used those exact words when Beck had demanded an explanation.

The volunteer kept fidgeting, and finally she beckoned him to sit next to her on the stairs. He did so with great reluctance, as if it were physically painful to be anywhere near her.

"What's your name?" she asked.

"Richard."

"I'm Riley," she said, keeping her voice neutral. This was hell for her, and it couldn't be any different for him. "Tell me what happened."

He sighed and adjusted his leather gloves before answering. "I set the circle like I always do. No problems. Necros came and necros went and—"

"Which ones?" That could be important.

He pondered on the question. "Mortimer and that guy who dresses all flashy. I think his name is Lenny."

"Anyone else?"

He shook his head. "I was reading a book, and then the wind picked up. I ignored it. That happens sometimes, and usually it's a summoner playing with my head. Then the ground in front of the circle began to glow like it was a pool of lava. It was a real strange red and gold."

"And?"

"Then *it* blasted out of the dirt like a rocket," he said, throwing his arms out like an explosion.

"It? You mean the dragon?"

"Yeah. I've always been afraid of them ever since I was little. My parents bought me a stuffed one because they thought it was cute. I was sure it was going to eat me, so I hid it in the back of the closet."

She'd expected him to blame someone else, but this guy was taking it all on his shoulders.

"Did you tell anyone that you were afraid of dragons, I mean like one of the necros?" she asked. Maybe that might give her a clue.

"No," Richard replied. "It's not something you go around telling people."

He had a point.

"What did it look like?"

He rubbed his face, his fingers making a scratchy noise on the stubble around his chin.

"It was huge, at least twenty feet tall. It had these thick mirrored scales that changed color when it moved. I could see all the candle flames in them. It was really eerie."

"It didn't fly into the graveyard," she said, more to herself than him. *Like you'd think a dragon would.*

"No. It came right out of the ground. You should have seen its claws. They had to be at least three feet long. It kept staring at me, hissing. I could hear it in my mind, telling me to break the circle or it'd roast me alive."

"And you did?" she asked, working to keep her anger out of her voice.

"No!" Richard retorted, shaking his head instantly. "I closed my eyes and tried to think of anything else but that damned thing."

"So how did the circle get broken?"

"When I didn't do what it wanted, it leaned back on it rear legs and roared," he said. "I saw tombstones shatter, and the roof exploded off the mausoleum. Then this wall of flame came right toward me."

Richard was shaking at this point, so Riley hesitantly put a hand on his arm. It seemed to comfort him.

There was no evidence of destruction near the mausoleum. "All illusion," she said.

Richard took a deep breath and then pushed on. "When the flames hit the circle, the candles began to rock. It got so hot I thought I was being baked alive. I dove under a blanket and tried to hide, but somehow I must have kicked over one of the candles."

Once the circle was broken nothing kept the necromancer from summoning her father.

"What was it like when my dad . . ." she began, tucking her hands into her lap.

Richard looked over at her. "The dirt flew everywhere, and there was the crack of wood. I think it was the coffin lid. Then your dad just rose out of the ground. I tried to stop him, but he shook his head and pushed me away."

"Did he . . . say anything?"

"Yes, and that was *really* creepy. Your father walked up to the dragon, stared at it, and said, 'It just had to be you.'" Richard swallowed hard. "Then the thing just vanished, taking your father with it."

"But you never saw the necromancer?"

"No."

"How about a swirling bunch of leaves?" That was Ozymandias's favorite disguise.

"No."

Richard was no longer shaking, as if telling the story had somehow exorcised a portion of his fear.

"I'm really sorry," he said. "I feel really bad about this. If I hadn't been so frightened . . ."

She could blame this guy for everything or let it go. Hating on him for the rest of her life wasn't going to help. Well, maybe just a little hating, but he didn't need to know that.

"I understand. I almost fell for the 'Let's sacrifice a kitten' trick."

At his puzzled look, Riley explained Ozymandias's brilliant scheme, how he'd threatened to cut a kitten's throat if she didn't break the circle. Luckily the cat wasn't real, nothing more than a bit of his dark magic.

"Wow. I've heard about him. You think he's the one who took your dad?"

"Maybe."

Silence fell between them for a time. Finally Richard cleared his throat and rose. "Thanks for listening. I was afraid you'd be too angry to talk to me."

"You did what you could."

The young man shook his head. "All I did was let your dad's body be stolen. I don't deserve your gratitude."

He slumped down the road. Riley watched him until he took the turn toward the entrance. She wondered if he'd guard anyone else's grave or whether Paul Blackthorne had been his last gig.

"It just had to be you." Her father had known who had summoned him. Was it Ozymandias?

"Doesn't feel right," she said. Ozy would want *her* to make the mistake, not a cemetery volunteer. *So he could gloat.*

Her phone rang deep inside her messenger bag. She was tempted to ignore it, but it might be Amy giving her an update on Simon. It was Beck. She groaned.

"Ya on hallowed ground?" he asked without bothering to say hello.

"Yes." She was, though she wouldn't be once she crossed under the cemetery archway.

"Stay there." It wasn't a request.

"You know, I'm glad I never had brothers."

"Why?" he asked, clearly puzzled.

"If they'd been like you I'd have run away from home."

"Go ahead. Just make sure it's to Fargo," he shot back.

Jeez, you just don't quit. He'd been on this "Move in with yer aunt" kick ever since he found out she had a relative in North Dakota. It didn't seem to matter that her aunt had hated her dad and disliked Riley by default. Once Beck got something into his brain, it was as immovable as a lump of dried concrete.

Time to change the subject. "I'm sleeping in my own bed tonight," she announced, knowing that would set him off.

"I'm sure yer neighbors will really like that when they get barbecued."

"Huh?" He wasn't making any sense.

"Nothin' would keep a couple Pyros from torchin' yer apartment buildin' just so that Five can get ya."

She hadn't thought about that. It seemed pretty far-fetched, but fiends attacking the Tabernacle hadn't seemed like a possibility either.

"I want to be in my own place, Beck. I'm tired, I need a shower, and

I hurt all over." Her dad's things would be around her at home. Maybe that way she wouldn't feel so alone.

"I hear ya, girl, but that's not the most important thing in the world."

He was lecturing her again like he knew all the answers to life's questions.

"Good night, Beck."

"Riley . . ." he said in warning.

"I got the message," she said, hanging up.

And I'm so ignoring it.

Though she hadn't seen anyone when she'd climbed into her car at the cemetery, she was unnerved when a motorcycle fell in behind her. It followed her until the next intersection, then it pulled even with her driver's side door.

Oh, crap, now what? The motorcyclist flipped up the helmet's visor. *Ori.* He replaced the visor and fell in behind her again once they cleared the intersection. It felt strange having an escort, but she had to admit he totally owned that bike. Absolute bad boy. The kind you dream about but really shouldn't date because you know it would never work out.

They couldn't have been more different—saintly Simon of the most holy kisses, and Ori, who stirred primal emotions she didn't understand. Riley shook her head again. *Can't go there. Simon's perfect for me. And he's* all *mine.* Even her dad had liked him. She suspected that wouldn't have been the case with the hot guy on the bike.

When Riley parked in the lot near her apartment, Ori pulled into a slot next to her.

"I hope I didn't frighten you," he said, walking over to her car.

"A little. I'm not used to having guys follow me around."

"I'm surprised to hear that," he said smoothly.

Riley felt the warmth creep onto her cheeks. Luckily the parking lot wasn't well lit, so he probably didn't notice. "Just demons follow me around." How many guys could handle that statement? Only trappers, and most of them weren't that cool.

"Ah, well," Ori replied, "I'll just have to deal with that problem."

"You know, you don't carry a duffel bag or anything. How do you kill fiends without any weapons or Holy Water?"

He gestured toward the saddlebags. "I've got a few things tucked away."

But you don't carry them with you all the time, not like Beck.

"So this is where you live?" he asked. It was like he'd wanted to change the subject. He did that a lot.

Riley went along with the shift of topic. "This is it. It used to be a hotel. Now it's an apartment building with lots of dinky rooms."

Ori studied her home. "It's got a roof and four walls, so that's all you need, right?"

No. It wasn't all she needed. There was so much more to it than just a place to live.

Somehow her escort was closer to her now. "Sorry, I didn't mean to upset you," he said softly.

She looked up into his dark eyes. "Not your fault," she replied, shrugging. "Just the way it is now."

"Maybe that will change," he said. Ori gently brushed a strand of hair out of her face. "In fact, I'm counting on that."

Her cheeks heated up again. *What is it with this guy?*

A moment later he was rolling out of the parking lot. Apparently his idea of watching over her didn't mean camping underneath her window.

Probably a good thing. Or she might be tempted to invite him inside.

When Riley eased open the apartment door, it creaked on its hinges. The place felt wrong: It suffered from a severe lack of Dad. Her father's clothes still hung in the closet, his electric razor sat in the bathroom, and all his books were still here, but he wasn't. That's why it felt wrong. She'd hoped to find solace here, but the emptiness just made it worse.

There was a solid bump at calf level, and she jumped in surprise. The neighbor's cat.

"Hey, Max." She knelt to give him a scratch as he leaned against her, purring. His front paws stood on her tennis shoes, the claws kneading into the fabric as his whiskers tickled her hand.

Max was a Maine coon, a solid mass of feline that weighed in at close to twenty pounds. He was Mrs. Litinsky's and seemed to think Riley's apartment was just an extension of his owner's.

"Sorry, you can't come in tonight." Normally she'd enjoy the company, but now all she wanted was a shower and a good night's sleep. Max would expect a great deal of human fawning, and she wasn't up to it.

After another thorough scratch under his furry chin she managed to get through the door without him following. She heard a petulant meow from the hallway but didn't allow the guilt to get to her like it usually did.

She dropped her messenger bag on the secondhand couch and she joined it a second later. The timer had turned on the one light in the living room, and it illuminated the compact space. Since the building was originally a hotel, they'd made this apartment from parts of two separate rooms. Between the drab beige walls and carpet and the jigsaw layout, the end result lacked anything resembling coolness.

At least it's mine as long as I keep paying the rent.

Riley pulled herself up off the couch, yawned, and then eyed the answering machine on the table near the old computer. The message light was urgently blinking red. She needed an incentive to tackle whatever lived on that machine, so she retrieved a strawberry yogurt out of the refrigerator.

Last one. She dutifully added that item to the grocery list. The three entries before hers were in her dad's handwriting. Her heart constricted, and she was forced to swallow a thick lump in her throat that had nothing to do with the yogurt. Yet another reminder that someone she loved used to live here.

She sank into the chair in front of the computer, pushed the play button on the machine, then began spooning yogurt and strawberries into her mouth. Five of the messages were from the CDC—the Consolidated Debt Company, not the germ people. Her father had taken out a loan to pay for her mother's hospital bills, the ones the Guild insurance policy didn't cover. Now the CDC wanted their money back. The first message was polite, but they became less pleasant with each subsequent call. By the last one the caller was shouting into the phone about how she had to pay the debt she owed them and if she didn't they'd exhume her father and sell his body to defray their expenses. The date on that one was yesterday morning.

"Too late for that, guys," she said, pausing in her enjoyment of the yogurty goodness. "Someone else beat you to it." For half a second Riley actually liked the necro who'd screwed these guys over.

The rest of the calls didn't require her immediate attention, which was a blessing. The moment the yogurt was finished, a yawn erupted. *Shower. Bed. Sleep. In that order.*

But it wasn't to be a good night. Apartment buildings generate ambient noise, and though these sounds weren't any different than normal—someone on the floor above flushing the toilet and the occasional cry of the new baby down the hall—all of them woke her up.

"Thanks, Backwoods Boy," she growled, using the nickname she'd invented to describe Beck when he was getting on her nerves. Which was most of the time. He'd seeded the idea that the demons would come calling, and now she couldn't get that out of her mind, even with Ori doing sentry duty. With a sigh, Riley rose and walked to her window, pushing back the curtain. The moon glared off the car windshields in the parking lot below, but no sign of Ori.

"Watching over me, huh?" If he was, he was invisible.

After staring at nothing for some time, she trudged back to bed and pounded her pillow into shape. "Maybe I should have let Max in tonight." He would have curled up against her and purred her to sleep.

A slight shifting noise came from her dresser, and she remembered why an overnight cat wouldn't be a good idea—her fellow lodger. Max would destroy the apartment just to get the thing.

More movement, or at least the faint hint of movement. "I hear you," she said, quietly.

The sound halted abruptly, followed by a minute sigh.

There were a number of things a demon trapper was supposed to do: Riley was expected to trap fiends, keep the proper paperwork, protect the public, and prevent Hell's Minions from making a real mess of the world.

She was not supposed to be sharing an apartment with one.

This was a Grade One Klepto-Fiend, or Magpie, as the trappers called them. He was about three inches in height, with brown skin and dressed like a ninja. He even carried a little bag like a cat burglar. He wasn't dangerous, just prone to ripping off shiny items such as bright pennies or pieces of jewelry. Sometimes she'd find them in bizarre places in her apartment, like in the silverware drawer. Often they'd be stuff that wasn't hers.

Riley had trapped and sold this fiend to a demon trafficker but it had promptly returned, like one of those missing dogs you read about in the paper, the ones who travel hundreds of miles just to find its owner. Not that she owned this fiend. He was definitely one of Lucifer's critters. She wasn't even sure if it was a "he" but as she saw it, girl demons probably dressed nicer.

Riley rolled over, thumped her pillow, and tried to shut down her mind. Instead she heard a teeny voice, the demon talking to himself. Probably counting his stash of goodies.

At least you don't start fires.

And with that in mind, she drifted into an uneasy sleep.

SEVEN

Morning felt as cruel as a dull knife slicing across her throat. To Riley's annoyance her head ached as much as her body, like she'd overdone it with some of Ayden's highly potent witchy wine. Every little noise had made her think of crackling flames and the taunting cackles of the Pyros. As a result she'd slept poorly, bouts of being awake interspersed with seriously bad dreams that had featured fountains of blood and lots of screaming.

"I should have had Ayden's tea," she grumbled, but she'd completely forgotten that remedy until this morning.

It annoyed her that Backwoods Boy might have a point: If Hell really wanted her dead, the fiends wouldn't care how many people they killed to get to her even if the mysterious Ori was nearby. No way could she admit that to Beck's face. His flurry of unwanted advice would become an avalanche.

Riley sat at the kitchen table, face propped up by an elbow, watching the microwave carousel rotate her dad's favorite cup, the one that said STUPIDITY CAN BE HABIT-FORMING.

Forty more seconds and there'd be hot chocolate.

She felt miserable, partly because of the poor night's sleep but mostly because of the calendar. Today's date was circled and marked with a big D. She'd marked the calendar that way because this was Dad Is Free day, the day of the full moon. After today no necromancer could touch him.

"Yeah, that really worked, didn't it?" she mumbled. She rose and turned the page to February, even though it was a day early. Anything to keep from staring at that *D*.

Just as she returned to her chair and resumed the microwave vigil, her cell phone jarred her out of her misery. She answered it without looking at the display.

"Riley?" a gravelly voice asked.

"Good morning, Beck," she said, not taking her eyes off the cup. Thirty seconds. First the hot chocolate, then oatmeal. Maybe she'd be adventurous and make toast.

"I told ya to stay at the cemetery, but ya didn't," he said accusatorily. "I was outside, watchin' yer place all night; that's how I know."

"You've got to be kidding me." *You sat out there in the cold? What kind of idiot are you?*

That was why Ori was nowhere to be seen. He wouldn't want Beck to know he was around.

"What are ya thinkin', girl?" her caller demanded.

"I'm thinking my hot water is almost ready and I don't want to talk to you anymore, not if you're going to be a stalkery butthead." She hung up on him. He immediately rang back and she ignored it.

"I'll so pay for that," she mumbled, but right now breakfast was the only thing she wanted to think about.

Ding!

"About time."

As she stirred the hot chocolate mix into the cup, she realized Beck wasn't going to give an inch. He'd sit out there, night after night, watching her place like a vigilant bloodhound. If he kept it up, he'd be so tired a demon would make a meal of him. And if he was out there, it would make it harder for Ori to do his job.

"Ah, jeez," she grumbled. Why was everything so much hassle?

What she needed was a "bolt hole," at least until Ori caught up with that Five. Every trapper had a safe place on hallowed ground just in case the demons went to war. When her father had first told her about that, she'd thought it sounded really paranoid. After the Tabernacle, not so much. Beck's bolt hole was in a church, so it was heated and had a bathroom, both of which would be a major improvement over the Blackthorne mausoleum, her family's "sanctuary." Besides, if she could find a place to stay, that would get Backwoods Boy off her case.

"Until he comes up with something else to complain about."

The phone rang again, but it wasn't Beck's name on the caller ID. This wasn't someone she could blow off.

"Lass?" the Scotsman asked, his voice tight.

"Master Stewart." *Why is he calling me?*

"I'm hearin' that yer givin' Beck a hard time. Now let's be clear: Ya *will* be on hallowed ground after sundown, till I tell ya different."

"But why not during the day?" The Five had come after her in the late afternoon. Or, it might have been right after sundown. It was easy to lose track of time inside a library.

"The beasties are stronger at night. Ya might be thinkin' that ya might go about yer business and I'll not know if yer followin' my orders. That would be wrong."

"Yes, sir. I'll be on hallowed ground at night."

"Glad we got that sorted. Good day ta ya, then." Stewart hung up.

Riley dropped the phone on the table like it was red hot. "Cute, Beck. Bring in the big dog," she said, shaking her head. "You're such a jerk."

A sharp series of raps came from the apartment door. She ignored them. Mrs. Litinsky didn't knock that loudly, and she was the only person Riley was willing to see this early in the morning. At least until the hot chocolate was history.

"Miss Blackthorne?" a voice called out. It took a moment for her to recognize it: It was the guy from the collection agency.

"Go away," she muttered under breath, continuing to stir the hot chocolate. Almost all the little clumps were gone now. A few more stirs and—

"Miss Blackthorne? Your car is in the parking lot so I know you're here."

Well, at least she could see what this idiot knew about her father's summoning.

Riley opened the door, leaving the chain lock in place. The guy promptly wedged a highly polished shoe inside to keep it from shutting. He wore a black suit, white shirt, gray tie, and carried a black briefcase. His hair was so glued down it didn't budge when he moved. It made him look like one of those dress-up dolls she used to play with as a kid.

He offered his card and she took it. ARCHIBALD LESTER, CLAIMS AD-JUDICATOR.

"What do you want?" she asked. Her hot chocolate was cooling.

"I would think that would be obvious," the man replied, an eyebrow arched. He pulled a sheaf of legal-size paperwork out of his briefcase. That was never a good thing.

"If you'll just tell me where I can find your father's body and where the funds from his sale are located, we can get this taken care of without any unpleasantness."

Her sleepy fog vanished. "You think I sold my own father?"

"Maybe. Maybe not. It doesn't really matter who did the selling as long as we receive the money and the asset in question."

"Asset?"

"Your father's body."

Her stomach twisted. "No way." She tried to shut the door, but the guy's foot prevented that.

"You're not helping matters, Miss Blackthorne."

Riley jammed a finger in his direction. "Why don't you go find the necromancer who stole my dad and ask him for that *asset*."

"We'd rather deal with you. You don't wield magic. If you refuse to cooperate, I'll be forced to file a complaint with the police."

A giggle escaped Riley's mouth before she realized it. Then another. She wasn't a giggler, but this was just too stupid to think about. After everything that had happened, this guy was worried about money.

The man's face clouded. "You're not taking this seriously, Miss Black-thorne."

The giggles ended abruptly. "I watched people die the other night. Do you think I give a damn about your money?"

"You should. It's your debt."

"No, it's not. I'm seventeen, so I'm not responsible for anything my parents did. You people are totally hosed, and you know it."

He glowered. "Then we'll play hardball. We'll confiscate your father's life insurance payment."

Can they really do that? "Whatever," she said. She just didn't care any-more.

"You'll regret this," he called out.

"The regrets line forms to the right," she said.

The CDC guy retrieved his foot microseconds before she slammed the door.

In Riley's search for the Guild's priest, the church secretary used the words *temporary* and *mortuary* in the same sentence and sent her to a lo-cation just west of downtown. After a bit of hunting she located the building, a music shop that still had sun-faded posters in the windows announcing the latest albums from several years back. Now it was home to the Guild's fallen, as no mortuary would touch a trapper if the cause of death was demonic in origin. Another weird superstition, as if *death by demon* was somehow contagious. Apparently Father Harrison had found a sympathetic soul who had agreed to let them use the location until the trappers were buried.

Eight pine caskets sat in a neat row down the center of the store, their lids closed. Each had an index card attached with the name of the coffin's occupant. These eight were just the start: Not all the bodies had been identified by the coroner yet, and others were still buried under the rubble at the Tabernacle. Standing near the head of the coffins was a trapper about her father's age. That was tradition: A member of the Guild remained with the dead until they were buried. It had been Simon's choice to perform that duty for her dad. Riley didn't know this particular trapper's name, but he gave her a solemn nod, which told her the man wasn't an enemy. She made sure to return the gesture.

Father Harrison was attempting to comfort an older woman. "I didn't want him to do this," she said in between sobs. "I told him it'd get him killed."

The man next to her, probably her husband, mumbled something reassuring, but it didn't seem to help. The woman only sobbed louder. As they left the building, Riley stepped aside to give them space.

Father Harrison joined Riley in the doorway. About thirty with brown hair and eyes, today he appeared older, dark circles beneath his eyes.

"Ethan's parents," he explained. "He was their only son."

Riley dug for tissues as tears began to burn. The priest held his silence until she'd pulled herself back together. He'd probably been doing that all day.

"I heard about your father's reanimation," the priest said. "I'm so sorry."

"Yeah, I thought I had it covered." She blew her nose one more time, jammed the tissues in a pocket, then leaned against the building. "You know about the Holy Water problem?"

The priest nodded. "The Archbishop called me. He said you'd discovered the consecration dates were incorrect and that some of the Holy Water was counterfeit."

"I bought some from the vendor at the market and took it to the meeting so we could test it. Some of the bottles didn't react right."

"Tested? How?" Harrison asked. He, too, was leaning against the building now.

"I put my demon claw inside the bottles." Riley pulled the item out from under her shirt, all three inches of ebony lethalness. Its former owner, a Grade Three Gastro-Fiend, had not so kindly left it in her thigh as a souvenir when it had tried to kill her. Beck had made it into a necklace, and now she wore it with perverse pride.

The priest leaned closer to her, studying it intently. "Wicked thing, isn't it?"

"Totally," she agreed as she tucked the talon away. "The real Holy Water went nuts when it touched the claw. The fake stuff didn't do a thing. And I found out that the fake bottles have labels that smear when they get wet, so that's a quick way to check them."

Harrison swiped a hand over his face. "I'd heard rumors that the Holy Water wasn't working as it should, but I never thought someone might actually be counterfeiting it."

"I checked the labels on the bottles Simon used for the ward, and they were good." There was more to it than that. Riley lowered her eyes, not wanting to see the priest's face when she made her confession. "But I didn't check what was inside those bottles. Maybe if I had, those trappers would still be alive."

She waited for the condemnation. Instead she heard a profound sigh. "It wouldn't have mattered, Riley," Harrison murmured. "It's not your fault. There were a lot of demons in that building, am I right?"

Her eyes rose. "They were everywhere. It was *so* scary."

"Holy Water loses its potency in the presence of sustained evil, unless it's consecrated by the Pope."

"So if it had just been one or two of them they might not have gotten through?"

The priest nodded. "Even if the Holy Water Simon used was counterfeit, he'd created a ward for the previous meeting, and the ones before that. The effects wouldn't fade that fast unless there was an immensely evil presence or all the Holy Water was bogus."

"The trappers aren't going to believe that. They're going to think he made a mistake or that I did something wrong."

"Or that your father let them inside the ward."

Her eyes veered upward. "He didn't! He was trying to save me, not kill all of us."

"I know," the priest said, gently touching her arm. "Your father was an honorable man, but that doesn't mean others might not want to make him a scapegoat. Or you, for that matter. You have to prepare yourself for that possibility, Riley."

"It's already started," she admitted.

"I feared as much."

For one wild instant she felt the need to tell the priest about her deal with Heaven. Then her eyes shifted to the trapper standing vigil over the caskets. She didn't dare, not with him here. He might overhear her, and then he'd tell the others, who'd make fun of her, accuse her of being crazy. Master Harper might find a way to use that to force her out of the Guild.

I don't want Simon to know. He'd feel like he owed her something, and that wasn't the way she wanted their future to play out. She'd tell Father Harrison her secret someday. *Just not today.*

When Riley left a few minutes later she felt better for having talked to the priest and she'd received his permission to use Beck's bolt hole at the church for her temporary living quarters. No more cold nights in the graveyard.

One problem solved. That left countless others. On impulse, she dug out the list she'd made at the coffee shop and studied it. Nothing to cross off yet. The least she could do was buy her groceries.

If Harrison was right and concentrated evil had taken out the Holy Water ward, then neither she nor Simon had caused the deaths of their fellow trappers. That was a profound relief. *Simon has to know he isn't to blame.* It was what the priest *hadn't* said that weighed on her mind.

If the Holy Water isn't strong enough, how do we stop the demons?

EIGHT

Riley knew she should be at Harper's place by now, but dealing with her master rated a negative five on a scale of one to ten. The feeling was mutual. So she'd bought groceries, one thing off her list, and now she was savoring a big cup of hot chocolate at the coffee shop and wasting time by staring at nothing. If she stared hard enough she couldn't hear the sound of roaring flames. Or the cries of the dying.

"Hello?" a voice called out. "Earth to Riley."

Riley glared up at the unwelcome interruption. Her barista friend, Simi, was clad in a criminally short jean skirt, black tights, and blood-red T-shirt that said PHREAKS ARE PHUN, her hair a wild mishmash of electric blue and hot pink. On her, it all looked good because she was a potpourri of Irish, Native American, Lebanese, and Chinese. Simi had never really explained how all that global DNA had connected, which was probably for the best.

Her friend pulled out a chair and took a seat. Her purse, a plush vampire bat with huge purple fangs, dropped on the table in front of her.

"Why are you here? You're not working today," Riley muttered.

"Looking for you. I think it's time for a Simi intervention."

Riley groaned. The last intervention had been two years ago, right after Allan, the soon to be ex-boyfriend, had socked her in the jaw. It'd been Simi who'd figured out how to apply enough makeup to cover the massive bruise so there'd be no questions from her classmates, but not so much that Riley looked like a zombie.

"No one has hit me today," Riley retorted. "Just go away. I'm busy brooding, okay?"

"Not okay. You're coming with me," Simi said, jumping up from her chair so fast it spooked a couple of customers nearby. Maybe it was because the girl lived on coffee. "I'm going to take care of your follicular issues."

"My hair is fine."

"No, your hair is fried, toasted, and shriveled. It needs help. Just like you." Simi leaned over the table. "You know I'm right. You don't want your trapper boyfriend to see you like this."

"He already has."

"And he's probably praying he won't see you like this again."

"I don't want—"

But that was the problem with her friend—the world ceased to exist until Simi got her way, which she usually did by sheer force of will. Riley continued to protest as she was pushed and tugged out of the coffee shop and onto the street. She gave her friend the glare that always worked on her other friends. No response. Apparently Simi was immune, so Riley gave up.

"Where are we going?" she asked.

"You'll see," her friend trilled.

As they threaded their way through the city's streets, Simi kept up a running conversation about the club she'd been to the night before. Some place called the Decadent Vampire.

"Let me guess: They wear fake teeth and lurk a lot," Riley said, conjuring up an image of her faux-vamp classmate who lisped and wore overly frilly shirts.

"Some. Not all. It's a mixed crowd. I really liked the band last night and—" She lost track of what she's saying, distracted. "OMG! Hunk at two o'clock."

Riley wasn't in the mood, so she didn't bother to check the guy out.

What was the point? There were more important things to worry about than handsome guys, at least in her world.

"He's coming this way!" Simi said, primping a couple of her pink dreadlocks. "Could you, like, fake a heart attack or something so he'll stop and talk to us?"

Riley scowled at her friend. "Are you kidding? No way."

"Come on. Just for me? He's amazing."

Riley finally eyed the oncoming hunk and then smiled. It was Ori, dressed to kill. Literally, if you were a demon. *Simi is going to be so jealous.*

Actually, her friend fell speechless when Ori stopped in front of them, which had to be a first.

"Riley," he said in a voice that would melt steel.

"Ori," she said. Somehow the day felt better already. "How's it going?" At her side, Simi had fallen into full-stare mode.

"You . . . you know this guy?" she asked breathlessly.

"Sure. Ori and I met at the marketplace. He was trying to buy a sword."

"Occupational hazard. You slay dragons and you go through a lot of swords," he jested, turning those bottomless eyes on Simi and playing the rogue. Actually, it was more the default setting with him.

"God, you're so cute," her friend blurted.

Riley did a mental face-palm. "Simi works at the coffee shop. And lives on caffeine."

"Ah, that explains it," Ori replied politely. He didn't seem the least bit troubled by her friend's adulation. "Glad to meet you."

"You really slay dragons for a living?" she asked, her eyes locked on him.

"On occasion. And rescue damsels," he said, winking at Riley.

For a second she thought Simi was going to tackle this guy.

As if Ori sensed the danger, he said, "I best be going. Good to meet you, Simi. I'll see you later, Riley." Then he walked off, duster flowing behind him.

The barista grabbed Riley's arm. "You have been holding out on me, girlfriend. Give me the deets, now!"

"No details. He's got business in Atlanta, and we see each other every now and then."

"See each other? Has he kissed you yet?"

What? "Pleeeze. I'm dating another guy. You think I'm a skank or something?"

"A kiss wouldn't hurt. I mean, you'd probably explode from the ecstasy, but, hey, it'd be worth it. You just don't see guys like that very often."

Simi was right, Ori was top-shelf material. Which meant he wasn't in their league.

"True, but he's not in Atlanta for that long. Once his job is done, he's outta here. Simon is not going anywhere."

Simi herded her down a side street. "Don't be an idiot. This Ori guy likes you, or he wouldn't be hanging around all the time."

"Not going there."

"You're too stuffy, girl. You need to be wild every now and then."

"You do wild. I'll do sane."

Luckily the conversation ended as Riley was shepherded into a salon. The hair stylist had colors even crazier than Simi's, which didn't do a thing for Riley's confidence. But after the shampoo, scalp massage, and deep conditioning, she began to relax. The woman seemed to know what she was doing, deftly removing the frizzled hair, shaping it as she wielded the scissors.

"You are overdoing the curling iron," she said. "I've never seen hair this badly damaged." In the mirror Riley could see her friend gesturing frantically, trying to derail the conversation. The stylist kept on. "Just what are you doing anyway?"

Before Riley could figure out a way to avoid talking about just why she was in this state, Simi tugged on the stylist's arm and then drew her aside for a private talk.

When the woman returned she was repentant. "Sorry, I didn't know. We'll make your hair look good, and there's no charge."

"But..." Riley said.

"No. I should have recognized you from the television. Don't worry, you'll look great when I'm finished. You deserve that for all you've done for us."

Twenty-three minutes later Riley stepped outside of the hair salon minus the fried ends and with hair that *moved*, according to the stylist. And it did. Move that is. She had talked the stylist into a generous tip, but Simi insisted on paying it.

"Better?" her friend asked, beaming like a sun at high noon. She always did that when she got her way. Riley tried her glower again, but couldn't muster the proper level of aggravation.

"Yes." She had to admit the new haircut, which kept most of the length but had cool layers, looked awesome. Even better, her hair no longer smelled like burnt Tabernacle. That in itself was a blessing.

After a time, they sat on the steps in front of the Suntrust Building, soaking up the sunshine like a pair of human solar panels.

"You'll have to keep it trimmed or it'll look awful," Simi advised as she fussed with her lipstick, some deep purple shade called Nameless Sin. "You need to look hot now that you've got three guys giving you the eye."

"Three?" Apparently her friend's math was different than Riley's.

Simi capped the lipstick with a click and dropped it back into the bat bag.

"Sweet blue-eyed blond trapper," she said, raising one finger. Her nail polish was purple and sparkled in the sunshine. "Muscled blond trapper number two, who buys you cards," she said, adding finger number two. Finger number three rose. "And that gorgeous, 'Where have you been all my life?' dude with the raven-black hair and dark eyes."

"You read too many romance novels," Riley replied sourly.

"You don't know how good you have it," Simi countered. "Any of those guys are great. Me, I'd go for the dark and dangerous one. He's smoking."

"You would." Simi was an on-the-edge kinda girl. "Simon's just fine for me, thankyouverymuch."

"Of course. You go with safe and secure every time, but no guy's really that way. Might as well go for a wild one once in your life."

"Simon is right for me," Riley argued. "Ori isn't." It was pushing the envelope to even think in that direction.

"What about Beck?" Simi asked, wrinkling her brow.

"Backwoods Boy? Are you crazy? It'd be a threesome—me, him, and his overbearing ego. Definitely doomed to failure."

Simi laughed, then a few seconds later her brilliant smile faltered. She took Riley's hand and squeezed it. "You know, you're doing incredible and dangerous stuff, but I don't want you to forget who you really are." She perked up. "With your new hair, you're going to kick demon butt and look awesome doing it. That's the Riley Blackthorne way."

A lump formed in Riley's throat. "Thanks." They hugged, and when they broke apart there was a film of tears in Simi's eyes.

"I do not want to see any more pictures of you on the television," her friend commanded. "Unless you're winning an award or something."

"They don't have those for demon trappers."

"Not yet," Simi said, hooking her arm around Riley's. "Now you tell me all about this babelicious blue-eyed boyfriend of yours. . . ."

Like most places in Atlanta, Master Harper's place was on its second reincarnation. Once a car repair shop, now it was his home, an aging single-story concrete block building with twin overhead doors that led to what once were the repair bays. Harper had made a few changes, adding a small apartment behind the original office, but it was still a dump that stank of old tires, grease, and demons.

No matter how Riley looked at it, her time with Master Harper hadn't been good. He'd hated her dad for some unknown reason, was a drinker, and had a volatile temper. He was too quick to strike out at his apprentices if he thought he wasn't getting his way, often leaving bruises. She'd not seen him since the Tabernacle. What kind of mood would he be in? If she was lucky, he'd be drunk and asleep, then she could do a quick walk-through and take off.

No such luck; Harper was awake in what had been the tire shop's office, perched in a ratty recliner that gave used furniture a bad name. There wasn't a bottle of booze at his elbow, which had to be a first. Instead there was a bottle of pills that sported a thick red sticker on the side warning against taking them with alcohol. Who knew keeping the old guy sober would be so easy?

His usual frown was in place, along with a sheen of sweat on his forehead, though it was cool in the room. The long scar that ran from his left eyebrow down to the corner of his mouth was pulled tight like he was in pain. She kept her distance from him: He was vicious on a good day.

The old television was on, tuned to CNN, with yet another talking head standing in front of the smoking ruins. They pulled up a file shot of the body bags lined along the street like long black cocoons.

Her master scowled up at her, hitting the mute button. "What are you doing here?" he growled.

"Bringing you food," Riley replied, hoisting the bag of groceries on the desk. *Though you so don't deserve it.* "I didn't know what you wanted, so I just got what looked good."

When she placed a McDonald's bag on the arm of his chair, he glowered at it like it held a bomb. The smell must have gotten to him because he opened the bag and rummaged through it. The cheeseburger came out first.

"None of this adds up," he said around a mouthful of burger. "Demons don't work together." He frowned, opened up the sandwich, and discarded the pickles into a nearby trash can with considerable disgust. "Every fiend wants to suck up to Lucifer. If that means shivving another demon, that's the way it is." Harper's sour expression diminished. "You got something for me to drink?"

She dug into the grocery sack and then handed over a cold bottle of soda, one of a six-pack. Harper twisted open the top, and after two big gulps, he put it down. He didn't say another word until the burger was gone, then he started on the fries. As he ate, Riley put away the groceries in the small kitchenette that shared space with his bedroom. Harper's bed was unmade, and from its condition it looked like he'd done a good bit of thrashing around in it. A stack of books sat on the floor, and the titles all had something to do with Hell or demons. The image of Harper curled up in his bed doing his homework just didn't compute.

Her master fixed her with a smirk as she exited the kitchen. She figured it was for her new hairstyle.

"You sure that Holy Water for the ward was good, not that fake stuff?" he asked.

He hated her already, so the truth couldn't make it any worse. "I only checked the labels, not the Holy Water itself. Father Harrison said it wouldn't have made a difference, that there were too many demons for the ward to keep them out."

She expected a blast of fury from her master. Instead there was a thick huff of air.

"The priest's right. No matter how careful Adler was putting that stuff down, we were hosed."

Adler. Usually their master just called him Saint because of her boyfriend's religious habits.

"But that don't answer why your old man showed up," Harper said, eyeing her.

"He told me the demons were coming. He was trying to save us."

Harper's attention momentarily flickered to the television. "What about Adler?"

"He's going to make it."

Then his eyes swung back to her. "I told you to stay away from that Geo-Fiend. Why in the hell didn't you listen to me?"

"It was the one who killed my dad."

"Jonesing for revenge, were you?" He sneered. "You just had to go up and introduce yourself?" He shook his head. "Stupid move."

That angered her. "It said it wouldn't kill any of the others if I gave myself up."

Harper's bloodshot eyes searched her face. "And you believed the damned thing?" he chided. "God, you're a fool."

"It was worth the risk," she admitted. "After Simon . . ."

Harper slumped back in his chair, wincing at his cracked ribs. "In the future, you listen to what I tell you."

"Yes, sir," she mumbled. "What do you want me to do until you're better?"

Her master rubbed his thick fingers over his chin stubble. "Get yourself in here every morning. If there're Grade Ones to trap, you'll do 'em. If not, I'll find something to keep your ass out of trouble."

That she wouldn't doubt.

"I've had enough of you for one day," he said, running up the volume on the television with the aged remote. "Get lost."

If it were only that easy.

✢

It was late afternoon when Beck hiked into Demon Central, his trapping bag fully stocked. He was eager for the hunt, and he wasn't too fussy about how many of the demons he caught were still alive when they were sold to the traffickers. If the fiends gave him a reason, he'd kill them without thinking twice, especially after what went down at the Tabernacle.

Beck knew he shouldn't be in this part of town on his own, but time was running out. When the demon hunters came to Atlanta they'd kill every demon they could find, big and small. If he wanted to build up enough money to tide himself over until the hunters cleared out, it was now or never.

There were two problems with his "catch as many demons as possible" plan. First—he wasn't in peak condition, not with the healing leg wound. Second—no demons. He'd usually spot at least one or two fiends in Demon Central during every visit, sometimes as many as five in one night. Tonight all he'd seen was a mangy limping cat and a few scraggly pigeons. Those were usually scarce when the Threes were on the prowl.

Demon Central was the trappers' name for Five Points, a section of south Atlanta that never got any breaks. Even the casino they'd constructed a few years back wasn't doing that well, not with the depressed economy. Time and neglect had opened up numerous holes in Five Points' streets and sidewalks over the old steam vents. Since the city didn't have the money to repair them, this area was now home to Grade Three demons. The Gastro-Fiends lived in the holes and ate everything they could gulp down, even fiber optic cable. Didn't matter if it was a stray dog, a rat, or a trapper: If something looked like it could be eaten, the Threes were all over it.

Beck pulled his attention back to his surroundings: daydreaming down here was a one-way ticket to a fiend's belly. He wrinkled his nose at the stench from an overflowing dumpster. To avoid paying the city's exorbitant collection fees, people brought their trash here and dumped it, even at the risk of becoming dinner for a ravenous Three. The only plus was that the rotting garbage was prime Gastro-Fiend bait.

But there were no demons to be found. At least not down here. He'd heard scattered reports of sightings elsewhere in the city, but they sounded like tall tales. Demons had certain behavior patterns, and some of the stories were too bizarre to be true, like how a Three who had broken into a dress shop had eaten some of the mannequins, clothes and all. Gastro-Fiends would devour anything, but they didn't usually break into businesses for a quick snack.

As Beck hiked down a street littered with abandoned tires, broken hunks of concrete, and boarded-up buildings, his thoughts slipped to Riley. They did that a lot nowadays. It troubled him that he hadn't seen her today, despite his early morning phone call that had earned him an earful of aggravation. He liked talking to her, even if she gave him grief all the time. It wouldn't hurt to call her, would it? Check in and see how she was doing? See if she needed any help? That's what Paul would expect him to do.

He wavered for a time, then flipped open his phone and dialed. Maybe one of these days he'd feel good about using that text thing.

"Hey, girl, how ya doin'?" he asked as soon as Riley answered.

"I'm okay. What's up?" Her voice sounded neutral, like she wasn't looking to pick a fight. Maybe they could keep it that way.

"Well, some of the funerals are tomorrow afternoon. I was wonderin' if ya could pick me up at my place and drive me down to the cemetery. The services are at South-View."

"Okay," she replied. "You know how to get there?"

"Yeah." He'd been there for another trapper's funeral about a year back. "Make it about one-thirty."

Beck shifted the phone to the other ear, keeping an eye on his surroundings. Just because it seemed quiet didn't mean he'd let down his guard. That was usually when you got nailed.

"How's your leg? Is it healing okay?" Riley asked.

"It's better. So what'd ya do today?" he asked, trying not to sound like he was conducting an inquisition.

"A friend made me get my hair cut. It looks better now. And I checked in with Harper," she said. He heard the sound of a car door closing. "He's still a jerk, but at least he's not drinking. I'm in Little Five Points. I'm going to talk to Mortimer to see if he has any idea who took Dad."

Beck opened his mouth to tell her that might not be a good idea, then changed his mind. Riley needed to be doing something useful, keeping her mind off Simon and all the other bad stuff. Besides, she couldn't get into too much trouble in Little Five Points. It was mostly necromancer and witch territory, and because of that the demons usually steered clear.

"Sounds like a plan," he said. "Let me know if ya learn anythin'."

There was a momentary pause, like Riley had expected a lecture and was astonished when she didn't get it. "So where are you?" she asked.

"Demon Central. No luck so far." He did another slow three-sixty. No threats.

"Someone with you?"

He smiled at the concern in her voice. "Nah. I'll be okay."

"Beck..." she began, the worry clearer now. "You're still getting over those demon wounds. You need someone watching your back."

"I'm fine, Riley. No action down here anyways. I'm about to pack it in, maybe go to the lounge and play some pool. Haven't done that in a long time." *Not since yer daddy died.*

Her deep sigh of relief caused his smile to widen.

"Tough life you got there, Backwoods Boy," she jested.

"Yeah, it's a bitch. Ya gonna be on holy ground tonight, right?"

"You know, I don't appreciate you ratting me out to Stewart. I owe you for that one."

"Happy to help out, as long as it keeps ya safe." He did another perimeter check. Other than a rat crawling along a ledge of broken bricks about ten feet to his right, there wasn't anything to worry about. He noted she hadn't answered his question. "Yer at the cemetery tonight, right?"

"No, I'm not."

"Damn, girl, don't make me call the Scotsman again."

"You don't have to. I'm staying at Saint Brigid's, in your bolt hole."

"What? Oh. Why didn't ya tell me that right off?" he grumbled.

"Because you'd just bitch at me about something else."

She had him there. "Well, then, that's all good," he said, pleased he'd not have to pull guard duty outside of her apartment again. Last night hadn't been that much fun, not with his fever and feeling like death warmed over.

"Now do me favor: get out of Demon Central!" she ordered. "And don't you dare go down there until someone is watching your back."

"I'm fine with—"

"If you don't leave right now, I'll call Stewart on you. I swear," she threatened.

He grinned at how neatly Riley had turned the tables on him. She *was* worried about him.

"Yes, ma'am. I'm outta here. Say hi to Mort for me." He flipped his phone closed before she said good-bye. He'd always hated *that* word.

Beck adjusted the strap of the duffel bag and headed for his truck. "Why the hell didn't I think of her stayin' at the church?" he muttered. It was the obvious solution to the problem. Stewart hadn't thought of it, either. "Too much goin' on. We don't have a handle on this, and that's not good."

But for now, he'd gladly follow Riley's advice: The best therapy he knew was a few games of pool and some ice cold beer.

NINE

Little Five Points sat east of the city, a strange mix of head shops, tattoo parlors, and retro clothing stores. Unlike Five Points, its downtown cousin, L5P's natives wore cruelty-free cotton, adored health food, and sported dreadlocks or emo garb. They spoke of auras and ley lines and cosmic karma. Riley liked this part of town. It felt good here, like there was positive energy running under the streets.

Unlike downtown Atlanta, horses were welcomed here. Like keeping a horse fed and stabled was somehow cheaper. Of course every practical idea had its downside, and in this case it was the outlandish coaches. It was a status symbol thing: The more money a family had, the more ornate the coach. There was even a television show that went around the country showing the transportation choices of the rich and famous.

From the looks of the open-top coach in front of her—solid white with gold accents—this family had serious bucks. The gold had to be paint; real gold was too expensive to waste on a wagon, but the effect was almost the same. The coach came with a uniformed guy in a blue velveteen coat, short pants, white hose, and ruffled shirt. He even had black shoes with big brass buckles.

That has to be embarrassing.

Two girls trotted up, and after helping them to the plush burgundy seats, the uniformed servant placed their packages inside the coach.

Riley drummed her fingers on the steering wheel in anticipation. This was the first parking place she'd found in the last ten minutes, and she wasn't about to let it escape.

As she waited, she checked out the passengers. They appeared to be about her age, but their clothes were definitely not secondhand, and the plethora of brightly colored bags at their feet spoke of a monumental shopping experience. One was showing the other a new pair of heels, the four-inch, ankle-snapping kind. They were brilliant orange. Four inch heels weren't her thing, but Riley felt envious anyway. How long had it been since she could shop and not worry about every penny?

Not since Mom got ill.

Her mom's cancer treatment sucked up every spare dollar, and when that money was gone, her dad had taken out the huge loan to cover the bills. For Riley that meant no more new clothes, no more new shoes, at least until the old ones didn't fit any longer. Every penny was hoarded, and it hadn't changed now that her father was dead.

It's so not fair.

Riley winced, the envy waning quickly. Cool shoes and new clothes would be really nice, but she'd trade all of it to get her mom and dad back.

The coach rolled out of the parking spot, the fine black horse clopping its way down the street as the fashionistas engaged in purchase worship, extracting clothes from the bags and comparing them. Riley pulled into the parking place and sighed in relief, happy the fashion show was over.

It wasn't a surprise that Enchanter's Way was different from any of the other streets around it. For one thing, there was a copper archway at the entrance, and it was adorned with the symbol of the Summoners' Society—a jagged lightning bolt striking a granite tomb. Underneath it were these words:

Memento mori.
"Remember that you must die."

Riley puzzled on that—not because of the depressing Latin phrase but the fact the copper was still there. Why hadn't someone stolen it? Any piece of metal that could be cut down and sold for cash was history. Curious, she touched the archway and immediately yelped in pain, snatching her hand back. The copper was scorching hot, like it'd just come out of a blast furnace, though there were no burns on her fingers. A queer prickly feeling skittered up her arm and across her shoulders, making her muscles twitch.

Magic.

If someone tried to tear it down, it'd make them believe their flesh was roasting off their bones. Apparently summoner magic wasn't just for stealing corpses.

Enchanter's Way was paved in cobblestones, and dried ivy clung to the brickwork in twisted brown ribbons. Doorways lined either side of the street, and some displayed the distinctive summoner's seal. Just ahead, on the right, was a café with stained-glass windows and a menu taped to its open door. A little farther down the street, on the left, was a weathered sign—"Bell, Book, and Broomstick." She'd always wondered where the witch's store was located, the parent of the stall at the Terminus Market. The closer she got to the store, the better she felt, the prickles of magic no longer dancing across her skin. Was that some kind of witch thing?

As she moved forward the street narrowed until a solid brick wall blocked her passage. It was dotted with metal mailboxes, which were set at random intervals ranging from only a foot off the ground to near the top. Half bricks stuck out of the edifice like a climbing wall. Apparently the higher-level boxes required their owners to ascend to claim their junk mail.

Bet the postal dude loves that.

Every box was different. The one for Bell, Book, and Broomstick had an iridescent fairy perched on the top holding a miniature wand, while another box had a black-and-white cat with a wooden tail and gleaming yellow eyes.

Riley rubbed her temples to try to ease her growing headache, then took a swig from her water bottle. Any other time she would have enjoyed this weirdness, but she wasn't in the mood. As she sucked down the liquid, she pondered the twin alleys that branched on either side of her. Right or left? Mort's card didn't indicate which one. Riley had just decided to ask for directions at the witch store when a dead woman stepped out of the left passageway. She had silver hair, curled neatly at the collar, and was dressed in a pale ivory shell and navy blue slacks.

The woman paused, then she moved forward, her pumps clicking on the uneven stones. She popped open a mailbox with a pinwheel on top and extracted the contents, but as she turned away, a slick magazine escaped her grip and landed on the cobblestones. Riley picked it up. It was a *Summoner's Digest*. The label said its owner was Mortimer Alexander.

Found you.

The deceased woman attempted a smile when Riley handed her the magazine, but the effort failed as the facial muscles just didn't work right. At best, Deaders were half-imagined copies of their real selves. Some of their personalities carried over, but none of the joy.

Dad's like this now.

Riley waited a few moments before she followed the woman to a bright purple door near the end of the alley. To the right of the door were two plaques: the Society's lightning bolt symbol and one that read: "Mortimer Alexander, Summoner Advocate of Atlanta."

Screwing up her courage, Riley knocked. Eventually the door swung open and the dead woman peered out at her.

"Yes?"

"I'm Riley Blackthorne. I need to talk to Mortimer about my dad," she said, displaying the business card the man at the market had given her.

The dead woman waved her inside.

Now I just have to convince him to help me.

Because of Mort's appearance—he was short, wide, and wore a

trench coat and a fedora—Riley had always assumed he was unmarried and lived with his elderly mother. This place didn't have a silver-haired-mom feel about it. The entryway featured a gleaming white tile floor, a black ceramic umbrella stand, and an old-fashioned wooden coat rack. Mort's coat and hat dangled from it.

"This way," the woman said, moving noiselessly down a hallway to the left. As she followed, Riley's imagination fired up. A summoner's place should have all sorts of arcane symbols on the walls, huge oak bookcases full of ancient leather tomes, and at least one black cat skulking around. Maybe even a cool wand and a pointy wizard hat.

Which wasn't what she found. The room they entered was totally round, at least twenty-five feet in diameter, with painted white brick walls that rose to a vaulted wood ceiling and a series of skylights that offered a dramatic view of the sky. From somewhere nearby water ran in a delicate trickle, but Riley couldn't find the source.

The space smelled faintly of wood smoke. Not fresh smoke, like something you'd expect out of a fireplace, but an aged scent, like it'd been baked into the bricks.

I could so live here.

A redwood picnic table and two benches sat in the very center of the room under the skylights. On the right side of the table sat an ink pot and a black pen, the old kind that you had to fill yourself. A neat stack of books sat to the left. A quick scan of the titles revealed that Mortimer liked C. S. Lewis and books with German and Latin titles.

Her escort made her way to a dark wood counter that curved around one portion of the room, filled a kettle from a faucet, and plugged it in to an electrical outlet. Then she left. Riley took the hint and stayed put, tapping her fingers on the side of her messenger bag to burn off nervous energy. Near the picnic table she noticed smudged chalk marks and rusty brown splotches dotting the plank floor. The rust spots reminded her of dried blood.

He's probably a serial killer. The nice ones always were.

"Riley?"

She turned and stared in astonishment as Mort seemed to pass through the curved brick wall.

More magic. Riley didn't appreciate the joke, but she needed his help.

"You should see your face," he said, exhibiting a mischievous smile. Mort wore a crisp white shirt and blue jeans, not at all what she'd expected. He seemed thinner somehow, like the trench coat had added thirty pounds.

"I'm so relieved to see you're in one piece," he added. "When I heard about what happened, I was afraid you were gone."

"I was thinking the same thing." To change the subject, Riley gestured toward the odd pieces of furniture. "Why do you have a picnic table inside?"

"It's easy to move when I want to do a ritual," he explained. "Big desks require strong backs, and my people aren't that sturdy."

People? "You mean the Deaders?"

Mortimer grimaced. "I prefer 'reanimates.' Deader is so disrespectful."

"Sorry," she said. He shrugged like it was no big deal, but she could tell it was. "I'm here about my dad. He was reanimated without my permission."

"I heard. Word travels fast in our community."

"Then you know who took him."

Mort shook his head, then gestured for her to sit. As she settled on a bench seat, a shrill sound filled the room, causing Riley to jump. Then she felt really stupid: It was the teakettle.

Mort dealt with the kettle and returned to the table with a tray containing two china cups, a matching teapot, and a plate full of goodies. "Cookie?" her host asked, offering the plate.

Riley took one to be polite, wondering if all murderers gave their victims treats before they sliced out their livers. She took a test nibble. Then a bigger one. The cookie was really yummy, homemade and chewy, the best kind.

"This is so good," she said, around bites.

"Emalee makes them. She stays in the kitchen most of the time because she's rather shy. Right now she's working on strudel."

He has dead people baking for him?

"About my dad . . ." she said, hoping to get something out of this meeting besides the image of a dead woman puttering around a kitchen in an apron.

Mort didn't reply until he sat on the bench opposite her and poured the tea. "I don't know who summoned your father. Nobody's talking, which is odd, because if I'd pulled off that reanimation I'd be bragging up a storm, at least to my fellow summoners." He took a thoughtful sip from his cup.

"Could it be Ozymandias?" she asked.

Mort shuddered at the name, making his tea slosh in the cup. "Maybe."

"So why would Mr. Creepy want him?"

Her irreverence caused a faint smile to appear. "Lord Ozymandias doesn't bother to tell us lesser mortals what he's up to. In general he treats us like we're annoying pests. It's very irritating."

More than irritating, if the death grip Mort had on the cup handle was any indication.

"Why would a summoner want my dad? Is it so he can trap demons?" she queried.

"I don't think so. Master trappers have certain demonic knowledge that would be of interest to a summoner who doesn't keep on the straight and narrow."

"Huh?"

"A summoner might require a master's expertise if he intends to call forth a demon."

"Whoa. Get out of here. You guys summon demons, too? Are you crazy?"

"I don't go there," Mort said flatly. "Too much downside. Most of the time the summoner ends up being the fiend's lackey, not the other way around."

Riley shuddered. "But Ozymandias does?"

"There are rumors to that effect." Mort offered her another cookie, and this time she took it without hesitation. Oatmeal. With a hint of cinnamon. *Nom.* Even if a dead lady made them.

"How do you guys do a summoning?"

The necromancer seemed to be weighing his answer carefully. "Unless you are at the level of someone like Lord Ozymandias, spells require preparation. He can do them on the spot, but then he's not like the rest of us."

"So how do you do it, the summoning spell, I mean?"

"I collect something of the deceased's—hair, clothing, a favorite book, some part that I can focus on. If I can't obtain an item, it's harder. Then I do a ritual invocation and request that the dead person arise to rejoin the living."

"Request?"

Mort looked chagrined. "Well, *I* request. Most just order the deceased to comply, which I think lacks respect."

Respect was a big thing for this guy. Riley leaned an elbow on the table, intrigued. "Which is why you only do legal summonings?"

"Exactly. It's bad enough to lose a loved one and then have a pirate come along and rip that person out of their grave. As you well know, the heartbreak is unimaginable."

The passion in his voice told her this was personal. "It happened to you?"

Mort's eyes lowered to his teacup. "My wife. She was only twenty-five when she died, and within a week she was serving as a maid at a rich household here in Atlanta. I would see her sometimes, on the street." He took a tortured breath. "Then they moved to New York City, and I couldn't afford to follow them."

"Can my dad's owner do that?" she asked, horrified.

"It's not against the law to transport reanimates across state lines, at least not yet. Or sell them to someone else, for that matter."

"Were you able to get your wife back?"

"Not until her year was up," he replied, his voice torn with emotion. "By then she was just a . . . husk."

God. It was hideous enough to bury someone you loved, but to see them like that and have no way to help them pushed Hell into a new dimension.

"It's why I became a summoner," he admitted. "In the case of your father, I will file a report with the Society of an unauthorized summoning," he said. "Unofficially I'll ask around and see if anyone knows who raised him."

"If I can get him away from whoever bought him, can you put my father back in the ground?"

"Break a summoning?" Mort executed a low whistle. "That's asking for serious trouble. We had a magical . . . feud a few years back when two summoners interfered with each other's reanimates. It was a really bad deal."

"So all you can do is ask questions?" she demanded, sharper than she'd intended.

"There is only so much I *can* do, Riley. Your father has no civil rights," Mort explained. "When the time comes for him to be inhumed, we will need his summoner's assistance to reverse the spell. If that summoner is angry at you . . ." He spread his hands.

"What happens if my dad isn't returned to his grave after a year?"

"The body disintegrates while the living consciousness is still in it. That's *not* what anyone wants to endure—him or you."

The cookies in her stomach were no longer playing nice. "So you're saying I'm pretty much screwed?"

"No," he replied, sighing. "I'm saying you don't have many choices, but that shouldn't keep you from trying to find him. If whoever has bought him has compassion, they should let you visit him during his term of service."

"Like he's in jail or something," she said. That was a depressing thought. "Is there somewhere they sell them, besides at the market?"

"Yes," her host said. He toyed with the half-eaten cookie in front of him. "I'll go to the vendue and see if he's there."

"The what?"

"The vendue. It's from a French word meaning 'auction.' The next one's on Friday night."

"I want to go with you."

He shook his head instantly. "You won't be welcome."

"Don't care," she said, pushing her cup of tea aside. "I want to be there."

Mort's eyebrows knitted together. "My fellow summoners are a testy bunch. They won't like you asking questions."

"I want to be there," Riley repeated. Then she tried the magic word. "Please."

Mort sighed. "All right, just as long as you know this could get unpleasant."

Only if I don't find my father.

As Riley walked along the alley to the street, she tried to get a grip on her turbulent emotions. Did she really believe that once she'd talked to Mort that everything would be okay? That her dad would be waiting for her, ready to return to his grave? If she did find her father and the summoner reversed the spell, she'd have to bury him again. Another funeral.

Oh, God.

As she walked past the mailboxes, a figure caught her notice, a boy spray-painting something on the brick wall ahead of her. He looked about thirteen, and his hood had fallen back to reveal a shock of hair the color of ripe wheat slashed with black stripes. The smell of wet paint stung her nose as he made broad swipes leaving dripping red letters in his wake. When she moved closer he jumped in surprise, giving her a panicked expression. When he bolted for freedom, the spray can fell from his fingers, rolling across the uneven ground and bumping the toe of her tennis shoe.

The crimson paint began to change color, first becoming pale red, then pink, and finally white. It slid downward brick by brick, as if someone were wiping it away with a squeegee. When it reached the ground it crackled and then disappeared in a bright cloud of pale dust. *More magic.* It took a moment to puzzle out what the guy had written, spelling errors and all.

Nekros suk!

"No argument there."

TEN

"Home sweet bolt hole," Riley said. She stood in the doorway to the room in the basement of St. Brigid's Catholic Church. The room wasn't fancy, but she hadn't expected it to be. All of about fifteen by fifteen, there were two stacked wooden bunk beds, a table, a pair of kitchen chairs, and a mint green couch. There was a small television, a mini re-frigerator, microwave, and a counter with a deep sink. Down a narrow hall she saw a bathroom. If not for the white walls and the crucifix hanging by the door, it would have felt like a bunker.

After dropping her messenger bag on the table, Riley retreated to the undersized bathroom to change into her favorite PJ's, the ones with the frolicking pandas. The PJ's were totally dorky, but her mom had bought them for her and they held good memories.

If Beck sees these . . .

But he wouldn't, not unless something went really wrong and he had to take refuge here. In that case, panda PJs were going to be the least of their worries. After scrubbing her face and brushing her teeth, Riley placed her folded clothes on one of the chairs. A blast of hot air ruffled her hair from a vent in the ceiling. She glared up at it.

"Too warm," she said. Hunting around for a thermostat proved fruitless. That wasn't good news. It was either freeze at the cemetery or roast here.

After ensuring the door's lock was engaged, Riley tried the lower bunk. That rated a definite thumbs-up. After some determined pillow thumping to get it into the proper shape, she lay on her back and stared at the underside of the mattress above her.

The furnace turned off. Then on again. Then off.

She was dead tired, but sleep wasn't in the same room with her. It wasn't the heat that was keeping her awake, it was this time of day that things hurt the most. She'd replay her dad's voice in her head, then her mom's. She'd remember bits of Blackthorne family history.

Eventually Riley sat up in bed, barely clearing the top bunk by a mere two inches. Apparently tall people took the top bunk. She hadn't brought anything to read, sure that she'd be asleep almost instantly. To kill time, she dug out her cell phone and scrolled through the texts. Brandy, her nemesis at the new school, was wondering if she was going to be at class on Friday. Riley ignored that one. Three texts from Simi about a Gnarly Scalenes concert in March and asking if she'd like to go. *Maybe.* Nothing from Peter. She should text him, but what would she write? *Stuck in a church so demons won't eat me.* That wouldn't work, not with someone who'd always been there for her.

Instead, she dialed his number. "Peter?"

There was a lengthy pause. *This isn't a good idea.*

"What's up, Riley?" he asked. She processed his tone—upset and exhausted.

"I needed someone to talk to," she admitted.

"You know, so do I."

Maybe this would work after all. She tucked the comforter around her legs and leaned back against the wooden framework of the bunk bed. It creaked in response. She told him of her new location and what it looked like. "Master Stewart wants me on holy ground at night. He's worried some demon will come after me." Actually just one demon in particular, but Peter didn't need to know that.

"Is Beck there with you?"

"No. He's shooting pool." *At least he'd better be.*

Silence. She tried to wait him out, but finally she gave in. "Look Peter, if you don't want to talk to me—"

"It's not that. There's been . . . stuff going on here."

She shifted positions on the bed, caught by the lost sound in his voice. "Like what?"

"Mom and Dad are getting a divorce."

It took time for that to sink in. "Oh, man, Peter, I'm so sorry. I thought they'd worked through all that after your brother's death."

"No. It was never the same. They've been acting like it was, but Dad finally cracked. He just couldn't take Mom's Nazi control tactics anymore."

Her friend wasn't exaggerating. After Matt's fatal car accident, Peter's mom became The Warden, as he called her. She'd monitored all her kids' moves like they lived in a federal prison.

"She's been doing the same with Dad," Peter confided. "If he's a few minutes late, she freaks and hounds him with phone calls."

"I thought they went for counseling or something."

"They did. It didn't help," he said sadly.

"What happens now?" she asked.

"Mom wants to go back to Illinois. She thinks Atlanta's too dangerous for her kids."

Only if you drink and drive.

A tortured groan filtered through the phone. "They told us the news tonight. Then they asked who we wanted to live with."

If her parents had asked her that question, how could she decide? No matter who she chose, the other would be hurt. "God, that's brutal."

"Totally. David said he'd stay here with Dad. I wimped out and said I had to think about it. Mom was really upset. I guess she thought I'd just go with her automatically."

"What about the twins?" she asked, thinking of Peter's two little brothers.

"The ghouls go with her no matter what. Too young to be with Dad." There was a sigh down the phone. "So what are you doing to-morrow?"

"I have to check in on Harper, then I need to visit Simon and go to the funerals."

"So who's this Simon dude? Is he the guy I've seen on TV?"

"Yes. He's an apprentice trapper. We're . . . dating."

"Cool."

"It feels right this time, Peter."

"Well, that's something, at least."

More awkward silence. "I'm really sorry for you."

"Yeah, so am I. For a lot of things. Good night, Riley."

She disconnected the call.

"Don't you dare move away, Peter King," she whispered. "You're my best friend. I can't make it without you."

Ori leaned against his motorcycle across the street from the church, arms crossed over his chest. Riley had chosen her sanctuary well: No demon dared tread on holy ground and not pay the ultimate price. This church was old, and even from here he could feel the raw power of the Creator pressing against his skin, saturating everything around him. He sucked it in as if it were a breath of tantalizing spring air after a cruel winter.

"You are such an addict," a craggy voice said.

Ori failed to curb his displeasure at having the peaceful moment disturbed. "Sartael," he said acidly. "Slumming, again?"

A wry chuckle came from the angel standing next to him. Unless you were Divine he appeared unremarkable, a plain man who always managed to blend into the background. A Divine would see the real Sartael—that dark hair, those immense wings, and the sword strapped to his back, its hilt protruding just above his shoulders. The blade was dormant at the moment, but once he pulled it free from the bindings it would flame like the desert sun at midday. As always, there was a hint of madness in the angel's eyes.

I wonder if some say that of me.

"I do not like it in this realm," Sartael replied, gesturing contemptuously at the church.

"So you have mentioned, on more than one occasion."

"Why are mortals so ignorant?" He shook his head in supreme disgust. "They believe their faith is made of bricks and mortar."

This was an old argument between them, one of many. "To them it *is*," Ori replied earnestly. "Mortals need tangible proof of the Creator."

"*They* are tangible proof that He exists. How soon they forget that little detail."

"It is easy to become distracted when you're not eternal."

Sartael gave him a sidelong look. "Not only mortals have that issue. You have a task to perform, and yet here you stand gaping at an old pile of bricks."

"I am going about my duties," Ori said, stiffening at the rebuke.

"Is that rogue demon no more? I have not heard its death cries," Sartael chided.

"The girl is alive, and she is the key to finding the rogue."

"Ah, yes, Blackthorne's child."

Ori did not like hearing Sartael speak her name, but he hid his frown. "Is there a point to your presence?"

The other angel turned to him. "Time passes and you are needed elsewhere. Cease being amused by the mortals."

"Is that *His* Order?"

"Not officially. However, He will ask of your progress and I must answer. I cannot believe you are unable to find a mere weather fiend."

"I believe it is being shielded by its demi-lord."

"And who might that be?" Sartael asked, leaning closer, his eyes lit by some internal fire.

"I have no idea." He and Sartael had always been rivals, so the admission stung.

"Ah, I see. You make excuses to cover the lack of progress," Sartael said, nodding his understanding. "To be honest, I did not expect such weakness from you."

Ori squared up with him, his anger growing. "Then do you know who is behind this rogue demon?"

"That is not my problem. You know what is expected. Get it done. Fail and there will be a reckoning."

"Advice noted," Ori replied crisply, turning back toward the church.

"And ignored, I wouldn't doubt," Sartael replied. "Oh, well, it's not my pretty head on the block." At a wave of his hand, the angel vanished into the night air.

"No, it never is," Ori grumbled. "But some day it will be yours on the block, and I'll be wielding the sword."

ELEVEN

Beck pushed open the twin flame-embossed wooden doors that led to the Armageddon Lounge. As was his custom, he paused a moment and gave the place the once over. Old habits die hard, especially when one of the worst beatings he'd ever experienced was delivered by a jealous husband in a pool hall.

But not this pool hall. The Armageddon Lounge was neutral territory for him, and he meant to keep it that way. For that reason he didn't usually pick up girls here. No need to invite trouble.

The Armageddon Lounge's décor was trashy, even for this part of town. Garish flames decorated almost all the walls, except the far one with the black-veined mirror tiles. Figures writhed in those flames, most of them female and nude, someone's idea of what the end of the world would be like.

Fewer mirrors, more screamin'. At least that's how Beck envisioned it.

When he was assured that nobody was in the mood for trouble, he headed for the bar intent on enjoying his first beer of the day. A couple years back that wouldn't have been the case: By this time of night he would have already gone through at least a six-pack. It was Paul who changed that, early in Beck's apprenticeship.

"There's a time to drink and a time to trap Hellspawn," his mentor had advised. "You get those confused and you're demon food." When

Beck had protested he could do both, Paul had summed it up with one question. "Is a buzz worth dying for?"

The answer had been easy: Much as Beck loved a few good beers he preferred to remain aboveground. He'd cut back on his drinking that very night. He still would get a buzz on every now and then, but not as often now. It was a sad fact that the booze wasn't the solution; it just wanted you to think it was.

Zack, the bartender, acknowledged him with a broad smile. Stocky, his sandy hair was so short you could see his suntanned scalp.

"Hey, Beckster, how you doing?" he called out.

"Good," Beck said, though that wasn't the truth by a long shot. By the time he reached the bar, the Shiner Bock was waiting for him. He sighed, took a lengthy sip, and then sighed again.

"Mighty fine," he said, grinning over at Zack. The less he drank the more he appreciated a good beer.

"Quiet tonight," Zack observed, leaning on the bar. "Usually Saturday evenings are totally packed. I'm thinking it's because of what went down the other night at the Tabernacle. Folks are scared."

Beck nodded his understanding. There were only about a dozen patrons in the lounge, and he knew most of them by name, though none of them were trappers. Those were probably on the streets trying to take down a demon or two.

And gettin' nowhere fast.

"Lenny was in a while ago," Zack added. "He said he'd be back later."

Lenny the Necromancer. He was one of the summoners who'd been jonesing to pull Paul's body out of the grave, so he'd be a good one to pump for information.

"Heard ya had a Four in here the other day," Beck observed, leaning against the bar.

Zack snorted as he dried a highball glass. "And some trappers. Seems one of them broke a pool cue and didn't bother to pay for it. Really pissed off the boss. Gave me an earful about how all you guys are arrogant jerks."

"He'd be right," Beck replied, taking another sip. "At least when we're after demons."

Another snort came his way. "Boss said the trappers had a girl with them. You guys allowing that kind of thing now?"

"Yeah, we are. The world is changin'," Beck said.

"Tell me about it." Zack's voice changed tone, went lower. "So how are you doing after the other night?"

Beck turned back toward the bartender, hearing the concern. "Breathin'," he said. "Better 'n some."

"That's for sure. When I heard about it, I prayed for you guys."

"That's good of ya."

"Sounds like it's getting ugly," Zack remarked. "I had a regular in here this afternoon telling me he saw a couple demons downtown, right on Peachtree Street."

"Is this guy on the level?" Beck quizzed.

"Yup. He's a cop."

Some of those crazy stories just might be true.

Using his bartender radar, Zack headed down the bar toward a couple and refilled their glasses the moment they were empty. The girl was plain to look at, but they were totally into each other.

Beck had been that way once. Her name was Louisa, and they'd been in the same class in Sadlersville, their hometown. The other kids had known not to mess with them: It was always Den and Lou from the time they met in ninth grade. Then Louisa decided she could do better than a poor loser who had an alcoholic for a mother. He still remembered what it felt like to have someone think you were less than human just because of your family. From what he'd heard, Louisa moved from guy to guy after that, never finding what she was looking for.

Beck gave himself a swift mental kick, annoyed at wasting time dwelling on the past. Picking up his beer, he toted it to the back of the bar where one of the pool tables was open. He selected a cue and took his frustration out on the balls. One by one they went into the pockets like remote-controlled robots, just an extension of his hands and brain. When he finished running the table, something he'd been able to do since he was thirteen, he racked the balls again.

Part of his frustration was Stewart's insistence he talk to the press and to the city bosses, that he learn the ropes before he became a master. Beck knew those same ropes could turn into a noose with very little effort. Then there was that flame-haired babe he'd seen at the city hall. No surprise, she was a reporter and she just *had* to talk to him. She'd even gotten his cell phone number, courtesy of the Scotsman. Beck had dodged her so far, but the master had warned him to just get on with it. That it came with the territory.

"Not a good idea," Beck mumbled under his breath. He knew what his mind was like when he had a pretty lady in front of him: He said things he shouldn't, but in this case those words would end up in the newspaper, maybe even on the Internet. One slip of the tongue and he might lose his chance at becoming a master trapper.

The double doors pushed open and a man entered the lounge. The newcomer was a little taller than Beck, decked out in black jeans and T-shirt. A gray duster hung from his broad shoulders like a hero in an action movie. His midnight-black hair and eyes gave him a screw-with-me-at-your-own-peril look.

Trapper? Probably not. Freelance hunter? That was a possibility. Still, he should have some form of defense on him and Beck didn't see one. Their gazes met, sizing each other up, then the dude headed to the bar. After a short conversation with Zack, the bartender began pulling a beer from the tap.

Though this was more of a locals bar, every now and then someone new wandered in. Beck's mind chided him that he was just being paranoid. When the newcomer settled behind a corner table near the front of the lounge, Beck went back to his game.

Lenny was the next one to arrive. The summoner's biggest sin was that he dressed like a pimp with a limitless credit card. Tonight he was wearing a particularly unholy purple velvet jacket, black leather pants, and a frilly black shirt. He really needed an adult to dress him.

"Let me get a beer," the necro called out.

Beck nodded, then racked the balls, buying time until Lenny joined him.

When the man returned, brew in hand, Beck asked, "Ya playin' for the exercise or the money?" Best to establish that right up front.

"Exercise. At least when I'm playing with you," Lenny replied, stripping off his coat and carefully draping it over a stool. His shirt glistened with silver threads. Beck shook his head at the sight, but Lenny ignored him and chose a pool cue. He tested the weight, chalked the end, and stepped forward.

"Go ahead and break," Beck said. It wasn't going to matter either way.

"So who's the new guy?" Lenny asked in a lowered voice, angling his head toward the action hero in the corner.

Beck shrugged. "No clue." He could feel the guy's eyes on him since the moment the dude had entered the bar.

"Doesn't look like a local," Lenny said.

"No. Definitely not from here."

The necro leaned over, lined up the shot, and then straightened up again like he had something on his mind. "I didn't have anything to do with Blackthorne's reanimation," he said, a thin sheen of sweat on his brow. "I wanted you to know."

"If I thought ya had, ya'd be in a world of hurt right now," Beck replied.

The summoner nodded and broke.

As Beck walked around the table to choose his shot, he asked, "Any idea who did it?"

Lenny sagged against the mirrored wall behind them. "No. I warned the others not to jack with Blackthorne's corpse. I told them you'd rip them apart if they did anything. A summoner's bones break just as easy as anyone else's. Not that you heard that from me."

Beck grinned. He'd spent a lot of effort building that reputation.

"Someone didn't give a rat's ass what I'd do," he said.

"That's for sure," Lenny said.

Beck made sure not to sink the next ball. "What about Mortimer?" he asked.

A chuckle came his way, along with a quick shake of the necro's head. "Mort's totally by the book. He won't reanimate a corpse without the family's written permission . . . in triplicate."

"How's about Christian?" Beck asked, recalling the necros who'd been visiting Paul's grave over the last couple of weeks.

"Don't think so. From what I heard, the spell was one serious mother. Christian doesn't have that much juice."

"So who does?"

Lenny's eyes rose to Beck's then made a quick circuit around the pool hall. He straightened up again, leaning on the pool cue. "Only one summoner I know of." He went back to his shot and blew it.

"And does this bastard have a name?"

"He does, but I'm not saying it aloud."

Now that's interestin'. "Why would a necro want Blackthorne?"

"It's said your masters have hidden knowledge about every kind of demon there is, even the Archangels and the Fallen. That knowledge could be incredibly valuable if you wanted to summon any of the above."

Beck blinked in surprise. "I thought yer kind was just into dead bodies."

Lenny gave him a sour look. "Magic can be used for other purposes, but most of us are smart enough to stay away from the dark stuff."

"But not *him.*"

His companion shook his head and leaned his pool cue against the wall. "Another beer?"

"Yeah, thanks." Lenny headed toward the bar. The necro wasn't telling him everything, but Beck had gotten more out of him than he'd expected.

"Yer scared, aren't ya?" he whispered.

And it had nothing to do with Beck's badass reputation.

They were three games in when Beck heard the bar go quiet behind him. He had his back to the door but felt a gust of cold air strike the back of his neck. A faint tingling began in his limbs, then a peculiar dizziness. *No way.* He took a sip of his beer as a quick test and was rewarded with a heady mixture of hops, grain, and alcohol, tenfold what it should be. There was only one thing that could magnify the senses like that.

His favorite pool hall had just rated another Grade Four demon.

Beck carefully set his beer aside while scanning the room through the uneven reflection in the mirrored wall. Many of the other patrons stood slack jawed, eyes glazed, except the dude in the corner wearing the hero clothes. He was leaning back in his chair, arms crossed behind his head like he didn't have a care in the world.

So what gives here?

When a low voice began to whisper to Beck, he hunted for the source in the mirror and found it standing just inside the lounge doors. "She" was dressed in thigh-high boots, a tan leather micro miniskirt that barely covered her butt, a black bustier, and red fake-fur jacket. Her hair was wavy brown, and she looked barely sixteen. That would be what the demon wanted you to think.

This was a Mezmer. They were known by a lot of names—Jezebels, Tempters, Seducers—and they came in a few different varieties, but all of them sucked out your life essence and then took your soul if you gave them half a chance. And as they did you'd thank them for every minute of hellish torment.

Beck wasn't immune to her power, and raw desire struck him head on then migrated farther south. He heard her talking to him, promising delights that might be his if he'd just let her do her thing. The tingling grew stronger as the demon wove its spell, slowly encompassing all the men in the bar. The three women in the place just stared around, confused as to what was happening. One jostled her date, but he didn't react.

That was actually good news. If the demon were more experienced, all of the customers would be under its spell. That meant this one was a younger fiend, less powerful, and by casting such a wide net it was looking to suck up energy to grow.

Beck began to hum under his breath, trying to break through the allure of the demon's seductive message as it trickled through his mind. The humming worked, allowing the dizziness to ebb long enough for him to kneel like he was tying a bootlace. Instead, he cautiously opened the zipper to his trapping bag where it sat underneath the pool table. When he rose, still facing the mirrored wall, he had both hands full—a purple Babel sphere in the right and a Holy Water sphere in the left.

When he turned toward the threat the demon's eyes locked on him immediately. He couldn't see beneath the illusion, not until he used the Babel sphere, but there was no doubt this was Hellspawn.

Beck hummed louder, one of his favorite Carrie Underwood songs.

The Jezebel wrinkled her face in what passed for demonic annoyance. "You resist me," she said.

"That's for damned sure," he said. That took his attention off the song just long enough for her to send another message to his brain, one that would make a prostitute blush.

"No way," he said, shaking his head to clear it. He began to sing to himself. The song was a sad one, about a love lost, and it proved stronger than the fiend's seductive message.

"Trapper," she warned, moving closer to him. "Come to us. . . ."

Beck waited until the last moment, then slammed the purple sphere at the demon's feet. It burst open, setting off a fountain of flickering lights and scenting the air with cinnamon. The magic inside the sphere veered toward the demon, and the transformation began immediately. The girl's voice went from sultry to rasping, as her features melted away and the body contracted. Smaller and smaller she shrank, her clothes vanishing. Left behind was a short, squat body that looked like it'd been coated in brown mud. Hellfire red eyes gleamed at him, and a long barbed tail thrashed back and forth. The claws were black and sharp.

The other patrons' dull expressions rapidly changed from seduced to shocked.

"Oh, my God, that's a demon!" one of them spouted, backpedaling.

"No shit." Beck caught a glimpse of the bartender; Zack was shaking his head in dismay. Beck shrugged and turned his attention back to the fiend. It was gnawing on one of its claws in agitation and glaring up at him.

"Well done, trapper," Lenny said.

"Thanks," Beck said, pleased. "This one doesn't have much power to it."

He didn't have a proper container to put the thing in, but he'd find a way of getting it to a demon trafficker, and then he'd collect his money. Not a bad deal: Shoot some pool, drink some beer, and collect four hundred dollars for his trouble. To think he'd wasted all that time in Demon Central when the action was here.

A bizarre chuckle issued from the demon. Then it started to laugh. That wasn't right. It should be angry at being captured, spouting off a bunch of curse words, offering a boon for its freedom. Instead it was laughing like he was the joke.

"What's so funny?" he demanded.

"Ah, trapper . . ." Lenny said, pointing toward the entrance.

Beck swore under his breath. Another figure stood in the doorway clad in black leather with silver-white cropped hair and a fortune in body piercings. In her right hand was a whip, and she was grinning like she'd just won the lottery.

That was why the first one had said, "Come to us." There were *two* demons, and the younger one was the weaker of the pair, an apprentice learning the ropes while the master waited outside in case of trouble. Beck had proven to be that trouble.

The older demon flicked the whip and allowed her barbed teeth to show, causing some of the patrons to knock over their chairs and scramble backward.

"Time to play, trapper," it called out.

Beck had no choice but to bluff so he raised the Holy Water sphere. "Back off, demon. Ya don't wanna go there."

A sharp crack filled the air as the end of the whip caught the orb and shattered it in his hand. Cursing, he pulled his steel pipe from the trapping bag.

He sized up the situation, and it sucked. "Lenny, get the others out of here."

"But I can—"

Beck shook his head. "Don't try it. This one's too dangerous. Just get outta here."

"If that's what you want," the summoner whispered, then edged toward the others in the bar, urging them to follow him to the rear exit. Beck wished he could join them.

"What the hell are you?" a man called out, staggering toward the demon. The way he was moving, the guy had more booze in his system than blood. That made him prime demon bait. "This is our bar, and we don't take kindly to some skanky bit—" He was on his knees a second later, clawing at his throat for air. It was the only reason he wasn't screaming.

"Stop it!" Beck ordered. The Mezmer's eyes swung toward him. "This is between us, demon. The rest aren't worth yer time."

The fiend took a step closer. "Trapper," it said, sizing him up. It scented the air and smiled. "You are nothing," it said.

"Oh, but I *am* somethin'. I'm a journeyman trapper, not just some apprentice." He paused a moment for effect. "I was Paul Blackthorne's partner. My soul would win ya serious points with yer boss."

"Blackthorne?" the older demon hissed, and in response, the whip began to grow flames along its length.

Apparently that was the magic word. The drunk started to bellow, his ability to breathe restored. Two of his buddies pulled him away toward the back of the building.

Beck kept his attention riveted on the more dangerous of the two threats. As he watched, the female form had vanished to reveal a Hell-spawn as tall as he was with pale beige skin, blazing crimson eyes, long talons, and a wickedly barbed tail. Unlike the lesser fiend, this one had horns.

Ah, damn. This demon was close to making the leap to Archfiend. Some of them did that, working up through the ranks of Hell, slaughtering rivals with every step. Those that survived were the really evil ones. That it would show him its true form so easily told Beck he was in serious trouble.

"Killing you would be a pleasure, trapper," it said, licking its lips. "Harvesting your soul . . . priceless."

Beck didn't have the experience to tackle one of these things, and right now there wasn't a master in the city healthy enough to bail him out. Not that any of them would get here in time anyway. He swallowed his fear, like he had so many times in battle.

"So, demon, ya gonna just stand there lookin' damned ugly, or are we gonna dance?"

Chilling laughter burst from the fiend's mouth. "You will be perfect for my amusements, trapper. I wonder who will buy your soul from me?"

Then it began to whisper dark words. Beck hummed, louder this time, then started singing at the top of his voice. Nothing had any effect.

He could feel the demon sifting through his mind, looking for his weaknesses. It uncovered his hidden fears, his dreams, the future that could never be.

The fiend laughed, lower this time, knowing it had hit pay dirt. "That future is yours. *She* can be yours. . . ." it purred.

Beck felt his will cracking like an old piece of china exposed to the bitter cold. It would be so easy to let this thing take him. Why be a hero? He didn't owe any of these guys an ounce of his blood. He could have his secret wish. *Forever.*

"No," he said through gritted teeth. Once Hell had him in its grasp, it'd use him to destroy Riley. She would trust him even as he was leading her to eternal servitude or death. In a last-ditch effort to break the demon's hold, he rammed the steel pipe down on his own injured thigh, sending a burst of agonizing pain through his body. Though the pain made him cry out, it wasn't enough to break the demon's spell.

"Your soul, trapper," the fiend urged. "Swear it to me and I will make your dreams come true. I'll bring her to you, and she will be yours this very night."

Beck knew he'd lost. He felt the words forming on his tongue, the ones that would commit his soul to Hell for eternity. The words that would doom Riley at the same time.

God, no!

There was more laughter, but it sounded different. It hadn't come from the senior demon, because it was hissing now, low at first, then louder, like a cat threatened by a pack of feral dogs.

"Interference," it growled. "He is mine!"

Another voice cut through Beck's fog, one he didn't recognize. It sounded male and very, very old. He couldn't understand the words, but whatever they meant the pull on his mind snapped like an over-extended rubber band. The sheer force ricocheted him back on top of the pool table, scattering balls in all directions as his head pounded like someone had clubbed it with a sledgehammer. Tears ran down his cheeks.

When he finally opened his eyes, Lenny stared down at him, concerned.

"You okay?" the necro asked. Around them Beck could see other faces, all as worried as Lenny's.

The blazing pain receded. "Don't know," he mumbled. "What happened?"

"Something spooked the demons and they took off," Lenny reported.

"There was someone talkin'. Sounded really weird. Ya heard it, right?"

"No," Lenny admitted. "At least you're okay. Damn, I figured you were history."

Yer not the only one.

Beck closed his eyes for a moment and then smiled. He might not understand how it all happened, but the bottom line was that his soul was still his. The bad news was that Hell knew his greatest weakness now, and it was a safe bet they'd use it against him every chance they got.

As the bartender and the guy in the garish clothes saw to the prostrate trapper, Ori slipped through the double doors in search of the fiends. Normally he wouldn't have interfered, but the elder fiend had invoked Riley Blackthorne's name. That made it his business. Besides, having the trapper's soul in the clutches of Hell would only complicate Ori's job.

It didn't take him long to find the pair—they stood in a smudge of sulfured air in the parking lot, arguing.

"You had almost the trapper," the younger one snarled in that particularly convoluted Hellspeak younger demons employed once their true forms were revealed. Parts of that form still peeked out from around that of the young woman, a nightmarish mashup of bared flesh, clothes, sagging breasts, and talons. "Why us leave?" it demanded.

The older demon raised its hand for silence and sniffed the air. "Divine," it spat in warning.

Ori halted about ten feet away, not bothering to reveal his true form. They knew what he was, and he could get to his sword quicker than the Hellfiends could move.

The twin horrors spun to face him. Power ripped across the skin of the elder fiend. A succubus rarely had the chance to become this powerful, as the Archdemons killed them to ensure they didn't have any more competition. That meant this one was particularly vicious.

"I thought I smelt you," it growled.

"I'm surprised you could over the stench of the brimstone," Ori said, waving his hand to clear the air.

"Interfere you, why?" the younger demon demanded. It was a mere pup, or the trapper wouldn't have been able to shut it out of his mind. And stupid, or it wouldn't have challenged a Divine so openly.

Ori issued a casual grin in response, though all he really wanted to do was cleave these two in half for their arrogance. "Who set you on the trapper?" he asked.

"Why want you to know?" the younger one asked. The older one snarled and promptly cuffed it on the ear, causing it to whine in fear.

"We work for the glory of Hell," the senior demon responded, trying to regain the upper hand.

Too late. The younger Hellspawn had confirmed Ori's suspicions: Someone had deliberately targeted the trapper in an effort to get to Riley.

Ori made sure his gaze met that of the older demon. It winced at his power and averted its eyes. "Stay away from Blackthorne's child. If you tempt her, I will execute you like the cockroaches you are."

The elder demon hissed again and stepped backward, feeling the seething power of Ori's anger. The younger demon began to protest, but after another blow from its superior, the pair hurried away, changing into human form as they moved.

Ori watched them, curious as to whether they'd go back after the trapper. To his relief they didn't, but instead they encountered a young man on the street. His eyes glazed over as the elder demon put her hand on his heart and began to drink his life essence.

Ori wasn't about to interfere. They had their job. He had his.

And mine is the girl.

TWELVE

The sound of church bells brought Riley out of her vivid dreams. Waking up in a new place was always strange, but the bells calling the faithful to Mass sounded surreal. She rubbed her eyes, yawned and sat up. Another yawn. The bells continued and they made her think of Simon. After a quick trip to the bathroom, Riley crawled back under the covers and dialed his sister.

Please let him be better. She'd uttered that prayer right before she'd fallen asleep, along with requests to find her father and one that Peter would stay put in Atlanta. The prayer list was getting longer every night.

To her relief, the news was positive: Simon was improving, though still not talking much, and there was a chance he'd get to go home in a day or two. Amy said it was a miracle. She was right, but it had a lot to do with the fact that the wounds were demonic and being treated by freshly blessed Holy Water courtesy of Father Harrison. Between Heaven's intervention and the priest, Simon had no choice but to survive.

Riley disconnected the call with a broad smile. Once he went home Simon would loosen up. His family would see to that, and if not, his girlfriend sure would.

A cold morning greeted her as she stepped outside the church. A few cars along the street exhibited a layer of alabaster frost on their wind-shields. As she walked around to unlock her ride, she found a pure white rose stuck in the driver's side door handle. She carefully pulled it free, mindful of thorns, and sampled its fragrance. It was amazing. More surprising was the fact the hard freeze hadn't affected it.

Must not have been out here that long.

Riley's first thought was of Simon, but he was in the hospital. Beck didn't seem to be the romantic type. That only left . . .

Ori? But why would he give her a rose? After a quick look around and finding no sign of him, she decided not to tax her brain and just enjoy the gift. *Maybe today isn't going to suck after all.*

With no time for a trip home and oatmeal, she drove through the closest fast-food place and bought what her father used to call "death in a bag." High-fat, high-carb food. She was completely awake by the time she walked into Harper's place where there was the scent of fresh coffee layered on top of the old automotive smells. Apparently he'd felt good enough to use the coffeemaker.

As she entered the office, she braced herself. Harper liked to yell at her just for breathing. No shouting this time, in fact, he barely gave her a second glance. To her relief she found he was still sober. Despite that improvement, she kept out of range and spent time cleaning up, washing dishes, and emptying the trash cans, none of which had anything to do with trapping. It was expected that an apprentice would take care of the master, even if he was an asshat.

"Anything else?" she asked, hopeful she could blow out of there.

He shifted in his recliner as if no position was comfortable, which was probably the case.

"Get those Holy Water jugs out into the parking lot. A recycling truck should be coming by to pick them up this morning." Another shift in position. "I want every one accounted for. I'll need the money since I can't trap."

"Shouldn't we keep some of the counterfeit ones for evidence?" she hedged. "The ones I had were destroyed in the fire."

"Hold back five of them." Then he frowned. "Why didn't Saint catch that those bottles were wrong the last time he did the inventory?"

"Because none of them were. The screwed-up consecration dates just showed up in the last three weeks."

He chuffed in disgust. "I'd love to find the bastard behind that scheme. I'd throw him to a Three and watch the thing gut him."

Riley shivered: She knew exactly what that looked like. Harper caught her reaction, but he didn't chide her about it like she figured he would.

"There's an order on the desk," he said. "It's a Magpie. You've trapped them before, right?"

She nodded. Grade One demons came in two flavors—Klepto-Fiends, who stole bright objects, and Biblio-Fiends who chewed up books and swore like rappers. If she had her choice of what to trap, the Klepto-Fiend was it. They weren't malicious, just obsessive and stealthy.

"When you catch it, sell it to that new guy...Dan What's-His-Name," her master ordered. "Don't go anywhere near the fag, got it?"

The fag. That would be Fireman Jack, one of the demon traffickers. Harper had a real hang-up about homosexuals.

"I understand. Where is this Dan guy's place?"

Harper jabbed a finger at the desk. "His address is next to the trapping order."

Riley ignored the paperwork for the time being and concentrated on moving the plastic Holy Water bottles to the parking lot. After the first trip she devised a way to run a piece of rope through the handles so she could carry more of them at one time. As she made the trips back and forth, she noted that Harper's collection of scrounged metal in the fenced yard behind the building was diminishing.

Selling it off to pay the bills. The Guild's disability fund wasn't very generous.

Once she'd finished the recount, Riley leaned against her car and waited. As long as the bottle count matched the paperwork, Harper would have no reason to bitch at her. At least not about this.

Riley heard the truck from a block away as it ground through gears and eventually pulled up near her car, brakes screeching in protest. The truck bed had a substantial mound of plastic containers held in place by tall wooden racks on all four sides. A couple of guys hopped out of the vehicle. She handed over the clipboard with the required forms.

"Hey, I saw you on the TV. You know, at the Tabernacle," the younger of the two men said as the other one checked the count. "Damn, that was one helluva fire."

"So what happens to these bottles after you guys get them?" she asked, in an effort to change the subject away from one that fueled her nightmares.

To her relief he took the bait. "These?"

"Yeah, those," she said, indicating the bottles. That hadn't been a trick question.

"They go to the recycling plant," the other man said, his tone guarded.

"Then what happens?"

"Don't know. Don't care," he said. He counted out the money, then dropped it and one copy of the paperwork into her hands.

Riley pointed to the sheet. "Sign it, will you?"

"Don't need to," the guy said, frowning now.

"Please?" she wheedled, turning on the charm. "Master Harper will be all over me if I don't get it signed."

The two men traded looks, and the younger one scrawled something on the page and handed it back to her. The signature was unreadable. Her thanks yielded no reply as they backed out of the lot in a cloud of exhaust fumes and tormented gears.

While Riley rearranged the paperwork on the clipboard, something nagged at her. She stared at the driver's side door. There was no logo, no text, no nothing. All the city vehicles had Atlanta's official logo on their doors, the image of a phoenix rising from the flames.

So who just picked up those bottles?

✦

Beck didn't like hospitals. He'd spent some time in one during his stint in the Army so he knew how they worked. They harbored weird smells and seemed too sterile for his liking, so finding himself "makin' the rounds," as Master Stewart put it, didn't do a thing for his attitude. In Beck's way of thinking this was the priest's job, but here he was trooping around the different floors, talking to bedridden trappers and their families, acting like all Hell wasn't breaking loose. Why Stewart had insisted he do this he hadn't a clue, but he could take orders like any good soldier.

Beck had purposely made Simon his last stop, partly because he felt bad he hadn't kept the apprentice from being hurt, and mostly because Simon was dating Riley. He still hadn't sorted out his feelings about that. Not that he had anything against Adler, but it just didn't feel right to him.

Better'n some she could be seein'.

Like that Allan Something-or-Other, the abusive dude she'd dated a couple years back. Beck knew he was to blame for that: Riley had been totally hot for Beck when he'd returned from the Army. Anyone could see it. That would have been okay if she hadn't been Paul's daughter and only fifteen. He'd pushed her aside, hard. On the rebound, she'd immediately taken up with that abusive prick, a loser who had her steal stuff for him. That relationship had lasted right up until Allan had hit her.

But that's the point, isn't it?

Simon would treat Riley right. He wouldn't beat her or talk her into stealing things, but every time Beck tried to tell himself that, it stuck in his throat. Did that mean he was jealous?

He shoved that unnerving thought aside and entered Simon's room. He found the patient awake, watching something on television. Beck's eyes flicked toward the screen; it was a talk show about what had happened at the Tabernacle. Every now and then a picture of the inferno would pop on the screen.

Just what ya shouldn't be watchin'.

"Simon." A weak nod returned as Beck slowly approached the bed. "How's it goin'?" he asked, keeping his tone conversational. Just like a priest would.

A shrug returned.

"I hear the wounds are healin' good." A nod. It appeared that Beck would have to do all the talking. "I've been visitin' some of the others. Looks like they're gonna make it, though Barton needs more surgery on his leg."

"Good," the patient mumbled, his eyes not meeting his visitor's.

Beck hadn't figured Simon was going to be all perky, but he had to talk this out or it'd eat him alive. Beck knew about that firsthand.

He tried another approach. "Did ya see the angels?"

Simon's expression saddened. "No, I didn't."

"Well, they were truly awesome. I've seen the ministerin' kind before, but these were the big boys. They were seriously kick-ass."

"Jackson told me about them," Simon replied. "He said they had fiery swords and you could feel this sort of power around them."

"Ya shoulda seen the demons. They ran for it."

Silence.

Beck leaned on the bed rail. "Ya know, it's real hard after a battle," he said. "Ya can't believe half of what happened, and part of ya is too damned frightened to deal with it. Just know, it'll take time."

Simon swallowed heavily. "I thought I was going to die."

"Same here."

The apprentice's eyes met his. "Were you frightened?"

"Hell, yes."

"I shouldn't have been. I knew God was with me."

"That don't keep ya from bein' afraid. That's natural," Beck explained. "Nothin' to be ashamed of."

"I saw on the TV that the demons are all over the city now."

"A few. They're actin' strange, but we'll get 'em; don't worry."

Simon frowned. "Why hasn't Riley come to see me again?" he demanded, his voice harsher now.

That wasn't a question Beck had expected. "She's helpin' Harper out and she's tryin' to find Paul. I figure she'll be along directly."

"That's no excuse. She should be here."

Oh, lord. "I'll let her know yer askin' for her."

That seemed to mollify the patient. When Simon spoke again, his voice was quieter. "They're going to blame me for this."

"No one's blamin' anyone," Beck said. "There are too many things we don't understand yet."

Simon's eyes swung in his direction. "You mean like why Master Blackthorne was there?"

"Surprised the hell outta me, that's for sure," Beck replied. "We're tryin' to work it all out."

The frown returned. "What's to work out? Either the Holy Water was counterfeit or someone broke the circle and let the demons in."

"Riley said the Holy Water was good. I trust her on that. No one would break the circle. It'd just get them dead."

"Not if they were dead already."

Beck straightened up, knowing that the next words out of the young man's mouth would be condemning Paul. That he wouldn't tolerate. "I'd best be goin'," he said.

Simon's eyes closed, his mouth a grim line. "I think you should," the apprentice retorted.

He thinks Paul sold us out. That didn't promise a rosy future between Riley and her new boyfriend. She would stick up for her father no matter what.

Ya sure know how to pick 'em, girl.

THIRTEEN

Peter hopped into her car and slammed the door the moment Riley pulled to the curb near the Grounds Zero. He was in his usual jeans and sweatshirt, the one with the picture of a guy taking a sledgehammer to a computer keyboard. The caption said COMMENCE REBOOT.

He set his computer bag on the floorboard, then stared at her. "Your hair. It's different."

"It needed a trim. It got really frazzled in the fire."

"I like it. It looks good." Her friend handed over an insulated cup. "Hot chocolate with whipped cream," he announced, then swiped at his own brown hair to get it out of his face.

"You brought me hot chocolate. You rock, Mr. King."

"I do, and your timing's excellent. I've only been here a few minutes."

"You take the bus?" she asked.

"No, David dropped me off. He wanted out of the house as much as I did."

No doubt. "I've got a trapping run."

Peter swiveled in his seat, eyes widening. "What kind of demon is it?"

"It's just one of the small guys, a Grade One Klepto-Fiend. I figured you'd want to stay in the car."

"Why? This could be fun."

This wasn't the Peter she knew. He was always playing it safe to avoid getting grounded by The Warden. Now, with his parents divorcing, it looked like he had decided to branch out a little.

Riley gave him a dubious look as she pulled up to an intersection. "You sure?"

"Yeah, unless that Five is going to be there."

"It shouldn't be." *Not during the day, at least.*

At the next intersection a man stood in the middle of the chaos clad in an orange vest and white gloves, like a cross between a butler and a traffic guard. Since most of the city's traffic lights had been stolen by thieves, he was part of the city's new scheme of HTLs—human traffic lights. For a little over five dollars an hour he had the privilege of standing in the intersection, trying not to get squashed.

As she waited for her turn to move forward, Riley asked, "Is it getting any better at home?"

Peter slumped in his seat. "No. Mom's still guilting us, and Dad's not saying much at all."

"Who do you want to live with?"

"Dad, for sure. He's cool. He has rules, and some of them are kinda stupid, but he's nothing like Mom."

"What will happen if you tell her that?"

Peter shook his head in despair. "Cue total meltdown. If I tell her the truth, she'll just throw Matthew's death in my face."

"Sounds seriously hideous, Peter."

"It is," he murmured. "Mom hasn't been right since the twins were born."

Riley remembered the day her friend had announced that his mother was pregnant. He'd been thirteen at the time and majorly grossed out to think that his parents were having sex.

"I feel sorry for the ghouls," he said, his term for the twins. "They just don't get what's going on and so they're really fussy right now."

A pair of cranky three-year-olds. No wonder her friend wanted out of the house, even if it was to trap a Magpie.

"Well, I'd just tell her and get it over with, Peter. It's tearing you up, I can tell."

He nodded but didn't reply.

At least my parents never stopped loving each other.

With a gloved wave from the human traffic light she edged through the intersection and continued east to the jewelry shop in Poncey High-lands. Peter's sharp eyes spotted the sign before she did. Riley glided to a halt in front of the store, one of those mom-and-pop kind of places that looked like it'd been at the same location for decades.

As Riley turned off the engine and scooped up her messenger bag, Peter appeared to be having second thoughts.

"Is this dangerous?" he asked.

"No way. These guys are all about stealth. That's why we call them Hell's cat burglars. They're just into bling."

"What kind of bling?" he asked.

"The shinier the better."

He thought that through. "Okay, I'll see what it's all about. If it gets weird, I'm outta there."

That was fair.

Right before she exited the car, her cell phone pinged—a text from Mortimer: The vendue was on, and if she really wanted to be there, she needed to be available tomorrow night. Time and directions followed. A second message arrived before she could reply: IF YOU ATTEND, DON'T WEAR JEANS.

She was supposed to be on hallowed ground after sundown. Did she dare risk it?

"Riley?" Peter nudged. "Something wrong?"

"No, just trying to decide something." What if the Five came after her at this vendue thing? Then she remembered who would be there—summoners who wielded magic for fun and profit. She couldn't imagine a demon would take that on when it could wait for another time when she wasn't protected. Besides, Ori would be on her tail. She sent Mort a quick text telling him she'd be there.

Riley found her friend studying the contents of one of the store's display windows. It was full of sparkle. "How do you catch this thing?" he asked.

She dug in her bag, pulled out a sippy cup, and handed it to him.

"You're joking, right?" he said. "You trap demons with cups that have dancing bears on them?"

She glowered at him. "See the glitter in the bottom? Klepto-Fiends can't resist it."

He held up the sippy cup and compared it to the exquisitely cut diamonds in the store window.

"Wanna bet?"

And I brought him along why?

He returned the cup. "The 'rents can't know about this—ever."

"Got it."

Riley pushed open the reinforced door and looked around for someone who might be in charge. The paperwork said the complaint came from a guy named Abe Meyerson. There were two employees, but the elderly man near the watch case seemed to be the best choice. He had some serious wrinkles and was probably at least eighty, if not older.

After a deep breath to build her confidence, Riley put on her professional "I know what I'm doing" face and approached the glass counter.

"Mr. Meyerson?" she asked. The old gentleman nodded. "I'm Riley Blackthorne and I'm here to deal with your *theft* problem." Her dad had always insisted that she not use the words *demon trapper* in a retail store until the owner indicated he was okay with his customers knowing what was going on. In case the jeweler wasn't making the connection, she offered him the paperwork.

Mr. Meyerson took the trapping request out of her hand, held it closer to his nose than would have been comfortable for her, and then nodded again. Then he looked at her, squinting. "Oy, they're sending young ones now!" the man said with a spry grin. He looked at Peter. "Are you a trapper, too?"

"No, sir. I'm just watching, if that's okay with you."

"Fine by me. These little thieves are just the nature of the business, but this one isn't kosher. It ignores anything metal; only likes loose stones. I think it's a little off in its skull; you know what I mean," he said, tapping his temple for emphasis.

Not good. That meant this one would be harder to capture. She so needed something to go right for a change, especially with Peter watching her every move.

"How long has it been here?" Riley asked, refusing to let the disheartening news sidetrack her.

"A week."

"Does it have any particular time that it steals stuff?"

"Just whenever it feels like it."

She'd have to go through this place inch by inch to find the fiend rather than just wait it out. With the funerals this afternoon, she really needed to make this happen. Taking a deep breath, Riley recited the warnings and precautions that came with removing a demon from a public location. Mr. Meyerson had no questions, mostly because he'd been through this numerous times over the years, and he readily signed the form to indicate he knew the consequences.

"I leave it to you," he said. "Let me know if you need anything." The old man puttered off to sit at a desk that had to be as ancient as he was. Pressing a jeweler's loupe to his eye, he bent over a watch and began poking at it with a little screwdriver.

Cue demon trapper.

Riley retreated to the door and began a visual tour of the showroom, a technique her dad had taught her during one of her first trapping assignments. *Assess the surroundings. Look for obvious hiding places.*

"What are you doing?" Peter whispered.

"Trying to find where a three-inch-tall demon could hide."

"Ah, that's about everywhere," he said. "I don't think your glitter-in-a-cup trick is going to work."

Unfortunately, Peter was right. There were a lot of nooks and crannies in a building this old. Her usual bait was worthless with all those gems in the cases, each lit with their own internal fire and by carefully positioned high-intensity lights. She could put Holy Water at each of the exits and along the windows to flush the fiend out. Problem was, then it'd go nuts and tear the place apart. She already had a reputation for trashing libraries; no need to add jewelry stores to the list.

What am I going to do? She could call Beck and maybe he'd have an idea, but that would make her look like she couldn't handle things on her own. Calling Harper was *so* not an option.

As she thought it through, Peter parked himself at a chair near the watch case, laptop out, surfing an online gaming site. She looked over his shoulder; he was checking out pictures of dragons. He pulled one of the images into a program and then upped the size so he could see it easier. It made the thing look huge on the vivid eighteen-inch color screen.

Her eyes went to the closest glass case. The problem was that all these jewels were about the same size. Nothing really screamed BLING! What she needed was a humongous gem.

Peter's dragon now sat on top of a mound of gold and jewels, short puffs of smoke coming out its nostrils. It looked menacing, but not the twenty-foot-tall, pull-her-dad-out-of-his-grave kind of scary.

The idea that popped into her brain was crazy. She would bet no trapper had ever tried such a stunt, but she was out of options. Either she gave it a go or she had to call Harper and say she couldn't handle the job.

No way. He'd never let me live that down.

Riley cautiously ran her lunatic idea past the jeweler, and to her astonishment she received a vote of approval.

"Can't hurt," Mr. Meyerson said. He opened the vault and returned with a large emerald. It was marquise cut and two carats in weight, he said, though Riley had no idea what all that meant. She took a picture of it with her cell phone, e-mailed it to Peter, and then explained exactly what she wanted him to do. To her relief, he didn't tell her she was totally wacked. As her friend worked, the jeweler returned the emerald to the safe, made a quick check to ensure there wasn't a demon inside, and then locked it tight.

Luckily there were no customers at the moment, as it took time to set the trap. The jeweler turned off all the interior lights, including those in the display cases. There was still light coming in the front windows, but not so much as to ruin her plan.

Peter positioned his laptop on one of the main glass displays, clicked a key, and the image of the emerald appeared on the big screen. He'd done something to it so the image rotated, sparkled, and shone like it was lit from within by a solar flare.

If the gem could talk, it would be screaming, STEAL ME!

"You think this will work?" Peter whispered as they backed away.

"It better," Riley whispered in reply.

The jeweler and his assistant hovered by the front door, watching the show. They seemed amused by her high-tech trap.

"Such a thing I have never seen," the old man said. "Kids these days—so smart."

Only if this works.

Time passed. Peter nudged her with an elbow. "And this is going to happen . . . when?"

She gave him a dirty look. "Patience, dude."

Then she heard it, that pitter-patter of boot-clad demon feet racing across glass. A moment later the Magpie stood transfixed in front of the computer, its bulging bag of loot at its side. It looked like the one in her apartment—about three inches tall—except this one wasn't wearing a black bandana. In the glow of the screen she could see its tiny fingers twitch in nervous anticipation.

That's right. It's all yours. Just don't move.

Riley slowly approached, making each step as quiet as possible. If she spooked it, it wouldn't fall for this ruse a second time. The moment before it leapt at the screen she caught the fiend. She dropped the demon into the transparent sippy cup and slapped a hand over the top.

"Lid!" she called out. Her friend just stared at the cup in her hand, wide-eyed. "Peter! I need the lid. Now!"

"Sorry," he called out and hurried over. Between them they sealed the cup.

"Wow. That's really a demon. I mean, you can see pictures of them on the Web, but—"

The fiend in question rose on its feet, pointed at the bag, and then began to wail, pulling at its clothes like it was in mourning.

"What's he doing?"

"Freaking. He thinks I'm stealing his stuff." Riley brought the cup to nose level. "Hold on, I'll get it for you. I won't take it away," she said.

Mr. Meyerson opened the bag's drawstring, and the contents slid across the glass countertop.

"Look at all that," Peter said in awe. There were at least a dozen loose diamonds and sapphires, but no emeralds. They'd offered the demon the perfect bait.

The old jeweler separated out the merchandise with a wizened finger. "That's all of the gems. The rest is just glass. Who knows where it came from," he said with a toothy smile.

Riley put the remaining loot back in the bag and, with Peter's help, dumped it inside the cup without losing the demon. The Magpie clutched his horde to his chest and sighed in profound relief.

"Wow, he *is* obsessed," Peter said, staring at the fiend.

"Totally. Get rid of the emerald. He's forgotten it for the moment, but that won't last."

"Gone," her friend said, punching a key. The image vanished, and in its place was a thunderstorm rolling over Atlanta's skyline.

"Well done," the old man said, beaming through a sea of wrinkles. "Ingenious."

Riley grinned. "Thanks." She looked over at her friend and shot him a thumbs-up. "Who knows, maybe this is the future of demon trapping."

"Tech rules," Peter replied.

They left the shop with one demon in a sippy cup, signed paperwork, and two free coupons for lunch at a downtown deli courtesy of Mr. Meyerson. He'd also promised not to tell anyone about Peter's part in the job.

"Trapper scores," Riley said, feeling really good for a change.

This is how it's supposed to be.

FOURTEEN

It was nearly one thirty when Riley pulled her car up to Beck's house in Cabbagetown. His place wasn't much different than its neighbors', other than it looked better maintained. The trim and porch railing were stark white, and the house itself a pleasing shade of light green. She could almost imagine him out there on a ladder slinging paint all over the place.

How does he find the time? She was still behind on her laundry.

Beck sat on the porch in a wooden rocking chair clad in his black suit. From the dour expression on his face, all he needed was a shotgun and something to fill full of holes, and he'd be just fine.

She'd first heard about the new kid from South Georgia over the dinner table when her father had told them about this smart-ass sixteen-year-old in his history class, a troublemaker sprinting full speed toward a brick wall. "Serious lemming potential" is the way he'd described Denver Beck. Now her father was dead and the former troublemaker had taken it upon himself to watch over her so she wouldn't go all "wild child" on him.

It was a plan doomed to failure.

As she parked the car in the driveway, Beck rose with considerable effort. She didn't think it was because of his injuries: The Holy Water would have started to heal those. What hurt was way deeper and most likely permanent. She carried some of those same scars herself.

Beck climbed in her car, placed his trapping bag on the seat behind them, and then clicked the seat belt without so much as a "Hello." Like it was expected she'd haul his butt around town.

Maybe he doesn't want to be on his own.

She asked the question anyway. "Some reason I'm driving you to the funeral?" she said.

"Don't need a ticket." At her puzzled look, he explained: "After the service we'll go to the Six Under for the wake. Don't want to lose my truck if the cops pull me over on the way home."

Another trapper tradition: Bury your dead and then get drunk. There were a lot of traditions, which led her to believe they'd evolved over time. Anything that involved an excuse to drink was automatically trapper approved.

"I'll drive you home after the wake," she offered, heading back toward Memorial Drive.

"No, I'll walk. It's not that far."

"You could still get arrested for that," she said. "I'll drive you."

He eyed her. "Yer not comin' to the bar with us. Yer not legal."

"They serve soda. Besides, it's only right: I was at the Tabernacle when they died; I want to be there for their wake."

He ignored her from that point on. The silence held for longer than was comfortable, and finally she relented. She needed to talk to someone and Beck was the only option.

"The collection agency jerk visited me yesterday. He said they'll go after the life insurance money since they didn't get to steal Dad's body."

Beck huffed. "Don't worry; they won't get it."

Easy for you to say.

More silence. She almost turned on the radio, but the music she liked would only earn her hassles from her companion. "Trapped a Magpie today. At a jewelry store," she said, figuring that was a safe topic.

"It go okay?"

"Real well." She was about to tell him how she'd pulled it off, then changed her mind. He might not like the idea of Peter being there.

They made it through four more intersections before he gave in. "Ya see Simon today?"

"No. I'm going to stop by tonight."

"Good; he's askin' for ya. It's gonna take him a while to get over what happened."

"Same for all of us." She heard a grunt of acknowledgment. Time to move to more sunny topics. "Mort's trying to help me find Dad."

"Does he know who took him?" Beck quizzed.

"No. He thinks it's odd that no one's talking. I'm just hoping it's not Ozymandias. Ayden says he's into dark magic."

Beck looked pensive. "That must be the guy Lenny was talkin' about. I'll pay him a visit."

"He's not like Mort or the others. This one's evil."

"Evil I can do," Beck said, as if the problem were solved.

"I'll go with you."

"Not happenin', so don't even think about it," he retorted.

Why is everything a battle with you? Why can't you let me make my own decisions?

In response to the tension, Beck began to rearrange the contents of his duffel bag. From what she could tell, it didn't need the attention, but he focused on that rather than talking. A nervous habit. She had a few of her own.

He finally stopped fussing with the bag. "There were two Mezmers at the lounge last night."

"What?" she said, giving him a quick glance before returning her eyes to the highway. "Did you get them?"

"No," he said. "I tagged the first one, but before I could get it secured, the second one showed up. It was . . . more than I could handle."

She pulled up to a stop sign, jamming on the brakes. "Beck! You're okay, aren't you?" He nodded. "How did you get away from it?"

Her passenger shrugged. "Don't really know. It was workin' me over somethin' fierce, and then both of them just took off."

"Did you tell Stewart?" she asked, more worried now that he didn't have a solid answer.

"Not yet. I will, once everythin' settles down."

Riley could tell there was more here than he was admitting. What if that thing *had* gotten his soul? Would she be able to tell? A sick knot formed in her chest. "Beck . . ." she began, her voice quavering.

"I don't want to talk about it," he ordered. "It's over and I'm still in one piece."

But you might not have been.

Beck had been planning his move from the moment the funerals had ended. As Riley pulled into the pub's parking lot, he hopped out of the car, hoping to avoid a confrontation. "Thanks, girl. Call when ya get to the church so I know yer safe."

There was no way he could ignore the expression on Riley's face. He knew it well enough; it promised defiance, so it wasn't any surprise when she turned off the car, undid the seat belt, and climbed out. Beck watched her walk across the street toward the pub, her hair swinging back and forth, boots clicking on the pavement.

Ya shouldn't be here. It wasn't dangerous or anything, but it was a guy thing.

"We're gonna get drunk, we're gonna swear and tell a lot of war stories," he called out. "That's about it."

Riley paused at the entrance to the Six Feet Under Pub and Fish House. "I know. Dad told me about these things."

"It's no place for a . . . girl."

"But it is for a trapper," she said, and left him standing there like a moron.

"Why do ya fight me on everythin'?" he snarled. He had no choice but to let her have her way. Dragging her out of there by the hair would just make both of them look stupid.

He found Riley at the bar, ordering a glass of Pepsi. Just like he figured, the bartender was giving her the once-over.

"You're new," the guy said, turning on the charm.

"Uh-huh," Riley replied, laying a five on the counter and looking around. "Where are the trappers?"

"Oh, you're here for that, huh? They're upstairs, on the roof," he answered, pointing toward a set of stairs near the entrance. Then he plunked the glass down and gave her the change. As Beck approached, Riley picked up her drink and headed for the stairs, acting as if he didn't exist.

"Hey, man," the bartender called out. "I heard about the Tabernacle. Sorry."

"It was a bitch, that's for sure," Beck said. "Thank yer boss for the flowers. The families really appreciated them."

"Will do." The bartender stacked a couple glasses as he watched Riley climb the stairs. "Now that's a total hottie."

"Don't even think about it," Beck warned.

"Oh, sorry," the guy said, raising his hands in surrender. "I didn't know she was spoken for."

Beck realized he'd been a jerk. "No, not yer fault. I'm kind of . . . well . . . she's a trapper. She's Paul's daughter."

"I thought she was a groupie or something. Thanks for setting me straight." He went into bartender mode. "The usual?"

"Yeah. Make it a pitcher this time, and start a tab."

"You got it."

✝

The rooftop portion of the Six Feet Under was open to the air, so Riley made sure to sit near one of the radiant heaters. She selected an empty chair at the end of a long wooden table. Three tables, actually, all nosed together to accommodate the trappers. As she sat, heads turned. A few faces frowned. She was pleased to see not all of them did.

"Hi there, Riley," Jackson called out. He was drinking coffee instead of a beer, probably in deference to his wounds.

"How are you doing?" she asked.

"Not bad. Hurts like hell, but the doc said I don't need grafts, so I'm not going to complain."

"That's really good news."

"Amen to that. Where's Den?"

"Here!" Beck called out as he walked up. He set his pitcher and pint of beer on the table next to Riley's glass. Shooting her a snarky grin, he said, "Now don't ya get those mixed up, ya hear?"

Riley gave him a scathing look, which was a complete waste of time. The group went quiet, except for Beck, who took a long gulp of his brew.

"God, I love this stuff." Then he looked down at the others. "What's the problem, guys?"

McGuire angled his head toward Riley. He was in his early forties, tall with thin hips and thin brown hair that covered his collar. If the deep crease lines on his face were any indication, a scowl was his default setting.

"Apprentices are always at these things. How else are they gonna learn anythin'?" Beck asked.

"But she's—"

"A trapper," Jackson said.

"Not in my book," McGuire replied.

"You can bitch all you want, but I saw her take down a Three with a *folding chair*," Jackson replied. "We would have been burying Simon tonight if it hadn't been for her, so I think maybe you should just can it."

"The hell I will. First it'll be her, then there'll be more of them. We'll have to take anyone who wants to be a trapper," McGuire complained.

"I'd say the more the better. We could use 'em right now," Beck said.

McGuire rose to his feet. "No disrespect to the dead, but I can't be here if she is." He slugged down what remained of his beer and then stomped off toward the stairs.

Riley shook her head. *Another enemy. Like I don't have enough already.*

One of the trappers pounded the table enthusiastically. "Good deal. McGuire's such a downer." He gave Riley a hundred-watt smile. "I'm Lex Reynolds, by the way. Pleased to have you here, miss."

She nodded in reply. Reynolds had a full beard and hair that went below his shoulders. He looked like a surfer, muscled, with a deep golden tan. He wasn't a good ol' boy, that was for sure.

The trapper rose and lifted his glass. With a nudge from Beck, she stood like the others.

"Rest in peace, guys," Reynolds called out, and then everyone took a long drink. "You keep those Pearly Gates open for us, and we'll bring the beer."

"Amen!" a few of the trappers shouted.

Chairs skidded on the floor as the group returned to their seats.

"Collins owed me twenty bucks," Jackson announced. "I'm never going to see that, am I?"

"Twenty? He owed me fifty," another trapper called out.

"Y'all are screwed," Beck laughed. "I bet he's laughin' his ass off right now."

"God, I miss him. He was so much fun," Reynolds said. "Remember when he went after that Four at Georgia Tech, right after he became a journeyman?"

"I don't know that story," one of the trappers replied. He was an older guy with an exquisite handlebar mustache.

"Well, there was this Four eating up fraternity boys like candy. So Collins gets the job. He goes up to this chick and she offers him a good time, so he drops a load of Holy Water on her."

Jackson chortled. Apparently he knew how this story played out.

"You see, she wasn't a demon." Reynolds grinned. "She was an undercover vice cop. Man, did they bust his balls."

Riley laughed along with the others.

"Sounds like somethin' I'd do," Beck joked.

A trapper named Thomas jumped in with a tale about Morton catching a Three in a meat locker at a grocery store. Then someone related the joke they'd pulled on Stewart involving a goat in Demon Central. It was only then she realized the masters weren't here.

When she asked Beck why that was the case, he replied, "So the guys can say anythin' they want and not worry they'll get in trouble. They can blow off steam that way."

Riley settled back in her seat, letting the stories surround her. This wasn't about remembering the dead but honoring those that were still alive. These trappers were the real deal, and for a moment she felt a strong sense of pride at being one of them. *This was why Dad did this.* It wasn't just bringing in the demons or earning a paycheck. It was about being one of the guys.

But I never will be one of the guys. She didn't have the right equipment and that would make all the difference. Even if she rose to the rank of master, she'd never really belong. Depressed, Riley finished off her drink and stood. All eyes went to her.

"You're not leaving, are you?" Jackson asked. "The night's young."

"I need to get some sleep," she admitted, then wondered if that made her sound weak. It was a better explanation than having to stay on holy ground after dark.

" 'Night, Miss Riley," someone called out from the group, though she wasn't sure who it was. She called out her own farewell and headed down the stairs. Beck quickly fell in step with her, following her out to the car.

"I thought ya were gonna drive me home," he chided.

"Changed my mind."

"Glad to hear it." He hesitated and then added, "I need help with somethin' tomorrow. Will ya be home around noon?"

"Help with what?"

"Just somethin'."

Okay, be mysterious. "I'll be home then."

"Good. I'll bring barbecue for lunch."

"That works."

They'd reached her car. As Riley pulled out the keys, he said, "Call me when ya get to the church."

"Why do you do that?" she demanded, turning on her heels to face him.

"What?"

"You go all old on me, like you're a geezer or something."

"Ya don't understand," he said, running a hand through his hair.

"What don't I get, Beck? That you had a craptastic childhood? That you can't change what happened to you so you're going to micromanage my every waking hour?"

His face hardened. "Yeah, that's part of it. I had to take care of myself since I was little. I know what it's like."

"You keep it up and you're going to be like Harper, a sad old guy who hits people and bitches about everything."

"Ya don't understand," he repeated.

"Then tell me why you have to be like this. One good reason."

"Because . . ." He slumped against the car. "I don't know any other way to be."

Finally the truth. And from the expression on his face, it looked like she'd carved it out of his heart.

She leaned against the car next to him, hands crossed over her chest. "Promise you'll stop going all senior?"

He looked over at her. "Will you call yer aunt?"

Here we go again. "I won't be any safer in Fargo. If the demons want me, they'll find me."

Beck put his hand on her arm. "Please," he pleaded.

Riley stared at him. That word just wasn't one of his favorites. For him to use it meant he was desperate. When she didn't reply, he removed his hand in defeat.

"I just need to know that there's someone who'll take care of ya ... if ... somethin' happens to me."

Without another word her companion walked back toward the pub. At the last moment he looked back over his shoulder. This time his emotions were unmasked and she could read them easily.

Fear. For him and for her.

What aren't you telling me? What really happened at the pool hall?

FIFTEEN

It took some time for Riley to find Simon: He'd been moved out of ICU. As she drew closer to his room, a man passed her in the hallway. He wasn't hospital staff, so for a moment she thought maybe he was a priest, but he wasn't wearing a clerical collar.

Probably a friend of the family.

Riley paused outside the room to gear herself up for this. It shouldn't be this way. She should be really looking forward to seeing Simon, but something wasn't right between them. *I'm overreacting. He's just scared like the rest of us. He'll come out of it.*

She cautiously stuck her head in the door and found him in the bed closest to the door. The curtain was pulled, shielding him from his roommate, who was watching television.

Her boyfriend was staring at nothing, hands tangled around a rosary, his face as pale as it had been the last time she'd seen him. She moved to his side, set her messenger bag on the chair and waited for him to acknowledge her. When he did, he frowned like she wasn't welcome.

"Where have you been?" he demanded, scowling. "I called your house over and over, and you didn't answer. Are you blowing me off on purpose?"

Riley counted to ten so as to not buy into his anger. *He's just frustrated. He has to vent.*

"I'm not home much anymore," she explained. "Call my cell." Then Riley remembered why that wouldn't work. "I'll get you the new number. My phone got toasted so I'm using Dad's."

If she expected that to mollify Simon, it didn't work. "Why weren't you here this morning?"

"I've been busy. I've had our master to take care of, a Magpie to trap, funerals and a wake to attend. That doesn't leave much time for sitting around the house waiting for your call, Simon."

"Wake?" he replied. "Why would *you* go to that?"

Because I'm a trapper? "Don't start," she replied. "I had to listen to McGuire complain about me being in the Guild. I don't need to hear it from you."

Simon looked away, but no apology was forthcoming.

"Look, I'm really tired, so I'm kind of bitchy," she said, trying to salvage the conversation. "Let's start over, okay?"

When he didn't respond, she reached over one of the side rails and touched his hand. Simon flinched and pulled away.

"What is going on with you?" she asked.

"I would think that would be obvious," he replied, scowling over at her.

No, or I wouldn't have asked. "Look, just hang in there. You'll be getting out of here soon. You'll be coming back to work and maybe in a couple weeks we can go to a movie or something. Spend some time together. I'd like that." *I really need your strength right now.*

"A date?" he retorted, his knuckles white as he clenched the rosary. "How can you think about that? How can you be oblivious as to what is going on in this city?"

Riley's temper reared its head. "I know what's happening, Simon. I know better than anyone, but—"

"I never realized how shallow you are," he said, staring at her like he'd just learned her darkest secret. "Don't those dead trappers mean anything to you?"

"Now look here," she retorted, trying hard to control her voice so as not to disturb his roommate. "Don't give me this 'You don't care' crap. I'm not oblivious, Simon." *I just want to get things back on track with us.*

"That's not what I'm seeing," he said, waving a hand dismissively. "We have to find out what happened at the Tabernacle. We have to find out who betrayed us."

Betrayed? Riley forced herself to sound calm, though her emotions were seething. "No one betrayed us, Simon. You know that as well as I do."

"Do I?" he asked, a strange light in his eyes. "This is a battle for our very souls, Riley. Nothing is like it seems. We can trust no one until we know what happened."

Riley gave up. She was too tired for all this drama. "Then you work it out. I've gotta go."

When she dropped a kiss on his cheek, Simon's jaw tensed underneath her lips.

"I'm not giving up on you," she said, defiantly.

"And I'm not giving up until I find the truth."

Instead of dragging herself into the solitude of the church's basement and listening to the furnace do its on-and-off dance, Riley sat on the stone steps that led to the building's front entrance. It was after dark now, the streets alight with cars and busy with pedestrians headed home for the night. Right now the Five seemed a remote threat. A bigger worry was Simon and what was happening between them. The possibility of losing him weighed on her heart.

"Heaven can't be that cruel," she whispered.

A slight breeze made her tuck her coat tighter. She heard the light footsteps before she saw him. Ori. He settled onto the steps next to her, dressed in a black leather jacket and jeans. He said nothing for a long time, as if he was respecting her need for silence. Finally Riley knew she had to say something.

"I didn't see you following me from the hospital," she said, looking over at him.

"I'm very good at what I do," he replied. "Something happened there, didn't it?"

"It's more what *didn't* happen." She twisted the strap on her messenger bag in agitation, then realized what she was doing and shoved it away. It was a stupid habit. "My boyfriend's gotten weird. I know he's been really ill and all that, but . . ."

"But?" Ori nudged.

"Simon's changing. He used to be so sweet and kind. Now he's nasty, even to me, like it was my fault he got clawed up."

"Do you think it's your fault?"

Riley rubbed her face in thought. "Maybe. What if the Five brought those other demons just so it could get to me? What if I'm the reason all those guys died?"

Ori gently placed his hand on her arm, giving it a gentle squeeze of reassurance.

"If the Five wanted you, it just had to wait for the right time to kill you. It did not have to orchestrate an attack on the Tabernacle."

Riley searched his face and found only compassion. She needed that support right now. Simon certainly wasn't giving her any. "You really believe that?"

Ori nodded. "The demons are not acting normally. Something, or someone, is driving them to this grotesque behavior."

"Lucifer?"

"No. Not his style. The Prince of Hell likes order above all things."

"But who—" Riley let it drop, too tired to try to work through it. Stewart and the others would take care of it. She had her boyfriend and her dad to worry about.

"I thought that Simon's faith would help him through this. I mean, he's really religious. I thought we'd deal with this together, but he's not moving on, all he's doing is looking backward."

"While you're looking forward?"

Riley nodded. "That's what I do when it goes wrong. If I slow down I don't think I can handle my screwed-up life, so I just keep moving, hoping it'll get better. It never does."

Ori put his arm around her, drawing her close to his body, which allowed Riley to rest her head on his shoulder. She inhaled the crisp, cool scent that was him.

"Simon's journey is his own," he said. "If he's foolish enough to push you away, then that's his loss. Don't give up on him just yet."

"I hope he gets his head straightened out. I really like him."

"Then he's a lucky boy."

She straightened up, uncomfortable with how close they'd become in such a short time. She knew so little about this man, and it was a good bet once he caught the Five, he'd be gone.

"Do you ever look back and regret things you've done?" she asked wistfully.

Ori stared into the middle distance before he answered. "No," he said, shaking his head. "I don't have that luxury." As he rose, he looked down at her with a sad smile.

"And neither do you, Riley Blackthorne."

In Ori's experience it was quite easy to find a demon, especially the ones that ate everything. All you had to do was pitch your ears toward the snarls and home in. He'd already found two of them, older, more feral ones, but they hadn't been helpful. He'd left their bleeding corpses in the murky dark of this place the trappers called Demon Central.

Now he'd found another, a younger one who hadn't developed its second row of teeth yet. It was rounder, more bulky. It almost looked harmless, but in a few months it'd thin down and become a dedicated killing machine.

It had just caught itself a large rat. The rodent's head was already gone, but this fiend, unlike most of its kind, wasn't a gobbler. It seemed to be savoring the meal.

Ori moved quietly to a position about five feet from the thing. Then he let it see his true form, wings, sword, and all.

It shrieked and jumped back in terror, clutching its bloodied meal to its chest as its black hair stuck out like a porcupine. After a quick look around, it realized it had no place to run.

"Hellspawn," Ori said. "You know what I am." There was a whine of fear from the abomination. "And you know what I want."

The demon began to shiver. Gastro-Fiends, or Threes, as the trappers so quaintly called them, weren't very intelligent, all their brains geared toward acquiring food. This one had enough smarts to know that if it pointed Ori in the direction of another demon, that might mean its death. Especially when the other fiend was a weather worker capable of killing a master trapper.

"Where is the rogue demon called Astaring?" Ori demanded.

The fiend's face scrunched up in what passed for thought, then it cautiously extended the rat toward him. A bribe for its life, perhaps?

Ori sighed and shook his head. "No. That is not what I want." He took a menacing step forward. It got the reaction he'd hoped for: The Hellspawn cowered in fear.

"Tell me, pitiful one," he ordered, putting power behind the command.

The creature began to babble in Hellspeak. Most of what it said was a list of complaints about how badly it was treated by the other demons, but at the very end it gave Ori a glimmer of information.

"Thank you. Enjoy your meal." Finally he had a lead on the rogue that had killed Master Blackthorne. Ori turned on a heel and hiked down the alley. He knew not to check on the fiend; it would be down the closest hole by now.

A short time later, he stood in the middle of a street that looked like a war zone. It wasn't his doing, at least not yet. His quarry was close. He sensed the thing. Felt its power.

"Show yourself, Astaring," he shouted.

A second later he leapt upward to avoid the rush of brilliant flames that blew out of the ground at his feet. He twisted in the air, spreading his wings, sword ready for battle. The flames vanished, leaving a crater rimmed with smoking asphalt. If he had been a few seconds slower, he'd have been a pile of smoking feathers.

"You're a cunning one," he said. "Now stop hiding like a silly child."

A laugh cut through the air, cold and cruel, but the demon did not materialize. "The war comes, Divine," it said. "On whose side will you be?"

Then the fiend was gone, its power fading away in the night air. Ori hovered in the air, studying his surroundings, trying to determine if it was a trick.

"Coward," he grumbled.

He floated downward, tucking his wings behind him as his feet landed. Demons always spoke of war. They craved it. Like they had a chance of winning against Heaven.

But this time, the fiend was speaking the truth. "The war comes."

SIXTEEN

The only reason Beck was out this early in the morning was sitting in the booth near the restaurant's front windows. At 7:00 AM the red-haired reporter had called him and then sweetly but firmly refused to let him off the hook. The interview just had to happen *this morning.* Beck had finally agreed so he could get this woman off his back.

When the reporter saw him, she smiled warmly. "Good morning, Mr. Beck." She had an accent he couldn't place. Something foreign, maybe French or Italian.

"Ma'am," he said, sliding into the booth across from her. He'd shaved and showered and put on the best work clothes he owned, but he was still uncomfortable. There was no good reason for him to be talking to this lady, especially after the wake last night. He'd not gotten drunk, but it'd been close, and now his body was making him pay for that bar tab.

The reporter daintily offered a manicured hand across the table. "I am Justine Armando," she said. "I wish to speak with you about Atlanta and her demons."

Bottomless emerald eyes held his gaze.

He gently shook the hand and forced himself to relax. This babe was a knockout, and the way she said *deemons* was cute. She looked like a model, not a reporter, but then that probably worked in her favor.

Her olive skin glowed in the morning light streaming in through the windows, which also set fire to the gold highlights in her hair. It made him wonder if she had chosen that location on purpose. He also noted she wasn't wearing a wedding ring.

As the waitress poured him a cup of coffee, Beck pulled his head back to business. "What can I do for ya, ma'am?"

"Justine, please. I am not old and gray," she said, her green eyes twinkling.

"All right, then, Justine. What is it ya wanna know?"

"I want to tell the story of an Atlanta demon trapper. Your Master Stewart said you were one of the best, that is why I asked to interview you."

She was shoveling the crap pretty high. He took another slug of coffee to buy time to sift through the mixed signals he was receiving. Usually if you didn't talk, the other person would fill in the silence and you'd learn something. The reporter was a pro: She sipped her tea and waited him out.

"Who do ya write for?" he asked.

"I am freelance. I sell my stories to newspapers all over the world," she said.

"Must be a nice job."

"It has its benefits," she replied, flicking a switch on a sleek microrecorder that sat near a notebook and a gold pen. Then she smiled, pointing at the recorder. "Shall we begin?"

"Yes, ma'am." *Let's get this done.* Not that he minded the scenery.

"I have researched you, Denver Beck," Justine said. "You were born in Sadlersville, Georgia, moved to Atlanta, and then you were in the military. You were awarded medals for bravery in Afghanistan."

"Yes, ma'am." That was as far as he was going on *that* topic.

"Why did you want to become a trapper?" she asked.

"Because of Paul Blackthorne," Beck replied. "He gave me a future." He knew that sounded hokey, but it was the truth.

"He died recently. You were with him when that happened," the reporter said, her voice softer now. "I understand that his corpse has been reanimated and that he was at the Tabernacle the night the demons attacked."

"Yes, ma'am."

She put down her pen and gave him a pleading look. "I really need more than just a 'Yes, ma'am,' Mr. Beck."

"Just Beck. That's what folks call me."

"Well, then, *Just* Beck . . ."

He opened his mouth to tell her she'd gotten it wrong, but then saw the corners of her mouth curve up in a smile. She was pulling his chain.

"Yer messin' with me," he said.

"I am. So why don't you tell me what happened that night at the Tabernacle, and I will tell the world."

"I think they already know."

"But they haven't heard *your* story," she said, leaning across the table. "I know it's a good one."

"Why?" he asked, frowning.

"I can tell by looking at you. You are not like the others."

She's right about that. He got another cup of coffee and told her what he remembered about the demon attack, leaving out a few details the world just didn't need to know. She listened intently, taking notes. Only when he'd finished did she put more questions to him.

"How did the demons break through the Holy Water ward?"

"I think it was because there were too many of them."

She seemed to accept that explanation. "Do you believe in Armageddon, Beck?" she asked.

"I would have said no a few days ago, but after I saw those angels . . ."

"Then they were really there?" At his puzzled look, she added, "The photographs and videos don't show them in detail, only a ring of intense light."

"I was inside that light. They were angels alright."

Justine seemed to shift mental gears. "Do you believe the hunters will have better luck in subduing the demons?"

"I'm not sure," he said cautiously, knowing this would be going on the record. "We know the city better than they do, and from what I hear, once the hunters arrive more demons will show up."

"More work for you," she said.

He shook his head. "They'll cut us out of the picture. We're the locals, the hicks. We don't have the money, or the flash equipment."

"But you can kill demons in certain circumstances," she said. He nodded. "Is this one?"

"Hell, yes." They hadn't received the official word from the National Guild, but he didn't care. Everything from a Pyro-Fiend on up was fair game. If he could trap it, fine. If it fought back, it was toast. He'd get paid either way.

"I have an appointment with the mayor in an hour," she explained. "I want to hear his side of all this, and then I will follow up with you if I have more questions."

Beck grunted. "The mayor's all talk, no sense."

Justine grinned, revealing perfect white teeth. "May I quote you on that?"

"Better not," he said, shaking his head. He'd let his mouth get the best of him.

The woman pushed a business card across the table. Her name was written in a flowing script, and there was a cell phone number beneath it. "Keep in touch, Beck. I'm sure I will have more questions."

He looked into those deep green eyes and decided this hadn't been as bad as he'd thought. Actually, a pretty nice way to start his day. "I'll do that, Justine."

As she strolled out of the restaurant, he put the card in his jacket pocket and signaled for a refill on the java.

"Not bad at all."

✛

To keep her mind off Simon and his infantile behavior, Riley dug into the pile of bills that seemed to have grown overnight. Paying bills was like doing laundry and grocery shopping—never ending. With Beck's help the rent had been paid, along with a few of the other monthly debts, but she would run short of cash again in about a week. That made her eyes stray to the trapping bag by the door. It still had the claw marks from her last solo adventure.

"Been there. Done that," Riley grumbled, scratching the now healed demon wounds through her jeans. Instead, she made a list of the debts so she could prioritize them. She was nearly finished when a series of knocks echoed throughout the apartment. It was straight-up noon.

When she opened the door, Beck held up a large bag from Mama Z's, his favorite barbecue joint. "Brought ya lunch, as promised," he said.

Her nose homed in on the piquant scent of spices. "Yum," she murmured, her mouth watering instantly.

As Riley set the table, she waited for his usual Spanish Inquisition, in particular, "Have ya called yer aunt in Fargo yet?" But none of that happened. Instead he draped his leather jacket over the couch and headed for the bathroom. Water ran, then he was back and removing the food from the bag, placing the sandwiches and the coleslaw on the plates she'd pulled from the cupboard.

He noticed the stack of bills. "How ya doin' for money?"

Riley rolled her eyes. "I paid the cell phone bill, the utilities, and the rent. There're more bills due in about a week and I'll be short by then. Peter knows a place where I can sell a few of my old CDs for cash."

Beck nodded and then fell on his sandwich like he'd not eaten breakfast.

Maybe he hadn't. "How late did you stay last night?" she asked.

"Until about one. I had to get up early and talk to some reporter."

"How did that go?"

"It went," he replied.

Rather than ruin what was going to be a good meal with talk that she might not like, she focused on her own sandwich, savoring the amazing taste. Mama Z's had the best barbecue in the world. Mid-lunch her cell phone pinged in response to a new text. She wiped off her hands and checked it. Then grinned.

"Yes!" she crowed. "Simon's at home now. They cut him loose from the hospital."

"That's good news," Beck said. "He sure healed quick."

"On the outside, at least."

Her visitor gave a huff of understanding. "Ya see him last night?" At her nod, he added, "How'd that go?"

"It went," she said, parroting his words about the reporter.

"Not good?" She shook her head. "Sorry." He cleaned his mouth with a napkin, crumpled it up, and dropped it in the middle of the plate. "I'm hopin' the food was a fair-enough bribe for this."

Here it comes. He's going to use the meal to guilt me, I just know it.

"Stewart wants me to fill out the papers for the National Guild." At her puzzled look, Beck added, "They're for the dead trappers. They're forms so their families can get their life insurance."

"Oh." Now it made sense why he didn't want to do these alone.

After she cleaned off the table, Riley dropped back into her chair. Beck placed a thick pile of manila folders in front of her. Each one had a name written in block letters.

"How many pages are there to these things?" she asked.

"The form's only got two. The rest is their files." She studied the first folder and deemed it a blessing the name wasn't one she recognized.

The form was pretty straightforward: a notification to the National Demon Trappers Guild that one of their members had shuffled off this mortal coil, and a request to release insurance funds to the listed beneficiary or beneficiaries. Riley opened the folder and found a picture of the deceased. It had been taken when he joined the Guild, which according to the paperwork was six years earlier. She didn't know the man.

Her visitor opened a folder and issued a tortured sigh. He'd know these guys—probably trapped with some of them, drank with all of them at one time or another.

She let her eyes skim over the paper in front of her. Russell Brody was forty-three, just about her dad's age when he died. He had a wife and two children. Riley forced herself to pick up the pen and begin filling in the form, though it was almost physically painful. His family needed the money and someone had to do this. She moved from section to section entering name, address, social security number, birth date, rank in the Guild, membership number, and then the hardest part—how he'd died.

"Ah, what do I put for cause of death?" she asked.

"Hellspawn," Beck replied. "They'll add the coroner's report when they send it in, so you don't need to do more than that."

"Hellspawn," she said, filling in the blank. It seemed too black and white for her liking.

After she'd completed the first one, she took the next folder and opened it. She didn't know this trapper either. The same thing happened with the next two files. *He did this on purpose.* She thought to thank him, but he might not take it right.

When she finished her fifth one, she set it aside and stretched. Beck was still working on his second form, hunched over the paperwork like a gnome. When he wrote a word, he did it slowly, forming each letter with a lot of effort. Like he was having to think really hard.

"You go much slower, and I'll end up doing all these," she said, not pleased at the thought.

"I'm goin' as fast as I can," he shot back.

"Fooled me."

His eyes rose to meet hers and flashed in defiance. "I'm not good at this, okay? But don't ya dare say I'm dumb."

Where did that come from?

Beck dropped the pen on the table. "Sorry. I'm tired and I'm not good company today."

Riley resisted the temptation to tell him he wasn't good company on most days.

"So what hot button did I push?" she asked, wanting to know for the future.

Beck winced. "I don't read or write good. Never had anyone show me, not at home at least. Teachers tried, but they couldn't do much because I wouldn't listen to 'em."

"You listened to my dad."

"He knew how to teach me. None of the others could."

It slowly dawned on her why he'd asked for her help. "Stewart doesn't know about this, does he?"

"No," Beck said, shaking his head. "I don't dare tell him, not if I wanna make master trapper. That's why I came here."

He'd put his inflated guy ego on the line, trusting she'd not make fun of him. That made Riley feel really good inside.

"That's why you don't send text messages, isn't it?"

"Yup." Beck looked down at the form in front of him. "I'm better than I used to be," he said. "The Army helped me a lot. It just doesn't come easy for me."

"You get around town without any hassles. I've seen you do it."

"I know the city," he said, his eyes meeting hers now. "I don't have to read the street signs to get where I need to go. It's when I'm doin' somethin' new I get into trouble."

"Like these forms." A nod. "You've been doing okay," Riley said encouragingly. "Your writing's a lot neater than most guys', and you're getting the stuff on the right lines."

"I watched ya, so I know where it goes."

She didn't dare pity him. That would make him furious.

Riley spread her hands. "Hey, I had it lucky. Both parents were teachers. It was hardwired in."

"I had a—" He stopped short, but Riley knew what he was thinking. *A drunken mom who didn't care how you turned out.*

"Do you read books?"

"Some of the kid ones," he said. "I get 'em from the library, that way folks don't know what I'm readin'."

So nobody will make fun of you. "How did you get through the Trappers Manual?" she asked, intrigued.

Embarrassment formed on his face. "I didn't. Yer daddy read it to me."

Which means all those hours Paul Blackthorne had spent with Beck weren't just about trapping demons or hanging together. *My dad was teaching him to read and write.*

She'd always loved her father, but now she loved him even more.

"How did you pass the journeyman exam?" she asked.

"I didn't cheat," Beck said, instantly defiant.

"Hello?" she said, rapping her knuckles on the table. "Did I say that?"

He half shrugged. "I knew all the answers, I just couldn't read the questions that good, so Paul had me learn 'em in order."

Which was okay since they gave the test questions out in advance to increase the odds that the apprentice might actually pass.

"I couldn't do that," she admitted.

"What?"

"Memorize all the questions. That would be way hard. You might not be able to read and write that well, but you're smart in other ways."

"Not sure of that."

I am. That's why her father had gone to such effort. *Now it's my turn.*

A thought twitched in her brain. "Do you have a computer?" she quizzed. A nod came her way. "My buddy Peter has a program that takes text and makes it into speech. You could listen to stuff off the Web and read along. Newspaper articles and things like that."

"That sounds cool. Is it really expensive?"

"I don't think so. I'll ask him about it." Beck instantly tensed. "Without telling him why I want to know."

"Thanks." He looked down at the form and then back up again. "I mean it."

The next folder in the stack was Ethan's. She took it.

"I'll do that if ya want me to," her companion offered.

Riley shook her head, feeling the prickle of tears. She flipped it open and studied the apprentice's picture. He wasn't that old, and now he was gone. If things had been different, Beck would be filling out Simon's sheet. Maybe even hers. She went to the bathroom to hunt up tissues, wiped her eyes, and returned to the table.

Beck dropped another file into the completed stack. "Only a few more," he said. She could tell this was hurting him as much as it was her.

Riley nodded and returned to the work. It wasn't until near the end of the stack that she actually read the fine print on the second page of the claim form. Under the name of the beneficiary was a place for a signature and an address, so the check could be sent directly to the person.

"Beck?"

"Hummm?" he said, not looking up as he painstakingly formed a letter.

"Why didn't I have to sign a form for my dad?"

He kept his eyes down, but he wasn't writing any longer.

"Beck?"

He set the pen down deliberately and leaned back in the kitchen chair, face pensive. "I signed it."

"Why?"

"Because the money comes to me."

"I'm not my dad's beneficiary?" she asked, totally sideswiped.

"If Paul left ya the money, the debt collectors might take it. With it comin' to me, they can't touch it. Don't worry, I'll have Fireman Jack figure out how to get it to ya."

"Why should you? It's your money. You can buy yourself a new truck with it. Nobody could say a thing."

Beck's face twisted in hurt. "How can ya think I'd—"

"I don't know what to think anymore. Nothing is like I thought it would be. I figured I'd get my license and then Dad and I would be together all the time and—"

She spun out of her chair and found herself near the big window, the one overlooking the parking lot. Below, someone was lugging groceries toward the entrance. It was proving difficult, as their poodle wanted to anoint every car tire it passed.

Beck was right behind her now. "I won't keep any of that money, girl. It's yers. Yer daddy wanted it this way, I swear."

"He didn't trust me."

"No, he didn't trust the debt collectors. He didn't want ya to lose the only thing he could leave behind."

Beck hesitantly put his arm around her shoulder and drew her close. She could feel him shaking.

"I won't let ya starve," he whispered. "I'll do whatever it takes. I promise that on yer daddy's grave."

Her father had trusted him. *Why don't I?*

They stood there for a few minutes, just looking out the window, neither of them talking. Finally Beck pulled away and returned to the table and the paperwork. Riley forced herself to join him. They worked through the remainder of the files in silence.

Once they were done, he placed the files in his duffel bag, picked up his jacket, and offered his thanks. Riley locked the door behind him, feeling she really needed to say something but wasn't sure what it would be.

It wasn't until later that she found the thick white envelope tucked underneath the pile of bills. The envelope was stuffed with twenties, and she counted them into one-hundred-dollar stacks. There were ten.

One thousand dollars.

Beck must have put it there when she'd gone in search of the tissues. Riley bowed her head in despair. She'd practically accused him of stealing her money, and all the while that envelope had been sitting there. He'd never said a thing.

She remembered him standing at the window, deep in thought.

How defensive he'd become because he could barely read and write. How her father had trusted him to do the right thing.

Denver Beck was a hard guy to like and even harder to understand. One thing was clear: His word was golden.

Why can't I accept that?

SEVENTEEN

"What is it about this place?" Riley grumbled as she drove past the Oakland Cemetery and then cut down one of the side streets in search of a parking place. "Why do I spend most of my life here?" The universe had no answer for her, so she kept driving up and down the streets. This field trip would be her first day back in class after the Tabernacle disaster. Her classmates would want to know what it was really like, badger her with questions because she'd been there when it all happened.

It wasn't like talking about it made it go away. It was just the opposite: The hellish images were too fresh in her mind, searing deeper every time she thought about them. If she could hold her classmates off today, maybe something else would have caught their interest by the next time. *As long as it has nothing to do with me.*

The schools made these mandatory historical education trips three times a year, dividing up the classes across different days. There'd probably be two hundred kids here today, and the school district didn't bother with buses anymore. Though the classes were designed to arrive at thirty-minute intervals, that hadn't lightened the number of bodies tromping toward Oakland's entrance like a herd of well-dressed zombies.

She finally found a place to park three blocks from the cemetery. As she approached the brick archway that led into the graveyard, a familiar face caught her notice. "Peter?" she murmured. Her best friend stood by the main gate, scanning the knots of students as they passed by. He brightened up the moment he spied her, and waved.

"Hey!" he said as she joined him. "I was worried you'd blow this off."

"No way. Mrs. Haggerty will take roll, and I don't need detention."

He shoved a package toward her. "A reprint of your father's Holy Water research. I read it this time. Your dad was amazing."

"Yeah, he was," she said, taking the package. "I think I might have a lead." She told him about the unmarked truck that had collected the recycled Holy Water bottles. "Maybe if I follow those guys around I might be able to figure out who's stealing the bottles and refilling them."

"Sounds like a plan," Peter said, nodding his approval. "Let me know if you need someone to ride shotgun."

Cool. "It's a deal." They passed underneath the brick arch into the cemetery. "I thought you were supposed to be here tomorrow."

"I've been transferred to your class," Peter replied, grinning.

When Riley stumbled to a halt, a student behind her swore when he almost ran into her. "Sorry," she said, then turned back to her friend. "Do you mean that you hack—"

Peter clapped a hand over her mouth. "As I was about to say, I'm happy to report that our educational overlords have decided I shall be in your class." He lowered his hand and winked. "Imagine my surprise."

Surprise. Right. Peter had managed to hack the computer system that housed the student data and set up a transfer. If he was caught he'd be expelled, exiled to darkest Illinois with his unglued mother.

"Are you insane?"

"Of course. It wasn't that hard, not once I figured out I had to transfer two or three others at the same time to cover my tracks. It's all about camouflage."

"You moved other people to our class?"

"Sure did." He smiled, clearly pleased with himself. "Easier than I'd thought, actually."

"But—"

Someone stepped in front of them on the road, blocking their way.

Oh, jeez. As if life wasn't absurd enough, the obstruction was her class's vampire wannabe, the kid with the jet-black hair and the alabaster skin. Today he had on a black frock coat and a bloodred shirt with decorative lace at the collar. A cameo sat at his neckline. The face on the cameo sported fangs.

You've got to be kidding.

"You are thtill alive," he lisped, glaring at Riley, his dark eyebrows furrowed. The fake pointed canines were definitely causing the speech impediment.

"Yeah, I'm alive. And your point is?" she asked, annoyed at the interruption.

"We will not be vanquithed," he replied. The lisp really came through this time, along with some spit.

Gross. "Can you move, please?"

The fake vamp didn't budge but continued to glower and display his plastic teeth. Riley strode around him, shaking her head.

As they moved farther down the road, Peter asked, "Ah, what was that?"

"That is our vamp wannabe. He drinks red soda and uses the imperial *we* all the time. He's harmless. Just ignore him."

Peter looked over into the graveyard. "Kind of hard to do," he said, pointing.

The kid darted among the graves, skulking behind trees and the larger monuments. Every now and then he'd leer out from behind a stone obelisk or angel.

"What's he got against you?" her friend asked.

"He thinks I hunt vampires. I told him I only trap demons, but he doesn't believe me. He has this need-to-be-a-victim thing going on."

Peter gave her a confused look. "Ah, correct me if I'm wrong, but that's so not a vamp's operating system, you know? They don't do victim."

"Tell him that."

"So what's his name?"

Riley shrugged. "I was afraid to ask."

Out of the corner of her eye she saw her vamp stalker trip over a headstone and do a total face-plant in the dirt, fake teeth and all.

Why me?

✛

Having a parent who was into the Civil War meant Riley'd been to this section of Oakland Cemetery more times than she could count. Her father had always found an excuse to swing down to the Confederate graves when they visited the family mausoleum.

"Soon all the flowers will be in bloom," she said wistfully. "It's so pretty then."

Peter gaped at the rows of white markers. "Wow. Look at all the gravestones. It's unreal."

"Never been here before?"

He shook his head. "It's seriously awe inspiring."

At least the first few times. After years of listening to her father talk about the war, Riley could quote death tolls from most of the major battles. She resisted the impulse. The neat rows of bleached gravestones spoke eloquently enough.

Peter was a numbers guy. "How many graves are there?" he asked, looking over at her.

"Almost seven thousand, and there're Union war dead here, too."

"I knew there were a lot of casualties, but you can't really deal with it until you see it in person," he said, waving a hand to indicate the scene in front of them.

A piercing sound cut through the air as Mrs. Haggerty gave a shrill whistle. The class gathered around her under one of the ancient magnolia trees.

"We'll be starting in a minute or two," she advised. Haggerty gave a stack of papers to the nearest student. "Pass these out. These need to be completed and handed in by the end of class." That set off a round of grumbles. "I know, but at least it's not raining, okay? It could be worse." Once the paper distribution was in progress, Mrs. Haggerty called out, "Riley, are you here?"

Riley waved a hand from the edge of the crowd, wondering what this was all about.

"Oh, good, glad to see you're still with us. I'm so sorry about the other night, dear."

Riley could only nod. There were a lot of eyes on her now, and that bothered her.

The teacher returned her attention to the group. "I got word this morning that we have new students in the class. I need to see your transfer papers, people, so all of you come on up."

Peter grinned and then dutifully headed for their teacher.

"Hey, Riley," Brandy said, gliding up. The brunette was dressed in black jeans and jacket and an unholy pink shirt. Her entourage wasn't with her. Instead they were a short distance away laughing over a text message on one of the girl's cell phones.

"Brandy," Riley said, testing the waters. When Riley had first joined this class, Brandy had gone out of her way to make the new kid feel right at home. Providing the new kid liked sabotaged tires and defaced windshields.

"So who's the new guy?" the girl asked.

"That's my friend Peter. He just transferred in."

"He looks like a nerd."

"He's smart but he's cool. Give him a chance." *You pick on him and I'll be on you so fast you won't know what happened.*

Her best friend returned and handed her the class assignment.

When he saw Riley wasn't alone, he issued a pleasant smile. "Hi, I'm Peter."

"This is Brandy," Riley said, more a warning than an introduction.

"Oh," he replied, the light dawning. "You're the one who vandalized Riley's car . . . twice."

Brandy blinked. Clearly she hadn't anticipated the nerdy guy to have a mouth. "Just playing with her head," the girl replied.

"I do that all the time, except I don't flatten her tires."

"We're okay now," Brandy added, giving Riley a meaningful look. *Until you decide we're not.*

"Okay, folks," the teacher called out. "Work on the sheets and turn them back in one hour. Off you go!"

Peter looked over at Riley. "Why don't you tell me about this lion statue," he said, waving her toward a massive marble sculpture. She gamely followed him to the metal fence that divided the world from the Lion of Atlanta.

A few seconds later Brandy joined them. "Ah, I have to write my paper on this. Can I listen in?"

Riley heard Peter's muted chuckle. "Sure. Any problems with that, Riley?" he asked, all innocence.

"No problem." *I love playing tour guide.*

Riley pillaged through her memories and recounted the statute's history, courtesy of her father. "It's called the Lion of Atlanta or the Lion of the Confederacy. It guards the graves of the unknown soldiers, and it was modeled after a statue in Switzerland. The dying lion is a symbol of courage, and it's lying on a Confederate flag."

"You can almost feel its pain," Peter said, his voice quieter now. "It's really haunting."

"This whole place is," Riley replied.

"I don't get why all this metal is still here," Brandy said, gesturing to the fence. "I mean, why hasn't it been stolen?"

"Don't know," Riley replied. That was a good question.

Brandy took a deep breath. "I'm so sorry about the other night," she said. "That had to be really bad."

Riley looked at her, shocked. She'd never expected the girl to care about anything else outside of her own little world.

"I saw a picture in the paper of you and that cute guy who was hurt so bad," Brandy added. "Is he going to make it?"

"Yeah, he is."

"That's good." A pause and then: "Is the TV show still coming to town? I mean, the demons didn't scare them away, did they?"

That's more like it. This was the real Brandy, the one who wanted Riley to get her an autograph of her favorite *Demonland* actor while the film crew was in town.

"I haven't heard anything about that." What with the Tabernacle fire, Riley had totally forgotten about the television series wanting to work with the trappers while they filmed in Atlanta.

"Well, just remember, I want Jess Storm's autograph. And a photo would be awesome," Brandy replied.

"If the show is in town, I'll get it," Riley said. This was the price of peace between them, and she was willing to pay it to keep Brandy and her crew off her back. She really didn't need any more hassles from her classmates.

Someone called out her name, and she shivered in response. The voice was familiar and not in a good way. Riley turned and then stared in disbelief.

"Allan?" she said as a figure approached.

Peter scowled. Her friend knew the tale of her ex-boyfriend, how she'd dated Allan and how he'd become the ex when he'd punched her in the face when she refused to steal a computer for him.

It'd been two years since she'd last seen him. Allan was taller now, wider, too. His body was football-player solid, and his brown eyes were just as piercing. An arrogant smirk seemed permanently chiseled in place.

That much hadn't changed. As he drew near, her jaw throbbed like he'd just struck her and she resisted the urge to touch it.

"I was hoping I'd find you," he said, just like nothing bad had fallen out between them. "I heard about your father."

Not a hint of sympathy for her loss. Of course, her father had paid his parents a visit after the hitting incident and had warned them that if their son came near his daughter again, he'd press charges.

And here you are, you jerk. But her dad wasn't in the picture anymore.

"Riley," Peter began. She could hear the concern in his voice. He was thinking she was going to repeat her mistake, fall for this liar's line of BS again.

"I'm good," she said. *Totally good.* She knew Allan's game now. She turned her attention to the ex. "What are you doing here?" she asked.

"Just checking out my new class." He angled his head toward Mrs. Haggerty. "I'm getting transferred in. The paperwork should be done in about a week."

Transferred in?

"Oh, God," Peter said.

You moved him to our class?

If Riley said anything, she'd reveal Peter's part in all this, so she fired up the attitude, putting her hands on her hips and glowering. "You just stay away from me, you hear? I don't want you in my face."

"Why? You dating this nerd now?"

Riley had her hand on Peter's arm before he could react. If he went after her ex, he'd get pounded. She knew from experience Allan had a wicked right hook.

"No. I'm dating someone else," she said, though the creep really didn't warrant an answer. "Let's leave it in the past."

He smirked. "You're a lot prettier now. Hot, even. I'm glad we're going to be together again."

"Not happening, so don't even think it." Riley spun on her heels and stomped away, Peter in tow.

Behind her she heard Allan call out, "See you later, babe!"

She made sure to go to the other side of the milling students, as far away as she could get from him. When she looked back, her ex-boyfriend was talking to Brandy. Riley pulled out her phone and sent a text to her clueless friend: TOXIC. DO NOT TOUCH OR YOU WILL RE-GRET IT.

A little while later Brandy glanced down at her phone, read the text, then went right back to talking with Riley's ex.

"She's not listening. That's a big mistake." She turned and gave Peter a full dose of the Riley Laser Eyes. "What *were* you thinking?"

"Oh, God, I'm sorry. I just saw the last name and the first initial. I had no idea it was *him*."

Riley really wanted to scream, just cut loose and shriek like a ban-shee. But it wouldn't do any good. Even if Peter managed to get him transferred, Allan would know she went to school in the old Starbucks on Fourteenth Street. He'd continue to haunt her no matter what.

"It'll be okay. He just wants to spook me," she said, trying to reas-sure herself that the ex didn't intend to pick up where they'd left off in that parking lot two years before.

Peter peered over at her former boyfriend. "I'm not getting that kind of vibe, Riley. I'm getting the 'You're going to pay for this' kind of feeling. Maybe you should tell Beck, let him deal with the guy."

"What?" she spat. "No way. I'll deal with Allan on my own."

"Like you did the last time?"

Peter did have a point. "If it gets scary, I'll turn Beck loose on him."

"Good. Sometimes you need backup, and I'm thinking this is one of those times."

"No more transfers, you got it?"

"I swear it."

"Unless you'd like to send Allan to like . . . Algeria or something."

"I wonder if that's possible," Peter pondered.

Brandy was smiling now, chatting up her ex. *Hope your parents have good health insurance, girl.*

Simon's family home was big, two stories and covered in pale peach stucco. Curtains hung at every window, and there were flowerpots full of pansies on the steps that led to the front door. Somehow they'd survived the winter frosts.

Riley adjusted her hair and clothes for what had to be the fifth time. At least the black denim jacket she'd found at the back of her closet fit. She'd forgotten it was there until the blue one had been fried, sliced, and peed on. Black would hide the stains better anyway.

She'd met Simon's parents, so this shouldn't be a big deal. *But it is.* It was the first time she'd been in their house, the first time she'd seen Simon since he'd left the hospital. Would he be better now that he was home?

He just has to be. She visualized what Simon had been like before the fire, before he'd been so badly hurt. The warm smile, the loving kisses. That's what she wanted more than anything.

Mrs. Adler opened the door wearing a pair of sweatpants and a worn Bon Jovi T-shirt. Her blonde hair was in a ponytail, and sweat glistened on her forehead. Riley had managed to catch her mid—exercise regimen.

"Come to see the fair-haired boy?" Mrs. Adler asked.

"If it's okay."

"Sure. He's had a few visitors, but he certainly needs the company." She waved Riley into the house. The entryway was paved in ceramic tile, and there were family photos along both walls. With a family as numerous as the Adlers, they'd need all the wall space they could get.

Riley followed the woman through what looked to be a living room into a small room at the back of the house. The shades were drawn giving the space a dungeonlike gloom. There was a flat-screen television and the kind of chairs you sink into and never come out of again. Simon was on the leather couch.

"You've got a guest," his mom called out. She left Riley standing at the door and headed toward the front of the house.

Riley drifted to the couch and sat next to her boyfriend, putting her messenger bag on the floor. Simon was in sweatpants and a long-sleeved T-shirt. The wooden cross he always wore was missing. Had he lost it at the Tabernacle? In his hands was the rosary, and he twisted it back and forth like a set of worry beads.

"Riley." The way he said the name didn't convey any meaning. No "Gee, I'm glad you're here" or anything personal. It was flat, just a word.

"So how are you doing?" she asked, trying to fathom where his head was at the moment. If he was in the same crappy mood as the previous night, there was little she could do for him.

"I'm home." Again that flat tone, like it didn't matter.

Riley took hold of one of his hands and squeezed it. "Simon, come on. What's going on in your head? Talk to me."

His deep blue eyes met hers. "Not sure what's going on."

"Having trouble sleeping?" A nod. "Nightmares?"

Simon seemed surprised she'd know that. "I see the demons and the blood and feel the flames. . . ." He kept rubbing one of the rosary beads between his fingers. "My dad says they'll get better, that they're the mind's way of dealing with what happened."

"He's right. How are your wounds?"

"Almost healed. The doctors don't know what to think of it. They've never seen anything like it."

Bet they haven't. Not unless angels routinely make hospital calls.

Simon's hand gripped hers tighter then released it. "I knew I was dying. I could feel it. I wasn't afraid, I was just sad," he said. "I thought I'd never see you again."

"Well, pretty soon you'll be healed and we'll go trap some of those demons. Teach them a lesson."

She expected a PC version of "Hell yes, let's kick some demon butt." There was no reply. Simon's fingers continued to worry his rosary as his blue eyes stared at nothing.

"You saved me," she said. "The demon came after you instead of me. I won't ever forget that."

"I did everything right," he retorted, frowning now. "The demons should not have been able to cross the ward."

"Of course you did it right. No one's blaming you."

He wasn't listening. "I put the Holy Water down in one direction, then repeated it in the other. There were no gaps. The demons should not have been able to get to us."

"Father Harrison says there were too many of them, that they over-whelmed the ward."

"No!" Simon replied, shaking his head vigorously. "Demons can-not cross the power of God."

"But you told me that Holy Water absorbs the evil. If there's too much—"

"When did I tell you that?" he asked, confused.

"When we were at the Holy Water vendor in the market."

"No, that's not possible. If demons can destroy God's power, then what's the point?" he argued. "We're doing His holy work, and He let us be ripped to pieces." He took a sudden breath, as if a memory had just hit him full on. She knew what it was: The demon's claws ripping at him, the smell of its rancid breath in his face. The certain knowledge that he was going to die.

When Simon began to shiver, she tried to hold him but he pushed her away. He ceased talking after that, refusing to meet her eyes. Not knowing what else to do, she dropped a kiss on his cheek and left him in the gloom. He had to find his own answers.

Just don't lose yourself when you do.

EIGHTEEN

It took Riley less time than she'd expected to drive from Simon's house to the old theater in Buckhead. By the time she arrived it was just after dark and the bright lights of the marquee had been easy to spot. She located a parking place in the lot just north of the building, sliding in next to a Mercedes with tinted windows. Then she just sat there trying to work up the courage to take this next step.

What if her father was here tonight? Could she handle seeing him again? It was one thing to say good-bye when he was lying in his coffin but another to watch him wander around like he was still alive. He'd remembered her at the Tabernacle, but what if those memories were gone now? What if . . .

The keys made a harsh, jangling sound, her hands shaking as her heart rate accelerated. Her vision tunneled as each breath became more difficult than the last.

Panic attack. She'd had them after her mother had died and thought she'd outgrown them. Riley forced herself to conjure up images of frolicking puppies and days at the beach, trying to think of anything but Simon, demons, and her reanimated father. Then she began to sing to herself. It was just nonsense words because she couldn't remember any songs at the moment, but it seemed to work. Finally her heartbeat slowed and she could take a deep cleansing breath. When Riley looked down, her hands were no longer quaking.

"Let's not do that again, okay?" she mumbled, as if her body would actually listen to her for a change. "It so doesn't help."

As Riley pulled herself out of the car, she paused. Was Ori somewhere nearby? She let her eyes search the area and quickly spied him leaning against a shiny black motorcycle across the street, arms crossed over his broad chest. He gave her a nod in acknowledgment.

My own personal bodyguard. That rocks. Bet Brandy wishes she had one.

Which left Riley no excuse not to go to the vendue.

She sucked it up and headed for the front of the theater. Mort was waiting for her clad in a necromancer's cloak of light brown, without his trademark fedora. The cloak halted just above the tops of his polished shoes and seemed to have an energy all its own, like magic was woven into the fabric. It made him look mystical, which she suspected was the desired effect.

"This isn't going to be easy for either of us," he warned.

"I know. What if my dad's not here?" she asked.

"Then I'll ask around to see if anyone's heard who reanimated him. Just let me handle this."

Riley hesitated. "What's this like?" If it was like the Deaders in the market, that wouldn't be so bad.

The summoner puzzled over the query for a moment. "It's a cross between a fashion show, a Roman slave auction, and a theatrical production."

"You're not kidding, are you?"

"No. If you're a buyer, it's one big party. If you've lost someone recently, it's pure hell."

Riley sucked in a deep breath. "Does it involve hordes of man-eating demons?"

Mort looked surprised at the question, then shook his head.

"Then it's doable."

✦

The old theater's marquee included running lights around the edges and it announced the place was closed for a private event. *Private* seemed to be the key word. There was only one line to get in, denoted by a pair of red velvet ropes like you'd find at one of the trendy Midtown bars. The two men at the door looked like bouncers.

A woman at the head of the line was waved away. When she protested, a third black-suited guy appeared out of the doorway and herded her back toward the parking lot. He held her arm tightly, and as they walked he was saying something to her. The woman's eyes widened. She shook her head and then skittered off into the night, clearly frightened by whatever he'd whispered in her ear.

Riley shot a questioning look at her escort.

"She's probably looking for a loved one," Mort explained. "The management can spot those a mile away."

"How can they tell?"

"Her clothes weren't expensive and she seemed ill at ease." He nodded toward the favored ones in line. "They think they own the world. That's the difference."

Riley looked down at her black slacks and scuffed shoes. She'd worn the best she owned. "Then why will they let me in?"

"Because you're with me," he replied, though she heard uncertainty in his voice.

Apparently necros had no DNA for queuing, because Mort didn't join the line, but walked right up to the door like he owned the place. The moment they saw him, the bouncers perked up. The heavier of the two beckoned them forward. There were grumbles from the well-dressed, but no one outwardly challenged them. Why annoy someone who could drop a magical cluster bomb on your head?

"Good evening, Summoner," the heavier bouncer said politely. He eyed Riley. "Your companion is . . . ?"

"An apprentice," Mort replied. "We're here on Society business."

That was smooth. She *was* an apprentice, just not with the necro-mancers.

One of the man's bushy eyebrows ascended. He turned away, holding his hand to his ear, talking to someone through a tiny microphone. When the man turned back toward them, he was all false congeniality. "You are always welcome here, Advocate."

"Thank you."

The two heavies parted to allow Riley and her escort to pass through the shimmering curtain that divided the real world from the obscene. She let out a puff of air in relief once they were inside. It was matched by one of Mort's.

He didn't think they'd let me in.

It began to dawn on her the risk the summoner was taking on her behalf. Clearly bringing a reanimate's daughter to one of these things wasn't business as usual, even though he was the Advocate.

"Thanks," she murmured. He didn't seem to hear her.

The lobby wasn't full, but it felt that way, and it took Riley a moment to realize why: Every person in the room acted as if they were bigger, more important than their physical bodies. As if every ego took up space of its own. Older, immaculately dressed women stood near a portable bar, chatting to each other. They glistened in the overhead lights like aged fairies on a summer's night. It was the jewelry. It had such weight that on anyone else the bling would be wearing them.

The next group was younger women in their perky dresses, wedge sandals, and cascading hair extensions. They sipped champagne from crystal glasses held in manicured hands and laughed in high tones. It was a safe bet they didn't have demon claw marks on their legs or have to worry if they'd be able to pay the gas bill this month. Why did they have it easy and she had to struggle for every dime? Why was she an orphan and they had everything? Nobody would dare steal one of these princesses' fathers. They would have professional vigil sitters and armed guards to ensure nothing happened.

Riley pushed aside the anger. It wouldn't do her any good, and if she tried to tell one of the princesses how she felt, what it was like to lose her father to some necro, it would be a waste of time. She'd just drawn a different life, and no amount of envy was going to change that.

On the other side of the lobby a knot of men clustered together. They ranged in age from young to old, from casually dressed to suit and tie. She heard words like *gross metric tonnage* and *FOB* being thrown around. To her surprise, a couple of the younger ones gave her the eye.

"How much money do you have to have to get into this place?" Riley whispered.

"More than you or I will ever see."

Figures.

Mort beckoned her toward a set of highly polished wooden stairs where a plush red runner greeted their ascent, as brass banisters and ornate crystal wall sconces led the way to the second level. He caught her elbow right before she reached the top stair.

"Don't do anything rash or we're both in big trouble."

The moment they reached the second floor she realized why he'd delivered the warning. There were only summoners up here, their voluminous robes ranging from pale white to black. Most of them were male, though a few females were present. One of the women wore a carmine robe, which stuck out like a bright robin in a flock of dull pigeons.

A necro spied Mort, smiled, and walked forward to greet him. The greeting died on the fellow's lips when he saw Riley.

"Sebastian, good to see you," Mort said warmly, taking the last few steps as if he hadn't noticed the man's reaction. "This is Riley Blackthorne."

"Ah . . ." Sebastian shot a look at her and then back to Mort like he didn't know what to say. He was older than her companion, maybe in his late forties, with a gleaming balding patch at the top of his round head.

Riley deployed the charm. "Nice to meet you, sir."

Sebastian frowned, then shook his head. "You really do like stepping on toes, my friend," he said, addressing Mort.

"Riley has asked for the Society's help. As Advocate, I am obligated to assist her."

"By bringing her *here*?" the man retorted. "Are you mad?"

"Her father was illegally summoned," Mort replied evenly. "I think it's best we solve this quietly before some reporter gets hold of the story. The name Blackthorne *is* newsworthy at the moment."

Sebastian's already pale complexion went a shade lighter. "But *he's* here tonight!" the man hissed. "By all the stars, have you no sense? The Eldest will not tolerate this infraction."

The pale and sweating necro had to be talking about Ozymandias, and this time there was no protective circle between Riley and that monster.

Ripples of goose bumps flooded across her forearms, followed by the sting of magic. "Summoner Alexander?" a smooth voice inquired.

Mort turned and gave a low bow. "Lord Ozymandias. How good to see you."

A dry chuckle returned. "Somehow I doubt that."

Riley took a deep breath. She could cower or meet this obnoxious asshat head on. If he was the one who took her dad, she wasn't going to let him do whatever he wanted just because he was the most powerful of the body snatchers.

Riley turned toward the necromancer who had terrorized her throughout her dad's vigil. Ozymandias was in his usual black cloak, but the oak staff was nowhere to be seen. That funky tattoo on his forehead gave off a faint sheen like it was radioactive. Now that she was so close, she could see his eyes were pale green with odd brown flecks.

He won't do anything here, not in front of the others. That was her edge.

She gave a nod in his direction, trying to keep her fear in check.

"Are you sober this evening, Miss Blackthorne, or can I expect a repeat performance of your juvenile belligerence?" he asked.

"No witchy wine tonight," she said. "Just the real me."

"And no little witch to guard you. You are foolish."

Mort cautiously cleared his throat. "My lord, Miss Blackthorne is seeking her father."

"I heard he was among the walking again."

"Did you yank him out of his grave like you said you would?" Riley demanded.

A collective gasp came from those around them.

Oops.

Ozymandias was suddenly closer to her, though Riley swore she hadn't seen him move. "So ignorant." The tattoo glowed brighter now. "The Society would never allow you to become an apprentice. You're only fit for that collection of scum in the Guild."

You . . . How dare he dis the trappers? All these necros did was rob graves and wear stupid robes. When she opened her mouth to reply, Mort's trembling hand on her arm cut her off.

"I think it is time for us to find our seats. By your leave, Lord Ozymandias."

The High Lord of all things necromantic delivered a gracious nod, but in his eyes she saw contempt.

Wait until I'm a master, you jerk. I'll teach you some manners.

As they entered the theater and walked down the ramp, Mortimer grumbled, "Which part of 'Don't do anything rash' didn't you get?"

"No one disses the trappers, not even His Creepiness," she retorted.

"Sometimes being humble keeps you alive."

"He's not going to go after me here. Too many witnesses."

"Who would say they never saw a thing."

"You would."

He eyed her. "Not if I'm dead."

The expression on Mort's face told her he was totally serious.

Riley was still seething when they reached their row, but at least her escort had removed his death grip on her arm. They'd no more than sat in the wide, plush seats when a cocktail waitress in an extremely short dress and heels hurried over to them. Riley wondered how she got up and down the stairs without falling.

The waitress handed Mort a piece of paper. He glanced at it and then stuck it under his robe.

"Champagne? Canapés?" she asked in a cheery voice that sounded rehearsed.

"Ah, no, thank you," Mort replied.

"What about you?" the woman asked Riley.

"No, thanks."

Mort produced a ten-dollar bill and dropped it on her tray. "We're good. You won't need to check on us again."

"Okay, thanks!" She headed off.

Riley took the opportunity to look around. No one was sitting near them, and even Mort's friend Sebastian was pointedly keeping his distance. She didn't bother to try to locate Ozymandias. He was here: Those goose bumps were still in place.

There was the sound of someone settling in a seat behind them: It was the woman in the carmine robe. She had wavy dark hair that touched her shoulders, and laugh lines at her eyes. The kind who could tell a really good joke and not screw up the punch line.

The necro leaned forward and placed her palms on Mort's shoulders. "You brought a reanimate's daughter to the vendue? I'm impressed. So what do you do for an encore?"

Mort noticeably relaxed. "Don't know yet." He allowed himself a pleased smile, then seemed to remember they weren't alone. "Riley, this is Lady Torin, one of our senior summoners."

"Glad to meet you," the woman replied. "Sorry to hear about your father. I'm hoping Mortimer can find him for you."

Riley studied the woman. She didn't seem to be blowing smoke just to be polite. The way her hands were resting on Mort's shoulders indicated she was fond of him. Or was she giving him her blessing in some way, telling the other summoners that she approved of Mort's actions and that screwing with him meant crossing her?

"Thank you," Riley said. *No matter what you're up to.*

"Just be very careful, dear Mortimer. You're treading into uncharted waters."

Lady Torin leaned back in her seat, rearranging her cloak. When the cocktail waitress appeared at her elbow she put in an order for a Scotch, neat.

"Do all the necros come to this thing?" Riley whispered to her companion.

"Don't call us that!" Mort pleaded. "At least not where *they* can hear you. You don't want one of us to download a spell on you, trust me."

"Okay, then the same question but with *summoners.*"

Mort shook his head. "You are only required to attend if you have a reanimate in the vendue."

"Then she . . ." Riley began, aware that the *she* in question was probably hearing every word.

". . . has someone on offer. Lady Torin doesn't like this any more than I do," Mort replied.

"How do you get to become a lord or lady in your Society?"

"The rank is awarded according to magical ability."

Which didn't tell her much. *Probably the point.* Trappers were equally cautious about discussing their trade. Since Mort and Riley were located in the front row of the balcony, she took the opportunity to peer over the wood rail into the rows below. There weren't any. Instead it looked more like a club than a theater. Tables sat at discrete intervals from each other, covered in fine white tablecloths, and in the center of each one was an iced bottle of champagne. A tuxedoed waiter approached one table and replaced an empty bottle with a fresh one.

"Champagne?" When Riley glowered at Mort, he had the good sense to look embarrassed.

"The auctioneers know how to cater to those who have money," he explained. "Each auction has a theme. Tonight it's . . . Gothic. Better than the last time. That was a salute to Hawaii. The luau was over the top."

Riley groaned under her breath. *This better not be totally stupid, or I'm out of here.*

The overhead lights flicked on and off a few times and then darkened, causing the crowd noise to die down like this was some popular Broadway show. A single spotlight appeared center stage showcasing a man in a tuxedo and a black satin cape.

"Good evening, ladies and gentlemen," he said in a deep, resonant voice, employing the same false smile as the waitress. "Welcome to our second vendue of the new year."

He walked a few paces, the spotlight following him. "Tonight we have a lovely collection on view. Do not hesitate to enjoy the refreshments, and remember that a small portion of tonight's sales will be sent to this month's designated charity. And now, without further delay, the show," he said, his hand gesturing toward the center of the stage.

The spotlight faded to nothing as the curtain rose with a soft mechanical whir. The low, ominous tones of a pipe organ filled the space, causing Riley's back teeth to hum. As her eyes adjusted, other details began to reveal themselves. A full moon hung over the stage like a huge silver eye. The skeletal branches of a gnarled oak tree draped over tombstones that rose out of a white fog sea like weathered teeth. A wolf howled and Riley shivered at the sound.

Mort sighed deeply. "I'm sorry you're going to see this," he said.

The fog parted in front of the largest tombstone as a man's head appeared like an oversize mushroom just above the stage floor. Bit by bit the rest of him rose until he was completely exposed. The guy was about her father's age and he held a skull in his right hand. He blinked his eyes rapidly in the bright lights. After an awkward pause he began to speak in a halting and raspy voice.

"Alas, . . . poor Yorick."

Mort groaned.

"I knew him . . . well . . ." the dead man intoned, misquoting Shakespeare. His forehead wrinkled in thought, as if it was taking every brain cell to remember the words. "A fellow of . . . of infinite . . . ah . . . jest. Ha! Ha!" Then he hoisted the skull up into the air and glanced nervously at the tables closest to him. Someone laughed and the poor guy heard it.

The master of ceremonies moved across the stage. "This, ladies and gentlemen, is Herbert. In his previous life he worked for the Internal Revenue Service as an auditor. His knowledge of corporate tax matters is his biggest asset. If you wish to avoid tangling with Uncle Sam over a few million dollars, this is the reanimate for you." Their host paused and then called out, "Do I have a first bid?"

"Ten thousand," someone shouted.

"Eleven," another said immediately.

They are really buying this guy. Riley had known this moment would happen, but seeing it in person was too much. When her stomach rolled over, she gripped her abdomen with both hands.

"Restroom?" she pleaded.

Mort pointed and she fled up the stairs. She could still hear the bidding as she pushed through the door to the women's room.

"Eighteen thousand!"

Riley's stomach opted not to revolt, so she wet her face with cold water and let it air-dry. As she examined her face in the mirror, a gruesome thought hit her.

How would they sell her father? *Own the city's most legendary demon trapper! Learn the secret mysteries of Hell.* Would they want him for his Civil War knowledge or maybe as a tutor to their kids?

There was a thrum of organ music and a clash of thunder. Applause followed. Herbert's auction was over. Riley made her way back to her seat, apologizing when she stepped on Mort's toes. The final sales price was displayed on the tombstone in bright red LEDs. Eighty-five thousand dollars.

There's always money to be made in death. The guy at the Deader tent had been right.

"So who gets all that?" she snarled. "You guys?"

Mort shook his head. "The family will receive eighty-five percent, tax free."

"They agreed to this? How could someone do that?"

"Herbert wanted it this way," Lady Torin's frosty voice said from behind them. "He wanted to ensure his wife and children had as much financial security as he could provide, even after his death."

"That's what life insurance is for," Riley retorted.

"Yes, but he wanted to go the extra mile. I just wish this could have been a private sale. Far more dignified."

"So what happens in a year? He ends up in a dumpster?"

The necromancer moved so close she caught the scent of whisky.

"My people *do not* end up in dumpsters, Miss Blackthorne. My people are given all the respect they are due. Don't you dare accuse me of not caring, do you understand?"

Riley nodded numbly. "Sorry. I'm . . ."

"You're not using your head, or you wouldn't be challenging me like this."

"Hey, why not? I already dissed Ozymandias. Why not make it a full sweep?"

What is it with my mouth tonight?

She tensed, waited for the searing blast of magic. Maybe she'd end up with a furry tail. It would be a good bet it wouldn't be the same color as her hair.

Instead, there was a wry chuckle. "You do like to live dangerously."

The next reanimate was a young man just a few years older than Riley. He held a sword like he had no idea what to do with it and stomped around the stage misquoting more Shakespeare. He went for five thousand, sold for his gardening skills. By the time they reached the seventh Deader, Riley had begun to wish she was legal age. Anything with booze in it would be great right now.

Three more Deaders crossed the stage, all sold for their various talents. Riley fidgeted in impatience. "Is my dad here?" she asked. She frowned when Mort shook his head. "How do you know that?"

"The server showed me a list of those up for auction," he replied.

"So why in the . . . ?" She counted slowly to five. "Why did you make me sit through this?"

"Because you have to know what you're up against."

The current offering, a middle-aged housewife whose rendition of a tune from *The Phantom of the Opera* had scarred Riley for life, went for considerably less. Thankfully the emcee called an intermission.

"Now what?" Riley quizzed as she and Mort filed out of the balcony.

"Now is when I get to ask questions."

NINETEEN

The summoners didn't hang with the moneyed elite, but had their own reception room, complete with crustless sandwiches and tuxedoed servers toting silver trays loaded with drinks.

Mortimer made his way through the group, Riley trailing behind. She knew everyone was staring at her. She was easy to spot: Other than the waitstaff, she was the only one not wearing a cloak.

Lenny walked up to them. "Miss Riley," he said. His usual pimp suit wasn't in sight, hidden by a light gray cloak. His cheeks were flushed red, probably because of the cocktail glass in his hand and the empty he had in the other. "How goes it?"

Lenny was pretty harmless, so chewing him out wasn't going to get her anywhere. Besides, he was friends with Beck. "Not going that well, Lenny. It'd be better if I could find my dad."

"Ah, I heard about that. Sorry, girl. I had three buyers lined up, and you would have got the money. I warned you it could get nasty."

You did. "Any idea who took him?"

Lenny narrowed his eyes then announced, a bit too loudly, that he needed to get his drink refilled. She watched him head for the bar.

"Better let me do the asking," Mort counseled.

Riley had come to a few conclusions by herself. "The guy who did this had a lot of power. That's not Lenny, right?"

"Right. To conjure up that sort of illusion requires something more than an entry-level summoner."

"So where are you on the scale between newbie and Dark Lord?" she quizzed.

Her escort didn't reply, suddenly uncomfortable.

"Mortimer is about three-quarters of the way there," Lady Torin said as she joined them. She held a plate full of cheese wedges and crackers. "Of course, he won't admit that. He likes to appear harmless."

Mort gave her a gracious nod and held her eyes a second longer than was needed. Was there something between these two? As if he realized he was showing more than he wanted, Mort headed toward another summoner, one who had made the mistake of getting caught with his hands full of food and drink and no place to run.

Riley turned her attention to the other necromancer. "So how about you? How close are you to being Dark Lord?"

Torin's mouth twitched in a grin. "I'm about seven-eighths of the way. Except in my case, it would Dark Lady."

"And Ozymandias?"

Torin's eyes met hers. "He doesn't even register on the scale anymore."

Whoa. "Who do you think took my dad?" Riley asked.

"Someone Mortimer's level or above," the lady replied. "That's his mistake, you see. He's asking questions of every summoner, rather than focusing on those at Theta level and up."

"But one of those lower dudes might know something."

"A lower-level summoner is not going to tattle on someone higher on the food chain."

"Out of respect?" Riley asked, curious.

"Out of fear." Torin finished demolishing the cracker.

Riley and the lady talked to five summoners before the lights flickered and it was time to go back into the theater. With absolutely no results. Mort joined them, and she could tell from the expression on his face he'd struck out, too.

"You might as well go home," he conceded. "I'll talk to the others, but most of them are too scared to say anything."

"Thanks anyway," she said, her heart sinking. As Mort and Lady Torin began to converse in lowered voices, Riley tromped down the stairs, her mood as dark as a senior necro's cloak. Ozymandias stood near the front door, like he was waiting for her. There was no one else around except for the bouncers outside. The only way to get to her car was to pass by him.

She halted and stared up into his really weird eyes. "If you took my dad, just tell me. I have to know where he is."

The summoner regarded her solemnly. "Stop hounding Mortimer to find your father. You're going to get him hurt if you keep interfering. Is that what you want?"

"No. I just want what's mine."

Ozymandias raised a silvery eyebrow. "As do I." He swept back into the theater, but the magic still danced across her skin.

How is that possible?

Riley pushed her way out the door, past the bouncers, and into the night. In the parking lot the woman who'd been turned away looked over at her, forlorn, her hands full of tissues. Was this Herbert's wife? Was she regretting his decision to support their family by making the ultimate sacrifice?

Riley had just made it to her car when her cell phone chimed. It was Mort.

WAIT FOR ME. I HAVE AN IDEA.

After one particularly lengthy yawn, she spied the summoner hurrying toward her, his cloak flapping behind him. When he joined her, he gave a wary look back the way he'd come.

"I hesitate to say this, but there is another way to find your father," he said. "It's risky, but it might be worth a try."

A sharp tingle of hope shot through her. Riley straightened up. "Go on."

"A certain type of summoning spell will call forth your father's spirit," Mort explained. "If he appears, maybe he can tell you who took him and where he's located, providing he can reveal that information."

Now we're getting somewhere. "Can you do this spell?"

"I can . . ." he started, ". . . but I won't. It will put me on the wrong side of the Society, and I'm already pushing the envelope as it is."

"What would they do to you?" she asked.

He sagged against her car, apparently not worried his cloak would get dusty. "The Society doesn't solve its internal problems by kicking someone out. In my case, I'd probably be found dead, just an overly large pile of ashes. It's not like I'd get a slap on the wrist."

"Oh." That *was* serious. "Okay, who else can do this location thing?"

"Anyone who is a magical practitioner." Their eyes met. "Like a *witch*, for instance. But you didn't hear that from me."

"Gee. I know one of those," she said, grinning.

"I figured you might. Most trappers do."

"So what keeps the Society from turning my friend into a pile of ashes if she gets in their face?"

"For all their New Age beads and incense, witches pack some serious power, and they protect their own. The last magical war we had with them ended in a draw, so we're not eager to repeat that mistake. There's still bad blood between us."

Riley had seen that animosity firsthand when Ozymandias had threatened Ayden and the witch had returned the threat without batting an eye.

"Okay, Mort, I got this covered," she said. Mindful of the High Lord's warning, she added, "You've done enough for me as it is."

"Just be cautious," he said. "Whoever took your father isn't going to appreciate you nosing around, especially if it's done with witch magic. It could get really unpleasant." He looked toward the theater. "And if it's Lord Ozymandias . . ."

With that, Mort trudged back to the vendue. Now it was time for

Riley to move the ball forward on her own. She sent a quick text to her friend Ayden with the unusual request. Now she'd have to wait and see what the witch thought of the plan.

As Riley turned to open her car door, she became aware of someone standing near her. A second before she realized it was Ori she gave out a squeak of surprise. And then felt really dumb. "Whoa, warn a girl, will you?" she complained.

A stunning white rose came her way. "Will this serve as an apology?" he asked.

Riley stared at the offering. Why was he doing this? "Where do you get these? They're way expensive." She knew that because she'd bought one on the anniversary of her mom's death to place on the grave and it'd cost her two weeks' worth of hot chocolate purchases.

"I have my sources," he replied.

She accepted it and inhaled its rich fragrance. It was just as amazing as the previous one.

"Where to next?" Ori asked, lounging against the car. "Shopping? The coffee shop?"

All of that sounded good, but . . . "Time to go to the church, I guess."

"No reason to go there. I'm watching over you."

"You're just hoping the Five makes its move on me."

"That, and I enjoy your company."

Give this guy points for knowing the right thing to say. "Thanks, but I am tired. It's been a long day."

"Your call." Ori straightened up. "Mind if I ride with you?"

"What about your bike?"

"I'll come back for it."

"Aren't you afraid someone will steal it?"

"No," he said. "No one will touch it."

He seemed so sure and Riley had no objections to the company. Ori waited until she'd unlocked the passenger-side door and then slid into the car. She set the rose between them, careful not to damage any of the petals. Part of her felt guilty accepting it—she *was* dating some-one else—but it was so pretty and had the most intoxicating scent. Besides, what would it hurt?

As she pulled onto the street, she looked over at him and frowned. "Seat belt, dude."

"I'm sure you're a safe driver," he replied.

"Doesn't matter. The city wants money, so the cops will ticket you. And me, for letting you be in the car that way."

Grumbling under his breath, Ori fumbled with the thing then clicked it home.

"Don't you get tired of following me all over the place?" she asked, heading south into the city.

"No, you lead an interesting life. Today you went to class at a cem-etery, visited your injured boyfriend, and then came to the theater and hung with a bunch of stuffy necromancers. That's not boring."

"You *have* been following me." *Everywhere.* It bordered on the creepy if she hadn't known he was trying to kill the Five. "But I thought the Geo-Fiend would only come after me at night."

"It's strongest then, yes, but I don't like to take chances." He turned toward her. "So what was it like, the summoner thing?"

Riley told him how awful it had been. How her dad wasn't there and how afraid she was of never finding him again. Tears blurred her eyes and she cursed under her breath. As she blinked them away, she felt his hand on her arm, warm through her jacket. He didn't say any-thing, but just his touch made her feel better. That's what she'd been wanting from Simon.

What is it about this guy? Why do I feel so completely different when I'm with him? When Ori's hand retreated, she missed it immediately. Her passenger was frowning now, and the temperature inside the car seemed to drop a degree. "I thought I had a lead on the Five last night, but it didn't work out," he admitted.

"What kind of lead?"

"I convinced a Gastro-Fiend to tell me where the rogue is hiding.

The silly thing tried to bribe me with a half-eaten rat. Absolutely pathetic." He sighed. "Unfortunately, someone else tipped off the Five and it disappeared before I could find it."

"Why would someone do that?" Riley asked, puzzled.

"Hell has its informers, just like Heaven."

"So I'm still bait?" she said glumly.

"I'm afraid so."

TWENTY

Usually Beck slept in until at least noon after a night of trapping, but for two mornings in a row he'd had to crawl out of bed early. Too early by his way of thinking. Now, as he stood in front of the Atlanta City Hall, he muffled a yawn with the back of his hand, earning him a bemused look from the Scotsman. The bandage on the master's forehead was gone, replaced by a neat row of transparent strips across a healing wound. He was dressed in a colorful kilt, which seemed odd, but maybe there was a rule about what a master wore when you met the hunters. Beck had opted for a clean pair of jeans and a blue shirt, topped off with his leather jacket. He felt naked without his duffel bag, but Stewart had insisted he leave it in the truck.

Where they stood gave them an excellent view of the street below. The street itself was clear, but the sidewalks on either side were jammed with people, eager to get a look at the Vatican's boys. It reminded Beck of the day after the Tabernacle attack. Some of the same sign wavers were back, and a new group insisted that Atlanta was doomed because of the gays and the unbelievers. Another yawn overtook him and this one he couldn't stop.

"Late night?" Stewart asked.

"Trapped a Pyro near Lenox Station. It was settin' dumpsters on fire." He tried to convince the fiend to tell him where to find that murdering Five. No luck. So he'd hauled the thing to Fireman Jack and sold it. At least that part of the evening was a success.

Beck zeroed in on the signs again. "I wonder if Jack knows he's one of the reasons this city is goin' to hell."

The master pointed toward a large sign with bold letters and blood-red flames around the border: "Kill Every Demon. Make America Safe for Our Kids." He shook his head in despair.

"What would happen if we *did* kill all the demons?" Beck asked. He knew that was impossible because Lucifer had an endless supply of the fiends. Still, it was something to think about.

"No demons and ya got no balance," the master replied solemnly. "I'll tell ya how it all works when yer ready ta become a master."

"Another year then," Beck replied. *At least.*

Stewart gave him a sideways glance. "I'd say sooner."

Before he could follow up on that comment, there was the sound of sirens in the distance. Beck perked up.

Stewart grunted. "That'll be hunters. They do love a show."

"So what's gonna happen here?"

"In front of the cameras they'll be all friendly-like," the master replied. "Behind the scenes it'll get dirty. The Vatican knows how ta pull strings with the best of them. Comes with centuries of practice."

"Ya sound like ya know them pretty well."

"Aye, lad. My family's been trappin' fiends for over eight hunnerd years. The hunters are the reason for that."

Beck looked over at him, confused. "What?"

"It's a tale best told over whisky." Stewart shifted his weight from one foot to the other. "I want ya ta trap with Riley every chance ya get. Where I respect Master Harper, I'm not fond of his methods."

"No way he's gonna let me work with her."

"As long as he gets a cut of the money, he'll be happy."

Beck doubted that but decided not to argue the point. If they did trap together he could keep a closer eye on Paul's daughter. Maybe keep her from getting hurt again. "Yeah, I like that idea," he said, but for an entirely different reason than the master's.

Sirens wailed and rose in intensity. The sound abruptly cut off as two police cars turned the corner onto Mitchell Street, lights flashing like they were leading a parade. Right behind were four sleek vans followed in turn by a white limousine. The black vans were identical and displayed the papal coat of arms on the side doors.

"Where'd they get their rides?" Beck asked.

"Airlifted them in from New York City. Money isn't a problem for these folks, not like it is for us."

The lead van halted in front of the building, the others quickly lining up behind it. Flashbulbs lit up as bystanders began to push against the barricades. Some were crying. The lead van's doors slid open and two men hopped out, one on each side of the vehicle. Both were clad in black military fatigues and combat boots and they carried specially modified assault rifles. The men scanned their surroundings then beckoned to their comrades. Five more men exited the van, remaining on alert. Once the first vehicle was empty, the third van in line followed the same drill, then the fourth.

"Smart," Beck said, impressed. These guys weren't mugging for the cameras, but eyeing the terrain for potential trouble, human or demonic. They were a mixed lot—white, black, Asian, and Latino. One thing for sure: They'd all be Roman Catholic. That was a job requirement.

Only when the scene was deemed secure did the side door on the second van slide open. A man stepped out. He was taller than Beck, six feet two or so, with a Mediterranean complexion and a goatee. Inky black hair ended at his collar. He was wearing a dark navy turtleneck with epaulets, navy trousers, and combat boots and was armed with a pistol at his waist. Over his left breast was the demon hunters emblem—Saint George slaying the dragon.

"Head dude?" Beck asked.

"Aye. That's Elias Salvatore, the team's captain," Stewart replied.

"He's thirty-two, the youngest leader they've ever had." Another man hopped out of the van. "That's Lieutenant Maarten Amundson, his second-in-command."

Beck scrutinized the hunter, watching his body language. He was older, beefier than his superior. "He doesn't like his captain. Not one bit."

"How can ya tell?" Stewart asked, intrigued.

"The way he looks at him. It isn't respect; it's somethin' else."

The master trapper nodded his approval at the assessment. "Amundson figured he'd be top dog by now and he's none too happy about Salvatore takin' his job. What else are ya seein', lad?"

"Their men are well trained. They're on alert, like they expected to be ambushed. Can't think that's just for the cameras."

"It's not. They were attacked in Paris by a pair of Archdemons a few years back. Got five of them dead, and they've not forgotten that humiliation. They're tired, too. It's not jet lag but somethin' deeper here. They're bein' pushed too hard, I think."

The master was right: Beck could see it in how the hunters held themselves. They were still deadly but not totally in peak condition.

"If they were trappers I'd say they need some R and R. Get drunk, get laid, get their attitudes adjusted," he said.

Stewart chuckled. "Well, that's not gonna happen, and the reason is in that limo."

Beck hadn't noticed the vehicle until the master pointed it out. As if on cue, one of the hunters marched back to the car and opened the rear door. A priest stepped out. He was older, maybe sixty, his dark hair lined with silver and his eyes sharp like a hawk's. He was wearing a cassock.

As the priest approached a wave of tension passed through the hunters' ranks, as if a wolf had just entered into their midst. "They can't stand this guy," Beck observed.

"He's nothin' like our Father Harrison. This one's the Vatican's man—Father Rosetti. He's here ta make sure the hunters stay on the straight and narrow and don't embarrass the Holy See. He's known ta be overzealous. Even Rome thinks so."

Beck turned to the Scotsman, astounded at the man's inside knowledge. "How do ya know all this?"

"I have contacts here and there. Comes with bein' a master. It opens up all sorts of doors."

The captain and his lieutenant had their photo op with the governor, the mayor, and a few of the city council members, all eager to be shown with the Vatican's team. Then it was the trappers' turn to meet the men who might turn this city into a war zone.

To Beck's surprise, the lead demon hunter made the first move, striding past the mayor and the governor, extending his hand toward the older trapper. "Grand Master Stewart. It is a pleasure. I've long wanted to meet you."

"Captain Salvatore. Welcome ta Atlanta."

Grand Master? Beck had never heard of that title before. He'd have to ask Stewart about that sometime. Hell, he had a lot of things to ask, once everything died down.

"I believe you met my father many years ago," Salvatore said.

"Aye, I remember it well," Stewart replied. "It was in Genoa. He'd killed an Archfiend that day, and you'd just been born. We shared a bottle of whisky ta celebrate."

"He recalls that occasion very fondly." Salvatore's face sobered. "The hunters are truly sorry about your men."

"Thank ya for that." Stewart looked over at his companion and gestured. "This is Denver Beck, one of our journeymen. He'll be yer contact while yer in Atlanta. He knows the city and her demons better than anyone."

Flustered by the compliment, Beck shook hands with the captain and murmured his greeting. The priest didn't look happy. Was it because Salvatore was being too friendly with the good ol' boys? Father Rosetti said something in Italian that caused the captain to stiffen like a dog at the end of a leash. Salvatore said something back and the priest frowned.

"Gentlemen, if you'll excuse me," the lead hunter said. He returned to the podium, where the mayor, never one to miss an opportunity, shook the captain's hand again knowing it would set off a flurry of flashbulbs.

"The citizens of Atlanta will sleep easy in their beds tonight knowing the Vatican's Demon Hunters are here," Montgomery proclaimed.

Beck ground his teeth. Funny how the citizens hadn't realized they'd been sleeping easy all these years thanks to the trappers. As the mayor droned on, Beck's eyes skimmed over the crowds at street level. It was funny how you can't resist trying to find someone you know in a pack of people. The red hair caught his notice immediately. Justine waved and smiled. He resisted the urge to wave back. Then suddenly it was all over: The hunters loaded back into the vans, and the motorcade drove off.

Stewart didn't budge. "A wee word of advice, lad. Be verra careful with the hunters. They're not a bad lot, but it'll get ugly if they think they're bein' made fools of."

Beck nodded his understanding. "What do ya want me to do?"

"Just try ta keep them from burnin' the city ta the ground. That's all I ask."

For a moment Beck thought the master was messing with his head. Then he saw the expression on the Scotsman's face.

Oh, God, he's serious.

"I do believe this qualifies as torture in most civilized countries," Peter groused. He was hunched up in the passenger seat of Riley's car, staring mournfully at the other side of the street where the recycling guys were loading Holy Water bottles into the back of a truck.

Riley speared him with a look. "Remember the Allan transfer disaster?" she retorted. "You. Owe. Me."

"I know. I just thought there'd be more excitement."

Riley took another lengthy slurp of her soda. "Yeah, this is a snore, but I have to know how this all works. Somewhere there's a break in the chain." Which was why they'd been following this one collection truck all over the city for the past two hours.

"You sure the counterfeit-water dudes aren't just buying new bottles?" her friend quizzed.

"I don't think so, not with a tax stamp on them. Those are specially made, and you can't buy them anywhere but from the city."

Peter gave her a dubious look. "How do you know that?"

"I went to the city's Web site and checked it out."

That response earned her a nod of respect. Any interaction with the Internet was righteous, according to Peter. "Can we get food after this?"

"Sure." She wasn't hungry, but her buddy seemed to eat his weight every day. Apparently he was in another growth spurt. She wondered how his dad could keep enough food on the table with two boys in the house.

Bored, Riley checked her phone for something to do. Not a word from Simon. She had the volume as high as it would go so she wouldn't miss his call, but that only worked if he actually made the effort.

"He's not talking to anyone," she grumbled.

"Your dude?" Peter asked.

"Yeah. He's all caught up in himself."

"Maybe you're not giving him enough time to pull his head together," Peter said. "You can be impatient, you know."

Harsh as it sounded, her friend was correct: She was expecting things to happen faster than they did in the real world. Maybe she was pushing Simon too hard. He'd admitted he'd never had any serious trials in his life, and then he'd landed a huge one. He needed time to get a grip on it all. *But his mom wants me to get him talking.* Riley typed out a text message to her boyfriend: THINKING OF YOU!

If he replied, she'd back off for a while. If not . . . There was a resounding lack of a response as the minutes crawled by.

Riley growled under her breath: Simon the Silent was definitely getting a visit this afternoon. She would not let him stew in his pool of depression any longer. It was time to move forward, even if he was confused and scared. *We can be that way together.*

"Ah, here we go," Peter said with exaggerated relief.

When the recycling truck pulled into traffic, Riley fell in two car lengths behind. Being big and loaded with plastic bottles made it easy to follow.

"So how many stops was that?" she asked.

"Four. No, five," Peter said, consulting his notebook.

"The thing's full." *So either they go to the plant or . . .*

But they didn't go to the Celestial Supplies plant. Instead they followed the truck to a large brick warehouse near East Point.

"So what just happened here?" Riley demanded as she maneuvered the car onto a side street. "This isn't the Holy Water plant. That's up in Doraville."

"Seems to be some sort of recycling center," Peter said, unbuckling his seat belt. "I'll go get a closer look." Before she could protest, he was out the door and hiking up the street.

This is a waste of time. Even my dad couldn't figure it out, and he was way smarter than me.

Her cell phone pinged. A text from Peter: IN POSITION. She rolled her eyes. At least her friend was enjoying himself. Then another text: I'M GOING INSIDE.

NO! she typed back.

I'LL BE OKAY. JUST HANG TIGHT.

It was a long fifteen minutes. Riley thought of sending him another text, but that might ruin whatever he was up to. Every minute increased her worry.

"I shouldn't have brought him with me. He's going to get into trouble, and his dad is going to go nuclear and . . ." Every possible scenario ended with Peter hurt or exiled to Illinois.

When her friend sauntered back to the car in no particular hurry, he sported a pleased expression on his face, which meant he'd learned something.

The moment Peter climbed into the car, Riley unloaded: "You're crazy, you know? You shouldn't have gone in there on your own. Who knows what they might have done to you."

"Crazy? This from a person who traps demons for a living?"

"This isn't about me!" she retorted. "So give it up. What did you find out?"

"I told the guard I had a report to do for school. I made sure to look like a nerd so he wouldn't think I was any threat."

Channeling a nerd wasn't really hard for Peter. "And?"

"This place is the city's only official recycler, at least for the Holy Water bottles. They collect them, strip off the labels and tax stamps, clean them out, then load them into trucks and haul them to the Celestial Supplies plant to be refilled, where they're relabeled and stamped before they're sent to the distributor."

"Then they're being stolen from here?" she asked, hopefully.

"Don't know yet. The guard says they count every bottle that comes in and out. But if someone can find a way to smuggle a few out before they're cleaned and stripped, all they'd have to do is put a new label on them and fill them with tap water."

"And as long as the new label has the original batch number and it matches the tax stamp number, it all looks kosher." Then she shook her head. "But they'd have to fake the paperwork to make up for the missing bottles."

"That's the problem with this theory," he admitted. "I can't imagine they're ripping off the bottles during the day, so we'll have to do night surveillance."

"You'd do that with me?"

"Sure." Peter interlaced his fingers and cracked his knuckles. "Tech rules. I'll find a way."

Her friend was beginning to plumb new depths of self-assurance. "You're really awesome, you know that?"

"I may be awesome, but I'm hungry."

"I'll buy you lunch, how's that?" She saw him open his mouth to protest, but cut him off. "I have money." Then she explained how she'd gotten it and just how much.

"Beck left you a thousand bucks?" Peter said, astonished. "And you think he's a butthead because . . . ?" He gestured for her to fill in the blank.

"Don't start."

Her companion checked something on his phone. "There's a Vietnamese restaurant four point three miles north of here. I want *pho*."

"Noodles it is, dude."

TWENTY-ONE

Though they'd been "invited" to meet with the hunters at the Westin, Beck and Stewart were stuck in the hallway, ignored. The longer Beck waited, the more pissed he became. When it appeared they weren't going to be ushered into the hunters' presence anytime soon, Stewart sweet-talked a maid into finding them two chairs, gave her a tip for her service, and then settled back in one.

"Sir . . ." Beck began.

The Scotsman waved him to a chair. "Don't let them psych ya, lad. It's all on purpose. We'll give them five more minutes and then we're outta here. Then I'll be talkin' ta the Archbishop."

They'd just risen to leave when one of the hunters appeared in the hallway and waved them inside. To Beck, the hotel room seemed huge, like three rooms in one. There was a galley kitchen to the right, a small bathroom to the left, and a big open area in front of them. In that area was a conference table and six chairs.

The smell of fresh coffee caught his nose, reminding him he was a few cups short for the day. Next to the coffeemaker was a plate of donuts. It appeared the hunters liked the frosted ones with the little sprinkles.

Sitting in padded chairs around the table were three men—Captain Elias Salvatore, Lieutenant Amundson, and the priest. Behind them was a massive window—Atlanta from a bird's-eye view. And another hunter. His eyes weren't on them but on the city below, an assault rifle in hand.

Vigilant bunch, that's for sure.

Captain Salvatore rose from his chair. "Grand Master Stewart, please excuse the delay." His tone told Beck he wasn't happy about it, either.

"No trouble, Captain," Stewart replied, choosing a chair at the end of the table near Salvatore. The priest gave them a cursory glance and then returned those dark eyes to the paperwork in front of him.

"Gentlemen, this is Father Rosetti and my second-in-command, Lieutenant Amundson," the captain said, unaware that Stewart had already given Beck a complete rundown.

Amundson delivered a crisp nod, but the priest pointedly ignored both of them. That didn't sit well with Beck. He could understand the priest blowing him off; he wasn't important, but Stewart deserved respect. To his credit, the Scotsman ignored the slight like he'd expected it. Uneasy, Beck sat next to him, which put the priest on his right.

"I'm actin' in Master Harper's stead," Stewart explained. "We're here ta help ya in any way we can."

Without looking up, the priest thumbed open a thick file folder stuffed with documents. "We have opened an investigation into the events at the Tabernacle," he said, his English heavily accented. "In particular what roles Paul Blackthorne or his daughter played in that tragedy."

Stewart frowned but didn't reply.

"Tell us what happened that night."

As the master delivered the report, Beck could hear the increasing tension in his voice. All the while Father Rosetti made notes on a sheet of paper.

"Who is the necromancer that reanimated her father?" the priest asked.

The Scotsman looked over at Beck.

"We don't know that yet," he replied. "The summoners aren't talkin'."

More notes went on the paper. Beck found it interesting that Rosetti was asking all the questions while Salvatore and his lieutenant watched from the sidelines. That meant he was really in charge of the operation, not the captain. *Wonder how that sits with Salvatore.*

"You are convinced the Holy Water used at your meeting was genuine?" Rosetti quizzed.

Stewart hesitated momentarily, then nodded. "Aye."

"I was not aware the Guild admitted females to their midst," the priest remarked.

"It's a recent change," Stewart admitted.

"This girl, what is she like?"

"I don't get your meanin'," the master replied.

"Can she be trusted?"

"Absolutely," Stewart replied, his tone prickly now. "The Guild is investigatin' the problem, and I've kept the Archbishop in the loop. It'll take some time, but we'll find the source of those bott-els."

"That is not important at the moment," the priest said dismissively.

"On the contrary, it is verra important. The public must trust the Holy Water will keep their homes safe. If not, there'll be citywide panic."

The priest put down his pen. "The more I look into this matter, all I see is one person in the very center of it all—the girl, Riley Blackthorne. Her father's papers only indicate he felt something was amiss, yet she claims the Holy Water is not genuine."

Beck jumped in. "She tested the bottles. Some of them didn't react."

The priest studied him, then flipped a page. "Yes, and for that test she employed the claw of a demon. A symbol of Hell."

How did ya know about the claw? Who told ya? "Why not? It came from the Three she caught. On her own, too."

Rosetti's eyebrow rose. "You cannot possibly have me believe such a young child could capture such a Hellspawn by herself."

What's goin' on here? All of this was about Riley, not about how to stop the demons.

Apparently Stewart was thinking along the same line. "So what is the official agenda, Father?" the master demanded.

The pen went down again. "We are here to take control of the city's Hellspawn problem. We cannot allow Lucifer to obtain a foothold in our world. To that end, if we find that anyone has sided with our enemy in this battle, they will be arrested and tried. That includes Paul Blackthorne's girl."

"Now wait a minute—" Beck began.

"Easy, lad," Stewart said. Then he addressed the priest. "Why are ya so interested in her?"

"Often there is a nexus, a specific individual that Hell uses to lay its plans. Often that is someone young and impressionable. In this case, perhaps it is Riley Blackthorne, especially since she was at the Tabernacle the night of the attack."

"She had nothin' ta do with that," Stewart replied.

"Either way, we need to speak with her on these matters."

"Not unless her master agrees," Stewart said, drawing the line in the sand.

"Master Harper's approval has little to do with the matter. We *will* talk to the girl," the priest replied, his face set.

"Not unless Harper agrees," Stewart retorted. "We don't throw our people ta the wolves."

The priest tensed. "You are impeding our investigation, Master Stewart. I shall be filing a formal complaint with the mayor . . . and the National Guild."

"Ya misunderstand me, priest. We came here ta offer our assistance, not have ya make one of our own a scapegoat."

"Your protest is noted," the priest replied. He shuffled his papers in an agitated manner. "We have nothing further to discuss."

That was as cold a dismissal as Beck had ever heard.

"Mind you," Stewart added, his voice rougher now, "somethin's afoot in this city and it would be a mistake ta think it's all Hell's doin'."

The priest studied him gravely. "Which is exactly what I would expect a trapper to say. Come now, Master Stewart, we both know who guards your kind, where your loyalties lay. That was so plainly evident the other night."

"That's not the issue, and ya know it," Stewart retorted. "We'll not have this city destroyed just ta make yer boss happy."

The priest bristled. "This is about evil, Master Stewart, not currying favor with His Holiness."

"Just as long as ya remember that."

With a curt nod to the captain, Stewart rose to leave the room, Beck in tow. Amundson had taken a position near the door. The master passed without incident, but the hunter purposely bumped Beck hard, bouncing him off the doorframe. Beck whirled, eager to take on this jerk, but never got the chance as Stewart's cane shot up between them.

"Stand down, lad!" With an oath, Beck stepped back, furious that he'd lost control in the first place.

Stewart stared up at Amundson's gloating face. "Another time, hunter. Mark you, that time will come, and I'll be damned happy ta turn this lad loose on ya."

Beck seethed all the way down the hall, wanting to hit something. He tried to chill, but the anger wouldn't fade. There was a showdown coming with the hunters—it was going to be bloody—and he was going to be in the middle of it.

As they waited for the elevator, the Scotsman called Riley's master and related the news. "Aye. I agree." He hung up, still frowning.

"Sir . . ." Beck began. "Harper isn't goin' to give her up, is he?"

"Not without a fight, that's for sure." The elevator dinged its arrival. "Let's head ta my place. It's time ya know what's really goin' on."

†

As Beck waited for the master to climb out of the truck, he checked out the man's house. It was three stories, fancy in an old-fashioned sort of way, and painted in different shades of blue. It even had a small tower off the front. His host led him into a room near the back. Beck liked this place. It felt like a home, from the big fireplace to the little crocheted things on the backs of the chairs.

Stewart took a position near a large cabinet and studied his extensive liquor collection. It encompassed three shelves. From what Beck could see of the labels, most of it was Scotch.

"Ya got a favorite?" his host asked, peering at him over his shoulder.

"No, sir. Never drank much whisky except for my granddaddy's."

Stewart hovered a hand over a bottle, then moved to the one next to it. "Aberlour a'bunadh, I think. Ya'd not take kindly ta the peat right off."

"Pete?"

"It adds a smoky flavor to the whisky. We'll build ya up over time."

The master poured a hefty amount in a tumbler, then something for himself from a different bottle. "Have a seat, lad," he said, handing off the liquor.

Beck settled into a red stuffed chair near the fireplace. Once the master had taken his place in a matching chair across from him, Beck gave the whisky a cautious sniff. *Not bad.*

"*Slàinte mhath!*" the Scotsman proclaimed.

Beck had no idea what the man had said, but he smiled and raised the glass anyway. The first sip told him he liked this stuff a lot, which meant it cost more than he could afford.

"Suit ya?" Stewart asked after taking a long pull from his own glass.

Beck nodded. "Real smooth."

The master propped up his left leg on an ottoman. After another lengthy sip, he smacked his lips in appreciation. He seemed in no hurry, though he'd been the one to issue the invitation.

Beck realized he'd have to get the ball rolling. "Paul told me yer family had been trappin' since forever."

"We weren't the first trappers, but we're some of the best," Stewart replied. "The Blackthornes were the same until they came ta America and got too much inta earnin' money rather than trappin' the beasties. At least Paul came back ta the fold."

"That took some doin', I imagine," Beck said, hoping to hear a bit more about his mentor.

"Paul had the Blackthorne tradition ta uphold, though he didn't see it that way. In times past, his family would send their sons ta Scotland and we'd train 'em."

"He never said a word about that." But then there was a lot Paul hadn't told him. "So what's this 'Grand Master' thing? I've never heard tell of it before."

"It's just a title we use in Europe. It means I'm one of the more senior masters."

Bet there's more to it than that.

"It made for hard feelings with Harper when I first came here," Stewart confessed. "Ten years ago, he was barely holdin' his own against some of the other masters here in Atlanta. They were a bad lot. Takin' bribes in a protection racket. If ya didn't pay their price, they'd set a Pyro-Fiend loose ta burn yer place ta the ground."

"What?" Beck spouted, horrified. "That's damned evil."

"Aye," Stewart said, nodding sagely. "One of the masters went after Harper and cut him up. That's how he got that wicked scar. While he was healin', the National Guild asked me ta come over and clean house."

"So that's how he got to be senior master—by ya kickin' out all the others?"

"Pretty much. Truth be known, he wasn't happy when I showed up. Felt like the National Guild hadn't given him enough time ta straighten things out."

"And now?" Beck asked.

"We've learned ta tolerate each other," the Scotsman said with a wry smile. "I tried ta recruit Paul when I first came ta town, but he turned me down flat. Then his teachin' job was gone and he was willin' ta listen."

The master rose slowly from the chair and refilled his drink. "More?" he asked.

"Not yet, thanks." No way he'd keep up with a Scotsman.

Stewart recapped the bottle with a *thwack* of his palm, then returned to his chair. "Back in the day, most demons were dealt with by the church. The priest would exorcise them. Some began ta hunt them, mostly as sport. The bishops encouraged that, partly because those men could be used as muscle when the Church felt the need."

Another long sip of the whisky. "As time passed," Stewart continued, "the hunters gained a reputation for bein' damned ruthless. There was a dispute between one of my ancestors, a Malcolm Stewart, and one of the local hunters. Somethin' about a bit a' land. The hunter claimed that Malcolm and his family were conspirin' with Hell, so the local bishop gave orders ta solve the problem."

"Solve it, how?" Beck asked. He suspected it didn't involve a lot of praying. These were Scotsman: They settled their disputes with lethal steel.

"A team of hunters descended on Malcolm's home in the wee hours and butchered everyone they could find. Hacked them ta death, even the bairns. Malcolm they burnt at a stake, claimin' he was a warlock."

"Sweet Jesus," Beck said, his gut twisting at the thought.

"Aye," Stewart replied. "Malcolm's son, Euan, had the good fortune ta be in Edinburgh that day. Knowing he'd be next for the stake, he came up with a brilliant scheme. He ordered the rest of the family ta trap demons and deliver them ta their priests, as many as possible in the shortest period of time."

"Smart," Beck said, seeing the plan clearly. "The Stewarts couldn't be workin' for Lucifer if they were trappin' demons."

Stewart nodded. "Euan was a canny one. After he'd trap a demon, he'd leave a few coins behind. Word got around. It was better ta get some brass for yer demon rather than havin' the hunters burn yer house and put yer family ta the sword."

Beck couldn't stop the grin. "Way smart."

"Aye. Because of that, the trappers became verra popular. That's why there's always been demon trappers in our family, even when some went Protestant."

Beck retraced to the beginning of the story. "What happened to the hunter who led the raid?"

A wolfish smile filled his host's face. "He vanished a short time after the massacre. They found him up in the heather. It took four men over an hour ta gather enough pieces ta bury."

"Righteous," Beck replied. He took another sip of the whisky, surprised at how things were playing out. Stewart wouldn't be sharing this knowledge unless Beck was going to make master. That stirred a rare feeling of pride.

"So that's why the hunters don't like us much," his host said. "That hasn't changed in over eight centuries. If anythin', it got worse once they came under the Vatican's thumb."

Beck's cell phone rang. He swore at the interruption and flipped it open. "Yeah?"

"It is Justine," a light voice said.

He didn't bother to hide the smile. "How ya doin'?"

"Very well, thank you. Is it possible for us to meet tonight?"

He shot a look at Stewart and then said, "I'm kinda busy."

"I am about to finish the article, and I have a few more questions."

Beck gave in. There was a triumphant lilt in Justine's voice as they worked out a time and a place to meet.

After the call ended, the Scotsman eyed him intently. "More whisky?"

"Yeah. I think I'm gonna need it."

TWENTY-TWO

Riley was met at the door by one of Simon's younger brothers, but which one she wasn't sure. Like his elder sibling, he had the trademark blond hair and deep blue eyes of the Adler clan. He said "the grump" was in the den and that no one could watch the television because of it.

"Have some of the other trappers been here?" she asked. Maybe they could get through to Simon, help him get back on track.

"A few. You just missed one guy, but I don't think he was a trapper," the boy said.

"Who was it?" Riley asked, curious.

The boy shrugged. "He visited him at the hospital, too. I wish he wouldn't come here: Simon just gets weirder after he talks to him."

"What's this guy look like?" Another shrug. *Maybe it was McGuire. He'd make anyone grumpy.* "So Simon's still not himself?" Riley asked. She got a sullen shake of the head. "Then it's time to change that."

"Good luck," his sibling muttered and then disappeared into the kitchen to raid the refrigerator.

Riley took a moment to check herself out in the hall mirror. She'd spent extra time on her hair and makeup and wore the nicest sweater she owned. It was bright blue and did good things for her complexion. She paused again outside the room, unusually nervous.

Please let him be better. She'd do anything to see that golden smile, know that everything was right between them again.

To her relief she found he had the lights on and the curtains open, but a tense frown settled on his forehead as she entered the room. In his lap was a Bible, its pages dog-earred, thin strips of ribbon book-marking different sections. On the table next to her boyfriend was his rosary, an uneaten sandwich, and a can of soda. A bright red afghan sat over his lap, the fringe tickling the carpeted floor. Probably his mother's handiwork.

"Hey, Simon," Riley said, "I brought you cookies from the coffee shop. I thought you might like some." She placed the bag on the couch near him. He ignored it as his blue eyes flickered in irritation.

"What's going on?" he demanded. "No one is telling me anything. I want to know what the Guild is doing."

So much for the "How are you, I've really missed you" part of this conversation. Riley gave in and delivered the news bulletins. "Beck and I did the paperwork so the life insurance policies will be paid. Harper is healing pretty well. He's wondering when you're coming back to work. Oh, and the demon hunters arrived today. Downtown traffic's a mess because of it." She'd have been down there, too, just out of curiosity, but Simon took precedence.

"That wasn't what I asked," her boyfriend retorted. "I want to know how the demons got through the Holy Water. I want to know what the Guild is going to do about it."

Back to that again. She'd tried to explain this before and he'd blown her off. *One more time.* "Father Harrison says there were too many of them, that they overwhelmed the ward. It's been known to happen."

"He told me that, too. I don't buy it."

He doesn't believe his own priest? "You saw them; they kept pushing until the ward broke."

"I didn't see that. I saw them swarm us. I saw them kill and . . ." He looked down at the Bible in his lap, his hands quivering now.

She knew how that was. Did he get panic attacks, too? His blue eyes rose to meet hers. There was no tenderness in them, not like in the past.

"Why did the Five come for you?" he asked in a low voice.

Simon had been too badly hurt to see the Geo-Fiend himself. *So who told you it was after me?*

"I don't know," she admitted. "It's the same one that killed my dad and tried to destroy the library. It must have this thing for Blackthornes."

There was a long pause as Simon shifted in his chair, his face suddenly flushed. He leaned over the side of the chair and picked up a pint water bottle, but he didn't take a drink from it. When he finally spoke, his voice was acidic, full of accusation. "Lucifer has sent his devils after you. What have you done, Riley?"

"Huh?" she spouted. "I haven't done anything." *Except save your life.*

"You're lying. Hell has you in its sights. Why else would your father be at the Tabernacle?"

"Whoa, what are you saying? My father has nothing to do with Hell."

"Your father was summoned by evil magic. That you can't deny. He was researching Holy Water. Why? Was he trying to find a way to break the ward for his unholy master? Did he tell you how to do it?"

Riley gaped at him, astounded at the venom coming from her boyfriend's mouth. "You're accusing my dad of killing those trappers? How can you say that?" She sucked in a hasty breath. "I don't even know if he made it out of that furnace."

He sneered. "Why would it matter? He's dead, or have you forgotten that?"

Riley's mouth fell open, astounded at his callousness. "What is *wrong* with you? You were never like this before. You actually cared about people. Now you're just . . . mean."

"I'm seeing things for what they really are. You, for instance," he said, his hands gripping the water bottle tighter. "If you've sold your soul to Lucifer, just admit it."

Sold my soul?

Riley pointed an accusing finger. "You know, I've cut you a lot of slack, but are you listening to yourself? You're, like, totally paranoid."

"He said you'd say that."

"Who has been talking to you? Is it McGuire?"

"It doesn't matter. All I can think of is what you told me before the meeting started."

"What did I say?" She just remembered the kissing.

"You said it was all part of your cunning plan. Now I'm thinking that's really true, that Lucifer is destroying the trappers from within, using you and your father as his weapons."

She'd only been joking with him that night; there was no plan other than falling in love with this guy. Now he was trampling on her heart, grinding it under his feet.

Riley grabbed the bag of cookies off the couch. "I'll keep these. You'll probably try to exorcise them or something. When you decide to be the old Simon again, give me a call."

He shook his head, resigned. "That Simon is gone. My eyes have been opened to the battle that lies before us. You have sold your soul, or you're a . . ." He took a shuddering breath that hitched at the end. "I have to know the truth." A second later she was drenched in water, launched at her from the bottle Simon held in his hands. Riley shot to her feet, stunned, liquid dripping off her face, chest, and hands. It tingled in a way she knew so well.

"That's Holy Water!" He'd just tested his girlfriend to see if she was a demon.

Immense sadness filled Simon's eyes, like he knew he'd crossed a line from which there was no return, but he wasn't willing to admit the mistake. "It's best we don't see each from now on. I can't be with someone I don't trust."

"What?" *He's breaking up with me? He can't do this. I saved his life.* Maybe if she told him about Martha, about the deal she'd made. *He'll never believe me.*

He waved her away. "You need to leave now, Riley. You're not welcome here anymore."

Tears broke loose and she didn't bother to wipe them away as they threaded down her already damp cheeks. Dropping the bag of cookies, Riley fled the house.

The demons had killed more than just trappers that night. They'd destroyed her future with the boy she loved.

✢

Beck worked on his second cup of coffee, trying to burn off the Scotch before he met Justine in an hour. He had one final question to put to the old trapper before he left, the one that had been nagging at him since the meeting with the hunters.

"What did the priest mean?" he asked. "Who guards our kind?"

Stewart was silent for a long time. Finally, he nodded to himself. "It's only right ya know." He took a lengthy gulp of his liquor. "More history," he said. "Sorry." Another long sip, like he was preparing to deliver bad news. "Some of the angels weren't happy when man was created, not likin' the competition for God's affection. Lucifer, in particular, refused ta bow his knee ta somethin' made of clay."

Beck nodded encouragingly, hoping to keep the man talking.

"God doesn't like someone challengin' Him, so He cast out Lucifer and all of the Divine who'd opposed man's creation. I've heard it was over a third of them; some say over two hundred; others believe it was in the millions."

Beck whistled. "That's a lot of damned angels."

"Aye. The demons first appeared when Adam and Eve gained the knowledge of good and evil. Not too many ta start with, but as we moved ta the cities they came with us and grew in number. The fiends serve a purpose, they're part of God's plan."

Stewart shifted his weight in the chair, gathering his thoughts. "Back at the beginnin', God told Lucifer, 'If ya think these humans are so awful, then test them for me, winnow out the wheat from the chaff. Find those whose faith is unshakable.' So He made Lucifer His Adversary, His *hasatan*. It's the Prince's job ta test our love of God, like a prosecutin' attorney, and he uses the demons for just that purpose."

Beck took a deep breath to try to clear his mind. It had to be all the whisky. Stewart couldn't be saying that Lucifer was on the level, could he? "But he's the Devil."

"There'd ya'd be wrong," Stewart said. "Now mind ya, there *is* a Devil and he's damned evil, but Lucifer is under God's thumb . . . more or less."

Beck worked on his coffee for a time, thinking things through. This was so confusing and made his head buzz worse than the whisky. "Then what did the priest mean?"

There was another lengthy silence as Stewart stared into the fire. "Even Harper doesn't know this, and it's best none of the others do, either."

"Know what?" Beck asked, his patience wearing thin. *Would this man ever answer the question?*

"Hell didn't want us ta die the other night."

"No way," Beck retorted.

"It's all part of the Grand Game, the one that keeps everythin' in balance. Hell does somethin'; Heaven retaliates. Back and forth across eternity. The trick is not ta push the other too far, or there's war."

"But—"

Stewart held up his hand for silence. "Neither God nor Lucifer want Armageddon. They both know it'll go badly and the balance will be upset. Now a few of the Archangels and the Fallen, they're hot ta fight. So there's always tension, in Hell particularly."

Beck ran his hand through his hair, frustrated. "I respect ya and all, but there's no way ya can say Hell wasn't tryin' its best to slaughter us."

Stewart locked eyes with him, his face somber. "Those angels, the ones that kept us alive. Who do ya think sent 'em?"

Damn silly question. "Heaven, of course. Who else would bother savin' our butts?"

"No, lad," Stewart replied, his voice almost a whisper. "Those warrior angels were sent by the Prince of Hell himself. I swear it on the Stewart name."

The old man is serious. He really thinks Hell saved our butts. Beck's mind fought against the obvious question: *If those were Lucifer's folk, then who sent the demons?*

TWENTY-THREE

Driven by some internal autopilot, Riley found herself at St. Brigid's. She parked and turned off the car's engine. Blowing her nose again, she flipped down the visor. Her mascara had realigned itself into vertical smudgy trails down her face. She mumbled a caustic swear word and mopped off as much as she could with a tissue. Hopefully the stuff would come out of her sweater. Not that she'd probably ever wear it again: It'd just remind her of *him.*

"I was such a fool." She'd daydreamed of their future, what it would be like if she and Simon had married, how many kids they'd have. She'd fallen hard for him, and now all that was gone, washed away by his irrational paranoia and a lukewarm bottle of Holy Water.

"You self-righteous hypocrite. How could you do that to me?" He'd really cared for her, she knew it. She'd felt it when they were together, and yet he'd thrown it all away as if it were nothing.

Once inside the room, she sat at the table. This was her life from now on. Once Ori killed the Five she wouldn't have to spend it on hallowed ground, but not much else would change. She would never find a boyfriend who would understand what she did, what she had to do. Beck had been right: There was a huge price for keeping Hell in line, and she was going to pay it for the rest of her life.

The twin roses sat in a glass in the center of the table—the one she'd found on her car and the one Ori had given her the night before. She pulled the glass closer and tested the fragrance. Still strong. The scent seemed to calm her. She closed her eyes and tried to remember Simon before he'd been injured, but the memories were there but too painful to address.

Her cell lit up. If it was Mr. Righteous and he thought he was going to apologize . . .

It was Beck. "Yeah, what?" she snarled.

"I just got a call from Simon. He's carryin' on like a crazy person; says yer workin' for Hell. What's goin' on?" he demanded.

Oh, no. She hadn't wanted Beck to know her love life had imploded.

He didn't wait for her reply. "Here's the deal, girl: I got too damned much on my plate as it is. I don't need this silly kid drama right now."

Kid drama? "Gee, you're all heart."

"Yer boyfriend issues are not my problem. Ya steer clear of him."

How's that's going to work? We have the same master.

And right on cue, her caller added, "Maybe now's a good time to call yer aunt."

Riley hung up on him. To her relief, he didn't call back.

There was more crying over the bathroom sink, choking sobs that felt more like she was standing in front of Simon's coffin than just breaking up with him. Then the doubts came to call, dark, insidious, like nightmares that never give you a moment's peace.

Maybe it's my fault. Maybe if she'd done something different and—

"Stop it!" she shouted at her reflection. "It's not your fault. You did what was right. You saved his life."

And lost him forever.

Riley crawled into the bed, her nose stuffy from crying. Simon's ugly words kept throwing themselves at her like missiles. How could he turn away from her so quickly?

Her phone rang, vibrating across the table and bumping into the drinking-glass vase. She ignored it. It rang a few minutes later. She turned to face the wall, unable to talk to anyone right now without melting down into an emotional mess. Then a text came through. Then another.

Maybe it was something really important. Maybe something had happened to Beck.

It was Peter. His final text message read: CALL ME NOW! I HAVE TO TALK TO SOMEONE!

That sounded ominous, so she gave in and dialed his number. "Peter? What's wrong?"

"Hold on."

There was the sound of footsteps across wood, a door opening and then closing.

"Okay, I'm outside now." His voice was as rough as hers, like he'd been crying.

Peter was never like this, and it scared her. "What's happened?" she asked.

"I finally told Mom I wasn't going with her and the ghouls to Illinois."

Riley winced as she climbed back into the bunk bed.

"She totally lost it. She cried a lot and accused my dad of brainwashing David and me. They had a big fight. It was totally nuclear here."

"That sounds absolutely ugly."

"Yeah. Maybe I was wrong, you know? Maybe I should go with her and . . ."

Her friend sounded so confused. "Where do you think you should be?" Riley asked.

There was a long pause. "With Dad. It's way less tense when I'm with him."

"Then you made the right decision. Your mom is going to have to straighten herself out, and you aren't going to be able to help her do that."

"Dad said the same thing. He wants me to stay here. He says it's time I had space to make my own mistakes."

"Well, if you're anything like me, they'll be stellar," she muttered.

He sighed heavily into the phone. "This is the part where you're supposed to tell me it's going to work out just fine," he said.

"No way I'm saying that. Not with Simon and . . ." Her sigh matched his. "He . . . we broke up this afternoon."

"But I thought you two were doing really well."

"We were until he lost his mind." She blurted out all the gory details, including the "you sold your soul to Hell" accusation.

"Damn," Peter said. "Is there, like, something in the water? First my mom goes crazy, now your . . . ex-boyfriend."

"Seems like we're the only sane ones," she said.

"Always have been," he agreed. "Don't worry, someday you'll meet some cool dude and he won't be an asshat."

Her mind drifted to Ori, but she yanked it back immediately. Two roses did not equal someone who wouldn't break her heart.

"You hold it together, okay?" she urged. "Your mom will be better once she's with her family. Maybe they can get her help."

"That's Dad's hope. Call me in the morning, will you?" Peter asked. "My uncle is going to be here with a U-Haul, and I'm helping Mom pack. I'll need the sanity break from the serious guilt trip she's going to lay on me."

"I'll call. Don't worry; you did the right thing, Peter."

"Then why does it hurt so much?" he murmured.

⁜

Beck pushed open the doors to the Armageddon Lounge, did his perimeter check, then moved toward the bar. If he was going to talk to the press, it would be on his home turf. As a peace offering, he placed a quart jug of Holy Water on the counter.

"That what I think it is?" Zack asked, drying his hand on a bar towel.

"Sure is. Put a line outside all yer doors. It'll keep the evil things out. I'll bring more when ya need it." He didn't like the expense, but he didn't want to have to change bars. Not when he had this one broken in.

Zack nodded his gratitude and asked, "Shiner Bock?"

"Soda," Beck said. That earned him a raised eyebrow. "Been hittin' the whisky heavy tonight; don't need to put beer on top of that."

"You go sober on us and we'll have to close."

"Ha, ha." Beck leaned against the bar, waiting for the beverage. "What did your boss say about the other night?"

"He swore a lot. Thought about banning trappers from the bar."

"Not our fault they were here. Maybe he should change the name of the place, ya know?"

"I suggested that. This"—Zack tapped the jug with a finger—"will help settle his nerves."

Beck paid for his soda and took it to a booth. An open pool table called to him, but he ignored it. A couple of the regulars gave him nods and he returned them. They seemed at ease with him here. He still couldn't wrap his mind around what had happened with those Fours. He'd have to tell Stewart about them once all the other hassles died down. Maybe between them they could take the fiends out.

Beck sipped his icy soda, deep in thought. He respected the old master a lot, but the Scotsman's claim that Hell had saved the trappers' bacon was just too far-fetched. Stewart had said the rest of the tale would have to wait for another time, which meant Beck had no clue who was fielding those demons. *Gotta be Hell. The old guy must have hit his head harder than we thought.*

At least the thing between Riley and Simon was over. He'd been hard on her, but right now his head was full of more important issues that her boyfriend hassles.

Beck groaned. *That's no excuse.*

He remembered what it'd felt like when Louisa had ditched him and now he'd been stone cold with Riley when she was going through the same thing.

Sorry, girl.

If he could talk her into visiting her aunt for a while, maybe Simon would get his head together. Not that she'd ever go back to him: Once you dissed a Blackthorne you were done for life. Simon had been all lined up and he'd managed to throw away the best girl he'd ever meet.

"What a dumbass," Beck muttered. "No way I'd have done that." *Like I'll ever have a chance.*

The twin doors to the lounge pushed open, and all his thoughts about Riley evaporated.

"Well, damn," he said. Justine scanned the room, then her eyes lit on him. Her smile appeared genuine, like she really wanted to be here.

As she headed for the booth with long, sure strides, every eye riveted on her. It was easy to see why: Justine was dressed in a pair of skintight blue jeans, a cream sweater that hugged her breasts, black boots, and an ankle-length black leather coat that flapped open as she moved.

Mighty fine. He rose. "Justine."

"Good evening, Beck," she said.

Remembering his manners, he helped her out of the coat, admiring the rear view as he did. It proved just as enjoyable as the front one. After stashing the coat on the bench seat, Justine slid in and placed her phone on the table.

Beck realized he should buy the lady a drink. "What would ya like?" he asked.

"Something fruity," she replied. "With alcohol."

He wasn't particularly sure what that might be, but he went to the bar and put in the order anyway.

"So who's the hottie?" Zack asked, keeping his voice low enough so the lady in question wouldn't hear him.

"A reporter."

"Niiice," the bartender said, then jammed a slice of orange on the rim of a tall glass and slid it across. Beck paid for it, grimly noting that the more fruit in the drink, the more it cost.

As he approached, Justine delivered a smile that would have knocked a lesser man to his knees.

"Thank you," she said. A quick sip of the drink, a nod of approval, and then the notebook, pen, and digital recorder appeared on the table.

Those implements of torture brought Beck back to earth. "So what do ya want to know?"

"I have talked to some of the other trappers," she said. "Is it true that you remained inside the Tabernacle longer than any of the others? That you saved lives that night?"

Beck felt an uncomfortable twitch crawl over his shoulder blades. "Not really." No need to have people thinking he was better than any of the other trappers. "I just did what I had to do."

"Some might call you a hero."

He frowned. "No. Don't go there," he retorted with more force than he'd intended. "I know what heroes are like; I fought beside them in the war. I'm not one of 'em."

Justine dipped her head in concession. "Then I will not use that word in my article."

"Thank you." He let his tension drain away. "Sorry. Sore subject."

"No, I understand." She took a long sip of her drink. "Why do you think the demons are acting this way?"

"Maybe Lucifer's testin' our defenses. He does that every now and then." That made more sense than Stewart's weird-assed notions of some game between Heaven and Hell.

"You have met with the hunters. What is your impression of them?"

Beck hedged, sensing a trap. "They're pros," he said. That was a safe reply.

"Is that all?" she pressed, smiling at his discomfort.

"Yup."

"They have an impressive track record."

"And one helluva body count," he said before he could stop his tongue.

"Can I quote you on that?" she asked, pen posed over the notebook.

There was no safe answer, so he decided to take the plunge. "Go ahead."

Justine took another long suck on her straw. He found himself watching her more closely than was warranted. *Might as well ask.* "Yer accent isn't anythin' I can place. Where are ya from?"

"I was born in Italy, raised in Ireland, France, and then America. I've been all over the world, so I'm a bit of everything. My Irish friends say I sound American. My American friends say I sound like I can't make up my mind what I am," she said, a full smile gracing her lips. "What about you?"

"Good old Georgia stock," he said. "Lived here and in the Middle East and that's about it."

"At least you know who you are." The reporter looked down at her pad and then up again. "Master Blackthorne's daughter is a trapper now. Does it bother you to have a female in the Guild?"

Sure does. He'd served with women in the Army, knew they could hold their own like any of the guys. He didn't care if a female wanted to be a trapper. His problem was that it was Riley.

"Not really," he lied.

Justine studied him intently. "You put a lot of thought into that."

"She's young and I'd hate to see her hurt." Which wasn't a lie.

"Are you two . . . ?" she asked, delicately raising an eyebrow.

Damn, yer nosy. "No, there's nothin' between us. She's too young."

"So you like your women . . . older?" she asked.

The come-on slid across the table so smoothly he almost didn't catch it. Maybe there was more going on here than he'd figured. "I like women who know what they're doin'," he said.

Justine began to run her slim fingers up and down the side of her glass in a way that made his head spin. "You're staring at me," she said, a touch of a smile at the corners of her mouth.

"Just enjoyin' the view," he said.

"So am I. I don't usually get to say that."

He reluctantly pulled his mind back to work. "Can ya tell me what the hunters are gonna do here?" When she didn't reply right off, he added, "Come on, I've been answerin' all yer questions."

"True," she replied. She reached over and clicked off the recorder. When their eyes met, he nodded in understanding. This was off the record. "They begin by surveying the most infested areas of the city."

"Demon Central, then," he said. "That's where the Gastro-Fiends like to hang out."

"Where is this Demon Central?" she asked.

"It's called Five Points. It's got lots of holes and abandoned buildin's. The Threes love those." He leaned closer, pushing his soda aside. "What will they do after this survey?"

"Once they know the types of demons and their locations, they'll move in and clear them out."

"And if folks get in the way?"

She shrugged. "They try to minimize the collateral damage, but sometimes that isn't possible."

"So who's this Father Rosetti?" he asked. "Are all Rome's priests such tight asses?"

A red eyebrow arched. "Father Rosetti was originally an exorcist for the Vatican. And no, the other priests are not as ardent in their duties. I find it odd: He usually doesn't go out with a team but remains in Rome."

"Then why is he in Atlanta?" Beck quizzed.

"I asked that question, but I did not receive an answer."

The lounge doors swung open and four guys entered, stepping right over the top of the still-wet line of Holy Water. Not demons, then. By the noise they were generating, they already had a significant buzz on. Beck frowned. These guys weren't regulars so they wouldn't know not to jack with him. Since he was with the hottest woman in the place, this might not go well. Especially with four of them.

He caught Justine's eye. "We gotta go. Now."

To his relief she didn't argue but scooped up her belongings. As they reached the doors, one of the guys called out from his place at the bar.

"Hey, where ya goin', babe? Come back here. I'll buy ya a beer."

Justine kept moving, Beck right behind her. When they reached his truck, he set his trapper's bag on the hood.

"Sorry about that," he said, his eyes still on the lounge's entrance. The quartet was still inside, the lure of more booze stronger than chasing tail.

"I am accustomed to it," Justine said as she ran her hand over the demon decals on the side of the truck. "What do these mean?"

"A trapper gets one every time we take down a Three."

She counted them. "Very impressive. Hell must hate you."

He chuckled. "I do my bit. Can I drop ya somewheres?"

She turned toward him, and he could smell her perfume now. Something flowery. When the reporter leaned forward and kissed him, it set his blood on fire. He didn't need a steel pipe to the head to see how this night might play out.

Why not? All he'd done recently was fret over Paul's daughter and work long hours to pay the girl's bills and the only thing he'd gotten was grief in return.

I deserve some fun.

"I am thinking," Justine began, running a hand through his hair, "it would be nice to talk to you about something other than . . . demons."

Beck didn't hesitate: He pulled her tight against him, enjoying the feel of her body close to his. She felt even better than she looked. "I'm game as long as this *talk* is off the record."

"I wouldn't have it any other way," she purred.

TWENTY-FOUR

It was never a good sign when your ex-boyfriend's mom called you at seven in the morning and asked to meet you after Mass. Though Riley was still enduring Category Five breakup grief, she didn't have the heart to turn Mrs. Adler down. Rather than just trudging around to the front of the church to meet the woman after services, Riley set the meeting at the Grounds Zero. She needed food and knew that standing on the church stairs talking about how Mrs. Adler's son was a crazed religious lunatic probably wouldn't be good for anyone.

Riley ordered a salmon-and-cream-cheese bagel, took it to a booth, and ate it without much enthusiasm. Food didn't taste good now, and though this coffee shop made the best hot chocolate, she hadn't ordered it as it would bring back too many memories of Simon. Like the night he'd said he'd wanted to date her. Riley closed her eyes, trying to erase that moment, but it didn't work. She could still hear his gentle voice, feel his hand stroking hers. How great it had felt to know someone cared for her.

"Riley?"

She found Mrs. Adler standing nearby. Her purple dress, matching coat, and hat looked really nice, but the outfit didn't disguise the dark circles under her tired blue eyes.

"I'm sorry I'm late," Mrs. Adler said, sliding into the booth. Her purse clunked on the seat next to her. "I wanted to talk to Father Harrison after Mass."

All the pain and brutal rejection from the day before slammed into Riley like a shock wave. She bit her lip, not wanting to shout her fury aloud, reveal to the world how badly this hurt.

How could you let him do that to me? Why can't you convince him he's wrong? That he made a mistake?

Riley felt the prickle of tears and brushed them away with the back of her hand. "Why is he doing this?" she said, her voice cracking. "He used to be so nice. That's why I liked him so much." *Why I was falling in love with him.* "Now he's . . ."

"Lost," Mrs. Adler replied, her eyes drifting down to her folded hands. "Father Harrison is finding us a therapist, one familiar with post-traumatic stress disorder. Maybe we can help Simon get past this."

There was only a slim thread of hope in the woman's voice.

"You don't think he's going to get better," Riley said before she could stop herself.

Mrs. Adler jammed her lips together while fumbling for a tissue from her purse. After she wiped her eyes, she took a deep breath. "Simon has always been different than the other children, so serious about everything. When he met you, he started to . . ." She struggled for the right word.

"Lighten up?" Riley suggested.

A weary smile came back at her. "That's it exactly. He smiled more and talked about you at dinner. He's never spoken of his girlfriends before. That's when we knew you were right for him."

"Not anymore," Riley said, feeling the tears massing for another assault. "He thinks I'm evil now, that I'm part of a grand hellish conspiracy." She sniffed and rubbed her nose. "I thought if he had time to get over what happened, he'd be better. He's just gotten worse."

Mrs. Adler reached across the table and gently took Riley's hand, much like her son had done the night he and Riley had begun dating. The woman's skin was cool despite having been in contact with the coffee cup and its heated contents.

"We didn't know what Simon had done to you until last night. He didn't tell us. Then some men showed up at our house. One of them was a priest, so I thought maybe Father Harrison had sent them." Mrs. Adler's hand retreated. "They were from the Vatican, and Simon had called them. He told them that . . . you and your father were the reason all those trappers died."

"He called the demon hunters down on me?" Riley cried. Heads turned in their direction. She lowered her voice, but outrage still owned her. "How could he do that to me? What is wrong with him?"

Mrs. Adler shook her head, more tears in her eyes now.

Don't yell at the psycho-ex's mom. It's not her fault. Riley counted to ten very slowly. She made sure her voice was steady. "My dad had *nothing* to do with the ward failing. Neither did I. There were too many demons. Period."

"I know," Mrs. Adler admitted, "but my son is fixated on this. He needs someone to blame instead of God."

That pretty much summed it up.

"Did the hunters believe him?" Riley asked. *Please say they think he's nuts.*

"I'm not sure," Mrs. Adler admitted. "I thought you ought to know about them."

Riley mumbled her thanks, but her mind kept screaming: *He called the hunters!* This was way bad news for both her and the Guild. Her attention snapped as Mrs. Adler rose from the booth, clutching her purse tightly.

Mournful eyes blinked tears away. "I'm so sorry, Riley." The woman swallowed heavily. "Please pray for Simon, pray that he might see the truth and be himself again."

Riley watched as her ex's mom made her way out of the coffee shop, each step laden with worry. *But I did pray for him. Then everything went wrong.*

✛

Justine was already up and in the shower by the time Beck came to full consciousness. It took some time to realize he was in a hotel room at the Westin. He didn't remember much sleep overnight, but that was okay. It hadn't bothered him that when they weren't going at it, she'd asked him a lot of questions about Atlanta and her demons and about the demon traffickers. Some girls did that. It meant they were interested in more than what he was packing in his jeans.

He rolled out of bed and used the toilet. Luckily it was one of those separate from the shower because the running water was getting to him. He moved to the sink and splashed water on his face. Then smirked. Justine had left marks on his neck.

Yer a fireball, that's for sure.

Beck dressed. He'd just finished tying his boots when Justine entered the room wrapped in a large white towel. Her hair was still damp. She came to him immediately, cupping his jaw in her small hands. Then she kissed him, tasting of toothpaste. He let his arms go around her waist, pulling her closer.

"Are you leaving already?" she asked, reproachfully.

"Got to. I'm meetin' with Master Stewart."

"Will I see you tonight?" she whispered after the next kiss ended.

He'd be with her whenever she wanted, but he just couldn't admit that right out. He had his pride to think of. "Maybe."

"So it's demons first, then me?" she teased as she sank onto the bed next him.

"Yes. No . . ." *Ah, hell, I don't know.* He kissed her again. Finally, he let go of her, but it took a lot of willpower. Claiming his jacket from a chair, he headed for the door.

"Beck?" He turned at the sound of her soft voice. She was curled up on the bed, sending him invitations he didn't dare accept. "If you speak to Elias Salvatore, don't mention you've been with me."

"Why?" he asked, curious.

"Elias and I were once lovers," she said matter-of-factly. "He is very jealous. It could go badly for you if he finds out about us."

I slept with the top hunter's woman? Part of him was jazzed, but the other part wasn't happy at the news. Without knowing it, he'd done the one thing Stewart had warned him against: He'd made a demon hunter look like a fool.

✛

Students streamed out of the old Starbucks, calling out to each other and hopping into their rides. "Feels strange not having to run home and check in with The Warden," Peter said as he and Riley walked toward her car after class.

Riley unlocked the driver's side door and dropped her messenger bag onto the front seat. "You'll get used to it."

"I called the city today to find out who picks up their empty Holy Water bottles, in case the guard at the recycling place was lying."

"Any luck?" Riley asked.

Peter leaned against the side of the car. "I got blown off. The secretary chick said it would be a breach of security to tell me that information, because someone might want to sabotage the shipment."

"Why would someone sabotage a shipment of empty bottles?" Riley asked.

"I pointed that out, but she wouldn't budge."

"That sucks," Riley grumbled.

"Don't worry, we'll find a way to get the info. I'll be able to help more now that I don't have to be chained in my room."

Riley eyed her best friend. "Think you'll be able to cope?"

"Totally. It's like I've been pardoned from a life sentence. I'm worried someone will realize they've made a mistake."

"They didn't." *Neither did you.* "So what are you doing tonight?"

"The house is just going to be a dead zone. I was thinking of going to the library, start on my homework. What about you?"

"No, I'm doing witchy stuff," Riley said. "A friend of mine is going to summon my dad's spirit so maybe we can figure out who stole him."

"Wow. Ah, can I come along?" Peter asked, his face alight.

"It could be kinda weird," Riley hedged.

"I'm good with weird. Come on, how about it? I need a little excitement right now."

"I'm not so sure, Peter. If something goes wrong . . ." Maybe she was being selfish, but Riley wanted him to come along. Still, he had to know what he was getting into. "When I say weird, I really mean it."

He debated for a moment, then extracted his cell phone. "I have to let Dad know where I am. It's part of our agreement. So how late and where?"

What would Ayden think if she brought him along?

Riley gave in. "Little Five Points and"—she consulted her own phone for the time—"I'm thinking we'll be done by eight."

"You'll drop me home?" When she nodded, he stepped a few paces away and dialed his father. As Peter pleaded his case, which did not include mentioning that they were going to visit a real live witch, Riley took that opportunity to check her text messages. She'd heard one arrive during class but she knew not to check it. Mrs. Haggerty was not into modern technology.

It was from Ori: MEET ME AT THE MARKET AT NINE?

Her fingers sent a YES before she had time to think.

Peter gave a thumbs-up. "Good to go," he announced, rejoining her. "Dad says I shouldn't get arrested or I will end up in Illinois sharing a bed with the twins."

"That's a brutal threat," Riley replied.

"Totally brutal. The ghouls have been known to wet their bed."

TWENTY-FIVE

Riley had expected she'd have to do a lot of explaining about Peter's presence, but Ayden only arched one eyebrow when they were introduced.

"Cool phoenix tattoo," Peter said, admiring the colorful artwork that spread from the witch's neck downward into her cleavage. Unlike Simon, he did allow his eyes to linger.

Phoenix? "Ah, what happened to the dragon tattoo you had?" Riley asked.

"I changed it," Ayden replied, still studying Peter intently as if she were weighing his soul. "It's easy when you wield magic." She shifted her full attention to Riley. "You sure about this summoning?"

"I'm good. It might get some of my questions answered. If this doesn't work, I'm out of options."

"So be it." The witch led them on a journey through the interior of the Bell, Book, and Broomstick, where they walked past displays of crystals, spheres, and all sorts of metaphysical goodies. The store reeked of incense. It was hard to pick out which scent was stronger than another, so it all became a nose blur. Once they reached the back room, Ayden loaded them up with boxes of candles and other paraphernalia. Peter got to carry a sword, which pleased him immensely.

"Is this like a real one?" he asked, gripping the scabbard tightly.

"No point in owning any other kind," Ayden said, her head deep in a closet. Out came a velvet cloak in rich purple. She draped it over her arm and then herded them toward the rear door. As they exited the building, their escort flipped a switch, illuminating a large courtyard with floodlamps.

"Do you know Mortimer Alexander?" Riley asked as her eyes adjusted to the garish light. "He lives down the street. He's the Summoners' Advocate."

"I've heard of him," Ayden replied. "Witches and summoners don't socialize."

"Because of the magical war?"

Ayden gave her a look. "How'd you hear about that?"

"Mort mentioned it. He said there'd been bad blood between you guys."

"Still is. Some of the necros are pretty decent, but their leaders have their heads up their butts. But then so do some of us witches."

Peter had wandered ahead and now stood transfixed by a circle of stones. There were twelve of them—old, stark white, and sticking upward about two feet out of the red Georgia clay. The whole circle was about thirty feet in diameter and included a fire pit and a stone altar.

"This is so unreal," he explained. "Like out of a movie or something."

While Ayden laid out her gear, Riley took the opportunity to check out the courtyard. The windows in the building to the left were bricked up, the roof too steep for anyone to climb up and see what the witches were up to. The buildings to their right and in front of them did have windows. Not a private site, but still better than most inside the city. A wall of concrete blocks, probably about six feet tall, surrounded the entire courtyard. Three-quarters of the wall was covered in a giant mural.

Riley wandered over to the closest section and studied the images. At first it just looked like an ordinary forest scene, then she spied the figures.

"Fairies!" she said. "There's like a zillion of them!" There were tall, stately fairies riding magnificent horses with flowing silver manes and tiny fairies peeking out from under mushroom caps and leaves. Some held swords, and others, chalices filled with golden nectar. Everywhere she looked there was a little face peering back at her. They were all unique. Farther down the wall the scene changed to marshy grassland. She soon found the fairies among the grasses and reeds, though they looked different than the ones in the forest scene.

Peter joined her at the wall and she pointed out her discoveries. "Aren't they amazing?"

"You really think they exist?" he asked.

"They do," Ayden replied as she placed a goblet and a ritual knife on the altar.

"You've seen them?" Riley asked.

"Sure," Ayden replied, in the same tone of voice as if Riley had asked if she'd ever seen a UPS truck.

"No way. They're just make-believe."

The witch cocked an eyebrow. "You mean like demons?"

"Oh." Maybe there was a lot more to this mystical-world stuff than Riley realized. *A Midsummer Night's Dream* was one of her favorite Shakespearean plays, mostly because of the fairies.

"Are they really cool? I mean, like Oberon and Titania cool?"

Ayden didn't reply until the brazier came to life, flicking pillars of flame into the air. "The Fey are a lot like us. They can be arrogant and vindictive or kind and helpful, if they're in the mood. The problem is you never know which mood they're in until it's too late."

"Are we going to see any of them tonight?" Peter asked hopefully.

"Not likely. If we were out in the country, maybe."

"Who painted this mural?" Riley asked, trailing her fingertips over the painted wall. The images almost seemed alive.

"I did, along with a couple of the others in my circle."

"*Your* circle?"

"I'm a High Priestess," Ayden replied.

You never told me that.

"So what's going to happen here?" Peter asked as they moved to join the witch in the center of the circle.

"I will set a circle and call up Paul Blackthorne's spirit."

"So no big deal, huh?"

"It could get lively," Ayden replied.

Peter chewed on that for a time. "Define *lively*, please."

Ayden continued her preparations, setting a green candle on the ground, then about ten feet away she put down a yellow one. "It all depends on what type of magical landmines I trigger."

"So we could get hurt?"

"Perhaps, but if you remain inside the circle you should be okay."

"*Should . . .*" Peter frowned. "If you were me, would you stay or take off?"

"Depends your freak factor," Ayden said, rising to her feet and dusting off her hands. "If you can handle creepy stuff, then I'd say it'd be worth staying. If not, best to wait inside the building. It's warded so you'll be safe there."

"Warded," he murmured to himself.

"Peter, you don't have to do this," Riley said.

He screwed his face up in thought. "Yeah, I do. Count me in."

"Then let's get this done," Ayden replied. "First, I will honor the four elements, lighting the candles that represent those elements." The witch adjusted the white tapers in the center of the altar. "Then I'll light two that represent the God and Goddess."

"Is that where we do the ritual sacrifice?" Peter joked, uneasily.

"Volunteering, are we?" Ayden asked. Peter clamped his mouth shut.

The witch turned and frowned at the building behind them like she'd forgotten something. "Could one of you turn off the outside lights? The switch is just inside the door."

Riley took care of the problem. As she returned to the circle, her nerves kicked into high gear. Her very best friend in the whole world was here. What if something went wrong? What if Peter got hurt?

"It'll be okay," she whispered as she crossed through the stone circle. "It has to be."

Ayden wore the velvet cloak now, her russet brown hair flowing over her shoulders. A circlet nestled among her curls, braided silver with delicate leaves. In a fluid movement born of practice, the sword slid out of its scabbard. The witch raised it reverently toward the sky like an ancient queen from an Arthurian tale. The light of the brazier threaded a thin, molten line of fiery gold along the blade's edge.

Ayden turned, pointed the tip of the sword toward the yellow candle at one of the four corners. In a clear voice, she said, "I call forth the Element of Air. Protect all within this circle from those who would do us harm."

Riley blinked when the candle burst into life. Ayden hadn't struck a match. She couldn't with the sword in her hands.

How did you . . . ?

Peter waggled his eyebrows and mouthed "Cool!" Maybe it was good she'd brought him along. He hadn't acted this happy about anything for a long time.

The witch turned toward the south and the red candle. "I call forth the Element of Fire. Guard us and warm us in our journey." That candle blazed. When Ayden completed the invocation with the remaining two candles, there was a weird popping sensation, like they'd been enveloped by some sort of force field. Riley knew how this worked: It was like when she'd set the candle circle at the cemetery to protect her father's grave.

Ayden carefully laid the sword on the altar then lit the two white candles with a match, invoking the presence of the deities in a clear voice. If Simon were here he'd be having kittens by now. Raising her arms in the air, the witch called for protection, for wisdom, and for knowledge. Then she waved Riley and Peter forward.

Edging close to the altar, Riley shot a quick look up at the window above them. Gazing down at them was a white-haired lady, her elbows resting on the windowsill.

"She likes to watch," Ayden explained.

"Is she a witch?"

"No. Just curious what kind of mischief we might be up to."

Knowing Ayden, there wouldn't be any. She took this stuff way serious.

"I'm going to cast the spirit summoning now. I want you to visualize your father. Try to pick a happy memory. That might make it easier to call him."

Riley's mind returned to one of the last moments they'd spent together. They'd been in the car after the emergency Guild meeting. They'd talked about a movie night, just the two of them. It wasn't the best memory, but the strongest right now. A sharp pang of loss cut through her, but she pushed it aside, focusing on her father's voice, his smile. How good it felt when he was around and how much she missed him.

As she held that single memory close to her heart, she could hear Ayden chanting something. There was the smell of aromatic herbs, then more chanting.

The air around them shifted as a strange prickle danced across her face and hands.

"We ask that Paul Blackthorne's spirit come to us," Ayden called out. "Come to his only child so that we may know that he is safe."

The prickling sensation increased, almost to the point of discomfort. Riley blinked open her eyes to find the stone circle around them glowed a soft white. Peter's eyes were wide in amazement, and his mouth had dropped open.

"Riley?" a voice said. It glided across her mind like a soft breeze.

"Dad?" she called out.

Paul Blackthorne stepped out of nowhere, like through a hole in the air. He wasn't in the suit he'd been buried in but in his Georgia Tech jacket, jeans, and a sweatshirt—the clothes he'd been wearing the night he'd died.

"Welcome, spirit of Paul Blackthorne," Ayden said solemnly. "You are much missed."

He gave a grave nod, then turned those sad brown eyes on his daughter. She was trembling now.

"I miss you, Riley," he said, his voice dry and thick.

This was as bad as when Beck had come to her door to tell her she was an orphan. "I want to get you back, Dad. I need to know who took you. Was it Ozymandias?"

No reply.

Maybe he doesn't understand. "We're being blamed for breaking the ward at the Tabernacle. The hunters are in town now. You've got to tell them the truth."

"Not yet," he replied.

"Is there anything you *can* tell us?" the witch urged.

Her father's eyes flicked to Ayden and then back to his daughter.

"I love you, Riley. You're stronger than you believe. I'm sorry for what has happened and for what will happen. It is my fault."

Then the spirit of Paul Blackthorne began to fade.

"Wait! No, don't go!" Riley shouted. *After all this and he's taking off?*

Ayden chanted again and the vision stabilized. The air just behind Riley's father began to boil in a red and gold maelstrom. Then something materialized in that very spot.

Towering over them was a dragon, at least twenty or more feet high. It was probably the one from the cemetery.

"Oh, my Goddess." Ayden latched on to Riley's arm and then did the same with Peter's. "Don't move. Don't break the circle!"

There was a screech of shock, and their spectator slammed her window shut, as if a single pane of glass would be any protection against this monstrosity.

"Can you make it go away?" Riley whispered.

Ayden didn't reply, murmuring under her breath. Riley caught the word *protection* more than once.

A low growl issued from the thing's cavernous mouth, sending a trickle of brilliant iridescent flames into the night air. "Cease!" the creature bellowed, and the witch fell silent.

Ayden clamped her eyes on the beast. "What do you seek, dragon?" she asked, her voice firm and level.

The creature ignored her, its glittering eyes only on Riley. "Blackthorne's daughter," it said. "Do not fail us."

"Who are you?" Riley demanded. "Why did you take my dad?"

It wrapped its powerful forelegs around her father's form. "To protect him from those who would use his knowledge for their own gain."

"I love you, Pumpkin," her dad called out. "I'll see you soon."

The summoning vanished with a loud clap of thunder that reverberated throughout the neighborhood, rattling windows and setting off car alarms.

"That was a bit over the top," Ayden grumbled, releasing her grip on Riley's arm.

"Oh . . . dammit!" Riley shouted. "We didn't learn a thing!" She had failed. Again. It was like her life was cursed.

She felt the panic attack coming but couldn't stop it. Her lungs collapsed, and she began to shake, her vision constricting to the section of the courtyard where her father had disappeared.

Her friends began whispering to each other, but she didn't understand what they were saying. Darkness crept in from the corners of her vision like twilight in a forest. The next breath hitched and she struggled to pull air inside her chest. The next breath was worse and she slumped to her knees.

"Riley?" It was Peter. He was close to her now, touching her hand. His fingers were trembling. "You remember the first day we met at school? How you didn't have a pencil so I loaned you one? Do you remember which one it was?"

Why is he asking me this? My dad is dead and that thing has him and I have to stop Armageddon and—

"Come on, Riley, you should remember this. It's easy. You gave me crap about it for ages," Peter urged. Then she knew what he was doing: he was recalling a good memory, trying to exorcise the fear that rode her like a fully armored warrior.

"Gollum," she panted, pulling her eyes to meet his.

Peter smiled through his worry. "Yup. You told me that any guy who had a *Lord of the Rings* pencil just had to be your friend for life."

Between the shallow breaths, she tried to match his smile. "I'm afraid, Peter. God, I'm so afraid."

"So am I," he whispered, then his arms went around her and he embraced her.

She hadn't lost everything. She still had her friends. Sometimes they were the only thing that kept you going. Her breathing eased and Peter noticed. He loosened his grip.

"You promised me weird," he said.

And I delivered. He only let go of her when she took a deep, full breath. "Thanks."

He nodded but didn't say anything that would make it harder for her. Ayden gave a relieved sigh then turned toward where the dragon had been. She stared at the spot for some time, unmoving.

"Ah, Ayden?" Peter asked.

"Give me a moment," she said. She took a deep breath like she was scenting the air, then blew it out a few seconds later. "And the verdict is: not a necromancer."

"What? It has to be," Riley blurted as she scrambled to her feet.

The witch turned toward them, perplexed. "That's what you'd expect, but it's not the case. I'm sensing older, more . . . primeval magic. Necromantic sorcery has a certain feel to it. This magic I've never felt before."

"Which means?" Riley asked.

"Which means there's a new player in the game. Remember what the dragon said: Your father was raised from his grave for his protection."

"But from who?"

"Whom," Peter corrected automatically. When Riley gave him a glower, he shrugged his shoulders in apology.

"Ozymandias is my favorite candidate," the witch replied, "but who wields the kind of power needed to cross the Eldest of the Summoners?"

Riley had no clue.

"I don't want to be a buzzkill here," Peter began, "but are you sure it was your dad?"

"It had to be," Riley said. "He called me Pumpkin. I always hated that nickname, but he thought it was cute."

Ayden was still pensive, her brows furrowed. "So what is the takeaway message here?"

"Dragons are damned scary, even if they are made of magic?" Peter quipped.

Ayden's frown diminished. "I'm beginning to like you, Peter King." He grinned in response.

"Do not fail us," Riley said. "Whatever I'm supposed to do, I'd better not blow it."

Riley and the witch traded looks. Then Riley shook her head: No way was she going to tell Peter about her bargain with Heaven. His life was complicated enough without him worrying about the end of the world.

Silence fell between them as Ayden released the magic and broke the circle. They helped her pack up the witchy supplies and tote them back into the store. When Ayden had stowed away all the gear, she unlocked the front door. They all stood there, awkwardly, like no one knew what to say.

Peter sniffed. "Food. I'll . . . catch up with you in a moment." Without waiting for her response, he headed down the alley toward the café.

"He eats like there's no tomorrow," Riley observed. *And he might be right.*

"He is a good friend to have," Ayden said. "Tell him what's going on. He has a role to play."

Riley gaped at the woman. "Was that, like, a prophecy or something?"

"I just know things." The witch looked in the opposite direction, down the alley that led to Mort's house. "You should talk to the summoner tonight."

It wasn't a suggestion. "You think he knew what we were up to?"

"He'd have felt the magic. I'd be interested to hear where he thought it came from."

Mort's housekeeper admitted her to the house without comment, like Riley had been expected, and led her to the circular room that smelled of wood smoke. Mort was at his desk, stacks of books mounded around him like a fortress of words. A plate of strudel sat at his elbow.

He rose. "What the hell was that?" he demanded.

The evening had been so outlandish, so scary, that Riley couldn't help herself: She started to laugh. What else could she do? When she finally regained control, she said, "I have no idea. My witch friend doesn't, either."

Mort sank back onto his bench, his fingers tented in a thoughtful pose. "What I felt was old magic, so old the summoners don't have a name for it. Tell me what happened."

Riley sat opposite him at the table. "Well, we got a dragon," she began and then related the rest of the tale. Mort didn't interrupt. "I've run out things to try," she said.

Mort nodded in sympathy. "Ozymandias has a reward out for your father's corpse, but no one has come forward to claim it."

"Everybody wants my dad," she said bitterly.

"So it seems. A loan company has filed suit against the Society, claiming we're preventing them from reacquiring their *asset,* one Mr. Paul Blackthorne. Apparently you owe them money," Mort said.

Riley groaned.

"Just so you know, I've issued a magical invitation. If for some reason the summoner loses control of your father's spirit, I've invited the spirit to take shelter here."

Riley stared at him. "You mean my dad might make a break for it?"

"Sometimes that happens, but in this case whomever conducted the summoning seems quite powerful, so I doubt we'll have any luck."

And if it wasn't a necromancer . . .

Riley stared down at her hands. There was dirt under her fingernails, probably from when she was having her panic attack in the courtyard. "What if I never find him?" she asked.

"Then in a year we'll just hope he's back in the ground and at peace."

That wasn't the answer she wanted. No, she wanted her dad's kidnapper to bleed, to hurt as bad as she did. After thanking Mort for all his help, Riley left the way she'd come. Behind her, she could hear the summoner mumbling under his breath, the thump of books falling open. He hadn't given up, no matter what he'd said.

Neither will I.

Her friends waited for her in front of the witch shop. Peter handed over a paper bag.

"Food. You need it. You get any skinnier and you can model in New York."

"Thanks," she mumbled. Riley opened the bag and found it contained a turkey sandwich and a supersized chocolate chip cookie. *Yum.* "Thanks," she repeated, this time with more enthusiasm.

Ayden lightly touched her shoulder. "What did the summoner say?"

"He had no clue who it was."

"As I figured. I think it's best you remember what your father said: You're stronger than you believe. That's important. Spirits don't usually lie."

The witch had spaced on the other thing her father had said: "I'll see you soon." Since it didn't look like Riley was going to retrieve him from whomever ripped off his corpse, that meant only one thing.

This might be the last cookie I ever eat.

TWENTY-SIX

The sensible part of Riley knew she should be at the church, but she was tired of hiding like some scared little kid. Everyone reached their breaking point, and she was way past it. If Ori was right, her being out like this might lure the Five closer, and he could kill the thing.

Then I'll be free.

She heard someone call her name and found the freelance demon hunter striding across the open field at the edge of the market. No way around it, Ori was made of awesome—yummy on so many levels you just didn't know where to start. Simon was handsome, but Ori redefined the word.

Just thinking the name of her now ex-boyfriend made her wince like someone had jammed spikes under her fingernails. This should be Simon hanging with her, laughing and being with her. *But it isn't.*

When Ori reached her, she murmured her hello, trying to sound upbeat. He examined her for a moment, as if he were trying to see behind her mask.

"You were up to something tonight in Little Five Points. Very noisy. And magical. I almost thought it was the Five for a moment."

"A witch friend of mine summoned my dad's spirit. I thought we could find out who stole him." She hitched her shoulders. "Not so much. He wouldn't tell us anything."

"I'm truly sorry about that," Ori said. "I know how much you miss him."

"This whole thing has been an epic failure. I promised him I'd keep him safe in his grave. Didn't do that. Promised him I'd find his body. Blew that one, too."

"Well, you're not the only one failing," he admitted, his tone darker now. "The Five is hiding, biding its time."

"So someone really is helping it?" Riley asked, puzzled.

"Hell *is* known for its alliances. Archfiends make pacts with lower-level Hellspawn, gathering in souls and power. The Five could owe its allegiance to another, one who wanted your father dead and is now sheltering his killer."

"Great. The manual never mentioned that whole 'dealing in souls' part."

"I'm thinking there's more weight on your shoulders tonight than just your father. What else is troubling you?"

Might as well unload it all. "My boyfriend and I broke up." On impulse, she told him the gruesome story. Including the part with the Holy Water.

Ori glowered. "Paul would not have harmed his fellow trappers. It was not in his character. Or yours, either."

Riley felt a surge of joy that someone believed in her dad. Believed in her. She slowed her pace, then stopped altogether. "Thank you. That means a lot to me."

To her astonishment, Ori cupped her face with his hands and carefully placed a kiss in the very center of her forehead. The merest brush of his lips sent heat racing through her veins.

"I will destroy that Hellspawn, and then you will not have to be afraid ever again," he said, his midnight-black eyes inches from hers.

"You would do that for me?" she whispered.

"For you . . . and your father," he said, then removed his hands. Before she could think of what to say, someone else called out her name. Riley knew that voice anywhere.

"Oh, no! What's he doing here?"

A familiar figure tromped toward them, the scowl on Beck's face promising trouble.

Riley hated to suggest it, but . . . "That's my dad's trapping partner and he'll be furious if he finds out you're here with me. He won't understand."

"That would be his problem," Ori replied simply. "I'm going nowhere."

Riley groaned. She took a deep breath and waited for the trapper to reach them.

"Beck." *Don't make a scene, please?*

That unspoken plea was wasted. "What are ya doin', girl?" Beck demanded. "The sun's down. Why aren't ya at the church?" He ground to a halt a short distance away, his hand knotted around the strap to his duffel bag. She could see his knuckles whiten.

His full attention moved to Ori. "Wait a minute; I know that face. Ya were at the Armageddon the other night."

Ori hangs out at a pool hall? He didn't seem the type.

"I remember you," her companion replied. "You were playing pool with a summoner. You were letting him win."

The trapper puffed up. "Who are ya? What are ya doin' with Riley?"

"Beck!" Riley retorted. That was just rude.

Ori moved closer to her, like he was claiming her in some way. His hand gently touched her elbow and gave it a reassuring squeeze.

"I asked ya a question," Beck said.

"The name is Ori, and I'm her date for the evening. Why is any of this your concern?"

Date?

Beck blinked a couple times before his eyes narrowed. "I'm the guy ya have to deal with if ya think yer goin' out with her."

"You didn't tell me you had a brother," Ori said, looking over at Riley. When he winked, she had to struggle to keep the smile off her face.

"Look, dumbass," Beck growled. "I don't know what yer game is, but yer not playin' it with her."

"Hey!" Riley said, stepping forward and snapping her fingers in front of Beck's face. "I'm not invisible. If I want to go out with someone, I'll do it, and you don't have any say in the matter."

He scowled. "Like yer a great judge of character. Yer first boyfriend was an abusive bastard, and the last one was a self-righteous dick."

"So where do you fall on that scale?" Ori inquired.

Riley almost choked.

In response, Beck's shoulders tightened like he was ready to charge into battle. "So what's your story?"

Ori's good humor disappeared. "I'm a freelance demon hunter."

She was surprised he'd let that one slip.

"Figures." Beck smirked. "Lancers aren't welcome here, not unless ya decide to become a trapper and join the Guild, do honest work for a change."

"You're very cocky for someone who almost lost his soul to a Mezmer in a pool hall."

Beck's face went pale. "Now look here, ya son of a—"

"Did he tell you about that?" Ori cut in. "Apparently not. I'd be ashamed, too."

Riley cringed. "Enough, guys," she said, tugging on her escort's arm.

"Girl . . ." Beck said, his voice a low growl.

She stepped between them again, though it was a dangerous place to be with all the testosterone in the air. "I don't care what you think, Beck, so just leave me alone. It's time I made my own decisions."

"Then don't come cryin' to me when it all goes to hell," Beck replied.

"Deal."

She turned her back on him and walked away, Ori at her side. Be-

hind them she could hear Beck swearing in both English and Hellspeak.

"Colorful fellow. Do you think he's watching?" Ori whispered.

"Oh, definitely."

Ori ran his arm around her waist and pulled her so close their hips
bumped. "Good. I hope he gets an eyeful."

"You're wicked," Riley said, grinning up at him.

"You don't know the half of it," Ori replied.

When the adrenaline from the encounter wore off, Riley found herself
more tired than she'd expected. It'd been a long and pretty much fruitless day. The only positive part was walking next to her. She felt good
around Ori, much like she had when she'd been with Simon. She wasn't
sure what that meant.

Abruptly her companion slowed his pace, then he stopped and
scanned the area around them.

"Is Beck following us?" she asked. A shake of the head. "Is the Five?"
Would it come for me here? Of course it would. Being in the market wouldn't
mean a thing to a demon.

"No." He mumbled something under his breath and then began
walking again, faster now, forcing Riley to catch up with him.

What's got him spooked?

As they turned the corner toward the road where she'd parked her
car, someone bumped her from behind. Her head spun for a second,
and then her vision cleared. When she looked around, whoever had
bumped her was gone.

A sharp stinging sensation came from her left hand. "Ouch," she
said, shaking it to clear the discomfort. There didn't seem to be anything wrong with it, but it still stung. From the way it felt, she'd expected to see a big welt or something.

Ori swore in Hellspeak.

"I'm okay," she said, rubbing the sore area. That only seemed to make it worse.

"Let me see." He took her hand in his, and the pain eased.

"Wow, how did you . . ." Riley looked up at him as she spoke, then all the air fled her lungs.

Ori shimmered in a harsh, pulsating light. She might have been able to ignore that, but the immense wings behind him pretty much sealed the deal. They sat tight against his back and were pure white, each feather shimmering in the lights from the tents around them. As she stared in wonder, a woman walked by them toting a basket and humming to herself, failing to notice that Riley's *date* glowed like a supernova.

I've been holding hands with an angel? Having hot thoughts about one of Heaven's peeps?

"You're an—"

Ori shook his head in dismay. "Not here," he said. He flicked his hand and the scene changed.

⁌

Riley found herself surrounded by a deep green carpet of grass, blades bending in the faint breeze. Nestled within the green were bluebells, and in the distance, white clumps. The clumps moved.

"Sheep?" she asked, surprised.

Every now and then one would raise its woolly head, move a few steps, and start grazing again. They didn't have sheep in the market, and there wasn't grass like this, or a big blue sky.

"What is all this?" A scent tickled her nose and she placed it immediately. *Watermelon.*

Riley found Ori under a broad oak tree that had to be at least a century old, his wings hidden now. A dark blue blanket lay on the ground, along with a wicker picnic basket. On the blanket was a white china plate with slices of succulent watermelon, the black seeds dotting the firm red flesh.

"I thought we needed privacy," he explained.

It was all so real. "Where is this place? How did we get here?"

"Just accept this as a gift from me." He waved her closer.

A picnic with an angel? Her mind finally completed its reboot. And went suspicious.

"You're not here to have me stop Armageddon or anything, are you?"

"No," he said smiling.

"How do I know you're not a demon playing games with my head?"

"You don't," he said. "You just have to trust me." He smiled and beckoned to her again. "Come on, the watermelon is really good."

Riley groaned to herself as she hiked up the hill. She paused at the edge of the blanket, arms crossed over her chest. She still wasn't buying all this. "Why haven't I been able to see your . . . angelness until now?"

"Because the timing wasn't right," he replied. "Unfortunately, one of the other Divines thought it would be amusing to alter that situation in the middle of the marketplace." From the low rumble in his voice it was clear he wasn't pleased by the prank.

"You mean I got bumped by an angel?"

A nod. Ori gestured toward the plate of watermelon. "Your favorite, I believe." He knelt next to the picnic basket and retrieved a bottle of red wine, followed by two crystal glasses. Then a plate of cheese, sliced peaches, and frosty grapes.

"How do you do that?" she quizzed.

Ori's face lit with a smile. "Divines are allowed small bits of creation," he said, as if it were nothing.

She took another look around, inhaling the fresh air. "This isn't small, Ori. This is amazing!"

Finally Riley gave in to the moment. What else could she do? It beat being bored to tears in a church basement. Besides, the smell of the watermelon was getting to her.

He fed her sliced peaches by hand, then the wine and the watermelon. They laughed as the juice rolled down her chin. The taste was extraordinary, like it was the best ever.

"Why does it feel different when I'm with you?" she asked dreamily. "Is it because of what you are?"

"That's it exactly." He seemed at ease here, not tense like he'd been at the market.

"So are you like my guardian angel or something?" *That would totally rock.*

"No, I'm not."

"Oh," she said, sincerely disappointed. "But you kept the Five from killing me."

"It wasn't your time to die," Ori said simply.

Which meant he knew when her time *was* up.

She couldn't ask that question. "So what do you do as an angel?"

"You mean besides giving pretty girls roses?" he said.

"Yes, besides that."

"I'm a problem solver. I handle difficult situations."

"Like . . ." she quizzed, beckoning with her hand for further information.

"Like that Geo-Fiend who killed your father. It's a rogue demon. It must be destroyed."

"So that's what you do all the time?" she said, sneaking another piece of watermelon.

"I told you I was a demon hunter," he said, brows furrowed. "I didn't lie."

"You just shaded the truth, a lot. You so didn't mention the 'I've got wings' thing."

"I didn't want to scare you," he said, his voice softer now.

"Do you always hang around pool halls?" she jested.

"Not usually. It was lucky I was there that night, or the Mezmer would have had your friend's soul."

Riley stilled. "Was it that close?"

"Yes. He was at the breaking point. I made sure it didn't happen."

She let out a whoosh of air in relief. "I wasn't sure if he was okay. Beck wouldn't say much about it. Pride and all."

"He is his own master. Pride and all."

Riley cocked her head. "Why did you save him?"

"Because he's important to you, so that makes him important to me."

She opened her mouth to protest, then realized it would be futile. "I do like Beck, at least when he's not being a jerk."

"I thought so," Ori said, then popped a grape into his mouth. "Besides, you've lost too much already."

"Like my dad," Riley said. "Do you know who summoned him?"

"No, I don't. It might shock you to know that Divines aren't all-knowing."

"Of course. That would be too easy."

Ori put his arm around her, drawing her close. Initially she wasn't sure if she wanted that, but eventually she snuggled next to him. She knew from the post-Allan experience that rebound romances weren't a good idea. A rebound with an angel? That didn't even register on the cosmic scale of "not a good idea."

"I disagree," Ori said. He delicately tipped her chin up with a finger. His eyes told her what he intended. And then he kissed her, without waiting for her verdict on the subject. Like the wine and the watermelon and everything else around them, the kiss was beyond what it should be. Every nerve in Riley's body tingled, a Simon-level kiss on steroids. They kissed again, this time more deeply. Her body began to hum, like it was lit from within by a strange erotic fire.

Riley pulled out of his arms, her head swimming. "Too much wine," she said, though she'd only had one glass.

Ori graciously allowed her the fib. He leaned back against the tree, one foot propped up. A scoundrel with that black hair skimming over his shoulders and those bold, dark eyes.

Get a grip, girl.

"Why are you are doing this? Spending time with me, I mean. You could have just followed me and I would have never known you were there."

"I feel alive when I'm with you."

She barely subdued the snort. "You're an angel. You hang with God and all those other divine guys. I'm just . . . me."

"You're Riley Anora Blackthorne," he replied, as if that settled the matter. "You deserve better than what you've had."

Her mind traitorously returned to Simon and how he found more comfort with his rosary than he did with her. And Beck, the constant annoyance in her life. What would they think if they knew she was hanging with an honest-to-God for-real angel?

Riley felt a faint touch on her arm.

"Neither of them can know the truth."

"Okay, that's way freaky," she replied. "You know what I'm thinking."

"Only when there's a lot of emotion behind the thought."

Then Ori was near her again, looking into her eyes, his lips barely brushing her cheek.

"One more kiss," he said, "then I'll take you home."

They took their time, and when they finally broke apart Riley could feel her heart hammering. *Amazing.*

"Amazing?" he said, that wicked grin blossoming.

He'd read her mind. Again. "Stop that," she chided.

"You'll get used to it."

"Only if I can hear your thoughts."

"Maybe that's possible. Let's find out."

The angel pulled her close. His skin felt warm, toasty even. There was nothing at first, then the silent brush of wings against her mind.

Hello, Riley.

She yanked herself away, blinking in surprise. "I heard you!"

He nodded, satisfied. "It is said if a mortal can hear an angel's thoughts, they were meant to be together."

Together?

He pulled her close again, putting his forehead against hers. She heard him as plain as if he'd spoken the words.

You will be my downfall, Riley Blackthorne.

She surrendered to another kiss, one that seemed to stir something deep inside her, like a flower unfolding in the glorious sunshine. For the first time wild, impossible futures began to form in her mind.

"Good night, Riley," he said, and then she was standing next to her car just outside the market, keys in hand. Ori was nowhere to be seen, but she could still taste his kisses on her lips, the brush of his fingers on her cheek, the warmth in her belly.

Then it all faded, like a dream. Even the watermelon on her tongue was gone.

As if it never existed.

Beck felt like an idiot. He'd been sitting in his truck for the past hour, playing the same Carrie Underwood song over and over until it sawed across his nerves. It was now close to eleven, and Paul's daughter wasn't at the church yet.

"Where the hell are ya?" he snarled. "If yer..." He clenched his teeth, trying hard not to think of what might be happening between that slick bastard and Paul's little girl.

One moment Beck knew what he was doing was right, then the next he felt like a damned stalker. She wasn't a kid, even if he tried to act like she were. He'd not been fair when he said all her boyfriends had been jerks. There were a couple boys between Allan and Simon who had treated her decently. But deep in his gut he was sure this Ori guy was a bad move.

During his hour's vigil he'd come to one conclusion: He was losing his mind when it came to Paul's daughter. He was jealous. No way to deny it. When he'd seen that man put his arm around her, he'd wanted to rip the guy to pieces.

I gotta get a grip on this. Can't keep goin' down this road.

Beck blew out a lungful of air in relief when Riley's car pulled to the curb and she stepped out. She had a strange look on her face and wasn't paying attention to her surroundings, so he tracked her until she entered the church and the door closed behind her. At least he knew she was safe.

And alone.

He started his truck, then just sat there. After a moment's consideration, he headed toward the Westin. Justine might know something about this Ori guy, and besides, she had her own brand of magic, the kind that would help Beck forget the one girl he'd never have.

Ori found his nemesis in the old cemetery near the master trapper's empty grave. The earth had been returned to the hole now, but it had settled, causing cracks to form along the edges where it met solid ground. He made no effort to cover his approach but landed squarely in front of Sartael, wings unfurled and prepared for battle.

"What were you playing at?" he shouted, his hands fisted. "Why did you reveal me? You nearly ruined everything."

Sartael observed his anger with cool detachment. "You know why."

Ori's fists unclenched and he ruffled his wings in agitation. "The rogue demon will come for her and I will kill it. That's been my plan all along."

Sartael eyed him gravely. "I have heard all this before. *He* is not pleased with your progress. If that does not spur you on, then you are a fool."

"I will speak with Him—"

"That is not necessary. You are to use your *special talents* this time."

Ori studied his foe, unsure if he could trust him. "Is that His order?"

"You would question Him?" Wings beating in unison, Sartael rose into the sky, sending decaying leaves billowing underneath him in a whirlwind. "If you do not prevail, I shall. And I promise, you will not like the outcome."

TWENTY-SEVEN

As the morning newscast droned on the television in Harper's office, Riley worked on the record keeping. It put her in the unpleasant position of having her back to her master, but he seemed less likely to leave bruises these days, what with his injured ribs.

"Done yet?" he asked, muting the sound.

"Yes, I got it. Between the money for the demons we've trapped, the disability payment from the Guild, and the scrap metal sales, you've got one thousand, two hundred and eighty-seven dollars coming in over the next three weeks." She turned in the squeaky office chair. "Is that enough?"

Harper gave a slow nod. "Better than I thought it'd be. I'll be able to take you and Saint out next week sometime. In the meantime, you trap with Beck."

Trapping demons with Beck? That had been okay in the past, but after last night she wasn't sure if she wanted to be anywhere near him.

"Okay," she replied. There wasn't any other answer she could give.

The front door to the warehouse pushed open, causing Riley to take a deep breath and hold it. Was it the hunters? What would her master do if the Vatican came calling?

"Master Harper, good morning," Simon said, moving slowly into the office. She noticed he didn't bother to include her in the greeting.

"Saint. How you doing?" their master called out.

"Better."

"Simon," she said. Only then did his crystal-blue eyes move in her direction.

"Riley." His voice was as cold as a tray of ice cubes dumped down her back.

More drama. Just what I don't need.

She moved out of the chair and let her former boyfriend sink into it. His face was as pale as his white-blond hair, and he had one hand placed on his abdomen like he expected his intestines to fall onto the floor at any moment.

The fact that he was up and moving at all was astounding. Heaven really did deliver on their promise, even if it did have unintended consequences.

"You sure you're good enough to be here?" Harper asked, rising from the recliner.

"For a little while. Thought I could do the paperwork."

"Give him the reports, then," Harper said and shuffled off toward the bathroom.

Riley moved the stack of papers in front of Simon. "I haven't gotten to these yet."

A nod. Then he picked up a pencil and began to work through the trapping reports. The moment Riley heard the bathroom door shut, she knelt down until her eyes were level with his.

"You sicced the hunters on me," she accused, keeping her voice low.

Simon's eyes bored into her like fiery blue lasers. "If you're innocent, no problem," he said levelly.

"How could you do that? I thought we had something, Simon."

"We did, until you showed your true colors."

"I haven't changed," she said. "You just think I have."

"Don't try to reason with me," he retorted. "I know what you are, and I know who you work for."

"And just how can you tell that?" she demanded. "Is there like some mark on my forehead or something?"

"I just know," he said, his voice less sure now. "I'm not the only one who's figured it out. He told me all about—"

When Harper exited the bathroom, she lurched to her feet.

"If you don't need anything else, sir," she said, wanting to put distance between herself and the cold-hearted monster sitting at the desk. This time it wasn't her master.

Harper waved her off. "Keep your phone on. If a call comes in, I'll need you to take care of it."

As she left the building, she could hear them talking. She bet Simon would waste no time telling their master all about her "deal with Hell."

And Harper will believe every word of it.

With time to kill before class, Riley flopped onto her own bed and stared up at the ceiling. She'd managed to cross off one item on her To Do list—groceries. The really big things were still undone, looming over her head like some ancient curse.

Though the tenant upstairs was vacuuming the floor and every now and then there would be a thump as the vacuum bumped into a piece of furniture, it felt good to lay in her own bed. The sounds of domesticity comforted her. The ache in her chest was still there, aggravated by seeing Simon in all his cruel and unrepentant glory. He really did believe she was evil. Maybe Heaven hadn't healed him as well as they thought. Maybe the lack of oxygen to his brain did do some damage.

Either way, Riley knew from past experience that this loss would eventually contract to a hard knot but never disappear. She still had one for Allan and one for Beck after he'd blown her off a couple years before. Simon's would be the biggest.

The vacuuming ended and there was relative silence. Riley's eyes closed, and for a brief moment she swore she could taste watermelon on her tongue as the soft brush of wings in her mind lulled her to sleep.

The knock at her door roused her out of a totally X-rated dream that involved a certain hunkalicious angel, no clothes, and much heavy-duty horizontal exercise. "Oh wow," she said, fanning herself. It was good she was at home. Having that kind of dream at the church was probably a mortal sin.

Another series of knocks. "Miss Blackthorne?" It was a female voice, one with a strange accent.

Riley relaxed. It wasn't the demon hunters; they didn't have women on their crew. Maybe they'd decided it wasn't worth the hassle to check her out.

And I'll be winning the lottery any day now.

She dragged herself out of bed and cautiously opened the door, leaving the safety chain in place. Her visitor was taller than Riley, probably five nine or so. She was a complete package: a sculpted nose, perfectly arched eyebrows, and thick hair that tumbled over her shoulders in a red riot. Her suit had to be custom-made the way it molded to her figure. It was green tweed with an asymmetrical collar, and the pants ended at just the right point above her sleek black heels. Her fingernails matched her hair. Even worse, the vivid green eyes weren't from contacts.

Riley instantly disliked her, an automatic response from one female to another when the other looked this good. Especially when Riley had opened the door clad in stained and ripped blue jeans and a T-shirt that had been tie-dyed by demon pee.

"Miss Blackthorne?" the woman asked. Her eyes flickered across Riley's clothes. To her credit she didn't gag.

"If you're here from the collection agency, don't bother. My dad's long gone and I have no idea who has him."

"I am not from any collection agency," the woman replied. Something floral wafted into the apartment as she offered up a business card with a delicate hand. "I'm Justine Armando." She stated the name as if everyone would recognize it instantly.

Riley studied the card: FREELANCE JOURNALIST. "I don't talk to the press," she said automatically. That was one of the first lessons drilled into an apprentice's brain: Talking to the media was a big no-go.

"I am aware of that, but Beck said it would be fine," the woman replied.

That didn't sound like Backwoods Boy. "I doubt that."

"On the contrary, I've already interviewed him . . . extensively," the woman added.

The words *interviewed* and *extensively* had a certain weight to them, like the reporter meant something entirely different.

Riley eyed her visitor again, assessing the package. "Stroke his ego, did you?"

Ms. Armando's mouth curved into a knowing smile.

Ah, jeez. You're knocking boots with a reporter? Come on, Beck. That's just wrong.

"I thought it would be wise to hear your perspective on trapping with the men," the woman explained. "That cannot be easy for you."

As much as Riley would love to tell her side of the story, if she talked to the press without Harper's permission, he'd be all over her. She just didn't need the hassle.

"Sorry, I can't do it, not without my master's okay," she said, and shut the door before she lost her nerve.

The reporter knocked again, calling out, but Riley ignored her, double-checking that the chain lock was engaged. She curled up in bed, trying not to conjure up the image of Backwoods Boy and the reporter chick doing what she and the angel had been up to in her dream. She thumped the heel of her hand against her forehead, hoping that might dislodge the slide show. It didn't work. In fact, the images only became more graphic.

"Euuuuu!" she said, grimacing. "La la la la la . . ."

If they were hooking up, there was only one reason that woman would pick Beck as a lover: The red-haired stick chick was using him to further her career.

"I mean, look at her. She's *so* not your type." Not that she knew what Beck's type would be, but Riley suspected it would be someone into country music and who liked to hang at the Armageddon Lounge and shoot pool all night. That was not Ms. Perfect Size Eight.

Riley finally drifted into an uneasy sleep. Seconds later, or so it seemed, someone pounded on the door. She sat bolt upright, glowering. It was like there was a neon sign on the top of the apartment building that said "Riley Is Trying to Sleep. Visit Her Now!"

"If this is the stick chick again . . ."

This time it was all guys, two of which were in military garb, wearing sidearms and sporting a special patch on their vests depicting a dude slaying a dragon. Behind them was a priest, clad in solid black like an aged crow. It wasn't Father Harrison.

Simon's call to the demon hunters had borne fruit.

"Miss Blackthorne?" one of the men asked, his accent thick and hard to understand. He was tall, Nordic blond, and pretty scary. "We are demon hunters, here by special permission from the Vatican."

Here being Atlanta, she hoped, rather than on her doorstep in particular.

"I can only talk to you if my master is present." It was a good response to about anything she didn't want to do.

"Those rules don't apply to us," the man insisted.

"They do for me."

"We have the power to detain you for questioning," he replied, his voice taking on a harder edge. "We will use that power if needed."

I so don't need this right now. "This is because of Simon Adler, right? What he said about me?"

The priest nodded. "Mr. Adler has concerns about your loyalties." He moved closer to the door at this point. Maybe he thought he had a better chance of convincing her to play along.

"Did he tell you we used to date?"

"He stated that you had coerced him into a romantic relationship."

"Co . . . erced?" she sputtered. Simon had been the one to ask her out, not the other way around.

"We need to speak at length about this issue, Miss Blackthorne," the priest replied. "Please let us in."

"I don't know what else Simon told you, but I didn't break the ward. Neither did my father, who is dead and has been reanimated, just in case you haven't heard. I have no idea why the demons came after us, and I have class in an hour," she said in a rush of words. "That's all you're getting from me unless my master is present."

"These charges are serious: You have been accused of working for Lucifer," the priest replied.

"Not a chance. Now good afternoon," she said, pushing the door closed.

The big blond man slammed his palm against the wood, straining the chain lock. With only a little more effort the chain would snap and they'd be inside.

Panicking, Riley backed off, grabbing her cell phone from the coffee table.

"You stay outside or I'll call the cops," she warned, brandishing the phone like a weapon.

"You let us in and the door stays in one piece," the big man replied.

She had no other option but to dial Harper, gambling that he hated the hunters more than he hated her. As the phone rang there was rapid-fire conversation between the priest and the Nordic guy, all in a language she didn't understand. When her master answered, she unloaded the situation in a breathy voice.

"What do I do?" she asked, crossing the fingers of her free hand behind her back where the hunters wouldn't see it. *Please don't make me do this.*

"Let me talk to the priest," Harper ordered.

Riley handed the cell phone to Father Rosetti through the wedge of open door. There was a brisk exchange, and then the phone came back to her.

"Sir?" she asked, her fingers still crossed.

"You're not to talk to them unless I'm with you. If they arrest you, call me and we'll take it from there," Harper said. "And don't think you're out of it. If you're working for Hell, I'll kill you myself." The phone went dead.

Oh goody.

The priest issued an order and the big man backed off. "You will talk to us eventually," the cleric said, giving her a thin smile. If it was supposed to reassure her, it did the opposite.

"The Guild won't let you touch me," she said defiantly.

"They will if we find evidence of your guilt. They will throw you to us just to clear their name. It is better to plead your case now. Unlike God, our mercy is not limitless."

"I haven't done anything," she insisted. "So just go away and leave me alone."

Riley pushed the door closed, then leaned against it, stomach churning. There was the thump of combat boots on the stairs and then silence.

They want a scapegoat and I'm it. The next time I won't be able to stall them.

TWENTY-EIGHT

The big blue tent at the far edge of the Terminus Market seemed an unlikely place to hold a trapper's meeting, but according to Jackson nobody else in the city would rent them space.

"Can't blame them," the trapper said as he parked himself in a folding chair next to Riley inside the tent. His arm was still bandaged, but he seemed able to move it without much pain.

"Do you want me to do the Holy Water ward?" she asked. It was usually Simon's job, but she doubted he could handle it right now.

"One of the others is doing it."

And Riley knew why. "You don't trust me to do it right," she said, more hurt than she cared to admit.

"If it was me you'd be doing the ward, but Stewart suggested a journeyman handle it for the time being. That way if anything happens, you won't be blamed."

"So will it always be this way? Nobody trusting me, that is?" Riley demanded.

"I honestly don't know," Jackson replied.

"We didn't do anything to the ward."

"I know that. Sometimes the truth is harder to accept than a lie."

Jackson was trying to make her feel better, in comparison to other trappers who kept frowning and muttering "Blackthorne" under their breath like it was a curse word. *Asshats.* How could they believe she'd let the demons in? All her father had done was protect his daughter.

When Jackson moved to the front of the tent, she looked over at her master. Harper hadn't said a word to her about her phone call this afternoon, like his apprentices were visited by the demon hunters every day. Which meant he thought she deserved their wrath. So did Simon, who sat next to him, grim. When one of the trappers said hello the apprentice only nodded, his mind stuck in some dark mire of conspiracy theories.

Why is everything so wrong now?

Someone called out Beck's name, and a moment later he appeared at the tent flap. He looked like he hadn't slept in days.

Bet it wasn't because you were hunting demons. Not with the arrogant smirk on his face.

He took a seat next to her, placing his trapping bag on the ground. "Girl."

The faint hint of something flowery caught her nose and she reacted instantly. "How's the reporter chick?"

Beck gave her a startled look. "What do ya mean?"

She took an exaggerated sniff. "The reporter chick, the one with the red hair? Unless you're letting your inner girl show, you smell just like her." When he began to protest, she waved him off. "She was at my apartment this afternoon trying to interview me, so I remember her perfume."

"Did ya talk to her?" Beck asked, suddenly worried.

"Was I supposed to?"

"No way. Ya know that. Everythin' goes through Harper or Stewart."

The stick chick lies like a pro. "You're always giving me advice; here's some for you: She's playing you. She lied to me, told me you said it was okay if I talked to her."

"That's what reporters do," he said, but his frown told her he wasn't happy with the news. "I thought ya knew that."

"I know a lot of things, Beck, and she's not your type."

"Ya sayin' I'm not good enough for her?" he said, his voice harsher now.

"No. I'm saying she's not on the level."

A scowl formed on his face. Riley knew what was coming. "Ya called Fargo yet?"

"No, I've been too busy trying to destroy the Guild and corrupt Simon's soul. Being evil is a full-time job."

Beck snorted. He angled his head toward where her ex-boyfriend sat at the other side of the tent. "No need to hang around for him anymore. He's moved on. That sure didn't last very long, did it?"

Ouch. Riley knew they should step away from this before someone went too far, but the need to retaliate became overwhelming.

"I'm not staying at the church from now on," she announced. "Ori's watching over me. He won't let anything happen. He'll get that Five, you wait and see."

A chuff of disgust came her way. "Bull . . . shit. Pretty boys like that don't know jack when it comes to demons. They're just flash."

Riley leaned closer to her father's favorite trapping buddy, eager to spear his insufferable arrogance in its heart. "Ori was the one who saved me from the Five at the Tabernacle."

"What?" Beck spouted.

"You heard me." She let three seconds pass before delivering the verbal knife-thrust between his ribs. "He was there for me when it counted, Beck. So where were you?"

The trapper's mouth flopped open in astonishment.

Jackson's timing was perfect: He called out for silence. As trappers settled into their chairs, Beck continued to stare at her in disbelief.

"I'm calling this meeting to order," Jackson said, waving his hands to gain attention. "We lost the gavel in the fire, so we'll just have to deal. The masters have asked me to be acting president until we have an election. Is that okay with you folks?"

There were murmurs of agreement.

"Fine. First thing, Pritchard is the only one still in the hospital. He'll be going home in a couple of days, but he's done trapping. That's a mixed blessing, but at least he's still alive."

"Thank God," someone called out. Riley thought his name was Remmers or something like that. He was the only other African American in the Atlanta Guild.

"I second that," another said.

"The remainder of the funerals will be out of the area, so I need volunteers to attend those services." Hands shot up and Jackson made note of the names. "Thanks, guys. Master Stewart, you want to give a report on the demon hunters?"

The Scotsman rose from his chair, leaning heavily on his cane. "As we expected, they're goin' ta do their own thing. My advice is ta stay outta their way. They'll kill a few demons and then leave, if we're lucky."

"And if not?" Jackson asked.

"Then it could get ugly. We don't want any more casualties, so don't cross these guys. Just back off and live for another day."

"We should just let them do whatever they want?" someone called out.

A wily grin settled on the Scotsman's face. "No, I'm not sayin' that. Ya have a problem with them, call me or Beck. We'll get it sorted."

"Anything from the Archbishop about the Holy Water problem?" Jackson asked.

"Not yet. He's checkin' his sources, but so far the city claims there's no problem at all."

Riley held her tongue. No reason to let the others know she'd been investigating on her own, at least not until she'd figured out the whole scam. Then she'd be happy to drop it in their laps.

"Anything you want to say, Harper?" Jackson asked.

Riley's heart began to thud. *What if he tells them about the hunters? What if he demands they toss me out of the Guild?*

The older trapper shook his head. "Not right now."

What? He'd had the perfect opportunity to ruin her career and he'd passed on it. *What's he up to?*

"On to other business, then," Jackson continued. "It seems like we've got more press in this city than we have demons, at least that's what it looks like. Be careful what you say to these folks. We need to present a solid front."

"Better tell Beck about that," a trapper called out. Riley didn't recognize the voice.

Her companion shifted uneasily in his seat. "I know how to handle 'em."

"So we noticed," was the swift response. Crude jests flew through the tent, followed by laughter. *Even* they *think you're sleeping with her.*

Jackson shuffled papers. "The National Guild is requesting trappers to come to Atlanta to help us out, at least in the short term. They're also trying to line up a master for us. It'll be a while before that happens."

"What about that television show?" Reynolds asked. "They still coming?"

"I haven't heard anything to say they're not," Jackson replied. "Let's talk about what happened the other night," Jackson added, opening the floor to whoever wanted to have their say.

There were different schools of thought: the Holy Water was neutralized or the bogus Holy Water was to blame. The third explanation cut too close to home: *Someone* had purposely broken the ward.

"Riley?" It was their temporary president and he was looking right at her. "Could you tell us what your father said to you that night?"

She rose, nervous when all eyes turned to her. "He said I should run, that *they* were coming. That there were too many of them."

"And he was inside the ward, wasn't he?" Jackson asked.

"Yes. He was right behind me."

Voices erupted from the back of the tent as she sank into her seat.

"I told you he did it!" McGuire shouted.

Harper rose, a hand pressed against his sore ribs. "That's not what I saw. The ward was still up when Blackthorne was talking to his kid. It didn't break until it was overrun by the demons."

Harper doesn't blame my dad? She had to be dreaming.

"What's yer theory on all this?" the Scotsman asked Harper.

"Same as yours—too much evil in one place," her master replied and sank back into his seat.

As Simon rose to his feet, all eyes went to him. "How can you . . ." He paused to suck in a tortured breath. "How can you believe that God's Holy Essence can be destroyed?"

"Not destroyed . . . neutralized. There is a difference," Stewart replied.

"Not to me," Simon shot back. "Either you believe Heaven has ultimate power to destroy evil, or you believe that Lucifer can win this war. There is no middle ground."

The silence within the tent became oppressive. No one wanted to challenge him, not after what he'd been through.

It was Harper who finally spoke. "No one is claiming that Heaven can't kick Hell's ass. What we're saying is that the Holy Water did what it was supposed to do, but there was just too much evil."

"I refuse to accept that," Simon replied, glaring at Riley as he lowered himself into his chair. "Hell had help that night. That's the only explanation."

She lurched to her feet, eager to tell him how wrong he was about her dad, about her. How much Simon had hurt her and how that agony would never go away.

"Anythin' ya want ta say, lass?" Stewart asked.

Her anger made her visibly tremble, and she cursed herself for that weakness. "My dad loved being in the Guild," she protested. "He wouldn't have done anything to hurt you, Simon. Or any of those guys."

"So if it wasn't him," McGuire called out, "how about you, girl? Did you break the ward?"

She turned toward her accuser. "And get myself eaten by a demon? Do I look stupid?"

"Maybe they said they'd let you go. Hell makes some powerful deals."

"Talking from experience, McGuire?" she snapped.

"Riley, he's a journeyman, and yer—" Beck warned.

"I know. I'm just a damned apprentice," she retorted. "I'm so tired of people blaming me for everything. I'm tired of the lies, the sick jokes, all of it. I should just . . . just . . ."

Quit. The word teetered on the tip of her tongue. If she just pushed it out, it'd be over. No more harassment, no more fingers pointed in her direction. She could be Riley Blackthorne again, high school student and hot-chocolate enthusiast, not some demon trapper wannabe.

Just tell them I'm out of here. She bit the inside of her lip, drawing blood. *If I do, they win.* The next female will have it twice as bad.

Riley swallowed the words. "But I'm not giving up," she said, staring right at McGuire. "I'm a trapper, from a family of demon trappers. And Blackthornes don't quit."

"You tell them, sister," Remmers called out.

Her anger exhausted, Riley folded into her chair, intertwining her hands in her lap so no one could see how badly they were shaking. Her muscles had knotted from the tension, and she had a dull headache thumping right behind her eyeballs.

Harper rose again. "If we fight each other, we can't beat the demons," he said simply. Then he shot a look at McGuire and some of the others at the back of the tent. "And just for the record, if anyone's going to run Blackthorne's brat out of the Guild, it's me. Got it?"

There were murmurs in the crowd: Message received.

"Okay, so let's move on," Jackson said, clearly relieved that was over. "Anyone know a church where we can meet?"

"The Tabernacle *was* a church," someone protested. "Helluva lot of good it did."

"It'd been desanctified," Stewart replied. "No services had been held there in years."

"We could meet in a cemetery," Beck suggested.

Riley groaned. *There's a plan.*

"We'll work it out," Jackson replied. "Let's get together Friday night at eight. We'll hold elections, try to get back on track."

"We meeting here?" Remmers called out.

"Sure," Jackson replied. "Look at this way: At least the rent's cheap."

Riley waited until Beck was deep in an animated conversation with Master Stewart to make her escape. It felt cowardly, like she wasn't brave enough to face him. She'd just stepped outside the tent when she heard her name. *Harper.*

"Sir?" she asked, turning toward him.

The moment her master exited the tent a piece of paper came her way. "Need some food. Drop it by my place. We have to talk . . . *tonight.*"

"Ah, I'm supposed to be on holy ground after dark."

"Won't take long."

At least Ori would watch over her. "Why didn't you tell them about—"

"Later," her master retorted, cutting her off abruptly. "Now get going, brat."

Confused at his behavior, Riley studied the list as she walked to the car. There was nothing out of the ordinary, just food and supplies, all of which could have waited until tomorrow morning. Which meant he wanted to talk about the hunters and their interest in Paul Blackthorne's daughter.

Jamming the list into a pocket, she rubbed her temples to ease the headache that had struck her the moment she'd unloaded on Beck. *Guilt.* That was what she was feeling. Industrial-strength guilt. She'd acted mean and childish, just as nasty as Simon, and Riley knew how that felt on the receiving end.

Why did I do that to him? Why did I cut Beck down like that?

There was an answer and she didn't like it one bit: The stick chick. Justine Armando just made her feel mean. It wasn't jealousy, not the usual kind anyway, it was because the reporter was so not in Beck's league. He was simple, plainspoken, no-nonsense. The kind of guy who always watched your back. The reporter was all flash and abundant money. And she was really pretty. No wonder Beck had homed right in on that.

She's going to hurt you, Backwoods Boy.

For all his bluster, Denver Beck had deep insecurities, and Justine was using those to get what she wanted. When she finally threw him away he wouldn't know how to deal, not with his history of one-night stands. It'd cut him deep. Riley knew how bad it felt, and no matter how much he annoyed her, she didn't want to see him hurt. *He's too good for that.*

TWENTY-NINE

When her headache didn't improve, Riley gave in to the craving for mood-altering chocolate. The moment she pushed open the door to the Grounds Zero she was instantly cocooned in the lusty aroma of fresh-brewed coffee. The place was busier than usual, and she noticed that some of the patrons wore name tags; apparently there was a woodworkers' convention in town.

A couple was just leaving "her" booth, and Riley hurried to claim the space with her coat. Then she joined the line behind two old guys discussing orbital sanders. Simi was at the counter and gave Riley a wide grin. Tonight her friend's hair was brilliant orange, with black spikes.

"Wicked," Riley said. "I bet they can see it from space."

"That was the plan," the barista replied. "The usual?"

Riley nodded. Simi always made sure the hot chocolate was topped with loads of whipped cream and chocolate shavings. Unfortunately, it would remind her of Simon, but the craving had to be fed.

"So where's the boyfriend, the one with the gorgeous blue eyes?" the barista asked. "He's *totally* hot."

"Simon's history."

"That sucks. How about the trapper?"

After what I said to him? "Also history."

Simi gave her a concerned look. "You're going through these guys like I do coffee filters, girl. Better slow down."

When Ori came to mind, Riley made sure to hide the smile from her friend.

Simi set the cup of hot chocolate on the counter and rang up the purchase. Riley automatically dropped the change in the tip jar: That would earn her a refill if she wanted one.

The trip to the table wasn't easy with all the conventioneers wandering around, but she made it without a spill and slid into the booth. While she waited for the drink to cool, Riley nibbled on some of the chocolate shavings.

I so deserve this.

A chiming sound came from her bag, barely audible in the midst of the boisterous coffee house. She dug out her phone, accessed the text message, and promptly smiled. Ori.

MISSING YOU. SEE YOU LATER?

She typed the YES before she could stop herself.

What could it hurt? Maybe he'd take her on another angelic picnic. Unlike Martha, he hadn't expected her to save the world or anything. As she watched, his text disappeared like it'd never existed.

How does he do that? Angel mojo apparently. She didn't even think Ori had a phone, but then sending a text without it was no big deal to someone with his job description. Making it disappear—just as easy.

Riley put her cell on the table and tested the hot beverage. The whipped cream deposited a white mustache on her upper lip, resurrecting good memories. The coffee-house run was a Blackthorne tradition. Riley would always have hot chocolate, and her dad would drink coffee, but in a real cup: He couldn't stand the paper ones. Now as she sipped she could visualize his mussed brown hair, the laugh lines at the corners of his eyes, that shy smile. This booth was his favorite, in the back, quieter than others. She wouldn't share this spot with anyone, not even Ori.

Riley closed her eyes, allowing the background noise to recede and in its place she heard the clink of a spoon against a ceramic cup as her dad stirred his coffee. She could smell his aftershave, hear him talking about his day, about her mom, about anything. It didn't matter. She could feel his presence, and that comforted her. As long as she could hold that moment, preserve it, he would always be part of her, even if he was slaving away for some rich creep.

The bench seat across from her creaked and she heard someone say her name. Riley's eyes flew open, her heart wanting to believe in miracles. It was Beck. A quick look around told her they'd have to stay put: There were no other places available.

He peeled off his Atlanta Braves cap, dropped it on the table, and ran a hand through his hair to tame it. It was longer now and it looked good on him. For an instant she saw something in his eyes, but whatever it was disappeared in a heartbeat, like he'd realized he was showing more than he wanted.

"I figured I'd find ya here." Then a nod of approval came her way. "Ya look pretty tonight. I like yer hair that way."

Riley hadn't expected the compliment, and she fought the blush. She'd just put on makeup, nothing special. "Thanks."

"It's for him, isn't it?" he replied, his tone darkening.

She knew who he meant, but she decided not to go there. "Harper? No way." That got her a puzzled look. "I'm going to his place after I finish my cocoa. He wants to chat."

"About what?"

Riley did a coin flip and this time Beck won. She told him about Simon's involvement with the Vatican's boys and how they'd shown up her place this afternoon.

"The little bastard," he said, shaking his head. "Do whatever Harper says. He won't let the hunters hurt ya, no matter what."

"Glad you're so sure about that. I'm not."

"I'll talk to Simon," he offered. "Let him know just how much a prick he's been."

"No, don't bother. It won't do any good."

Beck pried the lid off a cup and stirred the contents with one of the little sticks. It looked to be coffee, no creamer. "This stuff costs twice as much as it does at the Stop-and-Rob. I just don't get it."

You wouldn't. "What are you doing here, Beck?"

"Ya ran out of the meetin'. I wasn't done talkin' to ya."

That sounded for real, but she could never tell with him. One minute he was totally worried about her, giving her money to live; the next he acted like she was a brainless child.

You have to be angry at me. Why aren't you yelling? That, she knew how to handle. Instead he seemed morose. Lost even.

"You need to stop worrying about me," she said. "I'm doing okay."

"Then yer doin' better than me," he murmured. "I miss Paul real bad."

His stark honesty caught her off guard. She felt tears forming and blinked to keep them in check. "I keep thinking Dad will be in the kitchen when I get up in the morning," she admitted. "He always made me breakfast. His way of showing how much he cared, I guess."

Beck took a hoarse breath like something stabbed him deep inside. "I miss trappin' with him. He was always so cool. He never yelled at me. Well, only once."

"What did you do?" she asked, curious.

"I flipped off a cop," he said, shrugging like it was no big deal. "Paul gave me ten kinds of hell for that. Said I had a problem with authority."

"Duh."

Beck eyed her. "Yer the same or ya wouldn't be givin' me all this grief, girl."

He'd done it again. Just when she'd gotten a peek of what lay beneath that protective armor, he'd blown it.

"Girl?" he pressed.

"The name is *Riley*," she shot back. "Learn it. Use it!"

Beck's nostrils flared. Backwoods Boy never could stand being dissed. "I asked around. Seems no one knows this Ori guy."

"Ori's a Lancer." *And an angel.* "End of story."

"Seems too handy," Beck said, his face furrowed in thought. "Guys say anythin' to get laid."

"He's not like that."

Beck leaned over the table and lined his eyes up with hers. "Get a clue, *Riley*, we're *all* like that. We see a pretty young girl and we've got only one thing in mind. It's just a matter of pushin' the right buttons until we get ya naked."

"Like you and the reporter chick?"

He gave her a feral grin as an answer.

Riley felt her cheeks flame. "She's gonna screw you over; can't you see that?"

"And this Ori guy is any different?"

"Yes, he is."

"Then he's a damned saint," Beck grumbled, leaning back.

Weary of the sparring, Riley shoved her way out of the booth and headed toward the counter.

"Refill?" Simi called out as she approached.

"Make it to go." She'd had more than enough of Beck for one evening.

When the barista handed her the cup, Simi angled her head toward the booth. "He really likes you."

"Beck? No way." *Where did she get that idea?*

"Oh, yeah. I can tell by the way he looks at you."

"If that's the case, why is he such a jerk?" Riley asked.

"Some guys don't know any better."

Riley wasn't buying it. She wasn't surprised that the instant she returned to the booth, Beck started in again just like she'd never left.

"Ya have to be careful. This guy could be a Mezmer. They're way clever."

Riley shook her head. "Ori's not Hellspawn. He stood up to a Geo-Fiend."

"So? A lower-grade fiend will back off from a top-level demon."

"He sat on the church steps with me, Beck. He's not a demon." She knew the problem and it had nothing to do with Ori. "You're just pissed because that Four didn't get into his head like it did yours."

Beck's scowl deepened. "Yeah, and I wanna know why. Until then, I don't want ya seein' him. He's out of yer life, as of now."

"You're just bullying me to feel important. It's not working."

His face went crimson. "Call yer aunt or I will."

"You don't have the number."

Beck grew a grin: It wasn't a nice one. Then he pointed at her phone. "I do now."

Riley's jaw dropped. He'd gone through her cell phone address book while she'd been at the counter. "How dare you?" she growled, trying hard to keep her voice lowered. People were already staring at them.

"I promised Paul I'd keep ya safe," he said. "If that means packin' yer ass out of town so it doesn't get humped by a smooth-talkin' loser, that's the way it's gonna be."

Stunned at the menace in his voice, Riley pulled herself out of the booth. This was a different side of Beck, and it frightened her. Scooping up her phone and the drink, she pushed her way out of the coffee house. As she hurried toward the car, a street vendor called out to her, but Riley ignored him. All she wanted to do was run away.

Beck fell in step with her within a half block. She didn't dare look at him. Maybe he'd leave her alone if she ignored him.

"Wait," he said, grabbing her arm.

Riley yanked herself free and kept going. It wasn't until she reached the car that she realized he was still following. Her hands shook so hard she couldn't fit the key into the lock. Drained, she slumped against the car door.

In the distance she saw Ori leaning against his bike, on the alert, probably trying to figure out if the trapper posed a threat. Riley shook her head and he nodded in return, still vigilant.

Unaware she had backup, Beck halted a few feet away from her. "Riley, please listen to me."

"Why are you doing this? You're scaring me, Beck."

He recoiled, like she'd punched him in the face.

He sagged. "I don't know why I'm like this. Too much is happenin' I don't understand." She waited, knowing there was more. His eyes rose to hers, pleading. "I can't face losin' ya, Riley. Yer all I got left in this world."

That brutal honesty again. He'd peeled away more armor, and this time he'd exposed his heart.

"Ori's not the bad guy here," she said wearily.

Beck opened his mouth to argue, then shook his head in defeat. "That might be true, but that doesn't mean he won't hurt ya."

"It's still my choice," she said. "Just like Justine is for you."

"I know," he admitted. He took a few steps away, then turned back toward her. "I'm sorry it didn't work between us."

What? "Beck, I—"

"No. We'll leave it at that. Just be careful, girl."

As he walked away, his shoulders slumped like he'd taken a vicious beating. Gone was the overbearing bully in the coffee house, the arrogant man who thought the world should dance to his tune. In his place was someone she hardly knew.

It was late when Beck headed deep into Demon Central in search of the hunters. He'd already talked to his buddy Ike, the old war veteran who lived down here, and had learned the team was scouting the area. There was gunfire now, which meant the Vatican's boys had grown tired of scouting and were now reducing Atlanta's demon population one by one.

Beck adjusted his course through the darkened streets, keeping his eyes on the surroundings. It was hard to concentrate: He kept thinking back to what had happened between him and Paul's daughter tonight. The harsh words that had been said between them.

No matter what he did, Riley only pulled further away. Beck knew it was wrong to push her so hard, but he just couldn't stop himself. He cared too damn much. He hadn't lied: He was afraid of losing her to a demon. Or to someone else.

"This sucks." But as he saw it, there wasn't much he could do but run interference for her. Besides, he had his own problems: Elias Salvatore for one. If Beck was lucky, no one had told the hunter who his ex-girlfriend was hooking up with. If someone had, hopefully the hunters weren't looking to add a trapper to their kill stats tonight. Beck could just see the news report: "Journeyman trapper dies in tragic accident in Demon Central. Vatican issues formal apology."

Now that would really *suck.*

He caught up with them on Broad Street. There were six of the Vatican's crew all decked out in their commando gear, and there'd be more in the surrounding streets. From the five furry bodies lying in the street, they'd been busy. A single shot to the Threes' skulls did the trick, at least when the bullets were hollow points loaded with papal Holy Water. Fifteen hundred dollars' worth of demon carcasses had bled out on that pavement, and no trapper was going to get a bit of that money.

"What a damned waste," he grumbled.

Beck had expected to be challenged right off, but he was waved through the perimeter by one of the hunters. Captain Salvatore stood near one of the high-tech black vans. There was a map spread out on a portable table, and he was talking to his second-in-command.

"Good evenin'," Beck said politely. He got a nod from the captain and a glower from his subordinate.

"What are you doing here?" Amundson demanded.

Beck set his trapping bag down by the van. "Wanted to see how the big boys work."

Amundson opened his mouth, probably to order him to take a hike, but his superior waved him off. "It's okay, Lieutenant. Go check on Chavez and Rimsky."

From his frown, Amundson didn't like the order, but he obeyed and headed down the street, assault rifle in hand.

Beck pointed at the line of dead demons. "Ya know, if ya don't have to kill those things . . ." he said, just to stir up trouble.

Salvatore carefully refolded the map. "If we don't kill them, they'll just come back and eat more of your people."

"I thought y'all had that handled. Somethin' to do with monks and a lot of prayin'. I heard the demons just disappear."

"They do disappear," Salvatore replied, leveling his gaze with Beck's. "Then they return to this realm and start killing again. Hell has the ultimate recycling plan."

Beck wasn't sure if the guy was messing with him or not. "Yer jokin', right?"

The captain shook his head. "If we kill them, they don't bother us again."

"That don't track," Beck argued. "Hunters have been wastin' demons for centuries and we're not runnin' out of 'em. Maybe Lucifer gets 'em either way, livin' or dead."

The captain gave the theory some consideration. "That'd be a bitch, wouldn't it?"

Beck cracked a grin. *Maybe this guy isn't such a tool after all.*

"So why are you here, Beck? It's not to see how we do our work."

Busted. "It's about Riley Blackthorne. I heard that one of our apprentices told ya a wild tale about her and her dad workin' for Hell. That's not true."

"Of course you'd say that," Salvatore replied. "You wouldn't turn on the man who trained you, or his daughter."

Beck frowned, shifting his weight from one foot to another. "I would if they were shillin' for Hell, in a heartbeat. I saw too many of our guys ripped apart that night to let somethin' like that slide."

Salvatore gave a cautious nod. A gunshot in the distance was followed by a low, mournful wail.

"And another one bites the dust," Beck muttered.

"You sure the Blackthornes are on the level?" Salvatore asked.

Beck nodded. "Paul was a straight arrow. Same with his daughter."

"Grand Master Stewart says the same thing. So if Riley is not the nexus of the demonic power in this city, who is?"

"Don't know. The demons have changed their tactics, gotten bolder. They're actin' weird now."

"Not the first time," Salvatore replied. "In Moscow in 'ninety-three—"

The earth began to shake beneath their boots. It paused and started up again, triggering car alarms that howled into the night like electronic wolves.

"That's a Five," Beck said, his throat tightening. He grabbed his duffel bag and began scanning the area. There were shouts from the streets around them as the hunters sprinted back toward their captain.

Salvatore stepped to the van's open side door. "Where did that come from, Corsini?"

A dark-skinned man stuck his head outside the vehicle, holding some sort of electronic device. "Southeast of here, Captain, nearly two kilometers."

Two kilometers. That was near Harper's place.

Beck turned on his heels and sprinted up the road, his trapping bag slapping into his side. Behind him, he heard the captain calling out his name, but he kept running as if his life depended upon it.

Because it does.

THIRTY

To Riley's relief there were no demon hunters waiting at her master's place. Harper was in his office, in his recliner, eyes closed. The television was off. That had to be a first.

She set the grocery sack on the desk. "I found the soup you said you liked."

No reply. She took that as a hint and put away the food. When she returned to the office, Harper's eyes were open. She'd expected a smirk, but there was none. That made her more nervous. What if he trashed her apprenticeship because of Simon's allegations? She had no way to prove her innocence.

Instead Harper went in a direction she'd not anticipated. "Saint's going to be a problem," he said in a gravely voice. "I don't trust you any further than I can spit you, but I *will not* have an apprentice who is working with the hunters."

For some bizarre reason, Riley felt the need to defend her ex. "Simon is really confused right now and—"

"Don't alibi for him!" Harper shouted, his voice echoing off the open rafters. "He sold you out, called the hunters down on one of his own. What the hell is he thinking?"

"He's not. That's the problem."

She got a grunt of agreement. "His crisis of faith is chapping my ass," Harper said.

"Not doing much for mine, either."

Another grunt. "I'll be talking to him about this in the morning. Then as soon as possible we'll go trapping. We'll catch a Three and see if we can get Saint back on track. I don't want to lose him."

"You think Simon can handle that after what he's been through?" she asked, unsure.

"He has to or he's done. It's that simple." Harper eyed her. "Then it'll be your turn."

Riley figured that was coming. Could she face one of those slavering monsters again?

"I've seen this before," Harper conceded. "Until Saint settles his argument with his God, he's going to doubt everything and everybody."

"Just as long as he doesn't blame my dad for what happened."

"Blackthorne knew what was going down or he wouldn't have warned you."

Riley frowned, putting her hands on her hips. "Oh right, he gave me, what, *five seconds* to be out of there before it became a death trap? If he really wanted to kill all of you, he'd have made sure I wasn't near that building."

Harper's face sagged. She could see that simple fact was bugging him. "I talked to Rosetti right after they left your place. They're going to keep digging, seeing what they can find on you and your father. If you have sold your soul to Hell, you will bring down the Atlanta Guild, do you understand?" he demanded.

Riley shivered at the thought. She didn't like a lot of the guys in the Guild, but destroying it would put them all out of work and put the city at risk.

"Got it."

Harper sighed. "Stewart thinks something else is up. I don't buy much of his mystical crap, but he usually knows what he's talking about.

We'll get with him and see what we can do to settle things down. I want the hunters out of this town as quickly as possible, for all our sakes."

That was the longest conversation they'd ever shared. Since her master seemed to be listening to her for a change, she decided now might be a good time to tell him about her fruitless following-recycling-trucks-all-over-Atlanta investigation. Maybe he'd have some suggestions.

"I've been working on that Holy Water problem." The man's eyes swiveled in her direction. At least they weren't bloodshot like before. She told him about the unmarked truck and how the drivers hadn't been good with her questions. "I checked out the recycling place," she said, cautiously editing out Peter's part of the investigation. "The bottles go there for stripping and cleaning, then they're sent to the Holy Water plant. I think they're being stolen somewhere along the way."

Though Harper's brow furrowed, the smackdown didn't come.

"You might be right," he said. "Used to be the city would send their own truck to collect the bottles, then I'd have to wait for the check. Now they've made some deal with a recycler to pick 'em up and pay me right then and there in cash."

"When did that change?"

"About three weeks ago."

"Just about the time the consecration dates went weird." She knew that much from the paperwork she'd had to complete. When Harper's previous apprentices filled out the forms, all the bottles had proper consecration dates.

"So if I want to steal a bunch of empty bottles that just happen to have the city's tax stamp on them," she mused, "I make a deal with the city to collect them, skim some off the top, fudge the paperwork, and no one knows the bottles are missing. I fill those with tap water and sell them just like they're the real thing."

Harper gave her a hard look. "You've got a twisted mind, brat."

She couldn't argue with that. "So we just have to talk to the distributor, see if any bottles are missing."

"Might not be that simple. The distributor could be kosher, but someone is stealing from them or getting their bottles from some other place. Buying new ones, maybe."

"But they'd have to have a tax stamp."

"No reason someone inside the city isn't selling them under the table."

Riley hadn't even thought of that. "Now who's got a twisted mind?" she said. A second after she'd made the comment, it hit her what she'd said. Harper didn't seem upset. "The Holy Water vendor in the market is in on it too, I swear."

"We need to take control of this situation. Too much is getting by us," Harper said. "I'll talk to Stewart and—"

The ground shook, a tremor so light Riley could almost believe she'd imagined it. Harper sat up in his chair, flipping down the footrest, on alert.

Riley held her breath. *Please God, not here.* Another tremor followed almost immediately, rattling the plates in the kitchenette. She had to hold on to the desk for support, as items jittered across the top and tumbled to the floor.

"Oh, hell," Harper said, jumping to his feet. "It wouldn't dare . . ."

A blast of straight wind rammed into the front of the building, shattering the windows in the two overhead doors.

"Down!" Harper bellowed. A second later the doors exploded, converting the wood to lethal missiles.

Riley barely hit the floor before debris speared the room, burying wooden shards deep into the back walls like jagged arrows. Then came the laughter. Low, chilling, and totally demonic.

The Geo-Fiend had come for her.

Where is Ori?

Rolling waves coursed across the ground, causing the building's remaining window glass to shatter and its masonry to crack. Dust poured down in a choking fog.

"Pit!" Harper shouted, catching her by the arm and dragging her out of what remained of the office. Another tremor slung them to the ground. Harper crawled back on his feet, hampered by his injury. Above them, the metal supports shrieked in protest as the joints began to fail.

"Help me!" he called, scrabbling at something with his fingers. Through the swirling dust, Riley realized he was trying to pull up a piece of plywood covering a section of the garage floor. Putting her back to the wind and dust storm, she dug into the crevice between the concrete and the wood, attempting to gain leverage on the warped plywood. Lifting it proved impossible with the force of the gale, so with incredible effort they shifted it sideways.

Grimacing in pain, Harper pushed her into the pit. It stank of old oil and dirty rags.

"Cover your head!" he cried. Above them the building twisted on its foundations as concrete blocks ground into each other then dislodged themselves to tumble to the earth.

Riley beckoned for him to join her, but her master shook his head. "Stay here!"

With his trapping bag in hand, he wove himself through the falling debris, then crawled out a gaping hole in the side of the building.

What is he doing? The demon will rip him apart.

The other trappers would come to help them, or maybe the hunters would. He could not take on a Five by himself.

Harper had told her to stay here. That's exactly what she should do. Riley hated him, hated how he treated her and her dad. She remembered every bruise he'd given her, every insult.

But he's my master.

With a cry of anguish, she hauled herself out of the pit and ran to join him.

The moment she exited the ruined building the wind died, causing an eerie silence to beat against her ears. She found Harper in the parking lot thirty feet from the towering Geo-Fiend, guarding his injured side, his face coated with a thick layer of dust like a coal miner.

The demon was the one from the Tabernacle. The thing was tall, deep black skin stretched over a thickly muscled chest and bulky arms. Muscles rippled in its bull-like neck and horns adorned the sides of its head, tapering upward into wicked points. Brilliant crimson flames seethed inside its maw.

The demon observed her with blazing crimson eyes. "Blackthorne's daughter," it cried.

Harper turned, then glowered at her. "Get back in there!"

Riley shook her head, taking her place next to him. This was the demon who had killed her father; she would not hide from it.

Without asking permission she reached into the trapping bag hanging off her master's shoulder and retrieved two grounding spheres. When she handed one to Harper, he studied her for a moment, then nodded grimly, his pale scar stretched tight.

"You know what to do?" he croaked.

"Yes." Her fear felt so real she swore it was pouring out of her skin like water from a faucet.

Harper angled his head, indicating she should move to the right. As she took the first few steps, she heard the demon chuckle in amusement.

Where is the angel? Or Beck and those damned hunters? Why is it just the two of us?

"Now!" Harper shouted, but his command came too late. A solid wall of air hit them like a jackhammer, causing Riley to tumble backward. As she rolled, she cradled the sphere so it wouldn't break. Hail and rain slashed at her body like needles, the wind coming in unpredictable gusts so there was no way to brace herself against the onslaught. Through the torrent she saw Harper regain his feet. He didn't wait for her but threw his sphere toward the old mangled fence. Enough of it was metal that the sphere caught hold and began to run its blue magic toward the demon.

Lightning slashed out of the sky and struck the ground near Riley's feet. She yelped and jumped back, scorched earth filling her nose. She launched her sphere at the stretch of fence to the right of the fiend.

Abruptly, the wind shifted direction, coming from behind her now. It slammed her onto the ground, then relentlessly pushed her toward the demon. Riley skidded along on her belly, gravel imbedding itself into her knees and palms. She saw the demon's outstretched hand, pulling her toward it. Wicked spikes extended from the fingers, spikes that would impale her before the fiend ripped her in half.

"Die, you bastard!" Harper yelled and threw another sphere. It was luminescent gold and it exploded with an earsplitting concussion underneath the Five. The demon roared and then began to flail in agony. The wind propelling Riley vanished. She clamored to her feet and cheered.

Below the demon the gold magic spread across the ground, separating it from its source of power. The fiend struggled and rose higher in the air. Then it waved a hand, bellowing in pain, and a deep pit yawned open. The spreading gold sank into its depths. With a mighty effort, the demon forced the hole closed, sealing the magic beneath the earth.

They had failed.

Enraged, the fiend turned its fiery eyes toward Harper. "Die, trapper," it bellowed, and with a flick of a wrist, a blast of wind flung Harper backward toward the demolished building, rolling him over and over in the gravel. When he finally came to rest in a crumpled heap, the master didn't move.

There were sirens in the distance, but the cops wouldn't get here in time, not that they could do anything with a Geo-Fiend. There were no hunters, no angel, and no Beck. It looked like her dad was right: She'd be seeing him real soon. At least she'd be able to tell him she'd done her best.

The demon turned its Hellfire eyes on Riley. "Blackthorne's daughter," it called. "Your time has come."

Hands quaking, Riley armed herself with two Holy Water spheres. They would do no real damage, but at least she'd make a fight of it.

No way I'm dying without knowing why.

"Is this because of the Armageddon thing?" she asked.

The demon's reply was a roar that rivaled a jet engine. It filled her with such terror that her body went numb and the spheres tumbled from her hands to smash at her feet. The will to stand drained away and she slumped to her knees. "Why?" she demanded. "Tell me why!"

"You stand in the way," the demon replied. With great effort, she forced herself to look at the fiend. It was closer now. She could feel heat radiating off it, and the acrid stench of brimstone made her gag.

"I'd better take it from here," a voice said.

Ori?

He stood a few feet to her left, clad in light silver armor that seemed to generate its own light, his wings arched behind him. With a deep laugh that spoke more of revenge than mirth, he unsheathed a sword from the scabbard at his waist. The blade ignited in white-hot flames, crackling in the night.

"Omigod," she whispered.

Riley pulled herself to her feet and hurried to her master's side as the angel and the demon squared off. Harper was still breathing. She smiled, despite their turbulent history. He was like her—hard to kill.

𝒯𝒽𝑒 𝒹𝑒𝓂𝑜𝓃 𝓁𝒶𝓊𝑔𝒽𝑒𝒹 in derision, rising higher in the air, gaining strength as winds whirled around it. "You challenge me, Divine? Your bones break as easily as any mortal's."

"So do yours, Hellspawn."

The demon sneered, revealing razored teeth among the flames. "We shall destroy all of you at the End of Days."

Ori sighed. They were always like this—all Hellfire and retribution. He didn't understand how Lucifer tolerated them. "You have violated the Eternal Oath. You know the punishment, Astaring."

The demon snorted flames at the use of its true name. "I shall feast on your corpse, Divine, then I shall destroy Blackthorne's child."

"Not tonight," Ori said, raising his blade. "Not ever."

With a tremendous shout that even Heaven would have heard, the angel charged into battle.

A ferocious wind caught him mid-leap, but Ori used it to his advantage and spun in the air, landing a slicing blow to the fiend's left shoulder. It shouted in pain, then slashed at him with its claws. One caught the trailing edge of a wing, ripping deep into the feathers and tendons.

A second before the other claw would have hooked him, Ori spun out of its reach. A sudden downdraft pulled him toward the earth. His wings acknowledged it, but the injured one didn't have enough lift to counteract the plunge. As he fought to regain altitude, the demon cast a torrential rainstorm against him, drenching his wings and driving him hard into the red clay and gravel. Ori managed to scramble away to avoid being flattened by the fiend's taloned foot.

Killing a weather-worker should have been nothing for a Divine, yet this one had more power than he'd ever seen. "Who is helping you?" Ori panted. "Name your demi-lord!"

"I shall tell you as you draw your last breath," the demon promised.

A bolt of lightning sheared down from the sky, hitting Ori's blade. He reeled back from the blow but did not drop the weapon. Instead, he channeled the power of the storm upward, gathering the wind, the rain, the hail, and the lightning into one massive strike. Then he threw it at the demon with every ounce of power he possessed.

As the fiend fought against the onslaught, Ori drove his blade deep into the beast's chest. He carved through the ribs until its heart burst free, smoking black like hot tar. The demon's eyes widened in fear.

"Boon . . ." it cried. "Boon I grant thee."

"Death is thy boon," the angel replied.

Ori unsheathed his sword from the demon's chest and fell to his knees only a few feet away from his foe. The rogue was whispering, gathering in power, probably trying to heal itself.

The power around the demon shifted, grew stronger. With a final dying breath, it cast forth that energy in a shock wave that blew across the parking lot like a hurricane's winds. Ori cried out a warning, but it was too late.

⊹

Riley awoke in someone's arms as a soft voice told her she was safe, that the demon was dead. She blinked, trying to clear her vision. It didn't work. Everything was fuzzy, like she was looking through gauze.

"Hold very still," Ori said. He gently touched a finger above one eye, then the other, and a tingle spread across her face. Riley blinked again and everything became clear. Then the angel took her hands in his and performed the same miracle. The gravel embedded in her palms dislodged as the wounds healed. He repeated the healing with her knees.

"That's serious angel mojo," Riley said, trying to smile.

"Better be."

She forced herself to sit up. "You're hurt!" His one wing bled, a brilliant blue fluid leaking from between the feathers.

"It is already healing. Do not worry," he said. As she watched, the wing did knit together and the feathers grew back in place.

"Wow," she said. That was the only word that seemed to apply. She turned to look at where the demon had been. There was just a smoking crater now. "Please tell me it's dead."

"Dead and buried, just as I promised." He paused, as if hearing something she couldn't. "Time for me to go. Your master killed the demon. Do you understand?"

"Why should I lie?"

"It's for the best. They cannot know what I've done here."

"But when will I see you again?"

"At the cemetery, tonight. Come to me when you can."

"But what about—"

He touched a finger to the middle of her forehead and white light sent her into oblivion.

THIRTY-ONE

Someone held her, calling Riley's name. The voice sounded so worried, frantic even.

"Ori?" she asked. When she opened her eyes she realized it wasn't the angel. From the expression on the man's face, he wasn't happy she'd called him someone else's name. Especially *that* name.

"Beck," she said. His worried expression diminished.

"Thank God," he said. "When I felt the earthquake, I thought ya were done for."

Not yet. "Harper?"

"Bitchin' up a storm. He'll be okay." Beck looked around. "Must have been a helluva show," he said, his voice thick. "Sorry I didn't get here in time."

She swallowed and then grimaced. Her mouth felt like it was full of dirt.

"Water?" she croaked.

He laid her back down and dug in his duffel bag. Then she was back in his arms sucking down the cool liquid. It felt so wonderful. She struggled to sit up, cradling the water bottle between her hands.

"Easy," Beck warned.

She nodded, but sat up anyway. Her palms tingled. She inspected one: The skin was pink but there was no sign of the gravel burn.

No doubt about it. Angels are awesome.

She drank more of the water to clear her throat. "Harper went after it," she said. "He told me to stay in that pit thing inside the building."

"But ya didn't stay, did ya?"

She shook her head. "I had to help him."

A tortured sigh. "Well, yer alive and ya got the bastard. I just wish I'd been the one to take it down," he said.

She realized it was more than just scoring a Five; it was all about Beck extracting revenge for her father's death. "If you'd been here, you would have; I know it," she said.

He gave her a nod, telling her he appreciated the gesture.

A paramedic knelt next to her. "How about you lay back down and I'll check you out, okay?" the woman said.

Riley did as ordered, though she didn't think anything was broken. She answered the paramedic's questions until the woman was satisfied there were no serious injuries.

"I think it would be wise if you went to the hospital, just in case."

Riley shook her head. "I'm fine."

"Your call." The woman repacked her case and took off.

Riley sighed in relief and sat up again. Beck was near what was left of the building, talking to Jackson and a couple of the other trappers. Firemen milled around, and there were a few cops as well.

Her eyes skimmed across the parking lot to the smoking hole where the Five had been. Ori said he'd get the thing, and he had. He'd kept his word. *But why did he wait so long to show up?*

She heard Harper's voice, sharp and sarcastic. He was sitting upright, holding an ice pack to his head, growling at the paramedic who kept fussing with him.

You're just a tough old bird, aren't you? But when the time had come, he'd protected her. That she hadn't expected.

When Riley stood her head spun, so she waited until she regained her balance and then walked across the debris-strewn parking lot to her master.

He looked up at her with bloodshot eyes. "Brat," he said.

"Master Harper."

His paramedic tried the same "You should go to the hospital" spiel with him and failed just as miserably. Once the fellow had cleared off and they were alone, Harper eyed her.

"So where the hell's the demon?" he asked so quietly only she could hear him.

She knelt next to him. "Dead," she said. "You killed it." *Please don't ask me how.*

He frowned. "I don't remember doing that."

Time to change the subject. "You could have let that thing flatten me, but you didn't. Why?"

"I could ask you the same question."

She was too tired to edit her mouth. "You're my master. I couldn't let that thing kill another trapper, even if I think he's a total asshat."

Harper looked at her for a long time then cracked a toothy grin. "And you're one mouthy bitch, but you're my apprentice. I don't need the reputation that my people die because I don't protect them."

That was fair.

He slowly turned toward the building, and the grin fled. She followed his gaze. The back wall was still intact, but the front was a mound of concrete blocks and protruding metal. Steam rose from a couple of the piles, curling up into the air. Papers fluttered in a light breeze, and the office chair's legs stuck up into the air like an overturned turtle.

"Damn, I really loved that place," Harper murmured.

How could anyone love an old smelly garage?

"My dad was a mechanic," he replied, as if he'd read her mind. "I used to hang around and watch him work on cars. He could fix anything."

"So this place reminded you of him?" Riley asked, intrigued.

"Yeah."

"Was he a trapper?"

A nod. "He died taking down an Archdemon when I was sixteen." Harper swallowed and then coughed, hard. He looked up at her, no hint of arrogance in those ancient eyes. "It's why I became a trapper."

He'd suffered a loss just like hers. She never would have guessed.

"Riley?" Beck called out.

She welcomed the interruption. It felt strange having a regular conversation with Harper, and she suspected his next move would be to destroy this touchy-feely moment with a caustic remark.

Riley rose. When her balance faltered, Beck caught her elbow. They both turned as four black vans pulled into the parking lot, one after another, throwing gravel as they screeched to a halt.

"Took them long enough," Beck grumbled. One of the hunters stood out immediately: His body language told Riley he was in charge. He ordered his men to fan out, then headed her way.

"Who's that?" she asked.

"Elias Salvatore. He's their captain. Just be careful what ya say to 'em."

That was a given. At least the priest wasn't here tonight.

"Next time, tell us where you're headed," Salvatore growled, his frown aimed at Beck. "We could have been here sooner." Then he turned his attention to Riley. "You okay?" She nodded. "So what happened here?"

"It was a Geo-Fiend," her master replied, looking up at the man, his face stern.

"Grounded?"

"Dead," Harper said. His eyes met Riley's and the message was passed. No matter what really happened, the hunters weren't on their side.

The captain signaled to two of his men. "Check out the crater." He turned back to the master trapper. "Any other demons besides that one?"

Harper shook his head. "That was enough."

"You have my admiration, Master Harper," the captain said, tilting his head in respect. "They are very difficult to kill."

Harper coughed up more dust. "So I noticed."

Salvatore crossed the lot to join his men near the smoking hole, talking back and forth in what sounded like Italian. There seemed to be some debate going on, with lots of gestures.

Harper dropped the ice pack and then extended a hand to Riley. "Get me up off this damned ground."

Once she and Beck helped him up, he hobbled into the rubble, his shoulders bent and his gait uneven. Jackson joined him and they talked quietly among themselves. Then Harper pointed at something. The other trapper began to unearth it.

"So where the hell's yer fancy boy?" Beck asked. "Why wasn't he here keepin' ya safe?"

She wasn't going to take the bait.

"Whatever," she murmured. It didn't matter what Beck thought.

Any doubts she had about the angel had perished with the demon.

⁘

It was close to eleven when Beck finally made it to Stewart's place. Harper had refused to leave his scrap metal collection unguarded, so they'd loaded it into one of the trapper's trucks and stored it in Beck's garage. The rest of Harper's stuff was in the back of another truck headed for a storage unit. At least they'd been able to salvage his filing cabinets and business records, though his personal belongings were pretty much history.

Exhausted, Beck sank into the same chair he'd occupied during his last visit.

"Scotch?" Stewart asked.

"Yes, but not much." He didn't need to get drunk, he needed to sort out his feelings. When he'd seen Riley lying in that parking lot, he was sure she was dead. He'd run to her, praying to a God that he wasn't sure existed, praying for a miracle. Then he'd cradled her body in his arms. When her soft breath had touched his face, he'd almost lost it in front of her and the other trappers.

"Lad?"

Beck jerked out his thoughts. A tumbler half full of amber liquor sat on an end table next to his chair. He took a long suck on the whisky.

"Yer not lookin' good," Stewart said, settling into one of the chairs. "What's wrong?"

Beck shook his head. He wasn't ready to talk about it. "Where'd Harper end up?"

"He's upstairs, in bed."

"No, I'm not," the older trapper replied. He shuffled into the room and chose a seat near the fireplace. The way he eased himself into it told Beck the man was hurting.

"What would ya like ta drink?" Stewart asked. Beck noted he'd not offered the man liquor.

Harper fumbled in a pocket and produced a bottle of pain pills. "Water."

Beck did the honors, though it took some time to hunt through the kitchen cabinets to find a glass. Once he was back in his chair, they all stared at their drinks. None of them wanted to talk about what had happened tonight.

No choice. "How'd ya kill the Five?" Beck said.

The master shook his head. "I didn't. The last thing I remember is being rolled across the parking lot like a bowling ball. The Five was still kicking when I went down."

"But how . . ."

"Riley know how ta take down a Geo-Fiend?" Stewart asked.

Beck and Harper shook their heads at the same time.

"Then it appears we have a mystery, gents."

More silence.

This wasn't going to be easy, but Beck knew it was time to come clean. "I think I know who took out the demon."

The eyes of both masters shifted to him.

"There's a Lancer in town named Ori. He's been hangin' around

Riley. She told me he was the one who saved her from the Five at the Tabernacle. Maybe he was the one that killed it tonight."

"Why wouldn't she just say so?" Harper asked.

Beck shrugged. "Don't know. This one's an arrogant bastard, and I think he's got more on his mind than just killin' demons."

"Which means yer opinion of him might be biased," Stewart replied, a slight smile on his lips now.

"Yeah, maybe," Beck admitted. *Just tell 'em. If it kills my chances at bein' a master, so be it.* "This guy was at the Armageddon Lounge a few nights back. A couple Fours came in, workin' as a team. The older one had me dead to rights. Next thing I know the demons blew out of there like their tails were on fire."

When Stewart scowled, Beck knew his next question. "My soul's still my own. But this Ori guy just sat there and watched the whole thing go down. They didn't seem to bother him at all."

"Why didn't ya mention this earlier?" the Scotsman demanded.

"Too much hittin' the fan. And I wasn't proud I'd almost been taken down. That's the truth of it."

The master took a big jolt of whisky. "Next time, ya tell me, ya hear?" he said gruffly.

"Yes, sir."

"Did those demons know he's a Lancer?" Harper asked.

"Don't think so," Beck replied. "They didn't act like they knew he was there."

"A pair of Fours, and this guy doesn't make a move on them? That's not right," Harper said. "Freelancers are always after money on the hoof."

"Same thing tonight: If he'd killed that Five, he'd have stayed behind to make sure he got credited with the kill," Beck replied. *And to make me look bad in front of Riley.*

Stewart's face was pensive now. "Push yer personal emotions aside, lad, and do a gut-check about this fella. What are ya feelin'?"

Beck tried, but it was difficult. Too much of Paul's daughter was tangled up inside of him now.

"This guy's really smooth, but somethin' about him's not right, and it's not just because of . . . her."

"Could it be another Four?" Harper suggested. "Is that why the Mezmers ignored him?"

"I'm thinkin' not. A Geo-Fiend wouldn't back down from a Four," Stewart murmured.

"Riley said he'd been on holy ground. He's not a demon," Beck added.

Stewart sat straighter in his chair as if he'd realized something. "Is Riley stayin' at the church tonight?"

"No, she's at home now that the Five is dead," Beck replied.

"Call her and have her come here."

"But . . ."

"Just do it," Stewart ordered, his voice unusually crisp.

As Beck dialed the number he saw a look pass between the two masters.

"What are you thinking, Angus?" Harper quizzed.

Stewart gave a quick shake of his head. Which meant he didn't want to talk about it in front of Beck.

The call rolled over to voice mail. Same thing with her home phone. "She's not answerin'."

"Find her. Bring her here."

"I'll have to give her a reason."

"She doesn't need one," Stewart said curtly. "She's stayin' here until we know exactly who this Ori fellow is."

"What's goin' on, sir?" Beck asked. "Why ya so worried?"

"Just an old Scotsman's paranoia. Get it done, lad."

Beck left his whisky behind, heading for the front door. Behind him he heard muted voices—Stewart telling the other master just why he was paranoid. Beck couldn't catch the words, and part of him didn't want to.

THIRTY-TWO

True to his word, Ori leaned against the red brickwork of the cemetery gate, arms folded over his chest. He looked like he had the first time Riley had seen him: His hair slicked back into a ponytail, and wearing that black leather jacket. No sign of those wings, no hint that he took orders from Heaven. Just a hunky guy hanging around a graveyard.

Waiting for me.

It seemed silly, but after she'd called Peter to let him know she was safe just in case CNN covered the Harper thing, she'd showered and put on makeup again. She'd worn her best pair of jeans and her favorite shirt. She'd tried to tell herself it was just something you did, but that's not the way it felt.

As she climbed out of the car, Riley's finger brushed her mouth, remembering Ori's kisses, how they'd made her feel. Those had been real. Maybe Simi was right: Sometimes you needed to be a little wild, even if it was with an angel.

Moving toward the gate, everything else but Ori faded from view, his lazy smile drawing her in. She offered him one of her own.

"Riley." His smile widened as he took her hand, twining his fingers with hers. They were warm, though he wasn't wearing gloves.

"I wasn't sure you'd be here," she said, then regretted it. It sounded needy. "I mean, you've probably got better things to do now that the Five is dead."

"I have no other task but you at the moment."

As if to reassure her, the angel slid his arm around her waist, pulling her closer. She hesitated for a second, then nestled into his side as they walked into the graveyard. Leaves skidded along in front of them. As they passed the empty guardhouse, a gust of wind pushed against her, whipping her hair forward. Ori paused and looked back toward the main gate, his brows furrowed.

"What is it?" she asked, turning.

A slight frown crossed his face, then vanished. "Just someone trying to tell me how to do my job. It's nothing."

"I didn't figure angels had that sort of thing."

"You'd be surprised."

Ori squeezed her hand and they began moving again, but she could feel his tension. It hadn't been there when she'd first arrived.

"I don't know how to thank you," she said. "It feels weird not having to worry anymore."

"Enjoy your freedom; you've earned it," he said.

"That was an awesome battle. I just wish you hadn't been hurt," she said.

"Part of my job," he replied. He wasn't looking at her now, like he had something on his mind. "I should have been watching you closer. I am truly sorry about that. I was . . . detained."

Then he fell silent, like that topic was off-limits. The only way to find out more about this guy was to ask questions. She decided to start with one of the simpler ones.

"What do angels do all day?"

That pulled his attention back to her. "Divines are given a number of tasks," he replied. "For example, this cemetery has its own angelic caretaker who ensures that everything is as it should be. Most places have their own Divine."

"Are you talking about Martha?" she asked, surprised.

"I know her by another name, but yes, that's her. Have you never wondered why all this metal is still here?" he said, gesturing to encompass the graveyard. "She makes sure it doesn't get stolen."

"So that's why." She looked up at him hopefully. "All Martha told me is that I was to stop Armageddon. Do you have any idea how I'm supposed to do that?"

"If I did know, I couldn't tell you."

"Surprise," she murmured. "What she *didn't* tell me is that my boyfriend would go all nuts."

"Would you have let him die if you knew what was going to happen between you?" Ori questioned.

"Ah . . . no," she replied. "Simon has a family who loves him. I'll get over what he did to me." *In a few centuries.*

"Maybe sooner," the angel promised. A lock of dark hair had fallen forward on his face, making him look like a bad boy. A tingling sensation lodged in her chest.

Totally hot. And he's with me. Even if it was only for a short time.

She realized he'd probably read her mind, so she changed topics.

"What's Heaven like?"

Ori put a single finger to her lips. "So many questions." He gently caressed her cheek. When he drew her in for a kiss, Riley's world collapsed to only those points where their bodies met.

When the kiss ended, she swore she could see infinity in his dark eyes.

"Why are you doing this?" she whispered.

"Kissing you?" he asked, smoothing back a strand of her hair. "Because I want to. Because I find you so amazing."

Amazing?

She took a step back, though it proved harder than she'd anticipated.

"You're frowning. Are my kisses that bad?" he teased.

"No, it's just . . ."

"You do not think yourself worthy of love."

"No, it's just that I've not had a great track record."

"Then why blame me for the others?" he said, his voice cooler now. "I have been nothing but honest with you."

"Mostly because you haven't told me that much."

"So if I told you exactly how the cosmos works, how long an angel can withstand a star going supernova, and that I was there when it was all created, you would trust me more?"

Riley shook her head. "Then I'd think you were lying."

"Exactly. Accept that I enjoy being with you. Accept that when I'm with you I see Heaven in your eyes."

"It's hard for me to believe that."

"I know."

They'd reached her family's mausoleum. Things had been too heavy between them, so she asked, "Where are we going tonight? On another picnic?" *That would be so cool.*

"Tonight we shall stay here." He waved his hand, and the mausoleum's twin doors swung open on their own accord. No key needed when you were an angel. Riley stepped to the threshold and gasped. The interior was lit from within by a myriad of candles, like a great cathedral. The flames' reflections flickered off the stained-glass windows, igniting the vibrant colors of blood red, royal blue, yellow gold.

Ori pushed by her and settled into the niche at the back of the mausoleum. Riley hesitated: Something felt weird, which didn't make much sense. He was one of Heaven's own. He'd saved her life. If you couldn't trust an angel, things were really bad.

He studied her with those deep eyes. "I wish you didn't know what I am. It has changed things between us."

"No. It's not that."

But it was. He'd probably met God in person, polished His throne or something. It was like one of those books she'd read when she was a kid: The girl would meet an immortal guy, fall in love, and then everything would go wrong until they saved each other from a hideous fate. The books always had a happy ending, but she knew that was bogus. There was never a happy-ever-after in real life.

With a sigh, Riley closed the heavy bronze doors, troubled by her conflicted emotions. Behind her there was a *whoosh*ing sound. She turned and couldn't stop the gasp.

Ori's leather jacket and T-shirt were gone, revealing his muscled chest. A pair of white wings hung in the air behind him. They weren't fully extended—the mausoleum was not large enough for that—but still they were incredible. There was no evidence of the damage he'd sustained in the battle.

Entranced, Riley walked toward him. Each iridescent feather glowed as the candlelight touched it. She carefully ran a finger down the length of one. It felt like fine silk.

Pulling her to the floor, Ori laid her head on his shoulder, curving a protective wing around her. Outside, the wind gusted around the building and leaves pattered against the metal doors. All she heard was her heart beating in time with his.

"I could stay here forever," he said.

"But you won't," she replied.

Ori tilted her chin upward, looking deep into her eyes. "Maybe I will."

She wanted him to kiss her, keep kissing her until nothing else mattered. When his lips delicately touched hers, they felt like the brush of a dove's wing. The second kiss was more insistent. A fire ignited in her belly. She felt his fingers brush her neck, gently grazing an ear as he leaned closer and kissed her cheek.

As good as it felt, she was roasting. "Your wings are really warm," she said. He helped her out of her coat. She felt naked in front of him, exposed in ways she didn't understand. The fire in her belly burned hotter.

Taking her hand, Ori placed it on his naked chest. Riley could feel his heart beating underneath her fingertips. "You stir my blood," he whispered. "It's been a long time since that has happened."

When they next kissed, she found herself leaning into him, wanting him to touch her. Then she pulled back and shook her head.

"This is . . . crazy. This kind of thing only happens in books."

"You're sure of that?" he asked, wrapping her in those magnificent wings again.

"Angels can't, like . . ."

"Of course we can," he whispered into her ear.

At his urging, she skimmed her fingers through his dark satin hair, pulling it out of the ponytail. The pool of heat in her belly spread downward. Without thinking, she kissed his ear. He murmured in appreciation, drawing her closer. Another kiss, deeper this time, his tongue playfully touching hers.

Riley felt his fingers locate the top button on her shirt. He looked deep into her eyes, seeking permission. When she didn't protest, it came open. He worked his way down the shirt, button by button. As the last one gave way, he gently pushed it back, then brushed his fingertips across the lace covering her right breast. Riley hummed in response. The sensations were almost too much for her to bear.

This wasn't Simon or one of the other boys at school. This was for real.

Too fast. With a groan, Riley pulled out of his arms. She needed time to think this through, to let her head clear.

"I'm not sure I'm . . . ready for this," she said. It was a huge step, even with a mortal. She couldn't be the only woman he'd been with all these ages. What would keep him from getting tired of her?

"It doesn't matter. I'm with you now," he soothed. "I have a duty to protect you, Riley, and the best way to do that is in my arms."

His tenderness calmed her fears, and she settled back into his embrace. It would be so easy to let him make love to her. *Like in my dream.*

Ori gently pushed a strand of hair off her face. "It's your choice."

He'd read her mind again. He was right: This was her choice. "I've never . . ."

"I know."

He knows I'm a virgin? What *doesn't* he know?

"How to win your trust," he replied. He gently kissed her forehead. "So much sadness for one so young."

Riley curved into the hollow of his wing, feeling his breath across her skin like a whispering breeze. Outside, the wind skittered dry leaves across the gravestones.

"Tell me what you want," Ori urged.

Riley teetered on the edge. She was seventeen, not some kid. She could be with him, but what would happen after that?

"You will set our future, Riley. I surrender myself to you, body and soul."

His next kiss was surprisingly tender. It felt like a lover's kiss.

"Tell me what you want," he repeated.

Her final doubts melted away. "You," she whispered. "I want you."

"Then I am yours, Riley Anora Blackthorne, and you shall be mine."

Ori curved his wings around her, lifting her face, her body to melt against his. Raw desire surged between them. It surrounded her. Overwhelmed her.

Love me. Forever.

Nothing else mattered.

Riley awoke sometime later, covered by a wing that was toastier than any blanket. When she rolled toward Ori, he stirred, those dark eyes searching her face.

"You look content," he said.

"I am."

Did she feel different? Not really. Other than an intense heat that surged through her veins, she hadn't changed. Other girls had told her what it was like their first time, but hers hadn't been like that. There'd been no fumbling, no uncertainty. Ori was a born lover, and now he was hers.

"I want this forever," she said, tracing one finger across his full lips. Then she sighed. "But that's a very long time, and I haven't even finished school yet."

Ori chuckled. "You worry too much, Riley Anora, my *valiant light*."

She snuggled next to his body, mindful they were both nude. Underneath them was some sort of padding, almost like a sleeping bag only far richer in texture and comfort. *More angel mojo.*

Ori bent over her, running a line of tiny kisses down her forehead to her nose. "Morning comes soon. Let's not waste the night with talk."

"What happens in the morning, with us I mean?"

His answer was a breath-stealing kiss.

THIRTY-THREE

When Riley awoke again she was lying on the floor of the mausoleum fully clothed. The comfy padding was gone; so were the candles and the angel. For a few seconds she wondered if it had just been a dream.

No dream could have been that good.

Then she saw the rose. It was blood red, lying next to her. She sampled its fragrance and, like Ori, it was heavenly. After some time, Riley finally moved into a sitting position. So where was the angel? Doubts seemed to crowd her when he wasn't near. She wanted him here, holding her, telling her she'd made the right decision.

How long can this last? What would Heaven say if they found out?

She pulled on her jacket and then combed out her hair. A quick check of her pocket mirror generated a sigh of relief. Her makeup wasn't trashed. While she reapplied her lip gloss, Riley tried to recall every moment with the angel, but it seemed too magical to capture in mere memories. It hadn't been like she'd thought: It hadn't hurt that first time, and when she'd voiced her worries about becoming pregnant, he'd assured that wasn't possible, not with him. Still, something kept nibbling on her like a tenacious bug; she couldn't quite sort it out. Riley gave up and pushed open the mausoleum doors.

She found her lover a short distance from the mausoleum. His wings were tightly cramped against his back, a barometer to his mood. Something was wrong.

"Ori?" she called.

He turned toward her with an expression so sad it almost brought tears. He beckoned her over, but when she asked what was wrong, he shushed her.

"Enjoy the moment," he said, intertwining their fingers.

They faced east. The sun had just poked over the horizon, and it made the feathers on his wings glow as if they were absorbing the light.

"I always love the sunrise," he said. "It reminds me of Heaven." Then a tremor ran the length of his body.

"Ori, what's going on?"

He turned toward her again, taking both her hands in his. His expression was even sadder now. "You have a decision to make, dear Riley. It will be the hardest of your life, and I am so sorry you must make it."

He was spooking her. "What are you talking about?"

The angel hesitated. "I need you to pledge yourself to me. If you do, then I can keep you safe for as long as you live."

For a second she swore she felt the earth shake, but it was just her body.

"I have made my commitment by being with you," he explained. "I have placed my future in your hands, Riley. Do not think that was a light decision. In the past, any angel who lay with a mortal woman was punished."

"Punished? But isn't God all about love?" she asked. "I mean, wouldn't He want us to be together?"

"There are rules." Ori let go of her hands. "Your soul is . . . *in play*, as we call it. It happened the moment you made the arrangement with Heaven. That agreement attracted notice in the lower realms."

"That makes no sense," she said, stepping away from him. "The demons have always known my name. You're saying that just because I agreed to help Heaven, now I've got all of Hell after me?"

"Not all, only those who are truly ambitious."

Riley drifted up the path toward the mausoleum, troubled. She hadn't expected this, not after the night they'd spent together. She turned to face her lover. "What is this decision I need to make?"

Ori sighed deeply, his expression still troubled. "The fundamental measure of a mortal is his or her soul. Yours is very powerful, Riley. That is why you must pledge it to me. That is how Hell will know we have a bond, one that is lasting and true. Only then will you be safe."

He wants my soul?

"Yes," he said, reading her mind. "Nothing less will do." He was a few feet from her now. The wings were gone and he looked like any mortal. Harmless, if you didn't know what lie beneath.

Riley hesitated, so many questions pounding at her at once. *Why would an angel want my soul? Martha didn't.*

"That was different," Ori responded.

"It doesn't make sense. You're saying Hell's after me, but the Five tried to kill me *before* I did the deal with Heaven."

"The rogue wasn't after your soul, Riley. It just wanted you and your father dead."

"Why?"

Ori stepped closer, offering his hand. "Please trust me. I only do this to keep you alive."

He sounded so sincere, but she took a step back anyway. "I have trusted you. I slept with you, remember?" She'd given him something truly precious—her virginity. You could only do that once. Did Ori think so little of her that it meant nothing?

Something stirred inside her. Riley wasn't sure what it was, but it seared like a live coal in the pit of her stomach. She'd felt this before, in the parking lot with Allan right after he'd punched her.

"What does this soul pledging mean to me?" she asked.

"It means that we are bound together."

"That was a vague answer," she muttered. "You seem to be really good at those. Does that talent come with the wings?"

Ori frowned. "This is best for both of us. I'm the only one who hasn't hurt you."

"Give it time," she said, surprised at her bitterness. What was feeding that? Maybe the fact that almost every guy had lied to her.

Ori began to pace in front of the mausoleum, his moves disjointed, a mirror to his turbulent emotions. "I killed that demon for you, Riley. I have saved your life more times than you know. What else can I do to earn your trust?"

The coal in her stomach was a blast furnace now. She felt the tears slip down her face, and she swiped them away with the back of her hand. "Tell me the truth. How many mortals have you been with? Am I the first? The tenth, the thousandth?"

"This is for your own protection," he retorted. "You have no notion of how much danger you are in, from both Heaven and Hell."

"So God's going to smite me, too?" she replied. "If that happens, how am I supposed to stop the end of the world? You guys really need to get your stories straight."

"If you deny me, others will come for you, others more evil than you can imagine. Please, Riley, I am your only hope," he insisted.

"They can't get my soul unless I give it to them," she said, crossing her arms over chest.

"Oh, Riley," he murmured, "there are countless ways to lose your soul, most of them genuinely noble."

"You're lying. Why did I ever believe you?"

His wings reappeared, snapped tight against his back, vibrating with anger. "Clear your head, girl!" he shouted, his fist clenched now. "I am your last chance! Do not deny me!"

"Oh, dear, now you've upset him," a smooth voice said. "That is never a good thing."

Riley jerked in surprise to find a figure leaning against one of the gravestones clad in a black shirt and slacks, his collar-length ebony hair shot with silver. His eyes were bottomless midnight blue.

Ori started, then gave a deep bow. "My Lord, I did not expect you."

My Lord?

The newcomer laughed at the angel. "Of course you didn't. No one ever does." Those eyes fell on Riley again. They had a depth to them beyond anything she'd experienced.

"Who are you?" she whispered.

"I'm his boss," he said, angling his head toward Ori.

He sure didn't look like her idea of God.

The figure straightened. "You work it out, Blackthorne's daughter. You're a very smart girl."

Blackthorne's daughter. Demons called her by that name. Maybe Heaven did, too. They were on holy ground, so no way this could be Hell-spawn. Ori had called him "my Lord," which meant he was an angel, at least.

"You have that right," the figure replied.

Great. Mr. New Guy could read her mind just like Ori.

"I'll give you a huge clue," the newcomer said. Something flared in the air, and then a crimson doorway appeared next to him. The air seethed inside the portal, buoyed by unseen currents. Something waddled to the threshold, bouncing and giggling. It was round, black and white like a soccer ball, and about three feet tall. It had two feet tipped with claws, horns that spouted out of the top of its head, and pincers at the end of its arms. The moment it stepped across the portal and its clawed foot touched the hallowed ground, it shrieked and disappeared in a puff of black, acrid smoke. The unmistakable scent of brimstone stung her nose.

The newcomer rolled his eyes, snapped a finger, and the portal vanished. "Demons are *so* stupid."

"Omigod, you're . . ." she began, " . . . HIM?"

"Oh, indeed. I'm Lucifer," he said. "You'd be surprised how many mortals insist on using the S word. Or the D one for that matter." He shook his head in disgust. "I am neither. I am the Light Bearer, the Prince of Hell, the Chief among the Fallen, and *the* Adversary. Accept no substitutes."

Oh, shit.

"That's a very common reaction," he replied.

"You can't be here!" Riley protested. "This is hallowed ground. This has to be a trick."

"Hallowed ground is death to my Hellspawn but not to one who was created by the Light. Fallen can tread here as easily as you, child."

Another one of those things someone forgot to tell her.

Lucifer wandered over to the other angel, eying his servant intently. "So how goes it, Ori?"

"My Lord, I am fulfilling my tasks, as you commanded," Ori murmured. "Allow me more time, I beg of you."

"Tasks? And what were those?" his superior quizzed. "Refresh my mind."

Ori swallowed uneasily. His wings were no longer pure white but showed a thin line of ash gray at the tips. "I was to utterly destroy the rogue demon, which I have done."

"And?"

"I was to secure this girl's soul by any means necessary."

"About that *second* task," Lucifer said, "I note you have not fulfilled it. Losing your touch?" When he didn't reply, the Prince leaned closer. "Or is there some other reason?"

"You lied to me," she shouted, pointing an accusing finger at him. "You said you loved me."

The fire in Riley's stomach grew hotter, spreading into her chest now, threatening to consume her heart.

"I said I cared for you and that was not a lie," Ori said, stepping closer to her.

"Right. Try that one again," she snarled. "You're just sucking up to *him.*"

"Besides being one of the most arrogant of my servants," Lucifer began, "Ori is incredibly talented at seducing mortals. Male, female, doesn't matter. They're all the same to him."

"My Lord, please," Ori began, like he was embarrassed to have his sins paraded in front of her.

"Yes, this one is different for you," Lucifer chided. "But she is still at risk, unless you finish what you started."

Riley shook her head. "No go on the soul," she said. "No go on any of this."

"He was not lying," Lucifer replied. "Your soul *is* in play now. You can blame Heaven for that. We offer security. If you do not pledge your soul to Ori, others will seek it, and they will use every means to secure it."

"You can just tell them to back off, right?"

"I can, but that is no guarantee. Demons and Fallen are allowed to make their own mistakes. Like my servant Ori, here." He clapped a hand on the angel's shoulder, causing her seducer to grimace. "But we'll get back to that in a moment."

"Why is this about me?" Riley demanded.

She saw a flash of anger in the Prince's eyes. "Do not assume you are the very center of the universe, Blackthorne's daughter. There is more at stake than just your pitiful life."

"You know, I don't care anymore. I do one good deed and it all goes to—"

"Hell?" Lucifer quipped. "That's often the case."

"It'd be family tradition," Ori said in a bitter voice.

The Prince gave him a sharp look, followed by a frown. "Tread carefully, my servant."

"What do you mean, family tradition?" Riley demanded.

"Why do you think your father lived as long as he did?" Ori questioned. "Luck?" The smirk on his face made her queasy.

"My dad was an excellent trapper," she retorted. "One of the best."

"He was good, but he wasn't invincible. When that Archdemon was about to rip out his heart, Paul Blackthorne begged to stay alive. How could I ignore such a heartfelt plea?"

"No, you're wrong. My dad killed that thing. That's how he became a master."

"He did, after we made the deal," Ori said. "From that point on, no Hellspawn could harm him. In exchange, he would remain alive until you had become a master trapper."

These were more lies. That's what these monsters did: They twisted the truth until you couldn't tell day from night.

Lucifer bent over and picked up a withered leaf, examining it like he'd never seen one before. "Your father feared you being an orphan," he explained. "A very noble gesture, which cost him his soul." He blew on the leaf and it turned green, alive from the top to the stem. The moment it left his hand it returned to the dead, shattered fragments floating to the ground.

Ori started to say something, but his master waved him silent.

The lies had a kernel of truth to them. Her dad had changed after he'd captured the Archfiend. Quieter, more thoughtful. He hadn't shown any fear of demons from that point on.

"You understand now."

She did. Her father, the man she loved so much, had sold himself to Hell for his only child.

"I will do the same deal for you," Ori coaxed. "No Hellspawn will harm you. You'll do well in this life, and at the end there's just a small payment."

Like I believe that. "And what about you? Do you get a reward or something?" she chided.

Ori wouldn't meet her eyes, so it was Lucifer that answered. "If he does not take your soul, his power is diminished. Power and status are everything in Hell, much like Heaven. He will suffer for his failure."

If she agreed, she could trap and not get hurt anymore. She'd be as good as her father, and none of the other trappers could best her. She probably wouldn't even miss her soul. There was one glaring problem: "So if this is such a great deal, why is my dad dead?"

The Prince of Hell shrugged. "Shit happens."

Riley adjusted the messenger bag on her shoulder, dredging up the last bit of courage she possessed. It was pathetically small compared to the evil arrayed in front of her. "Well, this Blackthorne isn't playing ball. You had me once," she said to Ori, "you're not having me again. I'm out of here."

With her body shaking so hard it was difficult to walk, she turned her back on the two Fallen Angels. *This is insane.* How many steps would she take before they killed her? Five? Ten? Would they let her think she'd reached safety and then rip her apart? Throw her to a bunch of demons so they could eat her alive?

"Riley, stop!" Ori called out. "Your soul has to be mine. If you align with one of the others, there will be—"

"Enough!" Lucifer commanded.

A shrill cry of protest filled the air, and then silence. When Riley stole a look over her shoulder, Ori was gone. Lucifer leaned against the base of a statue, grinning that maniacal grin of his. Her eyes tracked up the plinth, then to the statue. At the top was a stone angel clad in blue jeans, his bare chest exposed to the air. Wings stretched behind him, and both fists were raised toward the sky in righteous anger.

Ori. In sculpted marble.

Lucifer cleared his throat, bringing her eyes back to him. "My order to my servant was for one task only—destroy the rogue demon."

"But he said there were two tasks."

"Indeed. He made the mistake of trusting another, one who lied to him. One who told him what he wanted to hear."

It hit her. "Ori wasn't supposed to sleep with me, try to take my soul?" she said.

"No." A pensive frown settled on Lucifer's face. "Ori had no idea he was being used, and now he is paying the price. As are you."

"Did you turn Simon against me?"

"That was the other's doing, not mine. However, it did push you into Ori's arms, which served my purposes."

One by one the pieces fell into the convoluted puzzle. She'd been herded like a sheep and never had a clue. "You test angels, too?"

"It is my job," Lucifer said solemnly. His expression changed to one of determination. "If you agree to act on our behalf, I will give you certain assurances."

"You're not getting my soul. That's just not on the table, no matter what you do to me."

A shrug. "Right now, you're more valuable as a free agent, though it does put you at greater risk." Lucifer peered up at the stone statue. "If you wish to keep those you value safe, you will owe me a favor. Should I set Ori free, he will not remember you with love and tenderness, not after this disgrace. He has pride, one of the Seven Deadly Sins, and you have damaged his reputation in Hell." Lucifer pulled a face. "Now just who would he destroy first? Maybe your little friend Peter, or how about that annoying trapper who takes my name in vain so often. You know, the one who loves country music so much?"

Beck.

"I'll even sweeten the deal," the Prince of Hell added. "You do what I want, and I'll grant you one wish. Oh, and I can't bring the dead back to life, so don't bother with that one."

It all came back to her dad and his sacrifice. "Who summoned my father from his grave? Ozymandias?"

A snort came her way. "A dabbler in the dark arts? Hardly."

"Then who?"

"Me, of course," the Fallen said, beaming. "Who else would be the dragon?"

It'd been right in front of her all the time. Even the hunters had the dragon on their patches symbolizing the battle between good and evil.

"Why did you summon my dad?"

"To keep him out of the hands of those who would use his knowledge against us."

"Where is he—"

The Prince waved her off. "Do we have an agreement?" he demanded.

The fight went out of her. "What do you want me to do?"

"A little task when the time comes," he replied. All pretense of good humor vanished. "Fail me," Lucifer said, jabbing a finger upward at the marble Ori, "and I'll set the avenging angel free. Trust me when I say that his wrath has been known to level cities."

My friends' lives. Atlanta. That's what hung in the balance. It was no longer just about her or her father. "No on the soul; yes on the deal."

Lucifer's blue eyes sparkled. "Excellent. Don't worry, it balances out the one you made with Heaven, and just might keep you alive."

A second later the Prince of Hell vanished in a flash of brilliant light, followed by an overly dramatic clap of thunder.

Riley slumped against the nearest gravestone. Her eyes took the tortuous journey from the bare toes to the handsome face of the enraged angel who had betrayed her. God help her, but she still half believed what Ori had said, that he really was trying to protect her. How much of what he and Lucifer had told her were lies? How much was the truth? And why hadn't Heaven warned her she was in danger?

Riley had gone too far now to walk this back, not after she'd slept with a Fallen and made a deal with the Prince of Hell himself. The longer she looked at it, Lucifer had set up his tests to ensure she'd fail. How else would he get her on Hell's payroll?

Harper was right, she was twisted.

"Just like my father."

THIRTY-FOUR

Riley sat on the wooden rocker on Beck's front porch, working up her courage. It was ironic she'd come to him for help, but she had no place else to go. He wasn't home, but if the number of calls on her cell phone was any indication he'd frantically been trying to find her, at least until about four in the morning. The messages had a common theme: Stay away from Ori.

"Too late." She hadn't heard her phone ring last night, but it was a safe bet the angel made sure no one could find her until he'd finished with her.

Beck answered on the first ring and he sounded sleepy. "Riley? I've been callin' ya all night. Where were ya?"

"At the cemetery. I stayed in the mausoleum."

"Ya weren't there. I looked. I walked all over the damned place."

More angel mojo courtesy of Ori. "It doesn't matter now," she said. "I'm at your house, on the porch." She blinked away tears as the final admission came forth. "I need your help, Beck. Something bad's happened."

When he asked what was wrong, she refused to tell him. No way she'd tell him over the phone. He gave her the alarm code and told her where to find the spare key. "I'll get there as soon as I can," he said and then hung up.

Once she was inside and had turned off the alarm, Riley stood rooted in the entryway. If things played out like she suspected, this might be the last time she'd ever be allowed in this house.

The morning sun poured in the front window, sending beams of light onto the wooden floor. The house smelled like fried chicken. Probably takeout. Riley made it to the couch, tucked herself into a ball, and pulled the crocheted afghan over her, even though she was too warm. The afghan's faint pine scent reminded her of its owner's aftershave. She tucked it closer to her chin. Of all the people she could have run to when things went bad, she had come to Denver Beck, even though she knew he'd be the one most hurt by the news. From this moment on, nothing would ever be the same. She had made the ultimate mistake; now she needed to find a way to survive it.

All along Beck had watched out for her. "He warned me. Why didn't I listen?"

Because Ori said all the right words.

Riley ground her teeth in frustration. It would be easy to blame it all on angel mojo, but that wasn't right. She'd been so desperate for someone to love her, not to challenge her every decision, she'd walked right into the Fallen's feather-lined trap. She could blame the angel for what happened—and Ori was good for a lot of it—but that would be lying to herself. She'd done the same rebound thing after Beck had returned from the Army and ignored her. That had earned her Allan's abuse.

Why do I do this to myself? Am I stupid or what? Why was it so important someone love and care for her? It wasn't like she'd come from a broken home. She'd been loved, knew what it felt like. And that made her want it even more.

The minutes crept by like a furtive mouse skulking along the baseboards. Soon Beck would pull into the driveway and she'd tell him what had happened. Tell him all of it. Well, not everything. He didn't need to know she'd made a bargain with Lucifer to keep him alive, or that her father's soul belonged to Hell.

Riley adjusted the afghan, sending another wave of its owner's woodsy aftershave into the air. There was a further reason she'd gone for Ori, and she couldn't deny it any longer.

I was so jealous. Beck's new girlfriend had turned Riley totally green from the moment the reporter had knocked on her door. That envy had colored almost every decision from that second on. Simon's betrayal had opened the wound, and Justine had poured acid into it.

Now I'm in a world of hurt and I have no one else to blame.

She heard a truck door slam and the sound of boots pounding up the front stairs. Her heart clenched, knowing what was to come. Beck was through the door and at her side in only a few steps. His duffel bag clunked down on the wooden floor, and then he was kneeling in front of her, his face wreathed in worry.

"What's wrong? Are ya sick? Should I call Carmela?" he panted.

"No." *He'll hate me when he knows what I did.*

"Riley? Tell me what's happened. Yer so pale." He reached out to touch her face. The tender gesture pushed her over the edge.

Tears burst out of her in torrents, her body shaking to its core. He wrapped his arms around her, and that made it even harder. Ori had stolen so many precious things from her, and Beck's friendship was one of them.

She heard him murmuring in her ear, telling her it would be okay.

No, it's only going to get worse.

Finally, when she'd cried herself out, she pulled back. Beck was still kneeling in front of her. There was a wad of tissues in her hand, and she had no idea how it got there. She blew her nose, wiped her tears, and then cleared her throat. "Ori . . ."

Beck's face went stony. "That bastard? Did he hurt ya, girl?" When she didn't answer, he demanded, "Did he force . . ." His voice faded and she could see the dread in his eyes.

Riley shook her head and laughed bitterly. "No. He didn't force me. I gave it to him."

The thick intake of breath told her she'd been right. Beck was going to hate her for this.

"Oh, God," he muttered. "Ya let him. . . . Why the hell would ya do that? I told ya he was no good."

She couldn't meet his eyes. "He said I was special. He said that he loved me." Even now, as she spoke the words, she could hear how weak they were. "He said . . ."

"Ya were one of a kind, that he always wanted to be with ya. We all use those lines, girl."

And we always believe them.

"Goddammit!" he shouted, jumping to his feet. His sudden motion frightened her, and she cringed back against the couch. "Why him? Why not . . . someone who cares about ya?"

Someone like you.

She had never considered that Beck might be interested in her in that way, but from the expression on his face, it was true. It was knowledge gained too late.

"So why the hell are ya here? Ya pregnant?" he snapped.

Am I? Had Ori lied about that, too? "That's not the problem."

Beck dropped into the chair across from the couch like he had no more strength in his legs to keep him upright. "Then why come runnin' to me?"

"I made a mistake, I know that, but there's more to it. I need your help because Ori . . . isn't human. He's an angel."

"Angels don't fuck mortals, girl. He's lyin' to ya again."

She grimaced at the raw language and the barely contained fury behind it. "He showed me his wings."

Beck smirked. "Bet that isn't all he showed ya." Then a frown came. "Why would an angel want ya?"

Riley had asked herself that a hundred times, but now she knew the answer. "Because I'm Paul Blackthorne's daughter. Because he wanted my soul." *So he'd have a matched set.*

"Angels don't want souls. Only Hellspawn pull that kinda—"

She could tell the moment the truth hit him.

"Sweet Jesus, he's a Fallen?" Beck retorted. "How could ya be so stupid?"

Her anger finally stirred. "I made a mistake, okay? I trusted him. You're doing the same if you believe everything the stick chick tells you."

"Leave Justine out of this," he said, his face growing crimson.

"Ask yourself why she wants you. Is it because you're good at knocking boots, or is it because of something else? You sure she's not after your soul, too?"

Beck grabbed up his duffel bag and surged to his feet, a feral snarl erupting from his throat.

"I'm not gettin' lectured by some dumbass girl who puts out for demons," he shouted. "I always thought ya were different than the others. I was such a damned fool."

He was out the door in only a few steps. Seconds later his truck roared to life. She stepped to the window, knowing this was the last time she'd see him. She'd have to go to Fargo now, get out of Atlanta. Leave Denver Beck, the Guild, all her friends behind.

The truck peeled rubber out of the drive and onto the street. As Beck drove away, he was talking to someone on his phone, gesturing toward the house. Probably telling Stewart how badly she'd screwed up.

Her mistake, her BIG mistake was already rippling outward like a tsunami. Her apprentice license was gone. No way they'd let someone who'd been with a Fallen stay in the Guild. Beck would hate her for life. That hurt the worst.

Damn you, Ori, you've ruined everything. And I let you.

Riley bent over the sink in Beck's small bathroom, splashing her face with cold water. No matter what she did, she felt like she was burning up inside, as if the lump of coal in her stomach had spread heat throughout every single cell of her body. Was it because she'd been with a Fallen? Would it ever stop? She stared up at her reflection in the mirror. Sweat beaded on her forehead, and her face was flushed, despite the cold water.

God, I look old. As if one night with Ori had subtracted three decades of physical payment. The dark circles under her eyes were more pronounced now, and her skin seemed translucent, but not in a good way. Riley plucked at a silver strand of hair that poked out at her temple. She was only seventeen. How could she have gray hair? She yanked it out, glowered at the strand, and washed it down the drain with extreme prejudice.

A sharp rapping noise brought Riley upright. Someone was banging on the bathroom window. It wouldn't be Ori. He'd just appear out of nowhere, grab her, and disappear them to a remote location where he could torment her. Like Hell, where those stupid soccer-ball demons lived.

The banging continued, more frantic now, and she thought she heard a familiar high-pitched voice. Riley pushed aside the window curtain and started in surprise. The Magpie from her apartment was gesturing frantically, jumping up and down on the sill.

"What are you doing here?"

He shrieked something.

"Settle down. What are you trying to say?"

"Deeemon hun . . . ters!" he shouted.

"Where?"

"Here!" the Magpie shouted back. "Coming for you!"

Omigod.

Riley bolted from the bathroom, grabbed her messenger bag, and fled out the back door. A few seconds later she was in her car and speeding down the back alley. As she slowed to make the turn onto the street, she saw a black van roll into Beck's drive. Then another. Their side doors opened and armed men burst out of them, heading for the front and back of the house in a coordinated assault.

How could they know about Ori? How did they know I was here?

The answer struck her like a brick to the forehead. Beck had been on the phone when he'd driven away. He hadn't called Master Stewart— he'd called the hunters down on her because she'd chosen Ori over him.

Riley's hands shook so hard she found it difficult to drive. The bile rose in her throat, but she forced herself to swallow it down. He had said he'd always look after her, honor her father's memory, but once his guy ego got bruised, Beck was all about payback.

Her phone rang. It was him. She tried to ignore it, but the fury was too much.

"Riley?" Beck said as she answered the phone. "I—"

"You sold me out, you hick bastard!" she shouted. "You're no better than Simon or that damned angel. I should have known you'd screw me over."

"What are ya—"

Riley jabbed the button on the phone, cutting him off. When it rang seconds later, she turned it off and threw it into her bag. With her luck the hunters could track her by it. Who knew what kind of crazy technology the Vatican possessed.

The shakes caught up with her seconds later, causing her to pull into an abandoned parking lot and lean her head on the steering wheel. This time her lungs didn't constrict, didn't fail to pull in the air she needed. If anything, they expanded. The anger fueled her desire to survive. She would never let anyone hurt her again. *Never.*

But where could she hide? Her apartment? No, they'd look there for sure. She didn't dare go to either of the masters; that would just make trouble for the Guild. Same with Ayden and the witches. Peter wasn't an option without causing a bunch of hassle with his dad. She had to disappear, make them think she'd left town until she had time to do just that. There was only one person who might be able to help, providing he was willing to accept the risk.

THIRTY-FIVE

It took only a few minutes to make it to Little Five Points. It took longer to locate a parking place. Finally she stashed the car behind a health food store, away from the main street. Maybe that would buy her time in case the Vatican was working with the local cops.

Paranoid much?

It seemed that just about everyone was out to get her. Well, except the Five, and that was because Ori had killed it. *Or did he?*

Absolutely everything she'd believed was up for grabs. She'd thought Simon was the perfect boyfriend, that they had a future together, but that relationship had gone down in flames. She was certain that Beck would always be there for her. Not so much. The only thing she could be sure of was that her dad was dead and that she'd slept with a Fallen. The rest was pretty much smoke and mirrors.

Riley hurried down Enchanter's Way, moving past the café, the witches' place, and then left into the alley that led to Mortimer's house. She kept turning around every few steps to see if she was being followed. After she knocked on the necromancer's door, she fidgeted with the strap of her messenger bag.

What if he won't take me in? Then she'd have nowhere to go.

The door slowly opened. She had expected Mort's housekeeper.

Instead it was the summoner himself. "Hello, Riley." His smile looked genuine. "It's good to see you." Then he frowned. "Are you okay?"

"I . . ." She looked around nervously. Any minute armed men might storm down the alley to arrest her. "I'm in deep trouble. The demon hunters are after me."

Mort's eyebrows rose in tandem. For a second she was sure he'd slam the door in her face, but to her amazement, he beckoned. "Then you'd better come inside." He shut the door behind her, bolting it. "What's happened?"

Riley couldn't tell him everything, but at least she could give him the short version. He deserved that if he was going to help a fugitive.

It came out in a rush. "I've got a Fallen Angel who wants to steal my soul, I owe Heaven a big favor, and the demon hunters want to arrest me because they think I'm working for Lucifer. I need a place to hide until I can get this worked out."

"That's all?" the summoner asked, quirking a smile.

Riley stared at him. How could he be so calm about all this?

"What are the hunters up to?" he asked.

"They're raiding Beck's place. They could come here, too."

"Wouldn't do them any good," he stated. "They won't find you, even if they come inside the house. Magic has its benefits, you see."

"You could get in big trouble taking me in," she cautioned.

"Most certainly. Where did you park?" She told him. "Give me your keys. I'll hide the car."

Riley handed over the key ring, along with the vehicle's description, knowing she just had to trust him.

Mort pointed down the hallway toward the circular room. "I'll have my housekeeper bring you some food. You look like you could use it."

"Thanks. I really mean it. I didn't have anywhere else to go," she admitted.

"I don't get to play the good guy very often. It's fun."

Not if the hunters arrest you.

Mort opened the front door then looked back at her. "He said you'd come."

Before she could ask who he meant, the necro was gone.

Riley walked down the hallway and into the big room, each step feeling like it was a mile long. The smell of wood smoke tickled her nose as she dumped her messenger bag on the picnic bench. She issued a heavy sigh. It was answered by an odd sound, like the shifting of dry leaves. It reminded her of Ozymandias's illusion at the graveyard. Had Mort sold her out, too?

Then she saw the figure as it rose awkwardly from a chair in the corner, a thin scarecrow in a suit and red tie. It slowly moved into the brighter part of the room, a strand of brown hair dangling across its forehead in a way that was so familiar.

"Pumpkin?" the figure called out.

"Daddy?" she cried.

Riley flung herself at her father, nearly knocking him over. As they embraced, the scent of cedar chips and oranges filled her nose.

"My beautiful daughter," he murmured, hugging her tight. "I've missed you so much."

"It's all gone wrong, Dad. I've made so many mistakes."

"It'll be okay," he soothed. "We'll get through this . . . together. I won't let you down."

She was with her father again. The whole world might be searching for them, but that didn't matter now.

As Riley's tears soaked into his suit coat, she made one final vow: *I swear that Hell will not have this man. Even if it means I take his place.*

Turn the page for a

SNEAK PEEK AT THE NEXT THRILLING DEMON TRAPPERS NOVEL!

Coming Winter 2012

ONE

2018
Atlanta, Georgia

Riley Blackthorne's tears were no more. She'd cried herself dry, but
remained in the arms of a dead man. If given the chance, she would
stay there for the rest of her life.

When she looked up, sad brown eyes gazed back. Her father, Master Trapper Paul Blackthorne, was a reanimated corpse now, summoned
from the grave by none other than the Prince of Hell. Like the day he'd
been buried, her dad was still wearing his suit and his favorite red tie.
The one she'd given him as a present.

"I never thought I'd find you," she whispered.

"I always knew you would," he said, smiling. The smile wasn't quite
right, like a cheap imitation.

Riley laid her head on his chest, but it wasn't like it should be. His
heart was dormant now. The essence of her father had been silenced.

Reluctantly they broke apart. With the Vatican's demon hunters
searching for her, she'd taken refuge in Mortimer Alexander's house;
she had nowhere else to run. She hadn't expected to find her missing
parent waiting for her.

Her father took her hand. "Come with me." She followed him

down a hallway, then outside into the morning light at a pace that was just above a shuffle. They entered a walled garden. Cardinals and blue jays flitted around a bird feeder. Water cascaded from the hands of a nude stone nymph perched in the center of a broad fountain. She was laughing, flicking water off her fingers as if her world was only this small courtyard. Riley and her father settled on a stone bench still covered with frost.

Too many questions careened inside Riley to be held at bay.

"What's it like?" she asked, her voice barely above a whisper.

"Very . . . peculiar."

That wasn't an answer. "You can't tell me, can you?"

"No. Not like I thought," he murmured.

The next question was just as hard. "You didn't get to see Mom, did you?" she asked.

There was a minute shake of his head as those eyes went even sadder, if that was possible. Her mother was dead and now that her dad had made a deal with Lucifer, he wasn't headed to Heaven. He'd never get to see Riley's mother again.

"Dad . . ." His eyes met hers. "Lucifer told me what you did. How you gave up your soul for me."

The truth still hurt: A few years before, her dad had faced death at the hands of an Archfiend and had pleaded for his life—for her sake. He'd pledged his soul to Hell in exchange for staying alive until his only child made master trapper, so Riley wouldn't be on her own, wouldn't starve or become a ward of the state.

"Did Mom know?" A nod. "Why didn't you tell me?" she asked.

"You were too young."

"That's crap and you know it," she retorted. "I was old enough. What else haven't you told me, Dad? What else is waiting to fall on my head?"

He didn't reply, his eyes not meeting hers now. Which meant there *was* more.

Her father pulled her into a tight embrace. Every time he moved there was a crinkling noise, like old paper. Something to do with being reanimated.

"I did what was best. My soul isn't important."

It was so important that Lucifer wanted it. Even though he hadn't wanted Riley's.

She closed her eyes, inhaling the scent of oranges and cedar chips, trying to find the good in all this. There was very little, other than she was with her father for a little while longer. Right now every second counted.

Soon you'll be in Hell with all those demons. How do I live with that?

To Denver Beck, there were many ways to welcome a new day—spread-eagled on his own lawn, wrists secured by flex-cuffs wasn't the best of them. Not to mention the rifle barrel jammed into the back of his head.

"What the hell is goin' on?" he bellowed into the dirt.

The response was the sound of combat boots tromping around inside his house as their owners' voices called out to one another in Italian. When there was a sharp shatter of glass, he swore, trying to lift his head to see what was happening. The rifle barrel only pressed harder, jamming his face back into the ground.

Beck closed his eyes to keep the dirt out of them and forced himself to relax. If he fought back, the demon hunter behind him might feel the need to put a bullet in his skull.

I'll be damned if I die like this.

His only choice was to remain here until the Vatican's elite team finished their search. Which, from all the commotion, involved tearing the house apart in the hopes of finding something.

When he heard a name in the midst of the voices flowing around him, he sighed into the dirt. They were searching for Riley Blackthorne, the seventeen-year-old daughter of Beck's dead trapper buddy, Paul.

The day had sucked even before this paramilitary-style raid, one Beck was sure his neighbors were enjoying with their morning coffee. Just after dawn Riley had arrived on his doorstep, weeping and shell-shocked. Through tears and sobs she'd admitted her blackest sin: She'd spent the night with a Fallen, one of Lucifer's own.

Beck had known this Ori guy was bad news from the first moment he'd seen him with Riley, but he'd never expected the bastard to be a Fallen angel.

Why him? Even now he could see her huddled on the couch, weeping, as he'd shouted that very question at her. After all Beck had done for her, she'd taken up with that . . . *thing.*

When he'd spat wicked slurs at Paul's daughter, she'd responded in kind. Fearing how bad it might get between them, Beck had bolted from the house. When he'd returned a short time later, he'd found his front door wide open and the Vatican's team on the prowl.

More rapid-fire conversation bounced around him now: Beck didn't need to speak the language to hear the frustration. Since Riley wasn't lying in the dirt beside him, this raid made the hunters look bad. They would need a scapegoat and Beck would do just fine. A new voice cut in—it was the hunters' captain. Apparently he'd finally decided to join the party.

Without warning, Beck was hauled roughly to his knees. Once he was up, he tried to wipe his mouth on a shoulder: It proved impossible with the flex-cuffs in place. The demon hunter with the rifle circled around to the side now, the weapon pointed at Beck's chest.

The captain of the unit squatted in front of him, his dark eyes flinty. Elias Salvatore was thirty-two, a decade older than Beck. He had a Mediterranean complexion, black hair, and a sleek goatee coupled with an athletic build. His navy turtleneck sported epaulets and the demon hunters' emblem—St. George slaying the dragon. Crisply pleated trousers tucked neatly into polished combat boots.

"Mr. Beck," he said evenly.

"Captain Salvatore. What the hell is goin' on?"

"We were informed that Riley Blackthorne was here."

Who told ya that?

"She was here a while ago. Must of left."

The man's eyes narrowed farther. "Where is she?"

"No idea." It was a safe bet one of the neighbors had heard them shouting at each other, so he went with the truth in case the hunters bothered to check. "We had words."

"About what?"

"That's none of yer business," Beck said. A second later he was facedown in the dirt, a heavy boot pressing on his back.

The captain issued a crisp command and Beck was hauled up again. He gave a look over his shoulder and found that the boot belonged to Lieutenant Amundson, the captain's second-in-command. He was a tall man, Nordic, and not known for his manners.

Beck spat dirt. "Get these damned cuffs off me."

Salvatore gave a gesture. There was the snick of a knife, then the cuffs fell away. Amundson had made sure to cut his palm in the process.

Beck wiped his hands on his jeans, revealing the blood.

The captain delivered a penetrating look over the prisoner's shoulder, then gestured for his lieutenant to move away. "I apologize."

Beck clamped down on his fury. Throwing punches wasn't a smart move right now. Instead he ran his uninjured hand through his hair to dislodge some of the dirt and to buy him time to think this through.

Did the hunters know about Riley and the Fallen? *They have to. Why else would they be looking for her?* Still, he didn't dare make assumptions.

"So what's this all about?" Beck asked.

The captain rose. "Let's go inside."

Beck stood, dusted off his jeans, and retrieved his trapping bag where it lay near the driveway. He felt the bottom of the canvas and was relieved to find it wasn't wet, which meant none of the glass spheres inside had shattered when he'd been tackled by the hunters.

After ensuring there was no one else in the house, Salvatore closed the front door behind them. Beck had expected the place to have been turned inside out, but that wasn't the case. The only damage appeared to be a glass that had been knocked off the counter. He ignored the mess on the floor and dropped onto the couch in the same place that Riley had occupied when she'd delivered her devastating news.

Where are ya, girl? If she ran to her apartment, they'd find her there. If she was smart she'd go to Angus Stewart, one of the two master trappers in the city. Stewart would watch over her.

The captain sat in a chair across from him. He moved as if he hadn't had a decent night's sleep in days. "We must find Riley Blackthorne as quickly as possible."

"Why?"

"There's a Fallen angel in Atlanta. His name is Ori. We believe he has targeted Paul Blackthorne's daughter."

Beck made sure he appeared shocked. It wasn't hard. He still couldn't believe that Riley had been with one of Lucifer's allies.

"Why would one of those want her?"

Salvatore shook his head. "We don't know. There is a strange pattern of events in this city, and that usually means there's an epicenter, a focus to that activity."

"If yer sayin' that Riley's the reason for all this—"

"What other conclusion can we draw?" Salvatore retorted. "She was nearly killed by a Grade Five demon. The same fiend pressed its attack during the trapper's meeting at the Tabernacle. That ambush alone cost you a third of your Demon Trappers Guild."

"I know the numbers, hunter," Beck replied sullenly. "Why a commando raid on my house? Ya could have knocked on the door like anyone else."

"But you weren't home," the captain observed. "Which leads to another question: Do you usually leave your house unlocked?"

Beck hesitated. "No. Why?"

"Both the front and back doors weren't bolted and your alarm wasn't engaged. The back door was partially ajar, indicating a hasty departure, perhaps?" The captain leaned forward, elbows on knees. "Did you call Riley and warn her that we were coming?"

By now they'd have gone through his phone and know he'd called Riley after they'd quarreled, so he opted for the truth. "I didn't know ya were comin' here."

"But you spoke to her."

"Yeah. We argued about this Ori guy. He'd told her he was a freelance demon hunter and I told her to stay away from. She wasn't listenin' so we had words. I called her to . . ." Why had he called her? Certainly not to apologize, that was for sure.

"Where is she now?"

Beck shook his head. "I don't know. Now I'm done talkin' to ya unless the Guild's lawyer is watchin' over me."

The captain sighed. "Look, I respect your loyalty to the girl's father. Paul Blackthorne trained you, brought you up through the Guild. You were there when he died at the hands of the same demon that tried to kill his daughter. I know what you're feeling, but we need your help."

"Bite me."

Salvatore scowled. "So be it." He triggered a radio on his shoulder and Italian filled the air. He'd barely finished giving the order when two hunters were through the front door.

The captain rose from the chair, his face set. "Denver Beck, as representative of the Holy See, I arrest you for obstructing justice, additional charges to be filed at a later time. You are duly warned that if you are found to be aiding Hell in any manner, the ultimate penalty is death."

"Go figure," Beck muttered.

TWO

"Syrup?"

"Thanks," Riley said. Her father pushed a tall plastic bottle across the table like it weighed a hundred pounds. She stifled a sigh as she squirted a thick line onto the stack of steaming buttermilk pancakes. Riley should have been thrilled: she was having breakfast with her dad one more time. How many mornings since he'd died had she wished for this very thing? Now that it had come to pass she wasn't so sure.

They were seated at a picnic table in a circular brick room that smelled of wood smoke. Mort had told her that the table was easier to move when he wanted to conduct rituals. The whole building had a different feel to it, one that Riley couldn't quite grasp. Something to do with Mort's magic, perhaps.

Her dad watched her eat in silence, not joining in the food or the banter they would have enjoyed in the past. A stray lock of brown hair curled onto his forehead like always. But something was missing—the part that made him so cool. Instead he was a human placeholder, a bookmark in a lost life.

There was a soft shuffling at the doorway that announced Tereyza, their host's reanimate housekeeper. That's what came with hiding in a necromancer's house—dead servants. The woman looked at Riley, at the plate full of pancakes, and then up at Riley again. Pancakes made by Emalie, another reanimate who never left the kitchen.

Great. Even the dead are guilting me now.

Riley obediently picked up the fork and dug in. Apparently that was enough for the housekeeper, as she returned the way she came. Though the food was excellent, after two mouthfuls Riley put down her silverware.

"Does Beck know about your deal with Hell?"

Her father shook his head. "You should eat. You're so thin," he replied.

Too much had happened in the last few weeks for her to have much of an appetite: her dad's death, the attack that had killed so many trappers, her boyfriend Simon's betrayal. Then there were Ori and Beck. Even more betrayal. Could she ever trust a man, or an angel, again?

But I am. She was hiding in Mort's house, trusting him not to turn her in to the hunters.

"Eat," her father repeated.

Riley returned to the pancakes. They were still warm. How could that be? After the first couple of mouthfuls, she began to eat in earnest. She needed comfort food and a nap. Then she'd figure out what to do. Where to go. Who else she could trust?

By the time she finished eating, Riley was so tired she couldn't think. When their host offered her a place to rest, she readily accepted the kind gesture. She found the bedroom bright, decorated with cream walls and peach accents. A girl's room. *Maybe he has a younger sister. Or a niece.*

As she yawned, Riley pulled the curtains to reduce the light, then did a test bounce on the bed. *Definitely workable.* Pulling off her shirt, her long hair fell over her face. With it came the unmistakable scent of crisp night air. *Ori's scent.*

"Damn you," she swore, flinging her clothes in all directions. Riley fled to the shower, adjusting the temperature as hot as she could stand. As the water ran, the night before rushed through her: meeting the angel at Oakland Cemetery, and how handsome he'd been. How right it had felt to let him make love to her for her first time. Then this morning had arrived, bringing betrayal and a broken heart.

"All lies," she said. He'd had only one reason for being nice to her, claiming she was special. Her soul. Riley couldn't scrub away the taint, the feeling that somehow she'd been violated by her own heart. At least she could mourn where no one would hear her.

While some would argue that the Westin wasn't a jail, the earnest demon hunter parked near the hotel room's door told Beck he wasn't free to come and go as he pleased. Since it looked like he was here for the time being, he took himself to the bathroom, used the toilet, and then washed his face and hands. Running a wet facecloth over his hair took most of the dirt out of the blond strands. All of this was busywork while he tried to unravel the knots in his life.

Riley's selfish actions had brought the hunters to his doorstep. That angered him, not only because of what she'd let that Fallen do to her, but because he'd promised her father he'd keep her safe. Still, Beck's wounded pride was the least of his worries: What would the hunters do to Paul's daughter when they caught her? Would they put her on trial? Lock her up? Or worse?

Knowing that his questions were not going to be answered by staring into the bathroom mirror, Beck returned to the bedroom. The hunter was still there, vigilant as ever. Dusting himself off, which left a trail of dried grass on the carpet, Beck unlaced his work boots and dropped himself on the king bed. It was one of those fancy ones you find in expensive hotels. He'd learned to sleep anywhere during his stint in the Army, so something this soft made him uncomfortable.

By his count there were two hunters guarding him: one in the corridor and one in the room with him. He could try to escape, but it'd probably buy him a bullet. Captain Salvatore had promised to call

Master Stewart, and for some reason Beck trusted him to do just that. If he was patient, the Scotsman would get him out of here.

The guard in the room was Hispanic with dark, intense eyes and a fighter's bulk. He kept his attention riveted on his prisoner's every move.

"Can ya not do that?" Beck growled. "Yer drivin' me crazy."

The guy gave a shrug, then settled back in the rolling chair, his attention a few feet to Beck's left. That was some improvement.

"How long is this gonna take?" No reply.

Knowing he wasn't going to be told anything of value until his captors were damned well ready, Beck pulled himself off the bed and went through his exercise regime to blow off steam. Fifty push-ups followed by fifty sit-ups. Then another fifty push-ups, some one-handed. As he worked up a sweat, he tried hard to block the memories: Riley crying in his arms, the knowing smirk on that Fallen angel's face. How disappointed Paul would be if he knew his daughter had been touched like that.

Dammit. I did what I could, but it wasn't enough. It's never enough.

He lost count of the push-ups and finally slumped to the carpet when his arms grew too weak to support him and his back felt like it had been scorched by molten lead. The pain did as he'd hoped, blocking things he didn't want to think about. Muscles quivering, he returned to the bed, tucked his arms behind his head, and stared up at the pebbled ceiling.

Someone had known Riley was at his house this morning and that list was pretty short, unless his neighbors had decided to spy for the hunters. Master Stewart knew she was there: Beck had called him the moment he'd left her at the house, seething in anger at what had fallen out between her and the angel.

Then there was Justine Armando, the woman he'd been with overnight. Justine was a new addition to Beck's life, a freelance journalist who'd arrived in Atlanta at the same time as the hunters. She trailed after their teams as they did the Vatican's wet work across the world, writing up newspaper reports on their exploits. Beck had been interviewed by her . . . twice. Then they'd taken it a step further and he'd landed in her bed. That's where he'd been this morning, in this same hotel, when Riley's panicked phone call had reached him. When he'd heard that terrified voice, he'd bailed out of Justine's arms and bolted out the door, sure Paul's daughter was in grave danger.

Had he told Justine where Riley was? He had to admit he wasn't sure. All Beck could remember was the petulant frown on his lover's face as he bent over to kiss her good-bye.

Couldn't be her. He wasn't willing to accept that, though he knew Riley would believe it in a heartbeat. He could still hear her warning him about Justine and how he was going to get hurt. If Riley had taken his advice, she wouldn't be in a world of hurt.

Ya wanted that damned angel, then live with that mistake. Forever.

His words were at war with his heart. Everyone made mistakes, and most didn't end up with Hell or the Church breathing down their necks.

When there was a knock at the door, the guard cautiously checked the peephole, then opened it to reveal Lieutenant Amundson. The second-in-command held Beck's cell phone in his hand.

"Your master wants to speak to you," he said in his heavily accented English, plain he wasn't happy about it. He tossed the phone on the bed, unconcerned if somehow he disconnected the call.

Jerk. Beck sat up and took the phone. "Sir?"

"What is goin' on, lad?" Stewart's Scottish brogue held none of its usual cheeriness.

"I'm"—Beck shot a surly look at his captors—"enjoyin' the hospitality of the hunters. It has somethin' to do with Riley."

"So I gather. Any notion of where she is?"

"No, sir. Not a clue."

"Well, then, let me talk to the Viking again."

Viking? Figuring he meant Amundson, Beck passed the cell phone back. After a short burst of conversation, the hunter ended the call, but kept the phone.

"You're here until we have her," Amundson announced.

"If that's the case, how about some breakfast?"

There was a grunt from the lieutenant and then the door shut behind him. The guard resumed his post in the chair as Beck stretched out on the bed again. Staring up at the ceiling, all he could think of was Riley. Her tears and his unrelenting fury. How sick he'd felt when she'd told him what she'd done.

How could you let him touch you? Was I just a meal ticket for ya, girl?

It was best he had no idea where Riley Blackthorne was hiding. The way he felt right now, he'd hand her over to the demon hunters himself.

All rileys boyfriends suck, riley + beck = perfection